VAULTING
THROUGH
TIME

VAULTING THROUGH TIME

NANCY McCABE

CamCat
Books

CamCat Publishing, LLC
Brentwood, Tennessee 37027
camcatpublishing.com

Hardcover ISBN 9780744309362
Paperback ISBN 9780744309379
Large-Print Paperback ISBN 9780744309386
eBook ISBN 9780744309409
Audiobook ISBN 9780744309423

Library of Congress Control Number: 2022952397

Book and cover design by Maryann Appel

5   3   1   2   4

FOR SOPHIE, AS ALWAYS

PART 1

PRE-FLIGHT

1

You know those dreams where you're flying? Suddenly your feet are no longer touching the ground. You're rising, weightless, airy and astonished. By force of will, you aim your body toward the sky and find yourself floating and soaring, amazed at your new skill. Why haven't you been doing this your whole life? It's as easy as walking or running. You've beaten gravity. Your spirits lift. You feel euphoric, no longer tethered to earth—or obligations, responsibilities, or expectations.

I've always been proud that I can fly without dreaming. I'm airborne when I swing from the high bar, flip across a spring floor, or launch into my beam dismount. It used to be that if I was in a funk, a fog, feeling blah, gymnastics could lift me right out of that, show me the world from new angles until I landed somewhere different from where I'd started.

Lately, not so much.

Lots of girls quit by the time they're sixteen, but not me. I'm one of the oldest girls on the team. Eventually, Coach Amy once said, a gymnast's body starts developing. Eventually a gymnast's center of gravity changes.

Eventually she gets distracted by hormones and life. I'm stubborn. Up till now I've stayed the course. But lately—secretly—I've begun to falter. After breaking my foot on a vault landing last year, I'm more nervous about throwing my body backward. And I've become even more distracted as I constantly chase thoughts out of my head of the boy I'm crushing on who is totally wrong for me.

It's a stormy Friday afternoon and I'm waiting for my turn on the bars. It's one of those nonstop late fall showers that brutalizes the last leaves, beating them off the trees. Then the rain turns to snow and all of the branches are bare and it's suddenly winter.

The downpour batters the gym roof as if someone is emptying jarfuls of pennies onto it. The sound nearly drowns out the level-4 compulsory floor music. Otherworldly strains reach my ears, my thoughts looping with the monotonous instrumental music that plays over and over. Warming up, little girls pitch forward, kicking over in unison, leaving behind one struggling teammate, legs flailing in the air.

Distracted and restless, I wish I could astrally project myself somewhere else. I keep feeling this way lately, like there's an old me and a new me in parallel universes. There's the disciplined one who still loves gymnastics, and there's the free-floating one who daydreams and follows whims. The daydreamy me cuts intricate patterns down the sides of my T-shirts and watches YouTube tutorials on how to weave my curly hair into fancy French braid variations and stays home in a cozy bathrobe editing selfies so that I'm wearing butterfly wings or floating among the stars.

Zach thinks I'm just a headstrong, driven athlete. I imagine proving to him that I can be geeky and creative and inventive too.

My thoughts are always floating involuntarily in that direction lately, the same way whenever I'm home my gaze drifts toward his bedroom window across the driveway from mine. Why do I care what my ex-best friend, a judgy guy with big, clumsy hands and big, stinky feet, thinks of me, anyway?

Zach and I have known each other all our lives. His family moved here when we were three. We used to make faces at each other across the driveway, our bedroom windows only a few feet apart. When we were eight, we rigged up a tin-can telephone between those windows. When we were ten, we entered the district science fair together with a project on sound waves. We won a blue ribbon.

Now I order my stomach to stop flip-flopping when I think about him. I mean, ick. He's like a brother to me. And also, he's boring—always talking about stuff like comic books and parallel universes and time travel and quantum physics.

I absolutely refuse to crush on Zach O'Mara.

Besides, I haven't spoken to him in months and I have no intention of resuming now.

"Have you thought about getting a straightening iron?" asks Molly, the girl waiting in line behind me. Her tone implies that she's making a helpful suggestion. But then, in the same overly earnest tone, she adds, "Maybe that would make your hair less witchy."

Molly has blond hair pulled up into a perky ponytail. It looks like the swirl on the top of an ice-cream cone, like something frothy and sweet, but she is anything but. I am darker than most of the other girls, tanning easily in the summer. Sometimes they make comments. "Are you sure you're not an Indian?" they ask.

"I think the term is Native American or Indigenous, but no," I answer, proving that I am totally my mother's daughter, because that's what she'd say. I do my best to ignore the way the other girls make faces and laugh at me.

Behind Molly, Callie, who wears her long, light hair in a tight French braid, giggles at Molly's jab about my hair. That hurts. Molly and Callie are both a year younger than I am, but I thought that Callie and I were friends.

Coach Amy strides across the floor toward us. "Hey," she says to all of us, but her gaze lingers on me. "I'm taking the top two from each optional level to the USAG meet next month. What do you think?"

"Sounds fun," I say, even though my first reaction is dread. As a YMCA gymnast, I should have been nothing but excited for the rare chance to compete with girls from private clubs, girls preparing to go elite and even compete internationally.

"You don't think you're going to be picked, do you?" Molly mutters after Coach Amy moves on to the group waiting for the beams. "You're such a baby about tumbling. I'm way better than you are."

Molly is fearless about throwing herself into back tucks and layouts. Fearless but sloppy. She and Callie have both surpassed my skills on everything but bars, though their technique, all bent legs and loose movements, pulls down their scores. Molly's constant deductions make her even more pissed off at me. During warm-ups, she tries to psych me out by "accidentally" crashing into me.

"If you're so much better than me, then do better than me," I toss back at her now, as if her words don't sting. She's not wrong. I am a baby about tumbling backward. And around Molly, I feel like I'm stuck back in middle school, not a junior in high school.

I turn my back on Molly's eye roll and the other girls' smirks as I step up to the bars. I close my eyes, shut out everything. My irritation, reservations, errant thoughts, the floor music, Molly's smug expression, the other bars groaning as a teammate swings into a handstand, the beam thudding as another teammate lands out of her split leap. All I have to do is score in the level-7 top two at the meet this weekend. Piece of cake. I'm almost always first or second all-around.

So what if I've been questioning the wisdom of blindly hurling my body backward? So what if I keep throwing in elements to avoid back tucks on floor and back walkovers on beam? I'm a stickler for technique, so my scores haven't suffered too much. And all gymnasts have fear issues, especially after an injury. Well, maybe except for Molly. Maybe if I try hard enough I can will my fear away the same way I can will away any inappropriate feelings I have for Zach. New energy sizzles through me as I springboard to the low bar, rising from my squat on to a high-bar kip, swinging continuously and big, casting to handstand and toppling into a back giant, arms and legs straight, toes pointed, no hesitation or extra swings. I defy gravity, flinging myself into a series of rotations and twirling into a flyaway dismount before I slam to the ground.

"You're on fire!" Coach Amy high-fives me. "Bring your birth certificate tomorrow and we'll get you registered."

I anticipate telling Mom about the USA Gymnastics meet as Callie's mom drives me home. We pass under street lights that bow over the streets, water cascading from them so they look like showerheads. Callie keeps her head turned toward the passenger-side window, making no attempt at conversation, like she's afraid if she's nice Molly will find out and turn on her. Whatever. I'm going to beat out her and Molly and go to the USAG meet. When Zach hears about it, he'll have to be impressed. It's a win-win.

As soon as I get home, I call Mom at the library, where she's working late. "I need my birth certificate," I tell her breathlessly. "Where is it?"

"I thought it was in the secretary downstairs, but last time I looked, it wasn't there. That's okay. There's another copy—" She stops abruptly, and then there's a long silence. "I'll find it when I get home." Her voice sounds funny.

I expect her to ask more questions. I expect her to be excited for me. Instead, she changes the subject, brushing me off. "Don't you need to submit your English research proposal online by tonight?"

"But—"

She ignores me. "I read it over. It's good. But look at the first paragraph. Where do you need a comma?"

I don't want to talk about my stupid English assignment. "Up your butt," I answer.

I hear a sharp intake of breath on the other end of the line.

So maybe I've gone too far. I brace myself.

But all she says, after a long pause, is, "No. That's a colon."

It takes me a second, but then I hoot despite myself. Mom starts to laugh too, and it takes us a few seconds to catch our breaths.

My teammates think Mom must be stodgy because she's so much older than their moms, so old they're always mistaking her for my grandmother. They think it's weird that we look nothing alike, and I guess I think so too: She's pale and I have a natural light tan even in winter; she has blue eyes and mine are brown; she had blond hair before she let it go gray, in contrast to my thick curls that people describe as black but are really dark brown—the darkest, richest-possible brown. I'm proud of my hair. Mom's always said that I take after my dad, but when I've asked to see pictures, she reminds me that they were all destroyed when our basement flooded. "Don't you remember that? We had to throw out so much stuff. That's why we got the sump pump," she says. Lately this explanation has nagged at me. I've suddenly started to wonder why she would have kept photos in the basement.

More and more things have been getting to me. Like whenever I have a fight with Mom, my teammates say, "Too bad you don't know your real mom," even though she is my real mom. Not to mention, no one says that to them when they have fights with their moms.

But they seem to think that conflict is different, less damaging somehow, if you look like your mom. Their moms are small and lithe, former high-school cheerleaders and track stars who now play on company sports teams and run marathons. They all have bodies genetically programmed to produce little gymnasts.

Mom never played any sports and claims she peaked at the cartwheel. We still have all of her old photos, like the school pictures where she's in the back row, towering over the other kids. When she wants me to think that she relates to me, she describes the back shoulder roll she did in her school's eighth-grade operetta.

But when we have moments like this, laughing so hard that she makes a honking noise and I have to wipe tears from my eyes, I'm sure she's my mom. I would never admit it aloud, but I think of Mom as my safe space, my reality check, the one who'll be supportive of whatever I do but won't hesitate to steer me back on track when I veer off.

Still, the doubts have been crowding in, so much so that I decided to do one of those genetic tests where you spit in a vial and send it to some lab. I had the hardest time working up enough spit. Finally I dripped some lemon juice in my mouth, and that made me salivate big time. I'm pretty sure my genetic results are going to come back any day now saying that I'm 99 percent lemon.

I feel a little guilty, going behind Mom's back, forging her signature. But I just want reassurance that we're really related.

"I'll be home late," Mom says. "I'll email my comments. Get your assignment done and get to bed so you'll be fresh for tomorrow. Also, I think your competition leotard is in the wash."

Idly, I click onto my email. "I put some of my leos in the dryer yesterday," I answer absently. "I think it's there." My heart jumps. The email arrived with my genetic test results while I was at practice.

"Is the copy of my birth certificate in the attic?" I click open the email. My eyes rove down the column showing my genetic heritage. I'm 70 percent Northwestern European, with strands of British and Irish, French, and German. No surprises there. Then my eyes stop on the last line.

"I'll find it when I get home." Mom's voice is tight and tense. "Don't get all impulsive the way you do and go rifling through papers and messing up my files."

"But what about—" I start before I realize that she's hung up.

By then I'm too distracted to even consider calling her back as I stare at that last line, which has to be a mistake. It says I'm 30 percent Han Chinese.

Or maybe Mom neglected to tell me the whole story of my dad's ethnic heritage?

Maybe my dad was part Chinese and somehow didn't know it?

Though Mom pays bills at the secretary in the living room, she periodically carries a new pile of insurance policies and bank statements up to the file cabinets in the finished attic room. I can't imagine anywhere else she'd keep documents like my birth certificate, and maybe it will be with other records that will make this make sense.

I close up my laptop and charge up the stairs, even more impatient to see what I can find.

2

I hurtle to the top of the stairs, then stop short in front of the attic door, suddenly afraid of what I'll find. I pace through the hall and then around my bedroom, adrenaline pumping like crazy, head spinning. There's got to be a rational explanation.

Sitting down on my bed, I reread the results of my genetic test. I reach for the phone to call Mom. Then I drop it. I look over at the window, wishing I could talk to Zach.

But I can't do that either.

The light is on in his room. He's been there, across the way, for as long as I can remember. Sometimes just knowing he's there makes my skin tingle, and I miss him terribly.

We hung out together all the time until middle school, when I began to find him totally annoying. If he saw me do a cartwheel or a split leap in the yard, he'd say, "But can you do a flip?"

"There's no such thing," I snapped. "It's called a handspring. Or layout. Or tuck."

After his little sister Zara joined the team and he accompanied his mom to a meet—conveniently, one where I got a first all-around—the pestering escalated. "Can you do a double full twist? Can you do a triple tuck?" His questions made me feel deflated, like all the stuff I *could* do wasn't good enough. And with all the pressure his questions put on me, I was terrified that I was going to mess up the next time he was watching.

"Don't come to another meet unless you want to die," I hissed.

He acted all casual, but I knew his facial expressions well enough to see that I'd hurt his feelings.

A few months ago, when she first joined the team and we were starting to be friends, Callie caught a glimpse of Zach when he came to pick up Zara from practice, and she said to me, "Whoa! He's hot!"

I raised my eyebrows. Zach, hot? For some reason, I found myself blushing. Then I started avoiding him even more than before. I was busy with gymnastics and school, and he was off geeking out over wormholes or science-fiction movies or whatever, and somewhere along the way, we completely stopped hanging out.

And then things got weird. Once last spring, too impatient to wait till Mom got off work, I walked home from gymnastics practice after dark. Zach happened to be driving by when a carful of guys passed me, shouting out the window. Zach pulled up to the curb, and I felt lit up, unexpectedly happy, when I caught sight of him. I tamped down that feeling as fast as I could and glared at him.

"Get in," he ordered. "You shouldn't be walking at night."

I hate being ordered around, but I was a little shaken by the yelling guys and a lot shaken by this strange new feeling, and I found myself ducking into his car. "Don't blame the victim, dude. I wasn't doing anything wrong. Those guys were cackling me."

"You mean catcalling? Or heckling?"

"Whatevs," I muttered. I was kind of proud of coming up with a new word that meant catcalling and heckling at the same time. Zach didn't have to act like he was so much smarter than me. Why, when I found him so irritating, did I suddenly find myself super-attuned to him, my stomach squishy, my skin raw, electricity sizzling along my leg when his hand brushed against it as he shifted the car into gear?

"It's dangerous to be out by yourself at this hour," he scolded me. His hair was sticking up funny, and I fought an impulse to smooth it down.

"Okay, Grandma," I answered. It irritated me to feel so vulnerable. Why did he have such an effect on me?

"Are you trying to get yourself abducted or something?"

"Those guys shouldn't be yelling at girls," I argued back. "And anyway, this is a small town. How dangerous can it be?"

When he pulled into his driveway, I jumped out, barely thanking him for the ride, my stomach so unsteady I just needed to get away from there.

Defying my new unwanted feelings, I snuck out one night last summer to meet a senior I'd talked to a few times. I made sure Zach saw me, slipping out my back door when he was in his yard with his dog.

The guy picked me up at the curb and drove too fast to a college party full of drunk people and smoke, the air reeking of beer and weed. I sipped from a red Solo cup of beer though I didn't really like the taste. I ended up in a bedroom making out with some guy who wasn't even that cute, and then I walked all the way home. I glanced up as I crossed our driveway in the moonlight and saw Zach's dark silhouette in his bedroom window, watching me.

For some reason, I felt pleased at this.

The next afternoon, Zach was walking his dog when I went out to get the mail. He winced when he saw me, like now he thought I was beneath him. Like those boring geeky girls he goes out with, with the fashion sense of middle schoolers, are so superior to me. "Don't be a creeper," I said to him.

"God, somebody has to watch out for you," he answered. "You are so bullheaded and impulsive. You are totally out of control."

"When did you get so judgy?" I asked him.

"When did you get so immature?" he asked me back.

I lashed out. "Yeah, right, like you're so much better. Just don't talk to me anymore."

Once I said those words, I couldn't figure out how to take them back, even though he winced, a hurt look crossing his face. "Just mind your own business," I muttered, storming away, resolving not to care. And ever since then, I've ignored him. I pretend like I am completely unaware of his presence, though actually it's like I have an internal compass that follows his movements whenever he's near me.

I hate feeling agitated all the time. I hate feeling my mood soar and dip depending on whether he's in the room.

And the more we avoid talking to each other, the more I miss him. It wasn't until I could no longer talk to him that I discovered all of these inconvenient feelings.

But I stand by what I said. He had no right to tell me what to do.

Still, I feel like I'm going to burst with this news. Somehow, I have Chinese heritage. With wonder I examine my tan skin and gaze in the mirror at my brown eyes and hair.

Zach would help me make sense of all of this.

Or not. I hear his sensible voice in my head, telling me to calm down and wait for an explanation from Mom. Telling me that maybe there was a mix-up in the genetic results.

I hate it when anyone tells me to calm down. Especially imaginary voices in my head.

I keep remembering Mom's tense tone, like she's hiding something. Why wouldn't she want me to find my birth certificate myself? Why would she be secretive about my heritage?

You are so impatient, I can hear Zach say.

Stop jumping to conclusions, I can hear Mom say.

I pace, second-guessing myself and feeling annoyed at Mom and Zach both. It doesn't take that big a leap to conclude that something's not right here, I argue with their voices in my head. People who've known you your whole life can be irritating, the way they're always trying to confine you to versions of yourself that you've outgrown, or see flaws in attributes that maybe have turned into strengths. Like, am I really so stubborn, and if so, isn't that a good thing for a gymnast? And why should I wait patiently till Mom gets home when I can investigate something she's had sixteen years to explain to me?

And so, resolutely, defiantly, I take the plunge through the attic door, heading up the stairs.

Something about this space spooks me. Sometimes I swear I hear creaks up here, and footsteps, as if the attic is haunted or someone has snuck into the house and is secretly living up here.

At the top of the narrow, steep stairs, I snap on the light, stumbling over a wadded blanket. Mom is a neat freak. It's not like her to leave things lying in the middle of the floor.

The file cabinet is locked. I yank and tug on the drawers, but they don't yield. I pull so hard I'm afraid I'm going to strain my shoulder or pull the file cabinet over on top of me.

I head back downstairs, where I rifle through the secretary. Mom's passport and birth certificate are there. I find our social security cards. But that's it.

Defeated, I settle in the living room to try to concentrate on the proposal for my junior research project. But I'm having a hard time focusing. All I can think about is how to open that file cabinet. I force my attention back to my assignment. I want to write about the history of body image in gymnastics, though I still haven't really found a focus. After glancing through Mom's suggestions and uploading my proposal draft, I scramble some eggs and make toast for dinner. I add some fruit so I can tell Mom I had a healthy meal. After I lay out my competition leo and warm-ups, I lie in bed, still roaming the house in my mind, trying to figure out where Mom put the copy of my birth certificate.

Maybe my dad's is tucked away in the same spot. Maybe there's something on it about his ethnicity. I keep picturing that file-cabinet lock, willing it to open.

When I wake at 2:00 a.m., it's like the quiet of the house amplifies the sound of rain ticking against the roof. My tabby cat, Simone Biles, is curled up next to me, and she purrs like a motor next to my ear. I lie there for a moment thinking about my genetic results and my birth certificate. I consider waking up Mom right now and making her tell me what's going on.

Instead I look up YouTube videos on picking a file-cabinet lock. Then I tiptoe down to the kitchen for a knife.

At the edge of my vision, I catch a flash of light from the deserted yellow house next door.

Startled, I move toward the kitchen window, straining to see beyond my own shadowy, ghost-like reflection, past raindrops standing on the glass. For a second, I imagine I see the silhouette of a woman in the shadows under the fog-rimmed streetlights, her belly rounded. I turn to flip off the kitchen light and swivel back to look out the window.

Our yards are empty. A tree branch from next door has wrapped around the partial fence that separates our properties, entwining with the slats like an arm casually slung across someone's shoulder.

Upstairs, the house remains quiet except for the steady hum of the fan, a branch that scrapes against a window, and the rain that spatters against the roof. Our old house has thick walls and doors, which made it easy for me to sneak out last summer. Still everything seems so noisy when you're trying to be quiet.

The creak of a stair, the pounding of my heart.

Up in the attic directly above Mom's bedroom, I aim the knife toward the file cabinet lock and insert it, shifting the lock counterclockwise. It's way too easy. The top drawer releases and slides open.

My heart is drumming. I find a thick pile of papers labeled "Abstract," consisting of four pages chronicling the house's legal history. In almost a hundred years, there have only been three owners. The entries go backward from Mom to someone named Abby Grant to a guy named Lucas Grant who built it in 1920. The deeds are monotonous and repetitive, mostly consisting of detailed discussions of the location of property lines.

Other folders contain boring stuff, receipts for home and car repairs, my parents' marriage license, my dad's death certificate. Receipts for property taxes on our house and, for some reason, the deserted yellow house, along with old electricity and water bills and a contract with a cleaning service.

Mom has been paying for years to maintain an empty house that belongs to someone else?

Score! My birth certificate, a single sheet of paper stamped with a Pennsylvania seal, is one of two thin documents tucked away in a manila folder. It says that I'm Elizabeth Arlington, born in Bradford, Pennsylvania to Joan Wilson Arlington and Philip Arlington. So this means I'm definitely their child? I wasn't adopted or something? The word *Deceased* appears under *Father's Occupation*. My dad was killed in a trucking accident eight months before I was born. The section under *Name and address of attending physician or midwife* is blank. I'm disappointed that there are no lines related to race or ethnicity.

I unfold the second paper, a letter signed by Mom with a notary seal near the bottom:

Elizabeth Arlington was born at home during a snowstorm. The streets had not been plowed and ambulances couldn't get through. Labor happened suddenly and there were no witnesses. I am requesting an affidavit of live birth. I enclose statements from my minister and my employer attesting that my husband died eight months ago. Grieving and on a leave of absence from my job, I didn't realize I was pregnant for several months. I did not seek prenatal medical care.

The sentences look wavy and disjointed as my eyes dart up and down the page. I read them again, and then a third time, trying to comprehend. I wasn't born in a hospital, but at home? Here, in this house? And Mom was all by herself?

Why hasn't she ever told me this?

The room tilts and whirls around me, as if I'm wandering through a dream that doesn't make any sense. My hands are shaking as if they aren't attached to me anymore as I sit back on my heels. I remember asking her once, "So you found out you were pregnant after Dad died? Were you scared about raising me alone?"

"Oh, yes," she said. "Terrified."

"But were you happy?" I prodded her. "Didn't you think it was sort of romantic to have something left of him?"

"I guess," she said dubiously, then saw the stricken look on my face. "No, no, I was thrilled," she hastened to add. "I mean, it was shocking at first, but once I got used to the idea of being a mom, it was the best thing that ever happened to me."

Wouldn't that have been the freaking moment to tell me about the weird circumstances of my birth?

I plop down with my legs crisscrossed, running my eyes over the affidavit again and again, trying to pull more answers from the short paragraph. It's true that there are lots of odd things about us. A mom who looks nothing like me. A dad, probably a mixture of Asian and Caucasian, who died before I was born. Both only children; no other relatives. My parents were in their forties by the time I was conceived. Especially in this town, where everybody seems to be related, it's always felt weird that I don't know anyone else who shares my last name. Sometimes we run into people who remember my dad. Why has no one ever said anything about him being Asian? It seems like that's something people would comment on in a town like this, where almost everyone is white. I reach to the back of the cabinet for another pile of papers: pages torn from a coloring book, yellowed around the edges. Matching pictures of dolphins and elephants, two of each. A gray elephant and a green polka-dotted elephant. Yellow daisies and purple ones. A rainbow striped puppy and one decorated with snail-like curlicues.

Mom saved embarrassing amounts of my toddler and elementary school art: streaky finger paintings; collages of magazine photos, thick with glue; wobbly clay bowls; drawings of lopsided houses next to bushy-haired trees under smiling yellow suns. They're stored in boxes stacked against the wall. Why did she store these particular coloring-book pages in a locked cabinet?

I replace everything in the drawer and ease it closed, then pull open the next. This one contains a hodgepodge of loose photos, mostly unlabeled ones of people I don't recognize. "J and A" is penciled on the back of one. Mom, no older than twelve, towers over a much older woman. She's always talked about the step-grandma she was close to when she was young.

And then I find myself staring at a photo of a little boy with hair so light it's almost white, the kind of hair that disappears altogether when it's wet. I turn it over.

"Phil, 6," someone has scrawled on the back.

My dad? Or some other guy named Phil? This guy has blue eyes and pale skin.

Below it are piles of packets of photos, bound with rubber bands so fragile they break in my hand.

I flip through them. A light-haired teenager in a tux as if he's headed to a dance, a man angling a fishing pole above a stream, a little boy waving from the window of a truck. In another photo, the man poses with Mom, both of them adults, in a restaurant with white tablecloths. The backs of all these photos are blank.

Maybe Mom had a brother she never told me about.

I pick up a thick bundle of school portraits, colors faded, this same guy turning from a chubby-cheeked boy with a crew cut to a teenager with shaggy hair, barely smiling.

"Phil, first grade," someone wrote on the back of one. "Phil, eighth grade."

Maybe my Mom's secret brother was also named Phil?

Otherwise, this doesn't make sense. This guy looks nothing like me.

"Are you sure I'm not adopted?" I've asked Mom a million times over the years, and she just laughs, says, "Oh, your grandmother was actually really petite," or "Maybe we don't look alike, but we have the same allergies and blood type."

And I've ignored the nebulous doubt that tugs at me.

I turn over another school portrait. "Phil Arlington," it says, confirming that this person with straight blond hair, with pale, pasty skin, with bright blue eyes, is my dad.

And suddenly my thoughts are whirling through space, flipping, tumbling, spiraling, unable to land on the simple fact that these cannot possibly be my parents.

Mom purposely hid these photographs.

Mom has lied to me my whole life.

3

From my bedroom window, under the cover of darkness, Zach's house has practically vanished, with not even a night-light or porch light visible. The whole neighborhood is sleeping—no blue lights of TVs or softly glowing bathroom windows. The rain has briefly let up, and the pavement looks slick and shiny. I wish I could text Zach the way I used to. I want to ask him if he's awake.

But I told him never to speak to me again, and I'm afraid that if I texted him, he wouldn't answer.

If I could talk to Zach, I know he'd put this into perspective. He would say something calm and logical that would smooth over this feeling in the pit of my stomach. He's always balanced me out when my imagination runs away with me. It will turn out that Mom had an affair with a curly-haired man or something. I would realize that it's totally overdramatic that I feel like my whole life is about to be overturned.

There's probably some simple explanation as to why Mom never told me about the circumstances of my birth. But what could it possibly be?

How harrowing, to have a baby all by yourself during a snowstorm.

That just seems like a story you would tell every chance you got.

I glance at Zach's dark window again and then at my phone. Maybe he'd be mad if I woke him up.

Or maybe he'd think it means I need him, and that might be even worse than him getting mad. I wish I hadn't been so impulsive when I told him not to talk to me anymore. I can't go back on it now, even if I regretted it the minute I said it. Even if I've felt this weird ache ever since.

The sky lightens. My thoughts are so tumultuous that I can't calm them. After my finger hovers over Zach's name on my contact list a few dozen times, I push my phone away.

After my dad died, was Mom too deep in mourning to realize she was pregnant? Once she told me that they'd wanted children, but she'd had two miscarriages and a stillborn baby and given up. And then she'd told me how hard it was when my dad had died, how she took leave from work and barely left the house, avoiding phone calls, rereading all the books on the shelves rather than going to the library, opening every can of vegetables and packet of oatmeal instead of going to the store.

It must have felt like such a miracle, I've always thought, when she found out she was pregnant. But why hadn't she gone to a doctor?

I close my eyes, but my brain still buzzes. It feels like I'm hovering in the air, perched above the delicious, soft, dark oblivion of sleep. Sometimes I'll drop, falling, falling, falling, waiting for my feet to hit the floor, steeled to plant them firmly and balance and salute. But I never land. I just keep going down, down, down until I wake abruptly.

I turn from one side to the other until the sheet is twisted and the blankets lopsided, pulled out from under the mattress and wadded loose around my feet. I jolt awake again from a dream that the mattress is tipping like the deck of the *Titanic*, about to dump me into the sea. The whole world feels askew.

Finally I give up on sleep, take a shower, and stare out the window while the sun comes up. The trees on our mountainside glow orange and red. New sunlight illuminates yellow and copper leaves piled haphazardly in yards. And lights flare on in the houses around me.

Zach's window is still dark. Down the hall, Mom is still asleep too. I try to distract myself by surfing the internet. I watch a hilarious video of the 1928 Olympics, the first one where female gymnasts competed. A group in white shirts and baggy black shorts do simple exercises in unison: lift a leg, fling an arm. The men's vault looks like a tall kitchen table; women skip together in flapper dresses.

In a video from 1936, an adult woman with boobs and hips moves slowly on the beam like a tentative level 3, not even pointing her toes. I feel a little jealous, glancing down at my own small breasts, wishing that competitive gymnastics today allowed for different ages and body types instead of favoring preadolescent girls. I skip through time: 1948, women in their twenties and thirties, moving sluggishly, dance with ribbons and pose on beam, while another woman swings on rings. They weren't allowed to do back bends or splits back then; those skills were considered unladylike. In sixties footage, a Czechoslovakian always lands with a forward lean that makes it look like she's going to topple over. The pert seventies gymnasts have impressively flexible spines, but some of the skills still look simpler than those we do nowadays, and I find myself longing to live in those less-complicated worlds.

I return to some footage I've been watching obsessively over the last few weeks, coming back to it as I look for sources for my research paper. It's of an eighties gymnast named Jillian Clayton, who won junior worlds at fifteen. She looks solemn on the podium. I click back to a recording of her floor routine. She's energetic and technically proficient, but there isn't anything especially distinctive about her. Despite that, I'm always mesmerized watching her, my skin prickling with a weird déjà vu feeling. Like I know her. And I keep replaying it, trying to figure out why.

This girl's skills are way more advanced than mine. The footage is grainy and the leo outdated, less shiny and with more coverage than today's sparkly back-baring elite leotards. The girl throws herself effortlessly into double back layouts way beyond my skill level, but the bounce of her dark ponytail, the angle of her head lifts and her pointed toes, the blurred speed of her tumbling, the slightness of her figure all feel eerily familiar. I switch over to videos Mom has taken of my routines. My ponytail bobs like hers, my tumbling speed is similar, but isn't everyone's in these blurry home movies?

A lot of girls in gymnastics have similar childlike figures. It's a sport that draws girls with those kinds of bodies, just like basketball tends to favor tall people. It's a sport that pressures girls to stay small and aerodynamic, which is why so many gymnasts are in danger of eating disorders, something Mom warns me about all the time.

In this regard, it's not that surprising that Jillian and I would look so much alike. And in motion, the girl is a little out of focus. It's probably a coincidence that we have some of the same moves. Like how, in Jillian's younger years, she mounted the low bar with a jump with half turn to kip, a B-value skill I've incorporated into my routine.

I idly watch a video of her for the zillionth time, wondering why I'm constantly drawn to it.

Suddenly I see something. I lean forward, press pause, rewind.

Watch again.

Something clicks.

My eyes follow her on the beam as she stretches upward and flicks her fingers in the air before connecting two back handsprings.

Every gymnast on my team has a ritual before she performs any backward blind element on beam, a signature hand movement, a bend at the wrist, a loosening shake of her arms, a quick jerk or snap or twitch or finger wiggle. They're like superstitious gestures to ensure that as we pitch backward into, say, a back walkover, our hands will find the beam, sight unseen. Our feet will land firmly on the wood block instead of missing it and doing that walkover right off into empty air.

And before I was too scared to go backward, before I could only perform the skill on the low beam or with a spotter supporting my back, my signature gesture was a finger flick that looked just like Jillian's.

I rewind again. Play forward. Watch her finger flick.

Before I started my research project, I'd never even heard of this girl. Now I realize with a chill that somehow I've replicated the gesture exactly.

I've practically memorized the Wikipedia article about her. Born in 1971, Jillian was fifteen when she became junior all-around world champion. She was considered a shoo-in for the 1988 Olympic team before she had a disastrous Olympic trials and suddenly vanished from public view. No one was quite sure what happened to her, although there were supposed sightings of her over the years, living an ordinary life in New York City, Boston, Houston. One person swore he spotted her in line at Starbucks, buying coffee, in the Catskills. Another claimed that she'd been buying grapes and bananas at a grocery store in Ohio.

The article is spare, raising more questions than it answers.

I search for other articles about her. But before I can follow the sparse links that pop up, I hear soft steps padding across my mother's floor, the flush of a toilet.

My heart jumps. I slam my computer closed and gear up to confront Mom.

4

"Mom, my birth certificate," I remind her in the kitchen, just to see what she'll say. I braid my hair tightly, moving my fingers swiftly over and under and over and under.

I watch for her reaction.

She's chowing down on a granola bar and gathering her purse and briefcase. "I'm going to drop you off at the meet and then I have to run to work for a few hours this morning," she says. "I'll come back and look for it later."

Outside, the rain has started up again. We dash to the car. "You don't have to bother," I say. "I found it myself."

Mom nearly runs into a car parked on the street. She jerks the wheel as she veers away at the last minute.

"Where?" she barks out, straightening the car.

"In the attic. Why didn't you tell me that you had me alone at home? And why was all that stuff locked up?" I know there's some kind of simple explanation. Mom will tell me, and I'll feel better and a little silly for suspecting some deep, dark secret.

When Mom gets stressed, when a leak from an upstairs bathroom caus-es the kitchen ceiling to collapse or when the car makes loud noises requir-ing extensive repairs, she becomes very still. She stares blankly at nothing. She's too distracted to carry on a conversation until she figures out how to take care of the problem.

That's what she does now. She checks out. And out of old habit, I feel like I should reassure her. I have to tamp down the desire to say, "Never mind." She signals to turn left onto Seward Avenue.

"What aren't you telling me?" I blurt out. "Why don't we look at all alike? You and me? Or me and Dad? I don't look anything like either of you. Why were all of the pictures of him hidden away?"

Mom fixes her eyes straight ahead as we cruise up to a stoplight. "I al-ways meant to tell you the truth," she says absently, and that's it. She doesn't offer anything further and the silence stretches on.

Who are you and what have you done with my mom? I want to ask. She's normally one of those parents who doesn't consider any questions off limits.

She lets me watch or read whatever I want, even inappropriate stuff. I'm still traumatized by the death scenes at the end of *West Side Story* and *Titanic,* which she let me watch when I was six. I had nightmares about the mental hospital scenes in *Amadeus.*

Mom never hesitated to answer my questions, the millions I shot at her from the time I was two or three: why doesn't E.T. wear clothes? Who in-vented cake? How did my dad die? Can you get pregnant the first time you have sex?

Except now that I think about it, when I was younger and asked where babies came from, she explained it in an age-appropriate way. But when I asked where I was born or where I came from, she'd say, "Under a cabbage leaf," or "The stork brought you."

Now Mom wrenches the car around a corner so fast it throws me off balance. "You're making me carsick," I protest. "I'm starting to feel wheezy and queasy."

"Wheezy, queasy," she repeats absently, and because I guess old habits really do die hard, we say at the same time, "CoverGirl."

"Mom," I say, urgently, angrily, as if saying her name could pull her out of her trance. "Why won't you tell me what's going on?"

She turns into a parking place in front of the gym and sits there frozen, statue still.

"It won't make any sense," she finally says. "I've thought for years about how to explain it to you, but I wasn't planning to do it in a parking lot before a meet."

Suddenly I don't care about this meet, or the USAG meet, or even Zach. I just want to know what's going on.

"There was this girl. And it was so cold and snowy and I wanted to call an ambulance—"

"A girl? What are you talking about?" I'm horrified. "You mean someone else was my birth mother?"

Mom goes rigid again.

Clams up.

Then bursts out, "You're my daughter. Of course you're my daughter. Can't you just let this go right now?"

I remember once someone pulled a chair out from under me just as I was sitting. I landed hard on the floor and for a second was in a daze before the pain radiated through me.

That's what it feels like now. Except instead of a chair, it's like my mom has pulled my whole foundation out from under me and all she's thinking about is how it affects her.

"Maybe I don't want to be your daughter," I snap.

She recoils as I jump out of the car and storm off to the gym.

I've never said anything so mean to Mom. I know how easily stressed she is, and now I've added to it. But what was she talking about? Who was this girl?

I'm in a daze. The last thing I want to do is compete. Why didn't I have my wits about me enough to demand that Mom take me home and explain?

But old habits kick in. On autopilot, I warm up on floor, every landing rattling all the way through my core. I feel like I'm in a dream. Any minute, I'll wake up, and my life will be back to normal.

Until then, I throw back handspring after back handspring until the whole world is whirling dizzily around me.

5

I t's like the adrenaline from my confusion and frustration has become a powerful fuel. During warm-ups I blaze through my beam routine, my bars. Molly does that thing where she crowds into my space when I'm throwing front handsprings across the floor, and I have to drop into a somersault to avoid running into her.

Callie chews on a fingernail and does that fake laugh that isn't accompanied by a smile. She's obviously afraid of Molly, even though they're supposed to be friends. Honestly, though, I just don't care. I'm too shocked to care about anything.

Girls from six other teams arrive, clustering in corners, waiting for their turns at each apparatus. The bleachers fill with parents and siblings. Zach's sister Zara bounces over to join the level 2s. She's tiny, with blond pigtails and missing front teeth. Everyone applauds madly when the little kids do clumsy somersaults and back kickovers.

I will myself not to look up into the stands, but my gaze travels there involuntarily anyway. Zach glances up from some geeky superhero comic book, and I look away fast so he won't think I've been scanning the crowd for him.

It seems strange that Mom is working instead of sitting up there in the stands, leaning against the concrete wall all the way up at the top. She hardly ever misses one of my meets.

The first three events go by in a blur. When I chalk up my hands, when I grip the low bar, no matter what else is going on in my life, I usually feel a glow of happiness, a sense that I'm exactly where I belong. Today it feels as if that joy is still there, somewhere, but buried under layers of scrambled emotions.

Still, I work the bars confidently, squat on to kip, cast to handstand, half turn, tap swing, underswing, clear hip circle, cast to horizontal, cast to 45 degrees from vertical, baby giant, flyaway dismount.

If I keep my body hurtling through space, I don't have to pay attention to the confusion and terror and anger that keep trying to break through the shock.

After bars, I practice my beam routine along a line on the floor until it's my turn. I'm the one who almost never falls, and I don't even wobble today. I move authoritatively through my handstand, front walkover, stretch jump with turn, my jumps, leaps, sissonnes and straddle jumps, back walkover, cartwheel to handstand dismount.

When we rotate to floor, I line up to warm up, staying on the move. Motion keeps at a distance that feeling of dread that is yawning through the chasm of my stomach.

Keeps at a distance the heaviness in my limbs that makes them feel feverish. Distracts me from that rawness, as if my insides have been chafed by rope burns, as if I'm on the precipice of losing Mom, my identity, my life as I know it.

If I think too much, I'll walk out right now, find Mom, confront her, and demand answers. If I think too much, my eyes stray toward the stands, to Zach, who I used to always be able to talk to. I catch myself before I glance toward him or catch his eye.

I'm determined to stay focused: front handspring to front tuck, leg swing hop, aerial cartwheel, back extension roll, pirouette. Even though I substitute a cartwheel for a back walkover on beam, even though I avoid the back tuck on floor and throw in a second back handspring instead, I do them flawlessly and still make decent scores. I'm confident that I'll be representing our team at the USAG meet. If I focus on that, I can pretend that everything is normal.

But then there's a lull. We have to wait for the team before us to finish on vault, and as my muscles start to cool, the dread takes hold and opens the door for an onslaught of agitation, a whole cloud of feelings I can't sort out. I can't stop thinking about Mom's refusal to answer my questions, and by the time we're cleared for warm-ups, I've lost all focus.

I race toward the table and smack my hands against it, but then I stop without going over.

My timing feels off.

I don't have enough brainpower to worry about it, though. Sometimes the warm-up doesn't go so well, but I always recover when it's time to compete. And anyway, the vault is the easiest event.

I'm up. The judge in a blue blazer signals.

I rein in my wandering thoughts, snapping in an instant into a robotic salute and intense focus. I gaze down the vault runway, telescoping until all I see is the table in front of me.

Shut out all thoughts except for the mechanics of what I'm about to do: take off, gather speed, hit the springboard, and slap the table, exploding off of it.

But as I launch my sprint, I see that I'm going to hit the springboard too far back for the height I'll need. I'm running too fast to stop.

I veer, jog back the way I came. In the wrong direction.

Skid to a halt in time to see Coach Amy fling her hands into the air.

I didn't touch the table. I have two more chances.

Sometimes I think how bizarre and random it is to base your whole self-worth on whether you can throw your body over a table or, for that matter, keep your balance on a thin plank of wood or cast over a bar. Those seem like kind of arbitrary skills to be proud of, like the ability to roll your tongue into the shapes of tacos and wontons, or a championship in competitive backward walking. But still, I pride myself on always being able to perform.

And if I don't go over the vault, if I scratch this event and get a 0, I'm not going to be one of the top two level-7 scorers. I won't be able to go to the USAG meet.

I don't really care anymore about the meet. But somehow, despite everything, I'm worried about letting down my coach and my team and Mom.

And also, Zach is watching. I can't stand for him to see me fail. I can't stand feeling like he could wound me with one word or look.

My teammates pound the floor and clap their hands in rhythm, except Molly, who sits with her arms folded. "Let's go, Elizabeth," everyone else chants. I used to love that. Now it just causes the pressure to build even further. I tune them out as the judge once again lifts her hand and nods.

Muscle memory used to kick in when I propelled myself forward, but now I'm overthinking everything, aware of each churn of my legs, the length and number of my steps, the importance of landing on the part of the board with the most spring and pounding my hands against the table in just the right place.

By the time I arrive, I've psyched myself out.

I can hear the intake of breath from the stands as I ram into the table and detour back the other way.

Again.

Someone snorts.

Did Molly just snort?

A blush works its way across my cheeks. Now everyone's going to think I'm a loser.

I'm down to one more try.

I'm itching to get out of here. To run as fast as I can from this feeling of humiliation and failure, to escape all of the eyes on me, the expectant faces of my teammates and coaches, the pitying, encouraging faces of strangers.

Zach's gaze bores into me.

I close my eyes. I need to channel all of my agitation into my run.

I'll run from all of the stares and fling myself over that vault.

I'm going to do it this time, no matter what.

All I have to do is go over. It doesn't have to be pretty.

My teammates clap harder and chant louder as I wait again for the signal from the judge, but she's left her table to confer with another one. They pass a scoring sheet back and forth. Waiting gives my muscles time to cool. Waiting gives me too much time to think. The heat of my embarrassment and shame spreads through me. My face feels like it's on fire.

My eyes are drawn to a youngish woman at the top of the bleachers who is watching me way too intently. Her dark hair is pulled back in a braid, a few loose strands spiraling down the sides of her face. She tears her gaze from me, leaping to scoop up her toddler daughter who is lifting her leg into a scale as if the bleacher is a beam.

Back at her table, the judge raises her hand.

My foot twinges, the one that I broke last year when I fell on my vault landing. I push aside the image.

I go for it one last time: salute, throw all of my power into my run, hit the board.

Think of Mom.

Fall out of my handspring.

Hear a low moan from the stands.

Freeze there, in shock.

I've never tanked an event before, and certainly not one as easy as the vault.

I plop down on a mat, barely noticing as my teammates take their turns. The tension and dread that have been hovering around my edges all morning now take up what feels like permanent residence. I'd give anything to crawl under the pile of mats in the corner and hide. I don't look over at Zach.

If he shoots me a single sympathetic look, I swear I will kill him.

Without a score on vault, I'll finish last all-around.

Last. Good-bye, USAG meet.

But honestly, I can't even remember why I thought I cared about that.

Gymnastics is the only sport in existence where the biggest loser has to stand in front of everyone at the end of a row of girls. Where everyone will know how much your scores suck because you're the one standing farthest from the podium, trying to smile.

Outside the high gym windows, dark clouds hang low, and the air is heavy, oppressive with humidity. It's like the world is on edge, waiting for the sky to explode in torrents of rain.

Every excruciating minute drags by as I wait for the meet to be over. The team behind us has just rotated to vault. The little girls, the level 2s and 3s, take running starts and do front handsprings onto piles of mats, a pre-vault exercise that they perform in competition instead of actually going over a table.

"Do you remember when you could make a nine just for somersaulting over a pile of mats?" Molly asks Callie.

Callie glances nervously toward me as we watch the little girls spring and flop onto mats while their teams applaud.

"At least they actually complete their vaults," Callie answers.

The betrayal is complete. Callie has taken sides with Molly. And even though this is the least of my problems, I feel like I can barely move. I'm catatonic with misery.

"Looks like I'll be representing the 7s at the USAG meet," Molly says.

I summon up my indifferent face. "Whatever," I mutter. I eye the door of the gym. I'll pretend I'm going to the bathroom, and then I'll walk right out instead of coming back.

I rise slowly.

Molly rises too.

"Going to go hide in the bathroom like a little baby?" she asks.

My hands whip out and shove her. She totters backward.

We both stand there, stunned.

Coach Amy storms over. "Elizabeth! Out! Now!" she says.

There's floor music playing and teams still competing on all of the apparatuses, but still I feel like everyone is watching me. I've never before been asked to leave the gym. I won the team sportsmanship award two years in a row, and two leadership awards after that. When other girls try to psych me out by bumping me during warm-up, I've always ignored them. When girls make catty comments about other girls' weight, I stick up for the others.

One time when Molly watched someone from another team on beam, repeating under her breath, "Fall, fall, fall," I was the one who said, "Don't do that! Karma!"

"Who's Karma?" Molly asked.

But now I've turned into a smoldering repository of rage. I'm a storm cloud waiting to burst. I'm the kind of girl who shoves a teammate. I remember how Mom used to tell me, when I was little, *Use your words, Elizabeth*, whenever I acted on impulse like this.

I'll probably have to go to anger-management class before I'm allowed back into the gym. I'll probably fail.

The rain has let loose, pummeling the roof, and someone has opened a window. Cool, damp air blows across the room as I grab my backpack and pull out my warm-up jacket and pants, sure that everyone is muttering about me as I make my escape.

6

Rain slashes and slams at me, trickling down my face and puddling over the ground as I trudge past Crook Farm and the bowling alley in my inadequate warm-up jacket and pants.

Rain soaks my jacket and weighs it down as if someone has sewn marbles into the hem. Rain batters me until all of my clothes cling like Saran wrap. I grit my teeth and keep going, even though I feel too heavy to move. Soaking wet, freezing, two miles from home, I can't imagine being any more miserable.

The quiet streets feel eerie, like I'm skimming the surface of secret depths, as if rain has washed away the dusty veil between the regular world and a strange shadow world beneath. Long fingers of light stretch along the pavement. Streetlights, headlights, stoplights become the pillars of the underworld, and it's like I can only travel the exterior of this mysterious, multidimensional plane.

For a second, my despair lifts a little. I forget that my sneakers are soaked all the way through and that Mom has lied to me and that I've just been kicked out of the gym. And then I remember and feel that hollow thud in my stomach all over again.

A car slides up behind me onto the shoulder. I turn to find Zach in his mom's Toyota Corolla.

Zach is the last person I want to see and the person I most want to see, all at the same time.

I glare at him to disguise the angry tears that have been running down my face alongside rivulets of rain. I hate the idea of giving him more power over me. It already feels like he has the upper hand, like he can make or break my mood so easily.

I hate that I'm so relieved to see him. That against my will I feel a rush of hormones, that a weird glimmer of happiness peeks through my misery, even though the last time he picked me up when I was walking home didn't go so well.

I'm tempted to stalk off and go on protecting my heart from him, but I'm so cold and wet and miserable that against my better judgment I open the passenger door and duck into the car.

"So you're skipping the awards ceremony and walking home in a monsoon?" Zach sounds cheerfully bemused. I fold my arms defiantly with no intention of explaining.

Zach's hair is disheveled and he's wearing his cross-country windbreaker, hazel like his eyes. The windshield wipers fly wildly back and forth, going all wonky as they try to keep up with the rain.

"Just take me home." I turn on the heat and aim all the vents at myself, refusing to look at him as he turns onto Jackson and stops at the sign at Petrolia. I try to maintain my grimace even though my mood ticks up in Zach's presence.

Instead of easing onto our street, he continues straight.

"What are you doing?" A part of me just wants to put on dry pajamas and pull the covers over my face. But I dread being alone with my thoughts and the bad feeling in my stomach. And what if Zach and I just go back to being strangers again? I don't think I can stand that.

Zach drives down Washington Street and swings into the Dairy Queen drive-through. "Want anything?"

"Are you kidding?" I can barely lift my rain-soaked sleeves, but he orders me ice cream anyway.

And I eat it anyway, hair turning stiff, the heat vents slowly warming me up as we park overlooking the overflowing creek. Rain rattles on the roof and fogs the windows, and as my clothes dry, the car feels like a warm cocoon. But there's no way I'm going to let Zach know how comforting I find it to be here with him. I plan my retort if he makes a lame high-school-boy joke about how we're steaming up the windows.

He doesn't. Maybe it would just never have occurred to him to flirt with me. Maybe it would never occur to him to like me that way.

But why should I care? I just have a dumb crush. I don't really want anything to happen between us.

I take a breath. "I almost texted you last night," I confess. It's amazing how quickly we've fallen back into our old rhythm, the casual good-friends vibe we've always taken for granted. We're much better as friends, I tell myself, resolving for the 80 millionth time that I will not give him the power to break my heart. Maybe after today we can just go back to being friends again.

He looks surprised. A slow smile appears, like he's pleased and sees no need to disguise it. "So what's with you?" he asks.

I reach for my backpack, where I've sealed my dad's pictures and the letter in plastic baggies and shoved them deep into an inner pocket. I pass him the pictures one by one.

Zach's phone flashlight lingers on each photo. "I don't really look like my parents either," he finally says, his first words to me after several excruciating minutes of silence. He examines my face as if he's never seen me before, and not like he's suddenly realizing he might like me that way. More like I'm a freakish plant he never got around to examining until now.

"You have the same eye color as your parents," I point out. "And body type." It's true that his hair is the color of molasses and Zara's the color of honey, but it's all syrup, right? And they're all tall and thin.

Zach shuffles the pictures of my tall, light-haired mother and my rangy, pale father, rearranging them, his eyes and his light moving back and forth between the pictures and my face, studying my mouth, my nose, my ears.

At first I tolerate his gaze. I notice the chip in one of his front teeth from the time he fell off his bike when he was six. The small scar on his chin from when he skidded into the corner of a kitchen counter when he was four. The green flecks in his eyes.

"Stop looking at me like I'm a specimen you'd like to enlarge under a microscope." I blush and shoo away his gaze like I would a pesky bee.

"I'm not," he protests, fixing his light on me. It blinds me.

"Hey!" I cover my eyes.

Zach emits a low whistle. "According to the biology genetics unit, this shouldn't be possible."

I pass him my birth certificate.

He frowns at it a second, then shrugs. "It has your mom and dad's names," he says.

"I googled it," I tell him. "When a kid's adopted, their original birth certificate is sealed and a new one is issued to the adoptive parents." I pass him the letter Mom wrote to the Department of Vital Statistics.

"Wow," he says after a few moments. "So there were no witnesses? No midwife or attending physician? Do you think she stole someone else's baby?"

Oh my God, I think. *She stole someone else's baby.*

But *Mom*? Mom, who is honest to a fault?

There was a girl, she'd said to me. *And it was so cold and snowy and I wanted to call an ambulance . . .* What did she mean? Who was the girl?

"If the weather was so bad that night, it would be a little hard for her to just go out and steal a baby from a hospital nursery or something," Zach muses. "I mean, they would have checked, right, before they issued her a birth certificate? They'd've confirmed the weather reports. They'd've checked to make sure there were no missing babies? Right?"

"I guess." I'm disoriented by this calm, rational, wise side of hyper, nerdy Zach. I feel a sharp stab of longing for him to go back to being himself, for all of us to return to the people I thought we were. I repeat Mom's mysterious comment about some girl.

His brow wrinkles. "Wouldn't it be great to have a time machine?" he asks suddenly, his voice tentative.

"Sure, I'd just pop back to the night of my birth and find out what really happened."

A million different revelations fight their way across his face. "You and your mom, you stand the same way and you talk the same way and you have the same facial expressions," he says. "So I always thought you looked pretty much alike."

I stare out the window at the rain pocking the surface of the creek. "Actually, if I could time travel, I'd go back to a week ago and never find out any of this."

"What else did your mom say?"

"Not much. She was kind of evasive."

He shuffles through the photos again. Takes a breath and lets it out like he's about to speak but then thinks better of it. Finally, he says, tentatively, "What if you *could* go back to the night of your birth?"

"Sure, and why don't I go to the moon while I'm at it?"

Zach is silent, as if he's trying to make up his mind about something. Then he scootches around. For a second, I think he's going to touch me, and I pull back, startled. It's funny how you can want someone to touch you and be terrified of it all at the same time. But instead he reaches into the back seat, rummaging around in his backpack.

"Do you remember this?" He produces a clunky-looking watch.

It takes me a second to place it. When we were young, on rainy days, Zach and I used to sneak into the yellow house on the south side of mine, pushing open the basement window and dropping into the concrete cavern. The house had long been deserted. Though for some weird reason the electricity and water still worked, and a cleaning service stopped in to clean it periodically. Now I know why—that for some reason Mom was paying the bills to maintain the place. The TV was hilariously old, an impressive square of furniture on narrow little legs with no cable box or DVD player. There were dusty dishes in the cupboards and silverware in drawers, cobwebbed clothes on hangers in closets, fading stuffed animals left on one of the beds, a car rusting in the driveway. It was like a family had been going about their lives and then suddenly up and left. I was prone to nightmares after we'd hung out there.

One day, while sifting through a drawer in the kitchen, we found, among hammers and screwdrivers and light bulbs and some mouse droppings, this strange, primitive-looking watch-like thing with a black strap, wrapped in a yellowed scrap of paper covered with an alphabet matched to strange symbols, like the key to a secret code. Underneath, there was faded writing: *If I don't return, please come find me.* "What if this is a time machine?" Zach had said, and I'd laughed. We glanced at it and put it back.

"I think it actually is a time machine," he says now. He watches me as if testing for a reaction. I'm pretty sure he's joking.

"Here." He passes it to me. "Try clicking these buttons. But whatever you do, don't push that one."

I click through the side-by-side window displays. A date flashes: 1928.

"Try the one next to it."

It shows an address in Amsterdam.

I look up, confused. Then I push the buttons a few more times: addresses in Antwerp, 1920. Berlin, 1936. Munich, 1972. Montreal, 1976.

"Those are Olympic dates and places," I say.

The furrows in Zach's brow smooth out. "Oh," he says, as if I've cleared up his confusion. But then his brow squinches up again. "But there's other dates too."

I stare at him, trying to remember when he got so tall. I vaguely recall his voice squeaking for a while in seventh grade before it deepened. Confronted by the reality of him, my crush-like thing feels even more ridiculous.

But I still feel weirdly happy to be in his presence. Even if my stomach bottoms out whenever he looks at me. The rain drums ferociously, swimming across the windshield so that now I can't see out at all. It feels like we might be the only two humans on earth. Like this day never happened. Like I didn't fail at vaulting. I didn't push a teammate. My mom didn't evade my questions.

I can't stop picturing her worried face. As I watch Zach studying the watch, clicking through dates, my brain keeps rushing. Ruminating about Mom's words: *There was a girl.* Cringing at the moment I told Mom I didn't want to be her daughter.

The moment I shoved Molly. The moment I gave up on the vault. I keep retracing my meet performance, every move, every mistake. I picture myself running, jumping, thumping the table, rising into a front handspring, falling back onto the board.

The warm car rocks a little in the rain and the wind. Zach finally tears his attention away from the watch. "I've actually been doing research. You know how, at the Zippo shop, they sell key chains and flashlights and stuff— merchandise in addition to lighters?"

I roll my eyes. I can't imagine why he's reminiscing about the Zippo Museum and shop now, especially when I've got real problems to worry about.

"Just listen." He gets that stubborn look on his face, the one that means his thoughts are following a track and can't be derailed for anything. "So, a bunch of medical research in the fifties and sixties confirmed that tobacco caused serious health issues. By 1970, all cigarettes sold in the US included a health warning from the surgeon general and cigarette advertising was banned on TV and radio."

I sigh impatiently. I can't believe I have a crush on someone so clueless, going on and on about boring stuff about cigarettes instead of really seeing me. I half tune him out.

"That's why Zippo recruited this woman, Abigail Lynn Key, to move here from Massachusetts. She would have been the youngest woman ever to hold a PhD from MIT, but she dropped out suddenly toward the end. She was only twenty-two and already had several patents. The popularity of smoking was declining with all of the health warnings and advertising restrictions, and Zippo was afraid of becoming obsolete. They were on a push to develop more products like flashlights and stuff, and she was specifically hired to develop a watch."

He rummages around in his backpack some more, then pulls out a folded paper. It's a printout of an ad. He reads it aloud:

The Chronowatch: designed with simple yet innovative features geared for performance, elegance, and sportsmanship . . . Keep track of the hour, the date, and everything in between with this multifunctional sports chronograph.

"God, Zach," I groan. "I know you think this stuff is exciting, but I just want to go home." And crawl under a blanket, hiding from my questions and humiliation and bruised feelings. But I know they'll catch up with me, sweep me up in a tornado of turmoil.

"Liz." Zach's voice is unnaturally quiet and patient. "Listen. This is about you."

I pretend to be exasperated to throw him off the trail of my crush, rolling my eyes again and sagging back in my seat, but not before I notice the rough jawline that has replaced his baby-soft skin. He smells like soap and coffee, and there are track marks in his hair, like he'd combed it after it got soaked in the rain. I look away quickly before he catches me staring.

"Gail Lynn Key lived in the yellow house," he says. "And while she was working on the watch in the ad, she was also secretly working on the prototype for this other watch. Then she abruptly left."

I remember finding a bunch of Zippo lighters in a drawer in the yellow house. I pretended they were dollhouse refrigerators, the tops popping open like freezer compartments.

He toggles through the dates and locations on the watch. "So these are Olympic dates," he says thoughtfully. "I think these are like the history button on a GPS. It shows where the wearer has been, or was planning to go."

"But GPS's hadn't been invented in the seventies. Much less the twenties. And why Olympic dates?"

"That's the part I don't get. But I'm pretty sure that this is a time machine."

"That's a sci-fi thing. It's not real."

"If you click all the way through, you'll see a bunch more dates. The day in 1976 a couple of weeks before Gail Key disappeared. And some others—I don't know what they mean. But what if you could go back in time to the day you were born? What if you could find out where you came from?"

"That's impossible."

"Well, according to the laws of physics, backward time travel is impossible. You'd have to move faster than the speed of light to break the time barrier, at least according to some theories. But that's impossible since the faster you go, the more mass you'd gain, and that would slow you down."

"Unless you have a phone booth," I joke. "Or a DeLorean."

"Yeah, I don't think we're going to find any radioactive plutonium." He sounds way too earnest. "Well, actually, all plutonium is radioactive. But anyway, we're probably not going to be able to harness the electricity in a lightning bolt either. Although in *Back to the Future*, they only had to go eighty-eight miles per hour to achieve temporal displacement."

We watched all of those old movies together when we were younger. "You know that stuff is all made up, right?" I say.

"So, maybe it is, but if there's the smallest chance that time travel is possible, and if it could help you figure out where you came from, wouldn't you want to know?"

"So, how would we find out?" I play along. That's all it takes for his eyes to light up. I feel sort of gratified that I can have that effect on him.

"Well, what you said earlier. What if you went back to the day of your birthday and witnessed your own birth?"

"Yuck?" I answer. So, how long has he been concocting this whole time-travel theory? Does that mean he's been thinking about me as much as I've been thinking about him?

"I'm serious."

He stares at me way too intently, so I humor him.

"Okay, say I could do that. If Mom was alone, though, wouldn't I be kind of conspicuous? Wouldn't that kind of freak her out?"

There's that thoughtful look again, as he takes his time to ponder this. "Yeah, maybe. And I think going straight to the night of your birth might be too much. I mean, it might be really emotionally overwhelming."

I bristle. "I'm sure I could handle it," I say. "I mean, if there were actually such a thing as time travel." I can't decide if I'm touched that he wants to protect me or insulted because he thinks he has to.

"What if we tried sending you back to the week that Gail disappeared?" he goes on. "Just as an experiment? You'd basically land in or near her empty house and there'd be no chance of anyone seeing you. If that works, we could figure out what to do next. But wait—"

I toy with the watch while he studies the dashboard as if trying to work out some equation. I try to remember when and where Jillian Clayton was preparing for the 1988 Olympic trials. I google it, then find an address in Dallas on my cell phone and tap a date into the watch: May 19, 1988.

"What are you doing?" Zach snatches the watch back.

"Well, if I'm going to travel in time, I want to meet this gymnast named Jillian Clayton. I want to know why *she* disappeared."

"You can't just put your own locations into the watch," he says. "It doesn't work that way. The only places you can go to are the locations that Gail preprogrammed."

"But it was already there. The gym in Dallas where she trained."

Zach's mouth twists in concentration. He clicks through the settings again. "Wow, this is so interesting. You're right, but that location was connected to a date in the 1960s. I wonder what the significance of that was?"

He muses for a second and then snaps back to his authoritative tone. He is taking this way too seriously. "So, the catch is, for this to work, you have to be moving through space as well as time. You can't just stand still and zap yourself to another time period."

"So you're going to drive eighty-eight miles per hour, and I'll time travel out of the front seat? Wouldn't that be dangerous?"

"I don't think you have to go that fast. This is a kind of time-displace-ment machine that is programmed to particular extra-dimensional vortices that can transport you through time if you move with sufficient speed and power."

"And how do I do that?" Another eye roll, just in case my skepticism isn't clear.

"By vaulting," Zach says.

7

BRADFORD, PA, NOVEMBER 10, 2018

6 P.M.

If I thought I was really going to vault into the past, I'd insist on taking a shower first. At least Zach's crazy scheme is prolonging my time with him and delaying the inevitable crash of turbulent feelings when I'm alone again. I'm tired of this clammy leo, so I make him take me home so that I can change into my shiny blue practice leo and switch into an old pair of warm-up pants. It feels good to finally be dry. I quickly run a comb through my wiry curls and hurry back out to Zach's car before Mom gets home.

"Maybe I don't have time to take a shower, but I am not going to time travel on nothing but ice cream," I tell Zach, so he takes me to Taco Bell for a burrito. I want to believe that this whole wacko time travel thing is really just his excuse to spend more time with me, but I'm scared that I'm deluding myself. We park outside the building next to the gymnastics center. By now, the sky is growing dark. Through the rain, passing cars are wavery bright spots of color and movement.

I squint out the window. The only car left in the gym lot is the coach's. There's a light in the window of her office, but the rest of the building is dark.

"I can't believe we're doing this." I finish my burrito and toss the wrapper on the floor. I'm pretty sure the old me, the one who wasn't running from a million tumultuous feelings, the one who didn't have a crush on Zach, would never play along with this. He frowns at me but I ignore him. I'll throw the wrapper away later, when he takes me home. "They'll kick me off the team for sure if they find out I'm breaking into the gym."

"Breaking in to practice vault, for all they know," Zach says. "They'd probably be proud of you."

"Yeah, right." I gather my resolve and make a dash for it under the foggy streetlights. The rain has let up again, at least momentarily. The front door of the gymnastics center is still unlocked, and I ease it open and stop to listen. Coach Amy is on the phone in her office, the door partially ajar. What if she sees me? I'll tell her that I forgot my grips. That I need to take them home to sand the fingerholes to widen them a tad.

She's staring at the computer with her back to the door, phone wedged between her ear and shoulder while she types. "Well, we were going to take her to the USAG meet, but now I don't think it's going to work," she says. "In fact, I wonder if it's time to ask her to leave."

My heart stalls. Is she talking about me? I duck into the locker room unseen, that feeling of dread and shame curdling in my stomach. Jamming a water bottle in the back door to prop it open, I run across the parking lot and fling myself in the car. "I don't want to play this dumb game."

Zach switches the heat back on. It blasts into my face.

"What are you going to do, hide and never leave your house again?" Zach asks.

"Yeah, pretty much," I mutter. Dread spreads through me like a thick fog.

"You can't do that. You're not like this. You don't give up on things."

"I heard the coach on the phone. They want to get rid of me."

"Get rid of you? Like, they're taking out a contract on you?"

"That is not funny." I fold my arms. "Just take me home."

"Elizabeth," he says earnestly. He never uses my full name. He's the only person I've ever allowed, however reluctantly, to call me Liz. But now, the way he pronounces it, almost tenderly, takes me aback. What if he really does like me back? What if he doesn't? All of the possibilities are terrifying. I rush to restore our old dynamic. "Can't you find someone else to be your guinea pig?" I ask.

"So you think I'm just doing this as a science experiment?" He sounds indignant, maybe even a little hurt. "I mean, yeah, it would be cool to see if time travel is real, but that's not the point of this. She left this watch for a reason. Why shouldn't you use it?"

I straighten up as Coach Amy emerges from the building. She chirps her SUV unlocked. Its lights flash.

She climbs in and sits there for an unbearable few minutes, fiddling with the radio. Finally she reverses and drives right past us, swishing along the wet street.

I resign myself. "Let's just get this over with." I'll go to the gym and vault and nothing will happen and then we'll go home.

"We need to go over the ground rules." Zach plunges on earnestly. "You're just going to go to the week that Gail vanished, prove that this works, and turn around and come back."

"So I'd have to find a vault?" I'm teasing him, but he takes me seriously.

"The schools have old equipment in their storage closets. We used an old horse during the sixth grade gymnastics unit in boys' gym."

"Seriously? A gymnastics unit? Is that where you learned how to do backflips?"

"By 'backflips,' do you mean handsprings, tucks, or layouts?" he cheerfully mocks me.

"No, really, what did you do in the gymnastics unit? Cartwheels and somersaults?"

"Back shoulder rolls." He's heard the story about Mom and her eighth-grade operetta. "No, actually, we just kind of jumped over the ancient horse and swung around on some parallel bars." Zach gets serious again. "Anyway, just remember, you can't do anything that might change the past. You can't kill Hitler or compete in the early Olympics or run over your grandpa with a tractor. That's called the grandfather paradox. Any of those things could cause you not to exist today."

I never realized there were so many rules. Not only am I not allowed to change the course of history but I also have to be careful if I run into myself from another time; my watch might implode if it accidentally intersects with itself. "You can't save loved ones," Zach goes on. "You can't undo the past. You can't stop a virus from spreading. You can't stop a bomb from going off. You know what a butterfly effect is, right?"

I nod in an attempt to be spared a long explanation, but I should know Zach better than that.

"When a butterfly flaps its wings in South America, it makes a minuscule change in the atmosphere that could have a ripple effect that could impact the formation of a tornado in Texas or a typhoon in Asia weeks later. You have to be careful. The smallest thing could affect history."

"So basically I can't even sneeze?" I conclude.

He doesn't crack a smile. "I've done some pretty thorough research, and I don't think small actions are going to make too much difference. But you've got to be careful. Everything you do has an impact. And if you were to change history too much, you could end up creating an alternate timeline. One where, say, you're a theater geek instead of a gymnast and you never met me."

"Okay, I'll be careful," I promise. "I don't like any of the theater geeks."

I still can't get a smile out of him. "Things won't be that different in 1976," he says. "Not like, say, if you went back two hundred years. Everyone would be shorter and you wouldn't be dressed right and things would smell funny and there'd be no antibiotics. But the world forty years ago will be a lot like this one. Except less technology. A lot less."

It's obvious that Zach has seen too many movies. Listening to him, I wonder if he's delusional. And what if I still can't vault? I don't think I can stand to disappoint one more person.

Especially if that person is Zach.

"Are you ready?" he asks. "I just want to be sure you're prepared. You've been listening to me, right?"

"Don't get killed," I repeat back. "Don't let anyone steal my time machine. Don't let my time machine meet itself in another time period."

Satisfied, he pushes open his car door. I follow. "What if I can't vault right now?" I ask. "There's not even anyone to spot me."

"Oh, I can do that," he says confidently. "The guys had to spot each other in gym class during the sixth-grade gymnastics unit."

He's just asking for another eye roll. "Is this supposed to make me feel confident about your spotting ability?"

We round the corner of the building. *Maybe*, I think hopefully, *Coach Amy noticed the cracked door and closed it when she was locking up.*

But no. It's still wedged open. I lead Zach through the dark locker room to the gym's double doors.

It's spooky in there, and cold, with the lights off and the heat turned way down. Streetlights through the high windows cast shadows across the high and low beams in the front, the bars in back, the spring floor in the middle, the tumbling strip and vault table all the way over on the side.

Zach wobbles along a low beam, taking exaggerated prissy steps. On the tumbling strip, he waves his arms and spins on his tiptoes in a fake ballet routine, then leaps up to grab the high bar. It creaks loudly in the quiet gym. Headlights cross his face, then mine, blinding, then gone.

"Come on," I urge him. "Let's just do this. I will be in so much trouble if we get caught." But I say it halfheartedly, because it doesn't feel like I have much left to lose.

Zach drops from the bar and becomes all business, heading over to the vault runway.

"First you need to strap this on securely." He passes me the ridiculously bulky watch or time displacement device or Chronowatch or whatever it is, and I tighten it on my arm. The only thought worse than getting caught would be getting caught wearing this ugly thing.

Zach picks up my arm, and a zip of electricity zings through me. Arranging my arm with scientific precision, he punches a button and checks the date on the device. He's standing so close I can feel his breath on my neck.

"Now look," he says. "You push this second button to program your destination. If you didn't set it, you would probably land in 1976 right here where the gym is—probably an empty field? Or did this building use to be a school?"

"Yeah, I got it." I'm having trouble concealing my impatience.

"So I'm setting this for a couple of days after Gail disappeared, just so there's no chance of you running into her. Also, if you need shelter her house should be empty," he goes on. "And her address is programmed here, in this window, see?" He hands it to me. "Okay, you're good to go." He pats my arm paternally before he releases it, like an afterthought, like he's decided he should acknowledge that my arm is connected to me and not just a handy place to store the watch. He stations himself at the end of the vault runway while I drag a springboard into position and check the height of the table. I strip off my jacket and pants and leave them in a pile.

"Is that a good idea?" Zach asks. "Can't you just vault in warm-ups? It's going to be cold."

I wave him off impatiently. "Nobody vaults in those. They'd get in the way." I jog in circles to warm my muscles and psych myself up. I visualize my run, my simple front handspring over the table. Then I'll land on my feet and prove to Zach that there's no such thing as time travel.

I focus, do a little hop like Jillian Clayton in the video, then take off running. I fling myself forward, then fall back onto the springboard.

"Just try again," Zach says.

He waits patiently as I run and swerve away, hit the springboard and take off, then fall out of my handspring without going over.

"I can't," I say. "I have too big a mental block."

"It doesn't have to be fancy," Zach says. "It doesn't even have to be good. All you have to do is go over."

At the end of the runway, I listen to the quiet gym and the distant hiss of traffic on the highway, tires splashing along wet pavement. I close my eyes, picturing all the gymnasts in all the videos I've been watching. How they salute the judges and then take a second to position the table at the center of their vision, closing out everything. Traffic outside, floor music, applause as a girl on beam connects her back walkovers and lands on her feet.

Nothing else exists except for that weird-shaped padded table.

The vaulters in the videos focus, hop, and run, accelerating, full speed, full force, leaping onto the springboard and letting it propel them onto the table, exploding from horizontal to vertical in a split second, bodies tightly positioned in flight. I picture the way Jillian Clayton rams her feet into place on the mat before she salutes the judges.

And then I open my eyes and take off running, throwing myself into a handspring, somehow in motion, sailing through the air.

All of a sudden a light flashes, followed by a series of bright explosions like flashbulbs, and maybe what I'm seeing is headlights from outside traffic or maybe this is what it feels like when time tilts and bends, and for a second it's like I'm losing consciousness. But then I'm landing, my feet touching down, the mat more firm than I remember, without any bounce. I stick it and open my eyes, ready to pump my fist and shout at Zach, "I did it! I vaulted!" Ready to say to him, "Can you take me home now?"

But I'm not on a mat in a dark gym.

The air has a crisp, clean winter smell, and I'm standing barefoot in a foot of snow, more flakes swirling through the air.

In front of the abandoned yellow house next door to mine.

Miles from the gym.

PART 2

IMPACT

8

BRADFORD, PA, DECEMBER 4, 1976
4 P.M.

Snow quietly heaps itself against doors and piles in helmets on stumps and fence posts, as tall as the guards outside Buckingham Palace in an illustration from a book Mom used to read to me. It blows in curvy hills across the lawns and smothers boundaries between yards and driveways.

"Very funny," I say. "How did you do that?"

But Zach isn't there, and a cold wind blows against my bare arms and legs. My feet are buried in snow. I lift them one by one in disbelief: Is this real snow? It feels soft and fluffy, but the cold is prickly and invigorating. It takes a second before the cold really penetrates my skin.

Before I think, *OMG, I'm cold. I should have listened to Zach and vaulted in my warm-ups.*

The narrow path that has been shoveled down the sidewalk reveals that it's made of brick, not concrete. A big old colorless car, white with salt, brown with grime, swishes along the snowy street. I do a double take. Was that woman in the front seat holding a baby? Where's its car seat?

Did Zach drug me? Is this some kind of elaborate trick?

Or maybe this is a dream, and I've sleepwalked out into the neighbors' yard. I was really tired, after all.

Or maybe I landed wrong. Maybe I've been knocked unconscious, and that's why I'm dreaming these vivid dreams.

I look down at the watch strapped to my arm. December 4, 1976, it says. Twenty-six years before I was born.

I'm wearing a thin leotard, and I'm barefoot.

In three feet of snow.

In 1976.

And suddenly I'm shivering so hard that my teeth rattle, and my shoulders shake, and my whole body vibrates uncontrollably, and I wrap my arms around myself to try to contain the spasms, and I can't tell how much of those shivers are from the cold and how much are from a mix of terror and crazy, disbelieving glee: I might have actually traveled through time.

I don't know how long I just stand there in the cold wind while snowflakes settle in my hair and on my shoulders. Eventually my toes begin to tingle. I come to my senses and realize what a bad idea this is, being outside with almost nothing on. But even as the tremors subside, I still can't think straight.

I stumble up the street past my house to Zach's, where a sign on the mailbox says Allen. I vaguely recall that Mom is friends with a former neighbor named Mrs. Allen.

Lifting my hand to knock on the door, I hesitate, because if this is really 1976, if Zach really isn't here, what am I going to say? Just then I hear voices in my own driveway, and I tiptoe over to the corner of Zach's house.

A guy wearing sunglasses and a stocking cap pulled over his head is standing next to a car, leaning down to kiss a woman with long blond hair. She's wearing a fluffy pink coat. "Be careful, and call me tonight," she says with my mother's voice.

And I feel a terrible pang: that's Mom. Mom, long before she was my mother, long before she spent years hiding the truth from me. Here she is, barely older than me, the sleeve of her coat pulling back to expose her arm as she reaches up to hug the guy.

The person I've always thought of as my dad. The dad I never met. She was nineteen when they got married. He wasn't much older.

I want to run over to them. Throw myself into Mom's arms, desperate and hysterical. Beg, "Help me, something weird is happening to me."

But I remember Zach's words: I'm not supposed to do anything that might change the past in a major way. Anything I do could cause me not to exist. But how am I supposed to know what actions are major and what actions are minor?

I shiver, watching them. This woman, really a girl, who is Mom but not Mom, and this guy, my dad. She has a tiny waist and sharp elbows. Snow lands on her hair and his hat, briefly white like dandruff, before it melts.

I must still be in shock, because I have that underwater sensation again, like feelings can't quite surface. Like hovering under there is the confusion and sense of betrayal and anger and dread and grief I've been carrying around the last twenty-four hours, suspecting that I'm not who I always thought I was.

Now, through it all, wonder pushes through. These two people in front of me are my parents. Or are they?

How could they possibly be?

"Would we have been friends if we'd known each other in high school?" I used to ask Mom, and she'd laugh and say, "Oh, no, you'd think I was too weird. You'd laugh at my music and my bell-bottom pants. You'd want to take me to the mall to buy something to tame my frizzy hair."

It's true. She's amazed that I can French braid my hair and use eyeliner and throw a back handspring without missing a beat in the conversation.

"I could never do any of that," she always says, and I wonder where I got it from.

Now, I watch her hand the guy, my dad, a suitcase, both of them so tall and blond. How could I have gotten any of my genes from them?

The young guy who will someday be listed on my birth certificate as my father but will die too soon to be my dad ducks into his car, a big old station wagon with wood panels on the sides. "Get back in the house," he says, laughing. "It's cold." He cranks down his window. Kisses the tip of his finger. Touches it to the tip of her nose.

That moment of affection seems all the more sweet, knowing that he will die young, knowing that I will arrive somehow in the middle of Mom's grief, that Mom will get older and sometimes I will catch that haunted look flickering across her face.

I have a sudden impulse to rush forward, to forgive Mom for everything even if I don't know quite what it is I'm forgiving her for.

"Will you be back in time for the meeting on Thursday?" Mom asks.

"Meeting?" He's playing with the radio dial.

"The one about being foster parents."

I lean forward, wondering if I heard that right.

"What's the hurry?" He laughs up at her.

"Phil!" she says, her tone sounding a little urgent, but he's cranking up his window and reversing out of the driveway.

Mom sighs, watching him go, then pads in her slippers, now full of snow, back into the house.

The shivering overtakes me again. My teeth are chattering, my toes are hurting, my feet are turning blue. I've got to get a grip. I've got to get warm.

I turn and run back down the sidewalk, to the yellow house. I move along the side of the house, wondering if I can push a basement window in, but I don't have to. The door into the basement is standing wide open. Guess no one locked their doors back then any more than they do now.

Right inside the door there's a washer and dryer with neatly stacked towels on top. I reach out for them, pulling them all down to wrap around my feet.

Can you get frostbite in a dream? Can you lose your toes even if you travel to a time where you don't actually exist?

But my toes are tingling painfully back to life. If this is really 1976, Zach's research suggests that the house should be empty, but there will be blankets upstairs, and probably clothes still lined up on hangers in this woman Gail's closet, and food in the kitchen. Once Zach and I rifled through drawers, finding stale vanilla wafers in the pantry and a bottle of liquefied ketchup in the refrigerator along with some containers of long-expired yogurt.

"You know you can still eat that." Zach looked speculatively at the yogurt. "Yuck."

"Oh, this stuff lasts forever. I read that you can eat it way past its expiration date," Zach said. "If I keel over, dial 9-1-1. But I should be fine."

But he didn't eat it. He just wanted to gross me out.

Now, as I head up the basement stairs, I'm still kind of expecting Zach to be waiting in the kitchen, laughing at how he's fooled me into thinking that I've time traveled to 1976, to a few days after Gail disappeared.

I start to shiver again. Dart into a bedroom and snatch blankets off the bed.

Then I hear a faint sound. I strain my ears. Is someone here? Or did Gail leave a TV on? I creep into the dark, quiet kitchen, listening. It takes me a second to identify the sounds from the back room: the tiny booms and crashes and bangs and zaps of a cartoon. The kitchen counter is littered with empty cereal boxes, a peanut butter container scraped clean, a bread wrapper with two slices left, dirty knives.

Zach said that with Gail gone, the house would be empty, but I suddenly flash on details that he overlooked. A twin bed in one of the bedrooms. Those stuffed animals on top of it.

Why didn't Zach find anything in his research about Gail Lynn Key having a child?

Or maybe she just liked stuffed animals. Maybe the twin bed was left over from a previous tenant or was for guests. Maybe someone else has been camping out here. Maybe a murderer is hiding out in the other room watching that big, old TV that doesn't get any stations in my time.

Shaking again, feeling like a girl in a horror movie obliviously strolling to her doom, I follow the faint sounds into a room that's dark except for the flickering screen. The picture window has been flattened by the fading light to a mirror of the dim room, the steady bright spots of lightbulbs from the dining room, the spasms and twitches of the TV's blue glow.

At first I think that the room is empty. And then I see her, a little girl sound asleep on the low-slung couch with broken springs. I retreat to the kitchen before she can see me. My heart is pounding.

It's a little kid. What am I so afraid of?

I creep into the room again and whisper, "Hello?"

She stirs and sits up abruptly.

"Mommy?" She flings her arms around my neck, jolting me.

Seriously, do I look old enough to be anyone's mom?

She looks into my face and slowly extricates herself. "Anna?" she says, like she knows me. "Where's Mommy?" She bursts into tears.

At first I'm alarmed, thinking she's having a seizure or something. Then I realize that she's shaking with terror.

She's tiny, barely more than a toddler, with a curly mop of brown hair a shade lighter than mine and two tiny freckles on her cheekbone. She reminds me of pictures of myself when I was small.

My skin prickles. Who is this kid?

For a second, I wonder if I'm in a dream encountering my own younger self. But the girl doesn't have my dimples, and I wasn't born until years later, and anyway, I would remember being alone in a house when I was four, wouldn't I?

The kid's tears are turning to wails, and I freak. "Where's your mother?" I ask. My teeth are still chattering. The couch vibrates, both of us quivering. The girl abruptly stops crying to take a breath.

"She's gone," she says. "I keep waiting but she won't come back. I did everything she told me. I take a nap every day and pick up my toys every night, but she won't come back. I thought she'd come back if I was good."

She's gearing up to shriek again. What are you supposed to say to a screaming kid who seems to have been alone for days, especially when you know that her mother never comes back? This is way beyond my skill level.

"Where did she go?" I ask, anything to head off the impending meltdown.

She sniffles. "I don't know. Sometimes she disappears." Her face screws up.

"Please don't do that," I say hastily. "Your mommy sent me to help you."

Then I want to kick myself. How am I supposed to help her?

But my words calm her down. She plugs her mouth with her thumb and stares at me trustingly.

I wonder again how Zach could have missed the fact that there was a kid. That Gail had left behind a little girl, too small to be on her own. I try to remember other signs of a child back when Zach and I explored this place around 2012. I'm pretty sure the bedroom closet and dresser were empty, though.

What happens to this kid? I feel responsible for her, and I search my memory for what my own mother used to tell me to do in an emergency. How she'd ask me, "What would you do if the house caught on fire? What if you got lost in a store? What if I was sick or hurt?"

I used to recite all the answers. Get out of the house, find a nice lady who works at the store. But Mom never prepared me for what to do if she didn't come home.

"Did your mom give you instructions in case of an emergency?" I ask.

The kid tugs me to the dark living room. Her tiny hand is moist and sticky. Pressing her nose to the window, squinting through the snow that has started up again, swirling thickly, she points at the light in my house's kitchen window, a beam that doesn't waver. "She said to go find the neighbor lady. But I was scared to go outside."

Mom. Instantly, I know that Mom will know the right thing to do. "I'm sure that's what your mother would want you to do."

The little girl looks at me shyly. "I can do a handspring," she says. "But I do it outside, like you told me. I only do cartwheels in the living room."

"Like I told you?" The kid obviously has me mixed up with someone else. I wonder who this Anna is.

I'm relieved to have a plan. "You need to bundle up," I tell the kid, and she keeps looking at me for approval while she pulls on a coat and hat and boots from a heap in the corner, arms tangling in the sleeves, buttons mismatched, socks forgotten. I realize too late that I should help her.

I open the door and we stare at the snow that coats the yard. New flakes settle over a dirty bottom sheet, replacing it with a layer like a fluffy blanket fresh from the dryer.

"Will you come with me?" she asks.

I remember Zach's rules. I can't do anything big that would change history. But is even letting this kid see me interfering too much with her life? I'm still here, though, so maybe it's okay. "You always have to test every limit," Mom is always telling me. I feel guilty.

"I can't," I say. "But I'll watch you."

She stands for a second, then runs to the TV room to grab a stuffed dog and a small pink plastic purse.

"What's in your purse?" I ask as she fumbles on her mittens. She drops them to open the purse wide. It contains things that I'm guessing belong to her mother. A ring, a shoelace, a big plastic watch that looks like the one I'm wearing, except it has a red strap and a plastic cover over the buttons. Another Chronowatch.

"What's that?" I ask.

"My mommy had a magic watch like this," she answers.

I know Zach will scold me for not asking more questions. But the kid seems so freaked and scared, and I'm terrified that she's going to start crying again. Also, I feel weirdly exhausted. I mean, I did time travel forty-two years today and nearly froze to death.

"I've never been outside at night all by myself," the kid says.

"Just go," I answer. "I'll be right here." I hold my breath, hoping that she'll go and no longer feel like my responsibility.

And then I breathe out as she steps into the dark cold, where moonlight illuminates the snow so it sparkles and glistens like a field of light. The white expanse almost glows in the dark.

I sink to the floor, my back against the door, and realize that I never asked her what her name was.

9

Aﬆter a second, I realize that sending a little kid out alone into the cold could be grounds for revoking my babysitting credentials, if I had any. I scramble to my feet and find a long coat on a hook by the door. A pair of boots sits underneath the hook. I put them on, ease out the front door, and stand there in the shadows.

My house has no curtains. I watch the little girl creep closer, past the partial fence, and hesitate in the falling snowflakes. Occasionally Mom appears in one of the windows. I picture her going about her usual evening routine: laying a fire in the fireplace, lighting candles, putting a teapot on the stove. Rinsing a cup and plate and bowl and stacking them by the sink.

The kid stumbles forward.

Mom's head snaps up. The kitchen light goes off and Mom goes still, peering out the window. The kid takes another step.

Mom moves away from the window. The kid stands still, shivering in the cold. The streetlights make yellow splotches on the snow and the pine trees cast blue shadows. The kid glances back at me. I give her a thumbs-up, but I don't know if she can see me. The footprints behind her form little blue pockets.

Then a side door opens. Wearing a puffy coat, Mom steps outside. "Hello?" she calls.

The kid moves out of the shadows. I move deeper into them.

"Hello," Mom says. "What are you doing out here by yourself? You live there, right?" She points in my direction, and the kid nods. "Where's your mother?"

The kid just looks at Mom.

Mom reaches for her hand. They walk back toward me, toward the yellow house, past the big, shiny car in the driveway. I slip into some bushes, crouch there as Mom taps on the door, then twists the knob and peers inside. Mom is wearing colorful striped pants that widen at the bottom, hiding her boots. They look like little circus tents.

It's all I can do not to burst out of the bushes and accost this younger version of Mom, trying to convince her that I've time traveled from the future. I want her to be my mom and say comforting words that will quench the panic that keeps threatening to rise up.

The kid stands behind her, head swiveling, looking for me. I don't think she can see me, but just in case, I put my finger to my lips.

"Hello?" Mom calls, then says, "I'm going to go look around, okay?"

I hear doors opening and Mom's voice calling into empty rooms.

"For now, you can come with me," Mom finally says. "We'll make up a bed on my couch, just until your mother comes back." The kid looks straight at me and puts her finger to her lips as if signaling that she will keep my secret. Then they trek back across the glowing snow. Now there are five sets of blue footprints, two big, three little.

"Would you like cocoa?" I hear Mom say.

"Coke?" the kid echoes.

"Cocoa. Do you know what cocoa is?"

"I like Coke," the kid replies, and I remember some empty cans of Coke and something called Tab on the TV room coffee table.

"What's your name?" Mom asks.

The kid tips her head up and doesn't reply.

"What does your mother call you?" Mom tries again.

"Doodlebug," she says, and Mom laughs, and they vanish into the house. I wish I could go there with them. If I could sit by the fire talking to this younger version of Mom, maybe my agitation and anger would dissolve.

I stare longingly after Mom and the kid, briefly forgetting how cold I am.

10

Even when I'm warm I can't stop shivering, huddled under a blanket in the back bedroom of the yellow house, the room that appears to be Gail's. It's like I'm still in shock, trying to absorb that I'm actually in 1976. That I saw versions of Mom and Dad from forty years ago. That I steered some strange kid toward Mom and safety.

The lights have gone off next door, in my house, and I'm not sure what time it is, but I know it's late. Still, my brain is whirring: Who is this kid now sleeping on Mom's couch, the little girl who looks so much like my own childhood pictures?

When I let Zach convince me to time travel to 1976, then come right back, I was expecting to find an empty house. How can I leave now without finding out who this girl is? But it feels even more urgent to just get home again. To make sure that I can.

Sometime toward dawn, my anxiety wears itself out and I drift off to sleep. Then I come to consciousness just enough to move from the chair to the bed.

When I wake, it's still snowing. Out the window, my house looks snug and still. From the den, the TV keeps making an obnoxious beeping sound. I go in to find school closure announcements scrolling across the screen. I file this away. I'm going to need an empty school gym to get home.

But first, I'm going to get one more look at the kid. And Mom.

llll ⟋llll⟋

In my time, my basement door is held shut only by a padlock, one that we frequently forget to close. I'm not surprised that there's no lock now. I tiptoe through the basement, past the workbench and laundry room, up the stairs. I'm in luck. Mom hasn't deadbolted the door, and I crack it open.

Mom is in the living room, talking to someone in a hushed voice. After a second, when I don't hear anyone reply, I realize she must be on the phone. "I don't know where her mother is," she says. "She hasn't come home for a few days, I don't think. The police? Social services? I wish she could stay here. I know, I know."

There's a long pause. "The weather's pretty bad. Maybe she just hasn't been able to make it back yet." Another stretch of silence. "I know this is crazy, but what if she doesn't come back? Do you think we could look into fostering or adopting her?"

I strain my ears, wishing I could hear my dad's voice on the other end.

Mom sounds sad when she says good-bye. Then she picks up the phone and calls in sick to the library.

Back in the kitchen, she cracks eggs. I smell the eggs and bacon that sizzle on the griddle. I ate the remaining bread and some jelly in the yellow house this morning, but the smell of bacon makes me hungry. I hear Mom and the kid scraping back chairs as they settle down to eat at the kitchen table.

"Your mom didn't take her car," Mom says. "Did someone pick her up? Or does she take the bus sometimes?"

It still sounds like she's having a one-sided conversation, because the kid doesn't answer. Maybe she's nodding.

"Do you have a dad?" Mom asks.

Again, no answer.

"Do you go to preschool? Day care? How old are you?"

Maybe the kid holds up fingers, because Mom says, "Wow, you're small for your age. We'll wait for your mother together, okay?"

Water swishes from the faucet, and there's a clatter of dishes. "I have some coloring books left over from story hour," Mom says. "Do you like to color?"

After that, they spend the morning sitting at the kitchen table with crayons and what I conclude from my mother's observations are matching coloring books. Outside the window, snow falls while Mom and the child color unicorns and stars and dolphins.

"Your tongue sticks out when you concentrate. My step-grandma used to do that," Mom says. "Everyone thought she was psychic. She could always guess who would be the next president and what stocks would take off. She had no idea who was going to win the Superbowl or World Series, though."

Mom never told me any of this.

"Did she disappear?" the kid asks. "Look, I colored inside the lines. Do you think my mommy will come back now?"

"Oh, no, she just—" Mom breaks off. "I'm sure she's trying to get back to you. We're going to find her."

"Do you have a little girl?"

"No, I have a husband, but he drives a truck so he isn't home much. Someday we'd like to have children." Mom changes the subject. "You have good hand-eye coordination. Most kids your age don't have that kind of control."

"Let's do an elephant," the kid says.

I hear pages turning, then a crayon tapping against the page.

"See my impressionist elephant?" Mom says. "Let me see your picture. Oh, yours is pretty too."

"You used the wrong colors," the kid says. "Elephants aren't green. And daisies are yellow, not purple."

"Really? I guess I just liked those colors. Let's do the puppy."

There's a long silence, and finally Mom says, "Ooh, I like your rainbow stripes." I smile. She has always been good at jolting kids into seeing the world in a new way. I remember the coloring-book pages in the file cabinet. One tankful of fish with jagged markings, another tankful of fish with colorful spots. A beach scene's house and umbrellas and sea outlined with dark strokes and then filled in, the same scene colored blue and green with an orange umbrella, the marks going outside the lines.

Right now, I think with a chill, *Mom and this little girl are coloring those very pages.*

There's a knock at the front door. "Who could that be in this weather?" Mom says, her footsteps crossing the floor, halting in the kitchen doorway. "Oh," she says. Slowly she proceeds across the living room.

"You called about a little girl?" asks the muffled voice of an older woman.

Mom sighs. "My husband did."

Suddenly, the peaceful room crackles with tension.

"Can't I stay with you?" the kid asks in a small voice.

"Can't she just stay for now?" Mom pleads.

"We could certainly place a child with you if you and your husband complete the screening and training," the woman says.

"That won't help now, will it?" Mom's voice is crisp, businesslike. I imagine her squatting to button the kid's coat in the long silence that follows. "I hope someday I have a little girl just like you," she says. She sounds about to cry.

The woman leans down and says gently to the kid, "We'll send someone back to pick up your clothes and things, okay? For now, though, we have to go."

The front door closes quietly.

I emerge from the side of the house to see a woman in a black coat usher the little girl, holding tight to her stuffed dog and pink purse, away to her car.

11

I feel sad and unsettled as I make my way down the slippery hill, the wind sweeping clouds of snow into the air, the cold bitter on my cheeks. But I'm also desperate to get home. The sound of Mom's ragged sadness as she said good-bye to the kid lingers in my ears.

It's shockingly easy to get into School Street Elementary, which I think used to be a middle school. The halls are shiny and silent, with no signs of life. The office door is locked.

I spend an hour searching a dusty equipment closet in the gym, rehearsing the story I'm going to tell Zach. I keep getting my feet tangled in volleyball nets and tripping over a pile of baseball bats. Nervousness edges toward panic. What if I can't figure out how to vault my way home?

I find a beam in the corner. There must be a vault table nearby.

Though the gym is cold, I'm sweating. I throw off the coat I've been wearing and then the boots, followed by layers of Gail's old clothes, until I'm sifting through containers of balls and helmets and old trophies in my skimpy leotard.

Finally I give up. Obviously, there's not going to be a vault table hidden away somewhere. Vault tables are pretty big.

I pace out into the gym again. Stop to look at a pile of mats in the corner. Wonder if I could just do the level 2 and 3 vault onto some mats. Would I achieve enough velocity to get home that way?

Maybe I could go even faster without the impediment of a table.

And so I set my watch for 2018. As I drag a pile of mats to the middle of the gym, I imagine the big hug I'm going to give Zach when I get back. We're not huggy people, but tough luck. I can't wait to see him and tell him about this. And then I'll go home, and after I hug Mom, I'm going to make her talk. I'll insist that she explain what she meant when she mentioned some girl. I'll insist that she tell me about the kid from the yellow house and what happened to her. Are the girl and the kid somehow connected?

Finally I'm ready. I make a run for it. As I leap into the air, into my front handspring, I hear a sound like cards shuffling.

Uh-oh, I think.

Lights flash. I feel a jolt and, unable to control my landing, stumble several steps forward.

I open my eyes. I'm not in a gym and if this is a dream, I can't seem to shake myself out of it. I've come to a halt on a manicured lawn swarming with people, mostly girls in warm-ups or leos, traffic whooshing by along the street.

The sign before me swims into focus: Dallas Women's Gymnastics Center.

12

I look at the watch. Instead of 2018, the watch reads 1988, the date I set when I was playing around earlier, in the car with Zach. I gape at it. Everything blurs. Panic travels along my limbs, until I'm hot all over. How did I get here? Why didn't the watch take me home?

I take shallow breaths, which make me feel dizzy. My vision blurs. This all feels like a really bad dream. I force my eyes open. Force my breaths to deepen. Try to just focus on my surroundings. Before meets, Mom has helped me calm my nerves by using the "three-three-three" rule for anxiety. "Look around you and name three things you see. Then name three things you hear. Then move three parts of your body—your hands, your feet, your elbows, your fingers." Following these directions helps you avoid feeding the panic.

I try to focus, even if I'm so nervous I feel like I've forgotten how to count. It's late afternoon, with school just letting out: a yellow bus pulls up to the sidewalk, and a minivan skirts around it. Even school buses were longer in the '80s, but I don't see any SUVs. Red and white flowers nod in a breeze.

Girls pile off the bus, preadolescents with legs elongated by their high-cut leos. A boxy car spills out three little girls in warm-ups. They toss down their gym bags to cartwheel across the lawn until they are stumbling dizzily and giggling. A toddler holding her mom's hand goes stock-still, watching in awe. Her mother tugs her on into the building. A grandmother with gray hair strides past me, heading in behind the mother and daughter.

A gym, I think. A gym full of vault tables. I'll just go in, find one, vault again, and travel home this time.

And then it strikes me: This is the gym where Jillian Clayton trained. Is training.

I was expecting to see Zach. I was ready to burst forth with the story of visiting 1976. I was raring to go home and talk to Mom. But now, I shift gears so fast it feels like whiplash. Maybe I can figure out what happened to Jillian. Why she mysteriously disappeared.

That thought is appealing for like two seconds before I dismiss it. No. I just want to go home. My heart stirs up with panic again, thumping crazily in my chest as I imagine never seeing Mom again.

I need to get inside. I need to find a gym and a vault table right now.

A girl my age shoves past me, throwing a skeptical look at my strange-looking watch. "I got a watch like that out of a cereal box once," she says scornfully.

Yikes, middle-school flashbacks. Every time my breathing turns shallow, dizzy terror takes over. I take more deep breaths and follow the girl into the atrium. She flashes her ID card and signs in on a sheet on the counter, then proceeds behind glass doors.

It's impossible to sustain panic continuously. My agitation settles every few moments into an exhaustion that feels almost like calm.

I can do this. I just have to take one step at a time. Things are not so bad. After all, in my time, there would be ID card readers at the entrance to the building, but fortunately for me, security doesn't seem to be a huge concern in 1988. I slip past the pro shop and front desk while the receptionist is distracted by a phone call.

I continue to cycle through waves of panic that leave my head spinning and then ease up briefly as I enter a long hall, peering into glass-fronted gyms where preschoolers practice forward rolls and elementary-school kids totter on rows of high and low beams.

I can't exactly interrupt classes to execute a vault, and it would be foolish to just hurl myself blindly through space anyway.

I have to take my time, I have to think things through. I have to get my bearings and try to figure out why the watch has malfunctioned. I will not be the impulsive person Mom and Coach Amy and Zach are always accusing me of being.

Taking a deep breath, I peer into gyms at instructors who don't look that much older than me. The halls and gyms are hung with banners up near the ceiling and lined with glass cases of trophies. One wall displays photographs of champion gymnasts. I stop to search for a picture of Jillian. It's in the section of club gymnasts who've been on the US National Team.

She looks so young, with a tilt to her smile and a way of holding her eyes wide in the photo that remind me of me, conscious of making sure one eye doesn't end up appearing smaller than the other. Her skin is paler than mine, her eyes rounder. I wonder if she's also part Chinese. I don't think so. But the way strands of hair spring out from her braid is totally me. These details ground me.

But even beneath the calm, there's still a hum of fear: What if I can't get home?

I stop. Look closer at the picture. Her braid isn't tied with a ponytail band or a scrunchie, but with a string. It almost looks like a shoelace.

I remember the kid in 1976 with the grubby shoestring in her pink purse.

Terror and hunger and exhaustion are all ganging up on me, making me imagine things. It's ludicrous to imagine that the shoestring I saw in 1976 is now dangling from this girl's braid.

Footsteps pound above me. I back up to watch a pack of girls running along the mezzanine's track. I sink down so that I'm sitting against the wall.

Putting my head in my hands, I try to focus on my breath. I imagine Mom talking me down before a meet, walking me through meditation techniques until I feel strong and sure and ready to take on challenges. I inhale and exhale and follow my breath.

I will get home, I will get home.

But what if the watch malfunctions again and I end up somewhere even worse?

I've been gone for two days now. Mom must be worried sick. I envision her on TV pleading with my abductor to bring me home. I can see her hollow eyes. I can hear her trembling voice. I imagine posters with my face on it nailed to telephone poles all over town. A reward for my safe return. I picture Mom lying in bed, imagining the worst. I close my eyes, trying to send her a psychic message across time: *I'm okay, I'll find my way back, don't worry.*

And what about Zach? Is he keeping quiet, consumed by guilt because he knows that I traveled through time but that no one would believe him? Does he lie awake at night wondering what has happened to me?

But maybe none of this is happening. Maybe no time has passed in 2018. Maybe no one has had a chance to miss me.

A couple of mothers walk by, glancing at me curiously. Their gazes linger on my watch. I have an irrational fear that someone is going to grab it off my arm. I itch to slip it off and hide it.

Then I think, *What if they know I don't belong here? Will I get kicked out of the gym? And then where will I go, and how will I find a vault table?*

I rise slowly to my feet. I can't just fling myself randomly through time. It's not in my nature to be slow and deliberate, but this time I have to try.

I have to look like I belong here.

I have to take my time and do it right.

I can't afford to make any more mistakes.

All I have to do is attain enough velocity to vault through time properly.

Pacing up and down the halls, I peer into workout rooms with treadmills and tumble tracks and pits. I remember how excited my team was to get our own dedicated gymnastics center, where we didn't have to put up equipment for every practice and then tear it down so that boys could get into the YMCA gym to shoot baskets. Back then, I would have found the idea of this huge complex to be unimaginably fancy, even if the springboards aren't as bouncy or the beams as padded as in my own time.

But the real luxury is the cornerstone of the building, a huge state-of-the-art gym that vibrates with a dizzying amount of motion—bodies hurling, swinging, kipping, spinning, snapping into dismounts from the bars and beam: the elite athletes. And it's so cool that unlike in my gym, not everyone is white.

In addition to a couple of Black girls, there are a few girls who look like they're Chinese or Korean or Indian. I'd fit in so much better in a place like this. I'm totally enthralled by all of the hairstyles too. Ponytails, low and lank and high and perky, tight French braids and loose, simple three-strand ones, and, surprisingly, lots of curly hair like mine. It seems that curly hair is fashionable in 1988. Half of the girls here have perms.

I don't know where to look, there's so much going on. White tape, chalky hands and legs, warm-ups heaped on the floor. Springboards banging, beams thudding, bars creaking, voices murmuring, bodies slamming to the mats. Snatches of music. Girls hurtling, triple twisting, wobbling, thumping, flying, launching runs, mounting the beam, pirouetting. An aerial here, an arabesque there, a flight series from one end of the beam to the other, a Yurchenko loop. A coach chalking lines on a mat.

I feel my younger self stirring, the one who would have been super jazzed by all of this, inspired by the effortlessly full extensions, precise technique, perfect positions, arrow-straight flights, flawless landings on two feet, falls covered with poise so that even mistakes have authority. In my own slower-paced gym, there's only two sets of bars, one vault, one spring floor, and two high beams, so that there's always a few girls working and a line of girls waiting, snacking, or gossiping, the most dedicated maybe doing back walkovers on the sidelines or balancing across a piece of tape on the floor. It took my gym years to afford a spring floor, which is so much bouncier than the hard mats where we had previously practiced our floor exercises. It took me ages to learn to control my landings on the new floor. I wasn't used to rebounding so high.

Here, there are multiple stations, including a set of apparatus designed around a foam pit for practicing new skills safely. Every girl looks focused, oblivious to her surroundings, to everything but her coaches and her routine. But if I watch long and closely enough, I realize that my perception of perfection is just an illusion. I begin to spot mistakes. Girls with so much power and momentum, they bound forward on their landings. Botched vaults when gymnasts hit the board or the horse too high or too low. Too many swings between bar skills, legs coming apart, dramatic crashes on knees and butts even after simple skills. Perfection, it seems, is timed carefully, meted out, saved for competition. Most don't try to stick the landings every time; they don't need to right now.

I keep scanning for a slim, graceful, elegant girl, but Jillian's body type is common in this gym. The muscular thighs and legs of gymnasts like Simone Biles have not yet completely taken over, despite the increasing influence of champions like Mary Lou Retton.

"Oh, hey, Jill," a woman, maybe a coach, calls to me. "I didn't think you were coming back till tomorrow. How was the photo shoot?" She circles back. "Oh, you're not Jill," she says. "Wow, you really look like her, though."

I stare at the woman mutely. It's all I can do not to beg this stranger for help. To say, *no, I'm not Jill. I'm lost and need to get home.*

And then what? She'll ask me what I'm doing here in this gym. Maybe she'll call the police and I'll end up in jail or foster care or a mental institution or something. Nobody is going to believe that I've traveled through time.

I break out into a sweat as the woman walks away.

I think about how alike Jill and I look. I think about that shoelace. What if I'm connected to Jillian somehow? What if she can help me? What if she knows something about the watch?

Right away, I know that this is farfetched. That I'm grasping at straws, or maybe shoestrings. But a little whisper of hope propels me back to look at her photo on the wall. I remember reading about how, that late spring before the 1988 Olympics, Jillian Clayton was riding high, considered an up-and-coming gymnast who was peaking at just the right moment, her position on the Olympic team a certainty. She shot commercials slated to run during the games, appeared on a Wheaties box and twice on the cover of *USA Gymnastics,* and probably, right now, is spending a lot of time traveling to competitions when she isn't being mobbed by reporters.

But that woman said that she'll be back tomorrow.

And maybe my certainty is just driven by wishful thinking, but suddenly I'm irrationally convinced that Jillian can help me.

When the gymnasts grab bottles of water and towels and rotate to their next events, my stomach rumbles so loudly I look around quickly to make sure no one's heard. I tear myself away from the gym.

Wandering past offices for coaches and athletic trainers, then a parent waiting area with vending machines, I stop before a door that says Staff Only.

Without thinking it through, I open the door and step in. Then I freeze. Going into places where I'm not supposed to is a great way to get myself thrown out of the gym.

But there are only a few coaches in here, playing cards and drinking beer. They glance at me and then away, politely, as if they know who I am but are giving me space, or they smile and say hello and go back to their conversations.

I guess it doesn't hurt that I look like Jill, but that doesn't mean I can fool them forever. At least I'm not out of place here wearing nothing but a leo. But the building is cold, and my stomach is still grumbling as I retreat to the hall to read the notices on a bulletin board. A practice beam and tumbling blocks for sale, a request for ride sharing, leos for sale, help-wanted posters advertising for coaches for beginning classes.

I wander back to the building entrance. Shivering, I gaze longingly at the new warm-up suits in the pro shop window, wishing I had money. I pace over to the reception counter, where an employee is tapping on a typewriter while pressing a big, clumsy old phone between her ear and shoulder.

She barely glances at me as I say, "I think I left my pants here last week. Do you have a lost and found?" Girls at our much smaller gym are always leaving things behind: watches and jewelry and grips and clothing.

The woman gestures for me to come behind the desk and flicks her hand toward a room off of it, past the copier. There, I hit the jackpot: two deep bins full of chalky items. There's an old gym bag, a tote bag, grimy pairs of grips, shorts, paperback books, a couple of jackets, several pairs of warm-up pants in different sizes, water bottles, a shoe, keys, some socks, a T-shirt. I quickly retrieve the gym bag and pick out a few nondescript clothing items.

Casually slinging the bag over my shoulder, I hope that the woman won't notice that I'm leaving with more than I asked about. As I exit the room, I hold up a pair of shiny warm-up pants triumphantly and call out, "Thank you." The woman, still on the phone, barely looks at me. She smiles absently and flicks through a file folder.

I try to remember when I last ate, but my sense of time is so messed up I only know it's been hours, maybe a day. The smaller gyms and halls are emptying, though crashes and thuds and music and shouts still reverberate from the main gym. I'm staring hungrily at a bank of vending machines, again wishing I had some money, when I turn and see the last thing I'm expecting: a girl with dark hair pulled tightly into a bun, slipping from the elite gym and coming down the hall, right toward me. A girl who looks even more like me in person than in photos and video footage.

Jillian Clayton.

13

My heart pounds as I flatten myself against the wall next to the vending machine. I feel like a stalker as I watch this girl, her skin flawless, as she strides by me, one muscled calf bound by white adhesive tape. She glances around as if to make sure no one is watching, then props open a back exit with her gym bag.

I resume my deep breathing exercises as she slips outside. Edging down the hall after her, I lean around to peer out the door. She's on her tiptoes, and I watch the way the long, sinewy cord-like muscles in her legs stretch and ripple as she kisses a tall guy. I edge closer, my heart stomping in my chest. Is he Chinese? He has high cheekbones and black hair so shiny it looks lacquered.

With one wrist hanging at her side, wrapped in the same white adhesive tape that swathes her legs, Jill flicks her other hand across his back. There's something tied around her wrist. A thick, grimy string. That shoestring again.

Now I'm really losing it, seeing shoestrings everywhere.

But it's like little electrical sparks keep shooting off in my brain, fire-crackers of revelation. Does this guy look kind of like me, or am I just imagining things?

Jill grabs at the boy like she's trying to hold on. She seems young and a little desperate.

And I imagined she could somehow help *me*?

"I thought you were supposed to be away all week." The boy is wearing a tank top basketball jersey with the name MARTIN on the back and form-fitting shorts rather than the baggy ones guys wear nowadays that hang to their kneecaps. He's really skinny, but he has muscular arms. "My coach is going to be pissed that I left practice early." He sounds nervous.

"We finished the shoot early and I wanted to see you. I missed you." There's something strategically seductive about the way she loosens her hair and lets it cascade to her shoulders, shaking it out. The weight of her long hair pulls out some of the curl. It's the kind of full, lush hair I've always wished for, waving around her face.

The guy watches her, blinking. I swear I see his eyes dilate. He is totally built and super cute, but he seems uncomfortable, his feet shifting backward, away from her, without interrupting the kiss. He seems so awkward I feel a little bad for him.

"Did you miss me?" she asks.

"Um, yeah, I guess." Not a very romantic response.

"After everything that's happened, that's all you can say?" Her eyes flash.

"God, Jill, I don't want to be all serious." He stares at the ground, scuffing his feet.

Something about their interaction makes me think of the first sixth-grade dance at my middle school. I was envious of my gymnastics teammates, because they all immediately found dates. But when I asked Zach if he wanted to go, he didn't even answer.

He just turned around and ran away faster than I'd ever seen him run. "Don't be too hard on him. He might not be quite ready for that," Mom said when I told her about it. But Jill takes offense at this guy's words. "You don't think what we've been doing hasn't been serious? You're the only thing I've been able to think about lately."

"You know that's not true," he says. "All you ever think about is gymnastics."

"I'm getting an ulcer thinking about gymnastics," she says. "After the Olympics, I'm going to retire and have a normal life. I can barely sleep or concentrate; I feel so pressured all the time. But after all this is over, we could really be together. Maybe even get engaged." I feel like my heart is an elevator sinking further and further as I watch this interaction. I don't know why I ever thought Jillian could help me.

Instead, I feel like I need to help her.

It's all I can do not to leap out of the shadows and scold her. She's way too young to talk like this.

The guy gulps and backs away. "Engaged? We're not even done with high school yet."

"I just want to be with you," she says. Her tone is pleading. I recognize the sound of burnout, but hasn't she ever heard of the feminist movement?

At the same time, I kind of admire her. I would never risk sounding so needy, even when I feel that way.

"I know a way we can escape from all of this." She waves vaguely toward the gymnastics center. "Go somewhere where no one can find us."

"I just want to play basketball," he mumbles. "And we're planning our senior prank." He lights up as if eager to elaborate, but she misses his cue.

"Who cares about that stuff?" she asks. "Wouldn't it be great if we could just be together?"

He stares at the ground. Right at the moment, he does not seem like marriage material.

"What about everything we've done?" Jill asks in a small voice.

"I think you're way more into this than I am," he blurts out. I wince. Sometimes I imagine that this is exactly what Zach would say to me if he knew about all of these feelings I can't seem to control.

"I thought—" She backs away, hurt all over her face.

He looks at his watch. "You've got to get back to practice, and I have to go. I'll call you later." He hurries away without bothering to kiss her.

Her shoulders slump while she watches his retreating back. I can't believe he's just walking away. She's Jillian freaking Clayton. Way out of his league. She droops, biting her lip, like any girl who's just been dumped.

Without thinking, I step out of my spot alongside the vending machine where I'd retreated and intercept Jill. "He's not good enough for you," I say, which I know is unfair. It's not like I really know anything about him.

She's hugging herself, staring into the distance in the direction of his departure, but as soon as I speak, her arms drop and her gaze swivels to me.

"Who are you?" she says. She does not sound pleased that a stranger has burst out of the shadows to offer words of comfort. "Weirdo," she says, and scoops up her gym bag, transforming from defeated teenager to confident gymnast. She squares her shoulders, tilts her chin up, gathers her hair and snaps a band around it, letting the door sigh closed as she returns to the gym, not bothering to give me another glance.

I want to kick myself for being so impulsive. I totally blew that one. Now she'll probably never talk to me again. And what if she reports me? What if my stupid attempt to comfort her is what gets me kicked out of the gym?

All of a sudden, I'm so dizzy with panic and weak with hunger that I have to hang on to the wall to steady myself. How can I make a plan to get home in this state?

I approach the athletic break room cautiously. Stand across the hall trying to look casual until the door opens and a gymnast emerges, gulping water, holding the door open just long enough for me to see that no one else is in there. As her footsteps retreat down the hall, I push the door open. Score: there's a box of cold pizza and a fridge full of water bottles and containers of yogurt.

Thinking of Zach, I sort through the yogurts, finding some expired ones in the back, and tuck them into my bag. No one will miss those. I find plastic forks and spoons in the cabinet and polish off a couple of pieces of pizza.

Back in the viewing area, I sit with chatting mothers, a grandmother reading a newspaper, and a couple of dads watching intently. I'm tense, waiting for someone to ask me who I am and why I'm there, but no one does. There's a grandma with braids coiled around her head. She glances at me almost like she knows me, and I tense up again, but the next time I look, her eyes are fixed forward.

The parents murmur, reporting rumors about who from the gym is going to be invited to Olympic trials in a couple of months. There's no question about Jillian. She'll be there. They speak her name with hushed awe.

I scan the gym, but I don't see her anywhere. As I study the other gymnasts, it's not their tumbling that I envy, not their power or strength so much as their artistry and attitude, their sassiness and the flow and musicality of their moves. Here in 1988, athleticism hasn't yet crowded out delicacy and grace like it sometimes does in 2018. In 1988, dance moves in the floor routine aren't yet treated as mere transitions, static breaks, moments to mark time by awkwardly and jerkily executing some self-conscious hip rolls and turns before appearing obviously relieved when it's time to set up the next tumbling sequence. In 1988, some elite athletes still study ballet to develop their flexibility and coordination, and it shows. My pulse picks up as I find myself singling out moves that I'd like to try in my own routines.

If I were going to keep doing gymnastics, that is.

I'm surprised to have that thought. Maybe I don't even want to.

If I can just get home, maybe there are other things I want to do.

I finally spot Jillian, icing her ankle in a corner. She looks serious and intent. She exchanges a few words with a passing coach. She holds out her ankle for a trainer to wrap with more white adhesive tape.

It's like the stuff is gradually taking over her whole body, mummifying her. She stands, wobbles, hops, and heads over to work on the bars, face still blank and serious. I get a creepy déjà vu feeling watching her.

I stare again at the string tied around her wrist. It's definitely a shoestring. I think of the little girl in 1976. She was what, around four or five? Which would make her almost seventeen now, the same age as Jillian.

A girl pokes her head into the waiting area, swinging a key from a chain. "Hey, could someone grab some chalk from the supply closet upstairs?"

"Oh, sure," I say. I'm surprised at how casual I sound despite my adrenaline-infused realization, my shock at this connection. I pretend I'm not shaking as I take the key and head off to find the closet.

I climb the stairs to the second floor and walk up and down the hall until I find a door near the locker room labeled Supplies.

Perfect. Inside, it's cool and quiet, with one long window high on the wall that lets in light. Mats are piled along the walls, and big containers of chalk are stacked near a couple of broken old wooden high beams, the slippery kind without padding. I hoist a container.

On my way out, I pop the lock. I'll find a hardware store to copy the key later. Except I don't have any money, I remind myself.

When the workout seems to be winding down—girls gathering water bottles and towels and trickling out to the locker rooms, janitors wiping down the beams and bars and vacuuming the carpets that cover the spring floors—I tuck myself into a bathroom stall. Lockers slam and voices echo and toilets flush and showers spray and then finally, the room goes silent. It must be 10 p.m.

For a quiet half hour, my heart thrums so hard I'm sure someone is going to hear it. The janitor's cart rolls down the hall, stops, continues. I listen hard, afraid that the janitor is going to come in to clean the bathroom. I hear a gym door close, followed by stillness. I slip to the restroom door and peer into the hall. There's a cart parked by the break room door and from inside the room drifts the sound of whistling.

I make a break for the supply closet.

As quietly as I can, I pull a couple of mats off the heap and arrange them in the crevice between the stack of mats and the back wall, where I'll be hidden if anyone comes in. I find a corner behind stacks of boxes to hide my bag, my watch safely tucked away.

I need a place to hide and think and process everything that's happened and get some rest before I do something stupid. But the building is so cold and I'm so wired, I can't imagine ever going to sleep, even in full warm-ups. My brain buzzes with so many questions.

Is Jillian the little girl from the yellow house? Where did her mother, Gail, go? Why did Jillian disappear after the Olympic trials? Is she in some kind of danger? What if I can do something to help? Will she report me to the police if I try to talk to her again?

And is the fact that we look alike more than a coincidence?

If Zach were here, he'd be all practical. He'd tell me I need to focus. That I'm all over the place. I argue with him in my head. *I'm just better at multi-tasking than you are*, I tell Imaginary Zach. Imaginary Zach folds his arms. He wants me to come home and stay put in my own time.

Not that I've ever done what he's wanted me to do in the past, but this time, Imaginary Zach and I are on the same page.

But, says that annoying little voice in my head, *what if it turns out I can't find my way home?*

My thoughts keep spinning and spinning, buzzing like a bee circling a flower, before I finally drop off into a restless sleep.

14

DALLAS, MAY 20, 1988
6 A.M.

I feel more decisive when I wake up, with the beginnings of daylight showing through the window high on the wall of the storage closet. Somehow, I've got to talk to Jillian more without freaking her out. That shoestring bothers me—what does she remember? What does she know about that watch she had that was identical to mine?

Somehow, while I wait to approach her again, I've got to look like I belong in this gym so that no one mistakes me for a crazy stalker and throws me out. I think back to the ad I saw on the wall for coaches for beginning classes.

The building is completely empty early in the morning, so I slip out and into the locker room, where I shower and wash my socks and the leo I've been wearing the last few days. Tossing on the clothing from the lost and found, reminding myself that the next time I time travel I should wear some actual underwear under my leo, I spread my wet clothing out on the edge of the closet hidden from the door by a pile of mats, grateful for the quick drying fabric of 2018.

After I finger-comb my hair and finger-brush my teeth, I hide out in my closet until I hear footsteps and jingling keys and shouting voices, the gymnastics center coming alive. It's still early—just past seven—but girls are flooding in for workouts and classes before school. I slip out of the closet and, on an impulse, head to the reception desk.

My heart gives a little jump when I see the guy from last night, Jill's guy, come purposefully through the doors, his long strides confident. Suddenly he stops in the middle of the reception area. He's so tall. Then I notice the confused, stricken look on his face as his eyes dart around, like he's totally out of his element.

"Hey," I say before I remember that he has no idea who I am. His gaze lights on me and his eyes widen.

"Is everything okay?" I ask him.

"I was hoping to talk to one of the gymnasts here. Jill," he says just as the college student working the desk emerges from the inner office and starts tapping on a typewriter.

"You're looking for Jill?" the college student says, barely looking up. "She's headed off to Atlanta this weekend. I doubt that she's going to be here."

The hope on his face crumples. "Okay," he says, turning away. "It's just that she wasn't answering her phone so I thought maybe I could catch her." He gives me another perplexed glance, but before I can think of what to say to him, he has pushed his way out the gym doors.

I watch him go. He's obviously more upset than he seemed last night, and I wish I could tell Jill that. My predicament is starting to sink in. I can't intervene. I can't be their go-between, even if I know stuff no one else knows: that both of them regret the way they left things. They'll have to figure it out for themselves.

"Can I help you?" the college student asks, yanking a piece of paper out of the typewriter and making a quick notation on it.

I'm still rattled and it takes me a second to remember why I'm here. "I want to apply to coach beginning classes," I say.

He does a double take. "Wow, for a second I thought you were someone else," he says. "Are you related to one of the gymnasts here?"

"I don't think so." I keep my face carefully neutral.

He escorts me to the office of someone named Misty, the education coordinator. She's really young, maybe just out of college, with cropped hair, impressive biceps, and an authoritative manner. She drops the chalk she's been using to write on a wall-sized scheduling board and says, "You could not have come at a better time." She gestures for me to sit, brushes off her chalky hands, perches on the side of the desk, and looks me over. "Are you related to Jill?"

"I don't think so."

"Never mind. You look so much like—anyway, yeah, I've got to hire a couple of people for the beginning classes. Nothing fancy, just basic skills for preschoolers."

She shoots questions at me. I tell her my name is Anna, the first name that pops into my head, the name the little girl in 1976—Jillian?—called me. I tell her I competed on a YMCA team back home in Pennsylvania.

The next thing I know, she's whisking me down the hall to a gym, talking the whole way. "Are you certified to coach? That's okay, we can get you started working on that with one of the progressive teachers. We have a four- and five-year-old class beginning in a few minutes. Have you ever worked with that age? What time do you have to be at school? Do you have time to work with them?"

"Yeah, sure. I coached a Tumblebugs class." It's not a complete lie. I did help out a couple of times. "And I think I can get a work release from school if you write a note. I don't have anything important first hour." And that's not a complete lie either. I don't have anything important any hour. But I'm starting to regret the impulse that led me to apply for this job. It feels like I'm digging myself in too deep.

"They've learned positions—tuck, straddle, pike, and stretch—and have started on handstands and cartwheels and backbends, so you'll help them with those. I'll try to pop in and observe. If everything goes well, maybe you can come back after school for a proper interview and we'll get you an ID card."

My panic from yesterday feels like it's lurking there under the surface as I spend a half hour with six little girls in tiny leos. I feel guilty because I don't really want this job. It's just my camouflage, my way of hiding out in plain sight. Of making sure I can look like I belong during odd hours in the gym. But it turns out that teaching is soothing too. I feel calmer when I focus on the task at hand.

I show the little girls how to balance and point their toes. Then we work on handstands. This small gym only has a mat pile set up for pre-vault practice. I'll need to get into another one to find a real horse.

Misty gives me a note to take to school and after pilfering some packages of peanut-butter crackers from a box in the break room, I slip back to my closet where I have a picnic lunch of crackers and yogurt. Then I nap all afternoon until it's time to meet with Misty again.

Once again I feel like an imposter as she has me perform and explain some basic skills: a cartwheel, a forward roll, a front hip circle on the low bar, a scale on the beam, a kip onto the high bar, a back handspring. She doesn't ask me to demonstrate my vault, thank God.

"Okay," she says finally. "If you could take the Monday/Wednesday nine-a.m. preschool classes, you could get to school by ten thirty. And then we'd need you after school at three on Tuesday/Thursday. And I'd like for you to find time in the afternoons to observe progressive classes and study for the certification test, which will probably amount to around three hours a week."

This all sounds really intense, but I just nod, not really paying close attention. I just want to talk to Jillian, figure out how to get home, and leave.

In her office, Misty slides me a paper application. "You only need to fill out the top part right now. Once we have your social security number, we can get you in the system."

Uh-oh. My social security number doesn't exist yet. I fiddle with the pen and then decide to come clean. Sort of. "I don't actually have a social security number," I say.

She stops clicking on the computer and raises her eyebrows at me. There's a long, awkward pause. Then she says, "Oh, that happened with a teenager we hired last year. You need to apply right away. You have ninety days after hire to get it."

I nod, but I'm a little disappointed. For a second I hoped that not having a social security number would mean I could end this charade. But then, until I can get out of here, wouldn't people wonder what I'm doing hanging around the gym?

Misty hurries me off to get my picture taken for my ID.

Late in the afternoon, still feeling exhausted from the panic and fear and excitement and wonder of the last couple of days, I watch the lean and light and wispy girls at elite practice. I can't figure out how to approach Jill without reinforcing her impression of me as a weird fangirl or creepy stalker. She looks like a normal teenager until she takes the floor or straddles the beam or kips onto the bars. Then she becomes intense and focused and fierce. Effortlessly she turns into a whirlwind, a blur of double backs or giant swings.

I need to go find something to eat, but as I stand, I drop my gym bag. It slides under the seat and falls to the floor under the bleachers. I scramble down to the floor.

"Jill's looking unbeatable," one of the moms says to another. "I don't even know why she's bothering to compete in Atlanta this weekend. She should be saving her energy for the Olympic trials."

In the dark cave under the bleachers, I crab walk over to retrieve my bag. Something glistens on the floor—a quarter. No one seems to have cleaned under here for a while. As my eyes adjust to the dark, I spot a wad of candy wrappers and a discarded cup. I think about Jill and the Olympics.

Even if it were somehow possible for Jill to help me, wouldn't I just be a distraction to her right now? What if I somehow derail her?

"Coach wants to keep her visible," I hear another parent say.

I find a half-empty container of Tic Tacs. I bypass a sticky pool of spilled Coke to get to my bag and come across a windfall: a dollar bill.

If time is a loop and everything that's happening now has already happened, does that mean that I have always been here, in the gym, during the weeks before the Olympic trials? What if I'm the person who somehow got her off track?

This thought makes my brain hurt. Pocketing the money and the Tic Tacs, I crawl back out and brush myself off. The parents are busy staring at the window and talking, not paying any attention to me.

Down the hall, I smooth out the crumpled dollar bill until I can feed it into the vending machine, poking the buttons for a ham-and-cheese sandwich on white bread. All of the available sandwiches are on white bread. I can picture Mom shuddering. With the quarter, I splurge for some chips. I grab a Dixie cup of water from the break room and then camp out in the back of my closet, spreading out my feast around me.

I'm kind of proud that I haven't made any wild, irrational moves, like flinging myself in a panic through time, but isn't this idea that Jill can somehow help me just as irrational? Zach warned me not to do anything to screw up the timeline. Not to change the past, because that could mean I wouldn't exist in 2018.

But how does that make sense? If everything that's happening has already happened, how could I change it?

Then I remember Zach telling me about the butterfly effect, and alternate timelines. *You've got to be careful*, he said. *Everything you do has an impact.*

My sense of purpose is starting to falter. I remember how Jillian called me a weirdo. What makes me think she would ever help me even if she could, anyway?

The last doors slam and the sounds of footsteps recede. The building settles down for the night at last as I lie down in my mat cave. The next few days stretch out before me, lonely and empty. Days of hiding out as I wait for Jill to return from Atlanta and my job begins, scavenging for forgotten sandwiches from the fridge and items people have dropped under the bleachers and otherwise trying to stay out of sight.

I'm still hungry now. I stare up at the window, where mellow evening light seems to flatten itself outside the pane rather than spilling through it like it did earlier in the day. A wave of desolation crashes over me, a wrenching tug of homesickness. Once when I was nine I went to camp and woke up in the night missing Mom, my cat Simone Biles, my room. That's how I feel now, except now I miss Zach too. Except now fears—that time has passed after all and that Mom and Zach are frantic, that I'll never get home—nag at me.

My real life seems so far away, like something that belongs to another world. Like something that doesn't exist.

The idea of winning Jillian over, of figuring out how we're connected, seems ridiculous. How is the brash, insecure girl whose boyfriend just brushed her off going to know how to make a time machine work correctly? How is the girl who has turned her single-minded focus to making the Olympic team going to help me?

All I want to do is go home. The want washes over me in a tide of impossible yearning, and all of a sudden, I'm on my feet, strapping on my watch. Bundling up my things and hiding them in a corner. Slipping into the hall and trying the door of a dark, empty gym.

It's locked.

The next gym is locked too.

Every obstacle fuels my determination. I finger the key in my pocket, the key that unlocks the small gym where I'll be teaching.

Maybe I just need to run faster. Maybe if I do that, the pre-vault mats can get me home.

But what if it doesn't work? What if I end up being trampled by a dinosaur or drowned by a tidal wave?

Wouldn't Zach have warned me if he thought that was possible?

I pass the elite gym, where I watched Jill only a few hours ago. I hope that I was somehow mistaken about her fate, that she goes to the Olympics after all. If she doesn't, at least it won't be because of my interference.

I hope that if my time traveling is changing the timeline, it will be for the better.

As I double-check the watch settings, then wave my hand around to make sure it doesn't accidentally reset, I imagine someday having the guts to come back to 1988 and figuring out how Jill and I are connected.

But I don't think I will. Once I'm home, I can't imagine ever wanting to leave again.

15

BRADFORD, PA, JANUARY 18, 1929
6:45 A.M.

R ight away, as I launch into a front handspring, I know that I've made
a mistake. I hear that sound like cards shuffling, but I don't have time
to freak out as the air around me goes all wavy and I find myself spinning
through darkness, lights popping. The next thing I know, I'm somersaulting
through a thin layer of snow.

Oh God, not 1976 again. I feel more drained than I did during my first
two time jumps. After I land flat on the ground, it takes me a second to get
up the energy to struggle to my feet.

My heart races and I feel so dizzy and nauseated that I almost sink to
the ground again. This is my street, but nothing looks right. Everything's
spinning.

I can't breathe.

I yank my arm up to look at the watch. January 18, 1929, it says.

WTF?

My teeth chatter and I'm shaking so hard that my ribs hurt. I'm freezing
cold, but just like in 1976, it feels more like terror tremors than cold shivers.

Fear rattles all the way through me. I feel like I'm being smothered as I gasp for breath. All I can think is, *I am so screwed.*

I think of Mom. Of the three-three-three rule for anxiety. Focusing on things around you helps you avoid feeding the panic.

Three things I see:

The house in front of me, a chocolate-colored wood-frame structure with a porch swing. It looks kind of like my house, but my house is green, and our porch floor is covered with all-weather carpeting like short, stiff fake grass.

The hill rising behind the house, completely bald of any trees, unlike in my own time. There's a light dusting of snow on the ground, brown dirt peeking through.

The street, like the sidewalk, brick. Each brick is outlined by snow in the cracks.

Three things I hear:

In the distance, a steady creaking that reminds me of a rusty swing or loose wheel on a trike, multiplied by a dozen. Oil rigs operating along the hillside, I think, remembering a demonstration at the oil museum in 2018. Panic rises again.

A train whistle in the distance.

A horse clopping up the hill. It pulls a wagon behind it, stopping before each house. A man in suspenders pauses each time to hitch the horse to the front porch, heave a block of ice off his wagon, and disappear into the side yard.

I add a new rule. Things I smell:

The air, funny, like oil, I guess, but also earthy, like soil and manure and livestock, like a farm.

More things I see: Next door, Zach's house is a lighter brown than it should be. And I discover as I walk down the dirt driveway, it's missing its back porch. Behind it, there's a barn and fenced yard, where two horses stand looking at me, manes rippling in a breeze. I guess that's where the livestock smell is coming from.

Wandering back to the front yard, I concentrate on moving three parts of my body. First, I lift my feet out of the snow. Before my recent adventures, I'd never waded into snow without shoes or socks. It's funny how invigorating it feels.

I lift my arms. I turn my head from side to side. My body parts still work.

By the time the man with the horse reaches my yard, he's staring back at me with an odd expression, but he doesn't break his rhythm. He strolls right over to the kitchen steps and goes inside. Bringing out a pan, he dumps water into the yard, fixes his gaze on me for another second, then picks up some ice and disappears through the side door again.

I fold my arms, shivering, barefoot and barelegged in my leotard and nothing else. I've always thought of leos as second skins that allow me to breathe and move freely. The fact that they are skimpy and shiny with frivolous rhinestones and sequins and glitter is secondary. But in the cold wind, they are relatively pointless coverings, and the man's stare makes me feel distinctly underdressed.

Like maybe I could be hauled away for indecent exposure or whatever they call it when you show up naked in public.

I feel like I'm in one of those dreams where you forget to wear your pants to school.

I've got to get home. Now.

"Are you all right, miss?" The man hurries up the lawn to unhitch the horse, politely flicking his gaze away from my attire.

I try to sound breezy despite my shaky voice. "Oh, yeah, just headed to the pool."

But who wears a watch to the pool? And do they even wear wristwatches in this time period? Much less, big, bulky ones like this? I remember the girl in 1988 who noticed my watch first thing and made fun of it. What will people here think of it?

With sudden visions of E.T. being captured by scientists and studied in a lab like a prisoner, I rip the watch off my arm and drop it into an empty flowerpot. It's still glowing: January 1929.

Yep, January 1929.

How did I land so far from my goal?

And then horror overtakes me: why did I take off my watch? My one means of getting home? Why do I do these wild, impulsive things?

The way the man furrows his brow at me, I'm guessing my explanation about the pool wasn't so plausible after all. I wonder if there are indoor pools in 1929. I itch to find a computer and google 1929. Then I realize with a jolt that Google doesn't exist yet. Or computers. Also, probably women don't wear skimpy swimsuits any more than they wear tight gymnastics leos.

Whatever. It's not like I can think that straight amid the panicked feeling that keeps crashing over me in waves.

Before I can summon up further lies to compound the man's confusion or dive after my watch, the front door of my house whips open.

A woman with bobbed hair and an apron over a knee-length dress rushes out and down the front porch steps. She looks vaguely familiar, but I can't place her. She's small-framed, with brown hair a little lighter than mine, a little darker than Jill's. Freckles spatter her cheeks and nose.

"Who the hell are you?" I burst out.

She flinches at the word *hell*, but then her voice goes all soft, her tone wondering, as she says, "You're here." She gently reaches out to touch my hair as if she doesn't quite believe her eyes. She stares into my face, so intense it almost feels rude. "I thought you'd never get here."

"What's that supposed to mean?" I pull away, startled. And who does she think I am?

But before I can ask, the iceman calls out, "Is everything all right, ma'am?" He fixes his gaze on me as he swings back up onto his wagon, but he's no longer addressing me.

"Yes, this is my cousin," the woman says, her tone brisk even as she gently takes my arm, staring at it like she can't believe I'm real. "I've been expecting her."

The man shakes his head, grabs hold of the reins, and continues up the hill.

"Your cousin?" I mutter, but the woman just says loudly, "Let's get you in out of the cold." She scoops up a bottle of milk from a tin box on the porch and holds the door open for me, as if it's perfectly normal to invite a practically naked girl in sparkly spandex into her house.

She ushers me into my own living room. Even in 1929 it has the same walnut floors and door frames, the same fireplace and built-in bookshelves. But that's where the similarities end. Around the room are different vases and books and rugs and chairs and drapes, an upright piano, an antique couch, floral wallpaper, floral area rugs. Magazines with titles like *American Watchmaker* and *Clocks*.

I can't stop staring at her, at that wild spattering of freckles on her cheeks, so unlike the small, demure ones that sometimes pop out on my arms when I've been in the sun. Her freckles somehow emphasize how strikingly beautiful she is. I've never before thought of freckles as glamorous, but on her, they are.

"I think you've got me confused with someone else—" I start, but she puts her finger against her lips.

"Just play along," she murmurs, then continues, more loudly: "Those clothes won't do. Luke's downstairs stoking the furnace. Let's find you a proper frock."

Bewildered, I follow her up the stairs to the front bedroom, the one where Mom now sleeps. The floors are less scuffed—glossier—and intricate pink floral paper covers the walls.

The woman sits down on the bed and stares at me like she can't quite believe her eyes. "You're so grown up," she says. "I knew you would be, but it's just hitting me. How many years I will never be able to get back."

"What are you talking about?" I ask.

A door slams in the hall and she jumps up, becoming all business again. "Where are your things? Don't you have a bag or something?"

"No, this is it." I gesture at my leo.

She looks puzzled. Footsteps pound through the hall and recede down the stairs, and she quickly jumps up. "We're about the same size." She tosses me some woolen underwear and black stockings and a long-waisted dress with a sailor collar and pleated skirt. She sorts through another drawer. "Maybe some knicker sport togs," she says, adding some checked wool tweed pants with cuffs that hit right below the knees.

There's something soothing about her matter-of-fact manner, like she has control of the situation. At least someone does.

I'm slippery with sweat and still shaking as I turn over the long underwear in my hands. It looks scratchy and hot.

"Here." The woman passes me some lace-up shoes. "If you tie them tightly, they'll keep the longies from riding up. Luke will be up in a minute and I need to wake the children, but just follow my lead, all right? I can't wait to talk some more. I want to hear how you got here."

She touches my face lightly with her fingertips before she backs out of the room, as if reluctant to turn around, as if she's afraid I'll disappear if I'm out of her sight.

As cold as I am, I'm reluctant to take off my leo. If I leave it on, I can be on my way the second I find a horse for vaulting. But my arms and legs are covered with goose bumps and I feel like I can never get warm, so I finally peel it off and hasten into the clothing the woman gave me, wondering the whole time who she thinks I am.

In these 1920s clothes, I feel bulky, and it's like waves of heat radiate terror all over my body. My hands are clammy. My head is light, spinning.

I take a deep breath. *Three-three-three*, I remind myself.

Things I can see: the space Mom's queen bed now occupies is instead fitted out with two twin beds.

A gas fire burns in the metal grate that is unusable in my time.

The mantel where Mom displays pictures of me holds a marble clock and a little cluster of vintage perfume bottles.

Move my body parts: I lean over to tie the shoes.

Then I get distracted by the realization that none of this stuff is really antique or vintage.

It's all contemporary for 1929.

Am I going to have to pee in an outhouse? I mean, if I have to pee before I find a vault horse?

I tiptoe over to the bathroom. There's a toilet, just like in my own time, though there's also a pile of catalogs in a basket, with some loose, wadded pages on top. Ugh.

My agitation subsides, then crests again as I think about my watch. Why did I leave it in the planter? It's my only way out of here. I need to go get it as quickly as possible.

Even when the panic dies down, it's still there, hiding under the surface, waiting to pounce again.

I take a breath and follow the sizzle and smell of frying bacon down to the kitchen. The woman stands before the stove, smiling to herself. I could go straight to the front door and down the porch steps right now.

But then she turns her smile on me and gestures me into the kitchen. I cast one more glance toward the front porch and reluctantly join the strange woman.

16

"I'm not supposed to be here," I tell the woman, but my words are interrupted by a slight man with curly hair in a bathrobe who comes up the basement stairs.

"Luke, look who arrived this morning," the woman says to him, a lilt in her voice. I'm not very good at judging ages, and the old-fashioned clothing makes this couple seem sort of timeless, but I think they're probably the same age as most of the gymnastics parents: late thirties or early forties.

"My cousin Anna," the woman announces.

Anna. Why is everyone in the past determined to call me Anna?

"I would recognize you anywhere," Luke says. "You are Abby's spitting image. But how did you get here so early?"

Who's Abby? I almost ask before the woman says, "She took the early train from Buffalo. Yes, we do look a bit alike. Now go dress and shave and call the children, Luke, and I'll get breakfast on the table."

"Who is that? Who are you?" I whisper, impatient, after Luke disappears up the stairs.

She pats me on the arm. "I've waited for you for a long time. Please just be quiet and follow my lead so you don't end up in a mental institution," she whispers before she directs me to set the table for six. She passes me boxes of cornflakes and Wheaties.

"But this is my house. I live here. Except in a hundred years," I try to explain as I open cabinets and drawers, finding blue-rimmed plates with bursts of flowers in the middle, matching bowls, and stainless-steel forks and spoons.

Another woman pokes her head around the kitchen door. She has gray hair in braids that are pinned to her head like a crown. Abby rears back like she's been caught in a sudden wind. "It's Mrs. Grundy," she mutters to me.

"I'm headed downtown. Do you need anything?" the woman, Mrs. Grundy, asks.

"No thanks," Abby says, and before she can say anything further, Mrs. Grundy whips around, calling back, "That ladder on the back porch is unsightly. Tell Luke to put it in the shed." Then she's gone. I hear her steps on the porch. I imagine her walking past the flowerpot, past my watch. I leap up to go get it, but Abby bars the kitchen door with her arm.

"You have to be careful what you say," she snaps at me. "You could put us both in grave danger. And I just couldn't bear it if anything happened to you again." Then she mutters, "I hope she didn't hear you. She's always hiding around corners and spying on me. I don't think she even saw you, though, or she'd still be here asking a million questions."

I've never been good at being quiet, and I hate being snapped at, but I think again of Zach's rules. *Don't change the past, don't kill Hitler, don't try to save loved ones.* He didn't tell me that I can't even *talk.* "Sorry," I say. "Who was that, anyway?"

"My mother-in-law," Abby says. "Be careful around her."

I focus on the front door. I'm poised to make a beeline for the porch to grab my watch. But Abby keeps her arm stretched across the entrance to the kitchen, like she is physically trying to prevent me from leaving. "Just don't go anywhere," she says. "At least not until we've had a chance to talk."

I feel uneasy, like I won't be able to focus on anything else until my watch is in my possession again. "I just need to—" I start, but she doesn't move her arm. "Please don't go," she says.

Does Abby really think I'm her cousin Anna? And what if the real Anna shows up? And why did the little girl I met in 1976 also call me Anna?

With all of the adrenaline that's been pumping relentlessly through my system, I've moved on to the panic-attack stage, where I feel detached, where everything feels unreal, like I'm watching my life from a distance. It feels almost like calm. It feels like I can think straight again.

I will be casual, finish breakfast, retrieve my watch, get Abby alone, make her talk. Figure out what I'm doing wrong so I can zap myself back to 2018. Make Abby find me a gymnastics horse, or some mats for my lower-level vault.

Or maybe not.

I remember how I used to leave the back door open, then get mad when Simone Biles escaped. "Insanity is doing the same thing over and over and expecting a different result," Mom used to say to me.

"Notice how you keep saying that, but nothing ever changes?" I asked her.

But she was right. Why would I repeat the pre-vault method when it's not giving me the velocity I need?

"Are you going to the club for luncheon?" Abby asks Luke over plates of eggs and bacon. I study the Wheaties box.

"Jillian Clayton was on a box of Wheaties once," I say, testing for a reaction from Abby. Her head swivels toward me, eyes startled.

"But you—" She starts, stops, and says instead, "Who?" Then she assumes an air of detached indifference though I catch her staring at the tablecloth, crinkling her brow. "Clayton," she repeats absently.

"Why was someone standing on a box of Wheaties?" asks a little girl at my elbow. "Wouldn't that crush all the cereal?"

"This is Catherine, our oldest." Abby laughs, but she doesn't sound very amused. In fact, she has a stricken look on her face. I feel as if I've somehow upset her. "Catherine asks way too many questions." She directs her attention to the girl. "You need to feed the kittens before you sit down."

"I have a Kiwanis meeting at lunchtime." Luke doesn't seem to notice all the microexpressions that have been flickering across his wife's face since I mentioned Jillian Clayton. "Will you be staying awhile, Anna?"

Before I can answer, the room erupts in chaos as two more kids clamor down the stairs, scrape back chairs, and squabble as they reach for bowls of food. Then, noticing my presence, they watch me curiously.

While they're all getting settled, Catherine pours the last drops of milk from a bottle into the cat bowl. In 2018, we know that cats aren't supposed to drink milk, but it will sound weird if I say anything. And then I'm distracted as Catherine softly calls the kittens: "Here kitty kitty." I can barely hear her over all the noise, but I practically jump when she says, "Come on Olga! Move out of the way and let Bela in, Nadia. Squeeze in, Marta and Rigby." I think of my own cat, Simone Biles.

I catch Abby's eye. She stares back intensely, like she's warning me not to comment.

Catherine is by far the tallest, ten or eleven with blond hair and green eyes, favoring Luke far more than she does Abby. The other two kids have smaller builds and Abby's dark hair, though only the boy shares her curls. None of them seem to have inherited her freckly skin. I glance between them and Abby and Luke as I often do my friends and their parents, ferreting out resemblances and all of the variations in the ways genes are passed on.

"Anna has agreed to stay for a few weeks. I know she'll be a great help." Abby turns to me. "We haven't had a hired girl for a while, so it's so good of you to come."

Is she freaking kidding me? A few weeks?

The kids clatter spoons and heave up from chairs to grab cereal boxes and argue over the last piece of bacon until Abby breaks it in pieces. The boy yanks the younger sister's hair and she screeches. Catherine, dreamily ignoring her siblings, sings under her breath. I catch the words, "Does the spearmint lose its flavor on the bedpost overnight?"

I thought kids from the past were better behaved than kids in my time. I thought they didn't speak unless spoken to.

Luke shakes a fresh milk bottle and takes off the paper cap. The cream rises to the top.

I focus on taking deep breaths.

"Catherine," Luke chides the girl, who looks up as if she's been suddenly jolted out of a trance. "That's not proper at the table. Our guest will think you're all hooligans." Abruptly, Catherine swivels her gaze to me and stops singing. She glances from me to Abby. The other kids also settle down, still eyeing me curiously.

"They *are* hooligans," Abby says affectionately. She tells me their names while I try not to stare too much. Catherine, Robert, Sarah. These kids were born in the 1920s, way before anyone I know, but I still keep looking for some sign that I've met one of them in my own time.

Catherine is examining me with the kind of eager-to-please slyly worshipful side-eye of younger kids toward older ones. "Your hair is berries," she whispers to me.

I touch my stiff curls. I have berries in my hair?

"The bee's knees," Abby murmurs absently, and I gather that this is a good thing. I try to remember if bees have any body parts resembling knees.

Robert, who's about eight, wears suspenders like the iceman's. Before sitting down at the table, he took off his golf cap, which made him look like a little French boy. He smiles briefly and without a lot of interest in my direction. Sarah, the four-year-old, continues to stare at me openly.

I take a bite of cereal. The cornflakes aren't sweet at all.

Outside, a horn beeps and the table erupts into chaos again, Robert and Sarah scrambling toward the door while Abby calmly goes on chewing and Catherine remains lost in a daydream, eyes glazed. I'm confused by all the commotion: are there school buses in 1929? Are the kids late for school? Or are geese flying overhead?

Then Robert yells, "A jalopy!" He's out on the porch, the girls spilling after him. My Chronowatch is in a planter right there at the foot of the porch steps. I strain to see the kids. I will them not to go down the steps and find my watch.

Luke extricates himself from the table, saying, "With all the new colors, we have to look every time we hear a car. We saw a Florentine cream last week." From the front door, he calls back, "Versailles violet. Very hotsy-totsy."

"Car colors," Abby murmurs to me, as if she's aware that I'm a foreigner who needs an interpreter. I'm not sure whether she means *Versailles violet* or *hotsy-totsy*.

I watch the door, trying to see where the kids are.

"Cars used to all be black," she goes on. "If you think all of this furor over car colors is weird, you should have seen Luke and his family right after this house was built. His brothers and sisters used to run over just to watch the toilets flush." Like Simone Biles, I think, remembering how my cat races to stand on her hind legs and peer into the toilet, fascinated by the whoosh of water.

"You must think we are country bumpkins." Luke returns to the table trailed by the kids. "Here, Abby. Mom just brought the newspaper up." He passes her a thin newspaper with tiny print.

I scan the kids for items in their hands or bulges in their pockets, any sign they've found my watch. Wouldn't they say something if they had? Sweat breaks out on my forehead.

"Anna, you are a dreamer just like our Catherine." Abby nudges me. "Luke asked if you've seen all of the new car colors in Niagara Falls."

"Yeah, right," I say absently. Abby knows full well that I'm not from Niagara Falls.

"She said *yeah*, Mom." Catherine sounds scandalized, like I just cursed.

"Well, people from different parts of the country speak differently," Abby says. "You're still to do as your grandma says and say *yes*."

"Yes, ma'am," Catherine answers. Now this is what I expected of kids in 1929.

Luke rises from the table and uncaps a bottle from the cupboard, pouring a spoonful of smelly dark liquid for each of the kids. They make faces before gulping down their share. Luke hands full spoons to Abby and then me. I look at her questioningly.

"I'm sure you take your cod liver oil every morning to prevent colds," Abby prompts me. As soon as Luke's back is turned and the kids are donning hats and grabbing schoolbags, she swiftly dumps hers into the sink, then snatches my spoon and dumps it too. Like she knows very well that the foul-smelling stuff isn't going to prevent colds.

Luke plants a quick kiss on Abby's forehead, and in a wild flurry, Catherine and Robert clamber off for school in tangles of jackets and shoes and rustles of books and papers and repeated slams of the door while Luke more sedately sets out for his own streetcar. Nervously, I watch them through the kitchen doorway, only resuming my breathing after they've clattered down the front steps and passed the planter without looking down or pausing.

In the suddenly quiet kitchen, Abby shoos Sarah off to the living room. "Go on, Little Bug," she says. *Little Bug.* I think of the little girl in the yellow house whose mother called her Doodlebug.

"I thought I knew, but now I don't. Who are you?" Abby asks me, her voice barely above a whisper, almost drowned out by the sound of the water filling the dishpan, the scraping of her scouring pad. "Where did you come from?" She speaks haltingly. "I had this babysitter once—do you remember—" She stops abruptly, looking confused.

"It's so weird," I start, ready to spill the whole story, but she suddenly raises her finger to her lips and nudges her head toward the window. Right outside of it, I catch a glimpse of Mrs. Grundy, right before she ducks as if looking for something in the yard.

"We've got to talk, but we can't do it right now," Abby says. "She doesn't like me." I follow her gaze to the white house next door that will someday be yellow. Frustrated, I finish piling breakfast dishes alongside the sink and wipe off the table. Standing behind Abby, looking out the kitchen window, I have a clear view of the white house. It's surrounded by bare dirt that shows beneath a thin layer of snow, as if the yard is devoted to a vegetable garden in the summer.

"Is that where she lives?"

"Yes. That's the house where Luke grew up. Luke's family owned this plot of land too, and gave it to him to build this house when he married the first time."

"The first time?" I'm not sure how nosy it is to ask questions in 1929, but I'm pretty sure that divorce isn't common.

"Delilah. She died in the flu epidemic. Soon after Catherine was born."

"And the other kids are yours?"

"This is not the way I thought I'd live my life," Abby says, then suddenly, defensively, adds, "but I don't know what I'd do without them. Or what I'd do without ever seeing—" she doesn't finish her sentence. She peers out the window as she rinses a plate and sets it on the drying rack.

"Are we related somehow?" I ask, but she says loudly, "Of course, Anna. Our mothers were sisters. Could you go check on Sarah?" She turns away, as if engrossed in her task, but I see her scanning the yard through the window.

I barrel through the living room, past Sarah, who is on the floor paging through a book with watercolor illustrations of birds. I throw open the door and shoot like a bullet down the wide porch steps.

I reach into the planter, anticipating the relief I'll feel after finding my watch curled there.

It's not there. My stomach bottoms out.

I've never regretted my impulsive nature more. Why did I rip off the watch and put it in the planter anyway?

But I know I dropped it here, on top of the packed dirt.

I remember watching it fall. I remember a soft thud as it landed.

Could I have missed it? Could I have dropped it in the snow alongside the planter?

I scoop up handfuls of snow, tossing them aside.

Nothing.

I pat the dirt in the planter. There's no loose soil, just a solid mass of earth.

My watch isn't here.

17

BRADFORD, PA, JANUARY 18, 1929
9 A.M.

"It is too cold to leave the door standing open." Abby stands in the doorway, glaring, hands on her hips. Then her voice softens. "I was afraid that you'd left without saying good-bye."

I'm still digging through the snow, brushing it aside, scraping aside the leaves under it. My panic has returned full force. I'm hyperventilating. Who has passed by this planter today? The milkman, the newspaper boy, the children, Luke, Abby's mother-in-law. Did one of them pick it up? "I dropped something—it's not here—"

Abby steps out and closes the door. Her eyes widen as if she's had a sudden realization. Her eyes flick down to my arm, then up to my face. "You dropped something?" she repeats. "I guess I thought—never mind. Why don't we get you a coat and we'll look for it, whatever it is?"

But I reject her invitation to go find a coat. "I'm having a panic attack," I say, plopping down on the porch steps, gasping.

"Close your eyes. Take a deep breath."

Abby descends the porch steps.

I watch her distrustfully as she glances around. Her eyes trace a path from the planter up the steps and across the porch. She casts a long stare at the white house next door. I follow her gaze. A curtain flicks at the window. She narrows her eyes.

"Whatever you lost, I'll help you find it," she says. "Just hold on. I've got to run next door."

A couple of minutes later, she's back, breathless, looking agitated. "She's not there," she says. "Okay, just come in and let me fix you some tea. We're going to figure this out." Her tone is confident and soothing. Reluctantly, I follow her inside and drink the tea she offers me.

"It's a watch," I say, and then I wonder, does she know what that is? Have wristwatches even been invented yet? Zach has an old pocket watch that belonged to his grandfather, and when he wants to be really weird, he wears it with a chain and fob. "It's like a bracelet with a clock on it. I dropped it when I first arrived and I can't find it anywhere."

"A wristwatch?" she asks. Her mouth sets into a grim line. "Don't worry. We will find it."

I have no choice but to trust her. To believe that she will help me. Gradually I stop shaking and my breath slows. She stands staring out the kitchen window for a long moment. "Just go look after Sarah and give me some time to think about this," she says.

In the living room, I plop down beside Sarah, who scoots over so I can look at her book with her. Her legs are folded over like origami, unnaturally limber.

I wonder if she's ever done gymnastics.

"Ducks," she informs me, pointing at two American scoter ducks, according to the caption, black-and-gray birds floating on water. She shuffles through the pages, pausing to show me her favorite birds while I strain my ears to hear what Abby's doing in the kitchen. She passes the doorway. She's cleaning the floor with a mop made of heavy rope.

How can she concentrate on washing the floor when a girl she's never met is in her living room having a crisis?

Then I notice that she keeps pausing for long moments, staring at nothing. Something definitely is wrong. Fear squeezes my stomach.

Sarah giggles at the American flamingo with its neck stretched out and bill pointing toward the water. I turn over Abby's words from earlier. *I've waited for you for a long time. Please just be quiet and follow my lead so you don't end up in a mental institution.*

Who has she been waiting for? Why did she look so surprised when I mentioned Jillian Clayton? And now why does she keep glancing next door? Why does it feel like she's barely containing her own alarm?

I hear her on the phone, calling in her shopping orders. I shift around till I can see her in the kitchen, speaking into the mouthpiece.

"Pel-i-can." Sarah sounds out the word. "This one's my favorite," she tells me shyly, pointing to the American swan, neck flowing into its body like a contorted "S," yellow flowers lining the water. "I like this one too." She points at a common buzzard, descending from the sky as if preparing to peck at a surprised brown rabbit. "I like the bunny."

When Abby said that about mental institutions, was she afraid for me or was she threatening me? Once again, I think about all of the people who tromped across the porch this morning.

Did one of them find the watch? Does Abby think that Luke's mother is responsible?

Abby's washing clothes in the kitchen, inserting wet items by hand through the barrel with a wringer on top. No matter her task, she never once stops staring out the window. I wonder how she ever has time to do anything besides haul and heat water and scrub and iron clothing.

When Sarah tugs me upstairs to see her room, I notice that she is light on her feet, moving in dancer-like steps. Her room is mine and not mine. Instead of purple walls or a computer desk, the room has green-flowered wallpaper, bunk beds stacked against the wall, an area rug and gramophone and small bookcase.

"How does this work?" Seizing on an idea, I grab a pogo stick leaning against the wall. It isn't until Sarah leads me downstairs and outside that I realize it's probably not the greatest idea for her to be bouncing on the snowy sidewalk. But I need to search the ground again. I edge toward the pot, running my fingers along the cracks between the sidewalk bricks.

When I overturn the pot, the dirt is packed in there so tight, it doesn't even loosen. I shake the nearby bushes. Crawl under them, feeling around for a fallen plastic object, branches snagging my hair and scratching my legs while I flatten myself and slither in further.

"Sarah!" Abby calls sharply from the door. "What are you doing out here without a coat?"

I back out of the bushes and straighten to my feet, brushing a twig out of my hair and dirt off the front of my dress.

Abby turns her wrath on me. "Anna, I know you're in the habit of running around half naked, but really?"

"I just wanted to look again," I say.

"I know you're worried, but you're going to have to trust me," she says again. "Come on in for lunch."

"I really need to find it," I insist, holding my ground, looking again in all of the places I have already looked as if it's going to magically appear.

"I can help," Sarah offers, and Abby freaks. "No!" she says. "Sarah, come on in the house. Anna, help her with lunch. I need to run next door one more time." There's something urgent and dire about her tone. I have a terrible feeling of impending doom as I sweep my gaze over the porch and yard yet again. Reluctantly, I head into the kitchen with Sarah while Abby breaks into a jog down the sidewalk.

Abby has put out a small feast of cold chicken, bread, celery stuffed with cream cheese and pimentos, fried cauliflower, clam broth, and an apple pie. I'm too distracted to eat any of it. Sarah has wound down, eyes glazing over, and she doesn't eat much either.

Abby arrives back in minutes, breathless, shaking her head. "Come on Doodlebug, it's time for your nap," she tells Sarah. Once again, I register the endearment. *Doodlebug.* Abby turns to me. "You've been traveling since early. You could use a rest also."

I'm still running on adrenaline, on worry and terror and panic. If I could rest, maybe I'd wake up with new perspective. But I don't think I can possibly sleep.

Abby shoos Sarah upstairs ahead of us as she shows me to the guest room. It's the same room Mom and I use as a guest room, though in 1929 it has heavy mahogany furniture and a canopy bed.

"There are some empty drawers in the bureau for your things," Abby says. "I put away your bathing costume here. It wouldn't do to let anyone else see it. I'll find you a nightgown and some extra frocks."

She says it like it's usual for visitors to arrive without any luggage.

"Look, I'm having an emergency," I tell her. I know I must sound obsessive, maybe even crazy, but I can't stop myself. "I have to find my watch."

She sighs. "I know, I'm doing my best. It was rather large, yes?" She looks around her as if she's afraid the house is bugged, and with the way Mrs. Grundy kept poking her head into rooms and eavesdropping outside of windows earlier today, I'm beginning to see why. Abby gestures for me to follow her. Back in the master bedroom, she opens a locked compartment at the top of her bureau and unloads pennies, pencils, compacts, and lipsticks.

"You have a lot of those," I observe, hoping that next she will reach in and produce my watch.

"When I first dated Luke, he was always giving me gifts," she says.

She fishes around in the back of the compartment. Pulls out some wool stockings and unrolls them. I suck in my breath. My heart begins to thump. Inside is a plastic wristwatch that's a twin to my Chronowatch, though a little more battered, with a white strap instead of a black one.

"It looks like this, but this isn't mine. Where did you get it?"

"It's a long story," she says. "This one is broken."

I open my mouth to barrage her with a million questions, but I don't know where to start. Suddenly, it's obvious to me who Abby is. But now I just have more questions.

"This thing has caused untold sorrow," she says. "If you lost yours, I will do everything in my power to find it right away. I don't want any of my children to get their hands on it. I'm going to go look some more while you take a rest. It's got to be somewhere. But listen. You have to be careful what you say. Maybe in—the place where you're from—people talk more frankly. But here, you have to blend in. Things have changed somewhat, but it wasn't too long ago that women who were considered deviant or out of control or off balance could be locked up. My mother-in-law remembers several such situations and likes to remind me of them."

There it is, that vague sense of threat once again.

"It's like she's always spying on you," I say.

"Yes," she says. "And she could cause me to lose everything."

"So you know that I'm not from Niagara Falls, right?" I say, wondering if we're always going to talk in code.

We both jump at a movement in the corner of the room. But it's just one of the cats leaping from the bureau to a chair.

There's a long pause. Then Abby lets out a peal of laughter. "And next you'll tell me you're not my cousin Anna!" Her eyes catch mine. There's no merriment in them, only warning.

She knows. She knows very well I'm not Anna.

"Do you even have a cousin named Anna?" I ask.

"We corresponded," Abby says. "You and I, Anna. We corresponded and you offered to come help with the children, don't you remember?" She bustles around, pulling drapes, turning off the light. "Have a good rest," she calls. "We will find your watch."

At first I'm way too wired and stressed and freaked out to sleep. I think of that watch in her room, identical to mine. Abby took care to lock up the compartment again, but I'll bet I could pry it open with a butter knife. I hear her in the hall and resolve to stay awake until she goes downstairs.

My sheets must have been dried on a line; they are stiff and have a distinctive smell, like the outdoors, like grass and sunshine. I close my eyes and breathe it in.

I half dream that I'm back home in my own time, that it's last summer and I'm lying in my backyard the way I did every afternoon after gymnastics practice, back when I thought I knew who I was and felt secure about where my home was.

I drift into a dream. It's late afternoon, and I'm in the hammock, thinking about Zach, wondering why he suddenly seems so important, startling when I hear a door slam next door and then see a silhouette at his window above me. My worst problem is that I really want him to come and talk to me, even though I'm the one who stopped talking to him. I lie in the hammock and think about ways to fly. I plan to take photos of butterflies surfing breezes, hazy bees dipping and swooping among flowers, my cat Simone Biles performing her own gymnastics contortions as she wiggles under bushes nosing for squirrels and mice. I can feel the breeze at my back as I glide on a longboard along wooded paths between trees, the waves lifting me as I surf through an ocean. Still flying.

I wake abruptly. All of the smells and tastes and textures of my real life, so real before, fall away, disappearing, realization and dread slowly blooming. I'm still in a bed in a room in 1929, and I miss Mom, I miss Zach, I miss my life with a longing so fierce it feels like it could carry me home on its own power.

I sit up. What if I never see Mom again? Or Zach? Why am I in 1929, of all places, instead of at least 1928, when I'd be able to witness an Olympics gymnastics competition?

If this was a random time jump, why does Abby look so much like me, and who is Anna?

Did Abby find my Chronowatch, or did Luke, or the kids? She seems to be convinced that it was Mrs. Grundy. What would she want with it?

Questions whirl and twirl and do back walkovers that throw themselves into back handsprings that turn into back tucks lifting high in the air, and I crawl under a warm blanket. The next thing I know, I'm waking, planning to tell Mom that I had the weirdest dream.

But when I open my eyes, I'm still in the mahogany bed, canopy arching over me.

18

The house is silent, the kitchen and front room empty. I peer outside, expecting to find Abby scouring the yard for my watch, but there's no sign of her. I edge toward the kitchen, wondering where she keeps the butter knives, when I detect the sound of a chair scraping in the basement. Tiptoeing down the stairs, I find her at a workbench covered with those boring-looking magazines like *Watchmaker*. Pieces from a kitchen wall clock and a pocket watch are scattered around her. She jumps when she sees me and makes a move to cover up the Chronowatch with the white strap.

"Oh my goodness, I lost track of time," she says. "Is Sarah still sleeping?"

"I think so," I say. "Did you find my watch?"

"No, and not for lack of trying. I've been next door every ten minutes but Luke's mother isn't there. I think she must know something." She sighs. "I've been trying to figure out how to fix this one for years. If we could just locate the other one, maybe I could compare them and see what's going on."

I just nod. She is, I know now, the one person who can help me find my way home.

"Come, we need to go upstairs," Abby says. I follow her up to the living room. She pops out the front door and across the lawn while I wait in the doorway, holding my breath, hoping my watch will magically reappear. But she returns sighing.

She has barely settled into mending garments by the fire when Sarah appears at the foot of the stairs, rubbing her eyes, and the older kids trample the porch, banging in from school. Abby puts the basket of shirts and socks aside.

Catherine squats to take off her shoes and Robert shoves her aside in his race toward the kitchen, but Abby heads him off, herding all three kids toward the door. "Don't take off your coats, we're going downtown," she says. She shrugs into her own, with a fur collar and cuffs. "Anna has lost something very important," Abby says in a carefully casual tone. "Have you seen a wristwatch?"

They all shake their heads as she throws a spare coat to me. "Put on your arctics," she tells Sarah, who fits rubber boots over her shoes.

"If you find Anna's watch, you need to tell us right away," Abby instructs them. "Don't touch it or mess with it. It's very valuable and you have to be extra careful."

We walk down the hill, the older kids running ahead, Robert circling back to take Sarah's hand. As we pass the house next door, a curtain pulls back and a face appears at the edge of the window, peering at us. Then the drape drops again.

"She's there," Abby gasps. "Hold on." She circles back and bangs on the door.

"Mom," she says when the door swings open. "It's urgent that I find something that my guest lost. A wristwatch. It was in the planter in the front yard."

There's a sudden laugh, a witch-like cackle, before Mrs. Grundy steps out into the light. I thought that she must be like ninety years old, judging by her gray hair. But now I realize she's probably really about the same age as Mom. Maybe even younger. Something about her hairstyle, severe expression, and 1920s housedress makes her seem ancient.

"Have you forgotten your manners, Abby?" she asks. "Aren't you going to introduce me to your guest?"

"This is my cousin Anna," Abby promptly replies.

"It's nice to meet you, Mrs. Grundy," I say, and Abby claps her hand over her mouth, stifling a giggle.

"Oh, you know what a bear cat I am," she says to Luke's mother. I feel like I've committed some kind of faux pas.

"I suppose you think that's funny too." Mrs. Grundy addresses me. "I hope you're not as slutty as your cousin."

I'm taken aback. I'm not sure if *slutty* means quite the same thing in 1929 as in 2018, but it doesn't sound nice.

"That means she thinks I'm a poor housekeeper," Abby tells me, but I'm not convinced that that's what Mrs. Grundy meant at all. "Listen, Mom, we've really got to find this watch. It's been in the family forever."

She frowns. "Don't go flying all off the handle, Abby, or people will think you're crazy. I'll let you know if I see it," she says. "But right now I'm in the middle of something." She closes the door firmly.

"A 'Mrs. Grundy' is an uptight person," Abby murmurs. "Don't call anyone Mrs. Grundy to their face."

That's when I realize that Luke's mother's name isn't really Mrs. Grundy, but in my mind, the name has stuck.

"I think she knows something," Abby murmurs as we continue down the street, catching up to the children who have run on to the corner. "Do you hear how she makes out like I'm completely wacko, though? If she had her way, *I'd* be committed to an asylum."

"Why would she think you're wacko?"

"I have modern ideas about rearing children." She speaks in that careful way. "And sometimes I let it slip how much I hate housework. When the little ones are older, I'd like to work outside the home. Things like that."

"That doesn't sound crazy," I say. No one is behind us, but now I'm getting all paranoid, too, convinced that Mrs. Grundy is going to sneak up on me. "Women from my—hometown—feel that way too."

"Yes, women from Niagara Falls have always been forward thinking," she answers, and smirks at me. "Women have been able to vote for less than ten years. I should be patient, I suppose."

As we near Jackson Street, a windowless car rattles by. "That's our school," Catherine says to me when she catches me staring at a wood-frame building that looks like a house. In my time, an old brick building stands here. It's where we went to preschool. Me and Zach.

We walk along a high wall where I used to practice beam poses and leaps, back when I never walked anywhere. Back then, I did handstands in elevators, cartwheels on curbs, wolf jumps in the living room. That was when gymnastics still felt exciting, and I couldn't wait to progress from one level to the next. I couldn't wait to get to optionals and design my own competition leo and pick out my own music. It's weird to think that none of that is really in the past. It's all in the future.

Down Davis Street, we stop at a barbershop with a red-striped pole like a peppermint.

"I'll be back," Abby says. "Can you watch the children?"

Abby leaves us there and darts off across the street to a watchmaker's shop. I'm hopeful. Maybe she'll find just the thing she needs to repair her Chronowatch. I refuse to think about all of the years that she's tried to fix it and hasn't.

The barber, in his crisp white shirt and string tie, wraps a sheet around Robert, clips his hair, and shaves his neck. There are three brass bowls in the middle of the floor, like dog bowls, and I examine the ceiling for leaks. Then a customer walks over and spits into one, and no one flinches.

Disgusting. The dog bowls are spittoons. And then I realize that the odd-shaped containers with funnels at the top I saw along the streets are also spittoons. Sometimes at my school, guys who chew spit their tobacco into the drinking fountain. That's even grosser.

Abby returns in time to pay with nickels that have buffalos on them. Then we stop at a small store for penny candy. Catherine wants a wax elephant, but the younger kids get rope-handled lollipops.

"Did you find what you were looking for?" I nod toward the watchmaker's shop.

"More parts. I'm going to figure it out," she responds. Then she changes the subject. "We have a little party this evening. You will join us and meet our friends." Abby studies me as if she's trying to decipher me.

"I can just stay home and look after the kids," I suggest. I'm not sure that I want to meet more people. Eventually I'm going to slip up, give up any pretense that I belong in this time period. "I mean, won't there be drinking? I'm not allowed to drink yet."

"No one's allowed to drink." Abby's mouth quirks. "Prohibition."

"Oh," I say, remembering.

"And Luke's mother is already planning to stay with the children."

The kids disappear into the house ahead of us. Abby catches me looking at the flowerpot. "We'll talk tonight," she says. "Luke will meet us at the party."

After a meal that would scandalize Mom—roast beef, mashed potatoes, and gravy, with no salad or green veggies—I help Abby clean up and then we hasten upstairs to get ready for the evening. She seems nervous and scattered, changing the subject every two seconds, avoiding my eyes. She tosses me a fresh frock and we powder our faces in front of the mirror. "Powder is common, but no paint. Lipstick is fine, but people still frown upon rouge," Abby informs me, sounding as if she's giving me a lesson.

"The children have eaten," Abby briskly tells her mother-in-law when we go downstairs a few minutes later. "They're upstairs having their baths and getting into their pajamas. They may listen to *Amos and Andy* before they go to bed." She nods toward a bulky, ornate wooden cabinet in the corner: a radio.

"I know how to take care of the children," Mrs. Grundy says stiffly. She seems like one of those people who sucks all the joy out of any room.

lllll〜〜llll

"She's always criticized me," Abby says, out on the street. "Early on, she used to constantly suggest that women who don't toe the line ought to be locked up. And it really does happen sometimes."

"Is that why you're so afraid of that?" I ask.

"I don't think she'd do anything to hurt Luke or the children. And she's gotten a little bit less critical of me over the years," Abby says. "But I still don't trust her. She's always snooping around, like she's trying to find out some scandalous secret about me." She's silent for a second, then says, "Things have been tough for her since Luke's father died last summer." Abby seems far more relaxed away from the house and her family, walking through the dark and talking too softly to be overheard. "I'd be really careful around her," Abby goes on. "If you were to mention odd things, like say, that you had traveled from another time, I don't know that people would look kindly on that."

I take the plunge, even though I know this is the kind of odd comment Abby is warning me about. "I know that you're Gail," I say.

Abby's eyes widen as if she's startled to hear her name spoken for the first time in years. She swivels her head to look behind her, eyes sweeping the empty yards and the cars that occasionally clatter by.

"You can't ever call me that. Don't let anyone ever hear you, okay?" she says, and adds quietly, "Who are you? When you got here, I thought you were her. I thought maybe you'd come from a time where someone had found a way to upload the contents of the watch into a chip or something. I didn't realize you'd left your watch outside. Why in the world would anyone do that?" She pounds her forehead with her fist. "I would have let you go get it if I'd known. I was afraid if I let you out of our sight you'd disappear. I was terrified you were going to leave." Then, without missing a beat, as if the question has been poised on her lips for ages, she says, "Do you know what happened to my baby?" The anguish in her voice and on her face are too much.

"I met your daughter in 1976. She was Sarah's age. But you never came home. I think she went to a foster home."

Abby looks stricken. But she just says, "Are you related to us somehow? There's definitely a physical resemblance."

"Well, I'm not your cousin Anna," I joke. "Honestly, I don't know. My name is Elizabeth Arlington. I grew up in the same house where you live, except a hundred years later."

"Arlington?" she says. "As in Joan Arlington?"

"You know my mom?"

"Your mom?" She looks confused.

"Yeah, I was born in 2002 here in Bradford."

"2002?" She moves her lips, calculating. Shakes her head. "Then I'm really not sure who you are."

"I just told you," I said. "Elizabeth Arlington."

"Joan's daughter," she repeats, more a question than a response. "But you look so much like me."

"She raised me. She's my mom. But there's something weird about the day I was born. I wanted to go back to that day and figure it out. First I did a practice run to 1976, because I thought your house would be empty and nobody would see me. But your little girl was there. And then I tried to go home and ended up in 1988, and then I tried again and ended up here."

"1988?" Her brow furrows.

"I programmed in that date myself." I don't explain further.

"So that watch was malfunctioning too."

"Who am I?"

"It's all so confusing." She shakes her head. She seems to be talking more to herself than to me as she says, "When you start messing around with time, nothing adds up mathematically." She shakes her head. "I guess we're both candidates for a mental institution."

"You mean I could be stuck here too? The way you're stuck here?"

"I hope not."

She has that troubled look again.

We turn the corner onto Jackson, a street that Abby has told me is known as Millionaire Row, and see Luke coming toward us from a block away. "We are going to find your watch. But we can't talk about this anymore," she says, before assuming a big smile and rushing forward to meet Luke.

19

BRADFORD, PA, JANUARY 18, 1929
7 P.M.

"Where is this party?" I ask as we meet up with Luke. "Is it at a speakeasy?" All I can think is that I have to get Abby alone so we can finish our conversation.

Luke and Abby exchange amused looks.

"There was one of those downtown a few years ago," Luke says. "The Bradford police made a raid on it and found fifty guests who were imbibing beer. I remember that the owner was fined fifteen dollars."

"Oh, yes, and remember the man caught with a couple of jugs of moonshine a while back? He got a lecture from the judge on the evils of his ways, a one-thousand-dollar fine, and eight months in jail," Abby says.

I can't stand the taste of beer, but I'm a little disappointed that Abby and Luke don't seem to frequent places that require secret passwords.

We approach a house with music pouring out the doors and silhouettes of dancing people in the windows. As Luke starts up the porch steps, I tug on Abby's arm. "Why are you bringing me to this party?" I ask her. "I'm going to be totally out of place."

"Sorry. I just wanted a chance to talk to you out of my mother-in-law's hearing. We won't stay long." Abby breaks away and follows Luke into a house that no longer exists in my time. In 2018, a building that used to be a synagogue sits on this land. Now it's owned by the Salvation Army.

Inside, the air is blue with smoke and something jazzy plays on the gramophone, though someone has to change the record every five minutes. The rugs are plush and the woodwork shiny. When I go to use the bathroom I'm awed at the intricate tiles and a bathtub set in a little alcove flanked by curtains that look like drapes.

Surrounded by women in bobs and flapper dresses and flesh-colored stockings and men in checked stockings, their caps hanging by the door, I feel kind of like I've stepped into *The Great Gatsby,* a book I read in school last year and the theme of the school's junior-senior prom when I was a freshman.

"Bushwa," a woman next to Abby suddenly exclaims, holding out her hand to a passing man. "Butt me!" she says.

I go to school with kids who routinely say "WTF" and "up your ass," but somehow this is much more shocking. My grandparents and great grandparents weren't supposed to say stuff like that.

"*Bushwa* means bullshit," Abby whispers. "She wants a fag."

"A fag?" I echo, still shocked. This town is small, but there are gay and lesbian and gender-fluid kids at my school, and we would never use language like this.

"A cigarette," Abby hisses as a man hands the woman one. Everyone is smoking, strewing ashes across the carpet and tables despite the ornamental ashtrays everywhere.

"Oh, phonus balonus!" one woman cries out, and I glance at Abby.

"Bullshit?" I whisper.

She nods, pleased that I'm catching on.

"Who's this choice piece of calico?" A young guy halts before us, looking to Abby for an introduction. This guy would be hot if it weren't for the tassels dangling from his knee. Not to mention the fact that he's ancient compared to me, considering that he's like twenty-five and I'm like negative ninety.

"James, she's a child," Luke protests, and I realize I've just been sexually harassed.

People keep looking at me strangely, like I'm too young to be here, and I really am, so I stay close to Abby and eavesdrop on the conversations around me. It feels like I'm at a twenties reenactment, people talking about things I vaguely remember from history class. I hear someone mention Sacco and Vanzetti.

Others discuss Colonel Lindbergh in worshipful tones. I almost chime in that I've seen the *Spirit of St. Louis*, hanging from the ceiling at the Air and Space Museum at the Smithsonian.

It seems like everyone has a hip flask, which puzzles me. "I thought that it was illegal to drink," I mutter to Abby, but then I think of all of the kids at my school who are underage and drink anyway.

"Oh, for now," Abby says. "But the saloons will be back. Prohibition is going to be repealed."

"She thinks she knows the future," Luke says affectionately.

I listen to a man telling a story about getting his car stranded in a mudhole, and, nearby, some women complaining about young people, with their petting parties and cheek-to-cheek dancing.

"We disapprove because we're jealous," Abby says. She's the only woman without a cigarette. "I hear about this and long to be young all over again!"

One woman blanches and opens her mouth as if preparing to scold, but the others smile indulgently, as if they're used to Abby's forthright comments. Abby turns to me. "I'm a bit shocking," she informs me.

The man who sexually harassed me earlier comes back, tottering and slurring his words, and Abby takes my arm and then Luke's, pulling us away. "He's half seas over," she says. "Luke, we need to go."

I look at her blankly, but follow her to gather our wraps.

"Half seas over?" I ask out on the street.

"Shit-faced," Abby translates.

"Abby." Luke's tone is scandalized, but then he says to me, not sounding the least bit perturbed, "I tell her, women are made of finer stuff than men and have to keep us on the straight and narrow. She's not doing her job properly."

"He says that, but he likes my devastating frankness," Abby responds. "Even if his mother disapproves of it and everything I do."

"She thinks the world of you," Luke insists. "She's told me that. That not every woman would accept a stepchild as her own the way you have."

"That doesn't make me a saint," Abby protests. "Of course I love Catherine like my own. Why wouldn't I?"

"Well, my mother loves you," Luke says. "You two are just too alike, that's all. You're bound to clash sometimes."

Abby turns to me and rolls her eyes.

We trudge up the hill toward their house, which will someday be my house. The stars seem so much brighter than in my own time, and as our breath puffs out in front of us, I think how beautiful a night this would be if it weren't for an undercurrent of terror that I will never find my way back home.

The house is completely silent when we arrive back, the kids all asleep, and Luke's mother, who I continue to call Mrs. Grundy in my head, is knitting in the living room.

She leans close to all of us, sniffing the air.

She's trying to figure out if we've been drinking.

By now, though, I'm so tired I might as well be half seas over. I can't walk a straight line. I feel almost feverish with exhaustion. Abby nudges me in the direction of the guest room, and when I get there, I collapse, more desperately homesick than ever.

In kindergarten, I memorized my phone number just in case I should ever get lost, but my mother didn't give me any instructions about what to do if I became lost in time. I was that kid who could never make it through a sleepover because I got so homesick, and now here I am, so far from home with no way to get back, a constant ache in my stomach.

Abby seems confident that my watch will turn up, and I want to believe her, or that she will figure out how to fix her own. Why didn't she fix it before now, though? As I lie in the dark, my hope leaches away, turning to despair.

Out in the hall, Luke pulls metal chains, winding a clock, and farther away, a train whistles. When we passed the railroad station on Main Street, Abby mentioned that there are sixty trains a day.

Sixty, I think with wonder, my last thought before I fall into a deep, dreamless sleep that I don't wake from for twelve hours.

20

BRADFORD, PA, JANUARY 19, 1929
10 A.M.

"And he did it! Yes, sir, he did it! It's a touchdown!" says a voice in the living room, accompanied by crackling static, as I descend the stairs mid-morning. Luke, in baggy pants and checked stockings like the men at the party last night, is working a newspaper crossword puzzle as he listens to a play-by-play on the radio.

I settle down on an uncomfortable stiff-backed floral chair and pick up a section of the newspaper, studying a Lucky Strike ad in which a "girl" implores a "man" to blow some of his smoke her way. Delicious smells waft through the house while Abby clatters around in the kitchen, filling a jar with freshly baked cookies. Bread and a cake cool on the counter.

I join her in the kitchen for some bread and butter. She seems moody, ignoring my attempts at small talk while she rolls dough, rinses pans, and casts pointed glances toward the living room and Luke. I lapse into silence. I don't really want to talk about the weather either, when all I want to know is what might have happened to my watch and how I'm going to get home again.

The radio goes silent and Luke appears in the doorway. "I'm off to the country club," he says.

"This afternoon we'll talk about the stocks," Abby informs him.

"Why would we withdraw all of our money from the bank and sell our stocks?" Luke asks. "The market is grand. The bankers say there's not a cloud in the sky."

"Luke, you know I'm right. I'm always right about these things," Abby replies.

"She is. She's always right," Luke says, tipping his hat.

"Anna, your father is in finance, yes?" Abby turns her head away from Luke and winks at me. "What would he say?"

And it dawns on me: it's early 1929, a few months before the stock-market crash and the start of the Great Depression. We learned about that in history last year.

Of course Abby wants Luke to get out of the stock market and put their money under a mattress. "He'd say you're right," I assure Abby and Luke. "That's exactly what everyone at home is doing."

"Where are the kids?" I ask after Luke leaves. The house is unnaturally quiet.

"They go next door on Saturday mornings for pancakes and pinochle with their grandma," she says. "We'll collect them in a bit for a show." She's hustling around now, wiping off counters and wrapping the bread in towels. "I'm still wondering if Luke's mother knows something about your watch. And I'll ask the milkman and the iceman tomorrow. If we could just get hold of it, I could figure out how to fix my watch before we send you back to your own time."

"And then what would you do?" I ask her as she buckles her shoes and throws on her wraps.

She looks up at me, furrowing her brow. "A part of me wants it to stay broken. There would be too many hard choices if it were functioning again."

As Abby, Mrs. Grundy, the kids, and I walk briskly toward downtown Bradford, crossing onto Main Street, I turn over Abby's words in my mind. If she goes back to the seventies, Jillian, and her work, she'll have to leave behind her 1920s husband and kids. Unless she could move back and forth in time, which sounds pretty stressful and unpredictable to me.

"Are you absolutely sure you haven't seen Anna's watch?" she asks Mrs. Grundy.

"You're really obsessing about that, aren't you?" It strikes me that Mrs. Grundy never answers any questions about the watch directly. "You're starting to sound a little insane. You need to be more careful. Do you remember Mrs. Peterson? She refused to have her children confirmed in the Catholic Church and her husband had her committed to a sanitorium. She was diagnosed with paranoid schizophrenia."

Abby rolls her eyes.

"And Maud Wilson? She protested because she thought her husband was having an improper relationship with her niece. He sent her to an asylum."

We turn onto Main Street, where I expect to find the movie theater that still exists in my own time on the bottom floor of a historic eight-story building next to McDonald's. But nothing is familiar, not the cobblestone street or the trolley lines running down them, not the stores and businesses: barbers and a Turkish bath, dressmakers, blacksmiths, a Chinese laundry, boardinghouses, a butter-dish manufacturer, a piano tuner, a fruit market.

"I appreciate your concerns about my sanity, but I really need to find that wristwatch," Abby says when Mrs. Grundy finally gives her space to squeeze in a word edgewise. "Are you absolutely sure you haven't seen it?"

"Does it look like that one you used to have?" Mrs. Grundy asks.

Abby freezes. "You remember that?"

"It was very odd-looking," says Mrs. Grundy. "If I find one like it, I'll let you know."

She still hasn't really answered the question. I raise my eyebrows at Abby, but she's distracted. "Wait for me, I need to do some things," she calls, slipping into the cabinetmaker's shop and then the jeweler's. My hopes lift again. I know that she's looking for materials to repair her watch. I try to ignore the fact that in the nine years she's had to repair it, she hasn't figured it out.

We wait on the street. Mrs. Grundy intervenes in a quarrel between the kids. She doesn't speak to me or acknowledge my presence. It's like I make her uncomfortable somehow. Like it's easier for her to pretend that I don't exist. Abby emerges empty-handed and my hopes sink again.

As we reach South Street, I tune out the gossip Mrs. Grundy is passing on to Abby about people I don't know, more stories about women committed to asylums for minor infractions. I see what Abby means. She seems to have a thing for these stories.

Finally we arrive at an unfamiliar structure with a sign that identifies it as Shea's Theater. The high-ceilinged lobby is hazy with the blue smoke and cigarette smell that seems to linger everywhere. The theater itself is breathtaking, with balconies, boxes, and pillars ornately decorated with rows of cherub heads. A gigantic screen hangs between red velvet curtains in front. We walk across a plush red carpet and settle in plush velvet seats.

The lights go out. Clouds swim across the ceiling. Theaters are obviously designed to distract people from their problems.

A newsreel flickers onto the screen. I half listen to economic and political reports, then snap to attention at an item about the 1928 Olympics in Amsterdam. A flag flies up a pole. Crowds clap and wave. The camera closes in on a girl on the sidelines who looks strikingly like me, but then she's gone as the camera flashes over to a windswept, grassy plane, where men hurdle into a mud puddle, prance out on horses, do the pole vault and shot put. While men work the parallel bars and rings, women in baggy outfits line up and perform a chorus-line kick. It's the first women's gymnastics competition.

After the newsreel, we watch a silent Charlie Chaplin film called *The Circus*. The main character hides in a circus to escape the police and accidentally becomes a hit. He keeps getting into trouble: he's trapped in a lion's cage, frees monkeys, teeters on the high wire. The kids find this hysterically funny, and I find watching the kids more interesting than watching the movie. Mrs. Grundy stares stiffly at the screen, barely cracking a smile.

We arrive back at the house before Luke, Mrs. Grundy peeling off to her own house without a good-bye. The kids go out to play in the snow. I follow Abby to the kitchen to help her prepare supper.

"I have something for you." My heart skips as she digs in her apron pocket. But instead of my watch, she pulls out a piece of paper. I unfold it while she gathers food from the icebox and cabinets. It's the alphabet, a strange symbol next to each letter, like a bunch of hieroglyphics or cartoon swearing. I feel like I've seen a similar list before. Then I remember: on the paper wrapped around the watch in the drawer of the deserted yellow house.

"What's this?"

"It's a code I made up years ago. I need you to memorize it as quickly as possible and then we will dispose of it. Whatever you do, don't let anyone see it."

"But why?" I ask, just as the front door clatters open, and Luke and the kids come tumbling in. I quickly tuck the paper into my pocket.

I study the paper until late that night, then report back to Abby after breakfast, after Luke and the older kids have left for church with Mrs. Grundy. Abby claimed that Sarah seemed a little feverish and stayed behind. Sarah seems fine to me.

"I memorized it," I tell Abby.

"Okay, good." She snatches it from me and rips it into little pieces, tossing them in the stove. "I need to get together some papers for you. Can you look after Sarah while I do that?"

Mystified, I throw on my leotard and the knickers and take Sarah outside, where it's warmed up considerably since yesterday, the snow almost melted. All morning I entertain the little girl and spend some of my pent-up energy practicing aerial cartwheels and wolf jumps. I shoot sharp glances toward the house when I hear noises or detect movement, but it's never Abby, just the sun bursting through clouds and glinting on the glass or a bird rising into the sky.

I need to be ready at any moment to vault my way home, and I'm determined this time to do a real vault somehow, to go faster and higher. So I go on practicing, while Sarah keeps yelling, "Do that again!" I wrack my brain for things that could serve as makeshift vault tables: the kitchen table, a big rock? Or maybe, instead of vaulting, I could just do a running front handspring and a front tuck, and achieve the height and velocity I need?

After lunch, when the kids have trooped off next door and Luke has gone to play golf, I'm washing up the dishes when Abby hands me a towel. "Wipe your hands," she says. "I need to give you something."

"Is it my watch? Did you ask the milkman and the iceman—"

She shakes her head.

"I caught them both this morning. Neither of them seems to have seen it. I just keep thinking that it has to turn up, though. Things don't just disappear into thin air. Are your hands dry?" She passes me a booklet with an orange cover: 5 cents, it says in the upper corner. "I know this is a lot. I filled most of a tablet."

"This is a tablet?" I crack, thinking of my iPad tablet at home. "Next you're going to tell me that a notebook isn't a laptop computer."

Abby raises her eyebrows at me. I guess tablets and computers didn't exist when she left 1976. I open the booklet and find page after page of brown paper densely filled with her code symbols.

"You want me to read this?" I'm dumbfounded. This looks like a foreign language. I sink down at the kitchen table, trying to decipher the words. This is going to take forever. "Dear," I read, then trace my fingers along the next word. "Jill." "Dear Jill?" I say aloud.

"I'd always hoped that she would show up someday. I started putting my story in writing years ago. I knew that someday, somehow, I was going to have to explain to her what happened."

I remember the shoestring, the string connecting the kid I met in 1976 and the girl I watched from afar in a gym in 1988.

And what about me? How does this thread lead to me?

"Leaving her behind is my biggest regret. There were so many moments that I almost hurled myself blindly through time, hoping to get back to her," Abby says. "But I knew that if the watch malfunctioned again, it would be like suicide. That I might end up in a much worse place than here. Still, there's not a day that I don't think about her. You said she was okay, though. That she became a well-known gymnast, right? I used to love to watch gymnastics on TV." She sounds simultaneously sad and pleased and anxious. "Is she the one you mentioned whose picture was on a cereal box? I remember that missing kids used to be on the sides of school-lunch milk cartons. Now they're on cereal boxes? But she's not missing, is she?"

Even though my thoughts are whirring, I laugh. "No, they put well-known athletes on boxes to sell cereal."

"Oh, I sort of remember some football and baseball players in the sixties," she says. "But few, if any, women. And Jillian is one of them?" A proud smile lifts her lips. "You said her name is Jillian Clayton? So that's the name of the family she went to live with? I had hoped that Joan would take her in—"

"I think she wanted to. But she hadn't been approved as a foster parent."

Abby pulls up a chair alongside me. It's rare for her to sit during the day. "Leaving her behind was by far the worst thing I've ever done. The worst thing I have to deal with," Abby says. "I've had to fight despair every single day. I tinkered with the watch for hours, tried resetting it again and again, but using it just seemed too dangerous. I love Luke. I love Catherine. I didn't know if I could bear to lose a whole second family on top of my first." She sighs. "And contraception hasn't exactly been readily available here, though clinics are becoming more common. With each new baby, I've felt even more bound to this time and this life. I would die if I lost any more of my children. You say that Jillian is all right?"

"I think she is," I answer, but I don't know for sure. After all, she disappeared after the 1988 Olympic trials.

"I want her to be," Abby says. "I can't tamper with her life anymore if she's all right."

"So you wouldn't try to go back?"

"I couldn't take that risk," she says, and I'm pretty sure she's being straight with me. "I mean, even if I could fix my watch and go back, I couldn't take the chance of screwing up timelines even further and causing paradoxes." She sighs and goes on, more forthcoming than ever before, as if now, finally, she trusts me. "Sometimes I wish I could get my old life back, you know? I mean, I'm a woman who nearly has a PhD in physics, but now I have to settle for a life of keeping house. I've already changed history by having children who wouldn't have existed otherwise. I can't risk doing anything else, like inventing anything that might impact the world even in a small way. I've accepted that."

"Isn't there something you could do that wouldn't change the whole world?" I stare at the symbols on the page, feeling a little despairing as I try to decipher the next couple of words: *I'm writing this . . .*

Abby perks up. "Maybe," she says. "I've been thinking about making artisanal clocks. That's a profession that requires artistry but also mathematic precision and scientific knowledge. Right now there's all sorts of cool research, like the switch from radium luminescent paint to phosphorescent light sources to make clocks that glow in the dark. And do you know that a couple of years ago, a Canadian clockmaker developed a timekeeper based on vibrations of a quartz crystal?"

I feel a wave of longing for Zach. I can imagine how the two of them would totally geek out together.

But then her mood shifts abruptly. "It's bad enough that I've had to put my own career on hold. But it's even worse that I can't step in and stop bad things from happening, even when I know they're coming. I know the stock market is going to crash. I know that Hitler is going to gain power. What use is knowing all that when I can't do anything about anything? I can make investments that will ensure the security of my family, maybe someday build my own lab. But maybe not. What if I inadvertently do something that keeps me from being born? Or Jill?"

Or me, I think, *because I'm sure we're all connected somehow.*

"We're going to find your watch." She doesn't sound all that confident. "We're going to figure out what happened to it and get you home." She stands, brushing her hands off on her apron. "You might want to put the papers in your room so they don't attract too much attention."

Abby whirls around suddenly. "Holy smokes!" Mrs. Grundy is standing in the dining-room doorway.

"Who's Jill?" she asks. "What papers?"

Abby gulps. There's a long silence, Mrs. Grundy's eyes passing from the tablet to my face to Abby's as if she's heard way too much of our conversation. "You have got to quit sneaking up on me like that," Abby says once she musters her voice. "How did you get in, anyway? The back doors were locked."

"With my key, silly," Mrs. Grundy says, but she still has a stunned look on her face.

"But you could have just come in the front door . . ." Abby's voice trails off, her gaze following Mrs. Grundy's. They both stare at the tablet. Abby seems calm, though. She knows it's in a code that Mrs. Grundy can't decipher.

"You were just talking about someone named Jill," Mrs. Grundy says, right as the front door bursts open and Sarah flies in the door, the other kids close behind.

"Can we go outside again?" Sarah asks me.

"Sure," I say, though I would much rather sit still and try to process what just happened.

I want to start reading the tablet. I hastily stow it in the back of the closet in my bedroom, under a pile of blankets, just in case Mrs. Grundy comes looking for it.

Outside, Sarah is waiting for me in her riding breeches, which are a little less puffy than my knickers.

What did Mrs. Grundy hear? I wonder, as I demonstrate a cartwheel. Why is she so sneaky? Maybe she really is gathering evidence to prove that Abby is insane so that she can have her committed to an institution.

Or maybe she's the one who found my watch. If so, what is she going to do with it? Why won't she admit it or give it back?

Sarah has almost mastered a cartwheel when Catherine joins us, also in riding breeches.

Robert wanders off across the yard while I instruct Catherine. "It's called a cartwheel because your legs are like spokes of a wheel turning quickly," I explain. This makes more sense to me now that I see the ice cart go by every day.

Catherine's legs are bent on her cartwheels and every time she tries to do a backbend she collapses in a sprawling tangle of limbs, giggling. "You have a flat tire," I tell her. She scrambles up to help me spot Sarah, who picks up basic skills astonishingly quickly. Even at four, she has a natural grace and remembers to point her toes, keep her fingers together, relax her shoulders. If she lived in 2018, it wouldn't take her long to be ready to compete at the lowest level.

"Look, Grandma," Catherine calls, and Mrs. Grundy pops up from behind the partial fence where she's been pruning some shrubs. I jump. I don't know what's going on with this woman, but she continues to appear out of nowhere, keeping me on edge. No wonder Abby is so suspicious of her, the way she creeps around so furtively all the time.

Now she watches Sarah cartwheel across the lawn, and a glimmer of a smile appears on her face. I didn't know that she could smile. Last night Robert made the family pose so he could take a picture with his Brownie camera. "Smile, Grandma," he ordered her.

"I am," she said, opening her eyes a little wider, not moving her mouth.

Now, she fights her face back into a stern expression. "It's not very lady-like to be teaching them to run in pants like hooligans," she scolds me.

These kinds of comments seem to roll right off the kids, as if they don't really believe that she means them.

Catherine dashes across the yards and taps her grandmother on the arm. "You're it!" Catherine yells.

Mrs. Grundy rises to her feet, brushing off her housedress. Then, to my surprise, she whirls around and hurtles after Catherine.

I had no idea she could run. I've thought of her as stiff and starched and stealthy, tiptoeing around, but here she is, ducking under a pair of pants clipped to the line, touching Robert's shoulder as he rounds the house to the backyard.

"You're it," she says before she dashes back to her yard and resumes raking old leaves out from under bushes.

I remember Luke telling me that his father had died only a few months before. I study Mrs. Grundy, her head bowed over her task. I imagine my own mother the months after my father's death, barely able to leave the house, and for the first time in my life, not sure if I'll ever see my mother again, I can begin to imagine what that grief was like. Is there more to Mrs. Grundy than meets the eye?

But she has such an odd way of looking past me as if I'm a ghost, as if she can't stand to speak to me. It doesn't make sense, how on the one hand she snubs me but on the other hand is always watching and listening. Am I a threat to her somehow? The mere sight of her has started to make me feel uneasy.

The tag game continues as Mrs. Grundy scoops leaves into her hands and throws them over the back fence.

Why do I feel that even though she doesn't appear to be paying attention to me, her eyes are boring into my back as I slip away back into the house?

21

BRADFORD, PA, JANUARY 20, 1929
7 P.M.

Dear Jill,

I'm writing this because I'm hoping it will somehow reach you, someday. I want you to know my story even if I'm not there to tell it. I want you to know that I would have never left you behind on purpose, that I made a mistake that has led to endless grief and worry. I often hope against hope that you'll find the extra Chronowatches I left behind and that you'll come to find me. I was so arrogant and sure of myself. I meant to leave those watches in a safe deposit box for you, as soon as I got back from my trial run. I wasn't planning to leave them behind in that kitchen drawer forever. Now it seems impossible that anyone will ever find them. And I'm terrified that if I write my story, it could get into the wrong hands. It took me a long time to realize how dangerous it can be to think I can manipulate time any more than I can control nature. Time and nature always win.

Yet still I find myself hoping that someday, somehow, I will be able to tell you my story in person. As the years pass, though, I become less certain that we'll ever meet again. And maybe writing this is futile, because if you never found the watches, how would you have ever found the code? Still I keep hoping that these words have somehow found their way to you.

I was born Abigail Grant in Cleveland, Ohio. I was the youngest of three children, ten years younger than my next oldest sibling, and I never felt that I fit into my family, that they understood my fascination with science or my drive to study and learn. As a child I voraciously read science fiction, especially stories about time travel. I skipped two grades, then graduated from high school at fifteen. I took a year before college to attend a watchmaking institute in Seattle. Later, when I applied to a PhD program at MIT, I claimed in my statement of purpose that I was interested in inventions regarding watch technology.

Since the Sputnik era, scientists had known it was possible to operate highly accurate atomic clocks in space, tracking satellites from shifts in radio signals. The government had started working on global positioning systems when I was in my teens, and I began to play with the idea of using these advances to locate the coordinates to traversable wormholes.

At twenty, I was deep into my research, experimenting with circuit diagrams and source code for receiving satellite signals and prototypes for a watch with a built in GPS system, only returning to my apartment to sleep.

Sometimes I'd look up from my work in the basement lab to see shoes walking by the high-set windows, sneakers and oxfords and the occasional secretarial high heels, the only signs of life some days. Or I'd emerge from concentration to discover that those windows had gone dark, or my stomach would rumble and I'd realize that I'd totally forgotten to eat. Or I'd suddenly notice the early morning light diffusing, the windows so aglow with the sunrise that I couldn't see outside. But I plugged on until I collapsed, slept a few hours, then got up and started again.

One summer night after hours in the physics lab, my head was falling forward, lights and words and equations dancing on the inside of my eyelids until I forced my eyes open, pushing on, telling myself that I'd take a break as soon as I found a stopping point. Hours later, I woke, head on the table, to the rumble of a cleared throat. Snapping open my eyes, I bolted up.

Professor Crake, my dissertation advisor, stood framed by the doorway.

22

BRADFORD, PA, JANUARY 21, 1929
7:30 A.M.

I wake suddenly. The tablet has slumped to the floor beside my bed. I fell asleep after hours of decoding the first couple of pages. I lie there, sunlight bursting through my window, a child thumping down the stairs, the smell of bacon wafting up. I feel despair at how much time it's taking to read this tablet, and yet I also feel a chill, reading these words meant for Jill, knowing how unlikely it is that they will ever reach her, how unlikely it is that I would be reading them, either. I pick it up again.

But as much as I want to know this story, my head is so achy that I immediately put the tablet aside again and just lie there, thinking. In just a few days' time, 2018 has begun to feel like a dream populated by shadowy people whose voices I can't quite remember. Not even my dream, but someone else's. I barely remember important events. The day I won beam at states. The day my biology teacher lectured about genetics in class. A trip to Disney World with Mom the time Nationals was in Florida. I cringe at the mean words I yelled at Mom the last time I saw her. That I didn't want to be her daughter.

Now, if I could just go home, nothing would matter except that I'm a girl from 2018, my mother's daughter. Will I someday have to write my own story in code, find a way to send it to the future, to let Mom know that I would have never stayed away on purpose? Will I have to write my story for Zach to let him know what happened to me?

If I could go back to 2018 now, if it were 1929 that became the shadowy world, I vow that I'd be more grateful for what I have. I'd try to repair things between Mom and me. I'm so homesick, I can't quite fathom how I was so angry with Mom when I realized that she hadn't told me the truth, whatever that is. I know I need to demand answers from Mom, but I vow I'll figure all of this out without any more traveling through time. I know I'll always be restless until I know where I came from. I mean, if I went home now, I'd be glad to be there. But eventually, if I never knew the truth, I'd feel like something was missing.

After the kids have left for school, Abby comes to find me, bringing me a plate. She perches on the edge of the bed while I eat breakfast. "Sarah's spending the day next door, so I'm going to take apart my watch again. It's probably futile. I've already done it dozens of times over the years, but I just don't have the equipment to figure out what's wrong with it. I don't have access to labs or computers or the right technology. If we could just find your Chronowatch, I could compare them and figure it out."

"I've only gotten through two pages of this." I rifle through the pages of the tablet. "It's taking forever. I'm getting a headache."

"Why don't you work on it a little bit more, or just get some rest?" Abby bounces up off the bed. "If you're still having trouble, we'll barricade all the doors after lunch and I'll help you with it."

I'm beginning to think that Mrs. Grundy is supernatural, that there's no way to get away from her. Would it be so bad if Abby just told Mrs. Grundy her story, though? Would that really give her any power over Abby? I can't imagine that Luke would go along with any plots that Mrs. Grundy might have to hurt her.

But the thought still nags at me: what if Mrs. Grundy has my watch? Why won't she give it back?

I ease the tablet toward me, drag my eyes across the next few lines, then settle in, working on decoding some more. It goes faster as I get into a groove, the process becoming more intuitive with practice.

23

BRADFORD, PA, JANUARY 21, 1929
9 A.M.

Professor Crake, my dissertation advisor, stood framed by the doorway. He was a compact man with a mustache and the faint beginning of a pot belly. I thought of him as ancient, but now I found myself staring into his gentle, handsome face as he loomed over me.

"I admire your dedication, but you're working too hard," he said. He wasn't that old, after all, I thought, maybe in his midthirties. "Go home and get some rest," he said.

"Oh, no," I said groggily. "I was just about to figure out something —"I looked at the computer terminal where I'd been working, trying to remember what I'd been doing when I fell asleep. Confused, I turned the pages of my notes.

"Show me tomorrow." He removed the pages from my hands and guided me to the door as one might a wandering sleepwalker. I felt the feather brush of his palm in the small of my back. "Go home and sleep now."

His concern made me feel connected to someone, cared for, after ear-ringing days of isolation. So that's how it started, the relationship with the man who would become your father. He brought me coffee and sandwiches. We ate and talked and I showed him my sketches and calculations and prototypes without mentioning the time-travel component of my research. He suggested some articles on global positioning systems and patents for me to read. And finally, one day over sandwiches he'd brought, the truth came out.

"What do you know about black holes?" I asked, cautious.

"It's not really my field. But I guess there are several theories."

"I started out looking at x-ray imaging from some of the telescopes that orbit the earth, focusing on possible signs of black holes—orbital motions near massive bodies, galaxies bent into pancake shapes, the light of stars bent inwards, stars that appear to be orbiting empty space, stars and disks of gas wobbling and spinning for no obvious reason."

"Okay." Professor Harry leaned forward, smiling. It felt like he found my enthusiasm cute rather than taking it seriously.

I was annoyed but kept going. "You know what a white hole is?"

"The other end of a black hole. Completely unproven."

I ignored that last part. "If a black hole is like a vacuum that pulls things in, a white hole ejects them on the other side, so a black hole entrance and white hole exit could actually be in different parts of the same universe or even in different universes." I made two pencil marks on a scrap of paper. "These are two points in space-time." I drew a line between them. "And this line is the distance from one point to the other in normal space-time." I bent and folded the paper and poked the pencil through it. "So if you could warp space-time like this, you'd find a shorter way of linking the two points. In other words, a shortcut through space-time."

"A wormhole. Like in science fiction."

"And possibly existing in black holes, which are getting closer to proven fact. Solutions to Einstein's field equations have yielded accurate

models of the properties of black holes. They've also reinforced the theoretical evidence for their existence. But it would take millions of lifetimes to get to one, right? And you couldn't approach them because of the huge amounts of radiation and the gravity that would crush you."

"Even if you located a wormhole, it would pinch closed. It would collapse before you could get to the other side." He drummed his fingers on the table thoughtfully. "But what about the Casimir effect?" He sounded excited. "That's a potential way to stabilize wormholes. Let me do some digging. I know I've seen some research on that." He pulled a piece of scrap paper out of a pocket and jotted something down, then folded away the paper. "But what does this have to do with watch technology and global positioning systems?"

I took a shaky breath. "So what if you could use GPS technology to locate wormholes? And what if, assuming you could stabilize them, you could use that GPS technology to build a time machine?"

I could see the war on his face, the little twitch of his mustache as his mouth grimaced and then tipped into a smile and then gaped soundlessly, this fight between his immediate impulse to cringe and his fascination with what I was saying and his responsibility as an authority figure to put a stop to such flaky ideas. I glimpsed a boyish light in his eyes, but his stern professorial tone won out. "You can't tell anyone about this," he said. "You'd be the laughingstock of the department. No one would ever approve this kind of research."

"Right," I said, trying to hide my disappointment as I rose to gather crumbs and crusts and crumpled napkins for the trash, changing the subject, dropping the conversation. But of course not the research. I would not drop the research no matter what anyone said.

24

BRADFORD, PA, JANUARY 21, 1929
3 P.M.

"Anna?" Abby pokes her head in the door, and I look up to discover shadows in the room slanting and lengthening. My stomach rumbles with hunger. "We both forgot about lunch," Abby says.

"Did you make any progress?" I ask her. I scramble up to get dressed before Luke and the kids get home.

She makes a face. "I feel like I've been having the same problems, again and again, for years. What about you? It looks like you've read quite a bit."

"It's getting easier to decipher. And it's like reading a novel."

"I've had years to write it." She shrugs. "Do you think Jill will stick with it if she comes across it some day?"

"I'm sure she will," I reassure her.

"I need to fix dinner." She hustles around the room, opening curtains. "Could you go next door and fetch the children?"

When I knock on the door of the white house, feeling an underlying sense of trepidation, Mrs. Grundy calls for me to come in. The front door opens into a dark living room where all the shades have been drawn and where large, heavy oak furniture looms, nothing that can be easily moved. In the 1920s, people decorated their houses with the intention of staying put. This room will be so much emptier in 1976 and my own time. The shadowy room feels ominous with all of this furniture looming over me.

As I make my way toward the voices in the kitchen, a pile of books on an end table catches my eye. I snap on a lamp to look more closely, thinking maybe I misread the title of the one on top. It's a novel by H. G. Wells called *The Time Machine*. Startled, I turn it over in my hands, then pick up the next book: *Memoirs of the Twentieth Century* by Samuel Madden, which I find, shuffling to the copyright page, was published in 1933. I flip through more pages and the words "time travel" pop out at me. The third book is by Edward Bellamy, *Looking Backward*. I rifle quickly through the pages and see more passages about traveling through time.

I desperately wish Mom and Zach were here to help me.

Mom is a librarian. She would know what to do. She'd find all the resources we'd need to conduct our research.

Zach is a geek. He would know what to do. He would focus his scientific mind on collecting data and getting to the bottom of this.

And maybe they would have some idea what to make of it.

There's an unholy racket from the next room, and I guiltily drop the books and flick off the lamp. The clamoring of something striking metal rings out followed by more gongs and clicks and clinks and scrapes and crashes. I enter the kitchen with my hands over my ears, my tension easing as I see Sarah on the floor with spoons and cast-iron skillets, banging happily.

In the ordinary brightness of the kitchen, no one else seems fazed by Sarah's noise. The older kids are clustered around the table, while Catherine mixes up some cookies and Robert and Mrs. Grundy play games. Robert is about to win one that reminds me of Sorry, with marbles moving along a board.

Mrs. Grundy glances up at me and nods. It may be the first time she's ever given me a direct look. The noise tapers off as Sarah loses interest. "You little stinker," Mrs. Grundy growls at Robert.

He giggles as he plays his last piece for the win.

"Let's play again," Mrs. Grundy says, and I watch them cycle through two games. She insists on a new game every time he wins and is only willing to abandon the game after she trounces him. She flicks Sarah peppermints from her pockets without breaking concentration. It's obvious that the kids love her, even if she never smiles. And it's becoming obvious to me that she loves them. Maybe Abby is mistaken. Maybe Mrs. Grundy isn't that bad.

But I still can't help but feel that with all of her sneaking around she is up to no good.

And what's with all the books about time travel?

I start hatching a plot in my head to get Abby to keep her occupied while I search her house. Somewhere in there, I'm betting, I'll find my watch.

"You all need to come home for dinner," I finally tell the kids, and as we're leaving, Mrs. Grundy hands me a pile of newspaper and magazine clippings. "Give these to Abby," she says.

What is Mrs. Grundy up to? I flip through the clippings on the walk home. There's a series of notices about couples renewing their vows and celebrating their fiftieth anniversaries. In an advice column, a woman complains about her unhappy marriage, and the columnist enjoins her to change her attitude and resolve to make her marriage work. Another article is about women who left their husbands and children and ended up outcast and destitute.

When I pass these to Abby, she flicks her eyes over the headlines. Then she sighs.

"What's the deal with these?" I ask her.

"She's afraid I'm going to leave her son," Abby says. "She's always sending me things about marriage to remind me of my duty. Reminding me that all of these other people have successful marriages and I shouldn't think too much of myself. Between these and those stories she's always telling me about women in asylums, she's obviously trying to keep me in line."

"Maybe she's overheard enough to know that you're torn between times?"

Abby's face twists and she does that thing again, eyes widening, head swiveling, checking that there's no one around to overhear. "First of all, she would never believe that time travel is possible. And I doubt she actually thinks that I would leave these three children."

"She's been reading about time travel. I saw a bunch of books in her living room."

Her brow furrows. "What books?"

"I've never heard of them but one is called *The Time Machine*. I mean, that seems pretty obvious, right?"

"It's a famous novel by H. G. Wells," Abby says. "Those are my books. She must have taken them off the living-room shelf." She looks spooked.

"Maybe she does think you'd leave your children. Or that you might leave and take them with you."

"That's ridiculous."

"Do you think she knows that?"

"It doesn't matter what I do. She's always refused to believe that I'm really committed. She's always thought that I'm flighty. I don't know how to prove to her otherwise."

"Do you think it's hard for her to read these articles about people's marriages?" I've been wondering about this a lot, picturing my own mom alone in the house grieving my loss, refusing to go anywhere, the way she did after my dad died. Up until recently, I'd just kind of thought that my dad died and she cried a little and then she went on with her life, no big deal.

Maybe you have to lose someone before you can really understand loss.

"Why would it be hard for her?" Abby's making bread, punching the dough with her fists. It makes her look angry.

"I mean, since her husband died recently and all."

"She's always been smug about her marriage. He died a few weeks short of their fortieth anniversary. She's always bragging about the fact that they almost made it to forty years, like she doesn't believe that Luke and I could ever rival her."

"Do you really think she means it that way?" I'm having serious doubts about Abby's portrayal of Mrs. Grundy, even if her fixation on these stories about happy couples and women sent to asylums is a little strange.

"Oh, if you get to know her better, you'll see what I mean," Abby says darkly, flipping the dough. "She always has to find a way to feel superior to me. She's a good grandma to our kids. But she's a hard person to be around." She slams the back door to go gather the laundry from the line, leaving me as mystified as ever.

That night, Catherine comes to my room and we read Milly-Molly-Mandy stories together. After a while she puts down the book. "Sometimes I don't feel like I fit into this family at all," she says. "Everyone is small and has dark hair. Like you. Even you look more like my brother and sister than I do." It's like she's me in reverse, experiencing an anguish I recognize as the small dark-haired child of a tall blond mother. But at least she knows why. At least she knows who gave birth to her.

As I turn off my light and crawl into bed, too tired to read, I worry that I'm beginning to forget things: the taste of the cookies Mom bakes at Christmas, the smell of summer barbecue that turns to fall woodsmoke, Zach's laugh. Sometimes I play with Marta and Rigby and I think about my fluffy kitty Simone Biles, who sheds so much that it's like she leaves another cat behind after she's been sitting anywhere. I remember the way she purrs when I stroke her nose. The way her claws get so long they get caught in things. Once I found her angrily dragging a blanket around the house, unable to shake it off.

I smile, remembering. For just a second my stomach unknots, my fear and trepidation and confusion loosening.

25

"We're going down to the dressmaker's to order some dresses for spring," Abby sings out to me the next morning when I come yawning down the stairs. "Would you like a new dress?"

"Why would I want a new dress?" Does Abby really think I'm still going to be here in the spring? "How about you take Mrs. Grundy, and I go over and search her house?"

"We can't just start going through her things willy-nilly, or we'll really raise her suspicions. And then I'm afraid that if she has the watch, she'd hide it somewhere we'd never find it. She's coming over to watch the children. Come on. We'll have a chance to talk without being overheard." Abby's tone is chirpy, but she doesn't look very happy. In fact, she looks downright glum.

After knocking briskly, Mrs. Grundy flings open the door and strides right in without greeting us.

The kids beat a path to welcome her, all talking at the same time as if they haven't seen her in years. Today is the first time I've seen her wearing anything besides one of her checked housedresses. She must have been out on errands earlier, because she looks kind of elegant in a tailored gray silk crepe suit with a drop waist and a collar that opens on the side to show off a faux gemstone necklace. My gaze travels down to her fashionable T-strap shoes.

As she fends off the onslaught of children, Mrs. Grundy's sleeve slides back. And there it is: my Chronowatch attached to her thin wrist.

She quickly pulls her sleeve down.

I utter a tiny, strangled yelp, my stomach pitching.

"She's wearing my watch!" I sputter.

"I don't know what she's talking about," Mrs. Grundy says.

"Grandma!" Sarah says. "Come see my roundoff."

Robert pulls on her arm. "Can we play Billy Whiskers?"

"I wanted to play Pegity!" Catherine interrupts him.

I keep squeaking, trying to find my voice, when Abby speaks in a low, menacing tone. "Lift up your sleeve."

Mrs. Grundy backs toward the door. "I'll be right back. I forgot something," she says. But I kind of get the feeling she wanted us to see the watch under her sleeve. She wanted us to know that she knows more than meets the eye.

Abby grabs her arm.

"Ouch!" Mrs. Grundy protests as Abby pulls up her sleeve.

"What are you doing?" Catherine shrieks, flying at her mother, trying to protect her grandmother. I'm sweating profusely as, in one deft motion, Abby pulls the watch off of Mrs. Grundy's arm.

"Sorry," Abby says to Catherine. "But this belongs to Anna."

"It's mine," Mrs. Grundy yelps. "I found it on the ground a while back."

"Finders keepers," Robert says.

"That's not necessarily true," Abby scolds him.

"It doesn't even tell time," Mrs. Grundy says. "It just has a bunch of buttons and numbers." Her lips turn up in as close to a smile as I've ever seen. There's a glint in her eye. But she can't have time traveled herself. She wouldn't have the first idea how to perform a vault.

I fold my arms, staring her down. "We've been looking for it for the last two weeks. Why didn't you say anything?"

"Children should be seen and not heard," Mrs. Grundy scolds me.

"I'm not a child," I argue, as Mrs. Grundy turns to Abby.

"You did not need to assault me like that. And in front of the children!"

"That looks like something from outer space," Catherine interjects. She sounds anxious. "Why wouldn't you give it back, Grandma?"

Mrs. Grundy softens. "It's not a toy, Catherine," she says. "You mustn't touch it."

We all watch as Abby slips it in her apron pocket, still clutching it in her hand.

Mrs. Grundy's gaze dodges back and forth between me and Abby. I wonder what lengths she will go to, to get the watch back.

Sarah tugs at her. "Come outside," she says to Mrs. Grundy, who, looking dazed, lets herself be dragged out to the backyard.

Abby's mood has lightened considerably as we head down the hill. "I've taken apart my watch a million times, but I'm just spinning in circles. I was about to give up until we found yours."

"It's almost like she wanted us to see that she had it," I point out. "Like she was taunting us with it."

"Didn't I tell you? She'll do anything she can to make me crazy."

"So now I can go home?" I interrupt impatiently. "Can we find a gym and a gymnastics horse this afternoon?"

"Can you please wait just a little longer?" Abby glances around nervously. "It's clearly malfunctioning. I need to fix it for you. No more mistakes."

The last thing I want is to be stranded again, especially not somewhere less friendly than my own neighborhood in 1929. But I'm bursting with impatience as Abby pores over patterns and fabrics in a claustrophobic small shop presided over by a row of dressmaker dummies and a black Singer sewing machine with gold lettering. I don't know how Abby can think about clothes at a time like this.

I'm so anxious that I feel like I'm about to levitate.

Finally we make our escape. "Honestly," Abby says as we mount the hill, "these days, most women buy factory-made clothing from Monkey Wards. Luke thinks that's tacky, but it would save a lot of time and money."

I barely listen. All I can think is that soon I'm going to hug Mom. Tell Zach to shut up. Apologize to my coach. Maybe even in a couple of hours, as soon as Abby has a chance to check over my watch.

"I wish I'd known when I was younger what I know now," Abby says, and I hear a warning in her voice. "That the problem with time traveling is that every time you make a new choice, you have to leave something or someone behind. There's always holes in you, no matter what you do. You're always split between times and desires. Between the life that suited you and the life you make instead, because you have to."

As we arrive at the house, she stops on the sidewalk. "Just give me a couple of days, okay?" she says. "Just a couple of days, and we'll send you on your way."

A couple of days? But I want to go today. I'm okay with taking my chances.

But if I don't get home this time, I don't know what I'll do.

It's only two days, I tell myself.

26

The next day, Abby neglects her household duties and sends Sarah next door. Sometimes I hear her working in the basement. Sometimes she hides out in her room with the door locked.

I pick up the tablet, losing the thread of sentences every time Abby pounds up or down the stairs, her bedroom lock clicking again. I stare at the page in front of me with a feeling of deep dread and an imagination gone wild. What if Abby is time traveling right now? Does she mean to disappear into the future and strand me in the past?

What if she does something that erases my existence?

I retrace the last line I read a couple of days ago: *I would not drop the research no matter what anyone said.* I fling down the tablet to go knock on Abby's bedroom door. There's no answer. I stop and listen. I can't hear anything, no creaks or shifts or shuffles or under-the-breath curses. There are no sounds indicating life beyond the door. Only silence.

I go back to my room and try to focus.

27

Professor Harry was the one who brought up time travel again a day later, and we talked through ideas and solutions late into the night and over the next several days.

I'd never dated, too busy with my studies, so it came as something of a shock that his interest in me, and mine in him, might be more than a teacher-student thing. I mean, he was my teacher. He should have been off-limits. But I was lonely, and I was drawn to him, and one night as he walked past me to lob his trash into the can, it was like little electrical signals pulsed between us. I had to restrain myself from reaching out and grabbing him.

Another night he insisted on walking me home in the dark, and he left my apartment two hours later. I'll spare you the details. I knew I shouldn't have gotten involved with my professor.

But I liked that he was smart and preoccupied with his own work—so buried in it, in fact, that there was no way he'd take over my life and ruin my focus.

But he became more and more possessive, over meals and walks to the lab planning my future aloud. He wanted me to get a post-doc and then a job in a prestigious think tank.

"That would be pretty all-consuming, wouldn't it?" I asked. "How would I have time to work on my time-travel device?"

"Look, at some point you're going to have to grow up," he said, smiling the whole time, like he was kidding, like we both knew that my ambition was cute and empty-headed. "You'll never be taken seriously if you persist along this route."

His words stung. For weeks, I'd believed that he respected me.

"You know everyone will think this is ludicrous, right?" He was oblivious to my dismay, or at least he pretended to be. "My colleagues will never approve it as a dissertation topic."

"Your colleagues, or you?" I asked.

This time, he was the one who changed the subject.

After that, I knew I had to end things.

28

B oth Abby and I have glazed eyes at dinner, but she manages to keep up a steady stream of chatter to Luke about ordinary things: the weather, his work, the progress of her dresses, her plan to send me to the library with the kids the next afternoon. Which means I'm stuck here for another day, when all I want is to find a way to get hold of my watch and go.

As Robert tells me about the home run he hit during recess, and Catherine chatters about the birthday party she's going to next week, and Sarah crawls up into my lap, I realize how much I'll miss them. I wish I could see what becomes of them.

That I could just drop in to visit sometimes. But no. Once I get home, I won't ever leave again.

The next day, while Abby works in the basement, I look after Sarah and then hang out with the other kids in the late afternoon. I find myself constantly staring out the window or startling when anyone comes into a room behind me, sure that it's Mrs. Grundy, but she is making herself scarce.

When he comes home, Luke looks around, puzzled by the haphazard state of the house, the unwashed clothes piling up, the hastily assembled meals. I wonder what is taking Abby so long.

I'm tired that night after trying to fill in for Abby, keeping the kids distracted, trying to put the house in some kind of order. But still I can't resist staying up way too late reading.

29

When I broke things off with Harry, he didn't take it well. I thought I would feel worse than I did, but instead I was distracted, if exhausted, suddenly physically incapable of going without sleep but also excited by the breakthroughs I was making, working evenings and weekends. I was in the midst of writing my dissertation proposal on global positioning systems and traversable wormholes when I realized that I was pregnant.

My dissertation proposal was turned down flat by my committee. It was 1972; abortion was not an option in Massachusetts unless I could prove that my physical health was endangered; and I was far enough along that even traveling to states where abortion was legal would be futile. And honestly, once I felt you flutter inside me, once you were more real to me, I wouldn't have considered it anyway. But I had nowhere to turn. I knew that my family would be scandalized.

I resolved that once I had a job, I would break the news to Harry. I would make sure that you had a chance to grow up knowing your father on whatever terms he chose. But for now, I needed a way to support us. Scanning trade journals in the library, I ran across an advertisement for a technician with innovative ideas in watch technology at Zippo Manufacturing in Bradford, PA, to begin in late summer. With a stable income, the help of babysitters, and access to labs at the factory and the nearby college campus, I thought, I could continue my research at night after you were asleep.

"Why?" my new dissertation director asked bluntly. He was in his sixties, with wild Einstein hair and a perpetual grimace. "That's a huge step down. You could get a research job at an eminent institution. This is a mistake."

I just shrugged. My pregnancy wasn't showing much, as long as I wore loose clothing; I planned to be out of the department before it became noticeable. "Maybe I'll come back and finish my degree," I said. "But for now, I need a break."

You were born in a Cambridge hospital in July, a little outer space creature with puffy eyelids and sparse swirls of dark hair and still-blue eyes that had never been exposed to light, such a funny-looking alien that I immediately wanted to protect. Your translucent purple eyelids, splotchy, wrinkly skin, and misshapen head made me feel tender and fierce, and for the first time ever I was just floating there, my brain ceasing to grind round and round like spinning tires.

But my fierce love for you turned my ambition even more ferocious. I wanted to achieve something not just for me, but for you too, to make you proud of me and give you a better future. You slept in a basket, fists tightly clenched, while I pored over my prototype and mathematical equations and diagrams, shifting my focus when it was time to nurse you.

Sometimes during those breaks, I flicked on the TV and watched bits and pieces of the 1972 Olympics. Something about gymnastics— the supreme feats of coordination—mesmerized me. "Maybe someday you'll be able to do that," I told you, propping you up to watch a blond, pigtailed Olga Korbut flip from the high bar to the low.

By the beginning of August, I'd begun preparations to move to Pennsylvania. After I advertised in the local newspaper for a house or apartment, a woman named Joan Arlington phoned me. She was looking for a tenant for her grandmother's old house. It was completely furnished, and I was shocked at how low the rent was. I agreed sight unseen.

Our possessions fit into a few boxes. I packed the car and we were off. Joan, away on her honeymoon, left the key under the mat, and after that, I left rent checks in her mailbox, and we always meant to connect in person but never did. You loved your day care, which relieved me since I was working long hours at Zippo. Joan worked equally long hours at the public library unless her husband was home; I didn't want to intrude on them. And anyway, I was so busy. So busy, in fact, that I never got around to sending that letter to Harry informing him that he had a daughter.

By the time you were three, you were trying to imitate what you saw on televised gymnastics competitions. You'd balance as you walked across the back of the couch; you hung upside down from rings on the playground. You were doing somersaults at two and cartwheels at three. I remember once you had a teenage babysitter who taught you to do back handsprings. I don't know if my tendency to gravitate toward watching gymnastics is what got you interested, or if it was your obvious natural ability that led me to become more obsessed with the sport. It was kind of a chicken-and-egg thing. Either way, it got so we never missed TV broadcasts that involved gymnastics.

30

BRADFORD, PA, JANUARY 24, 1929
8 A.M.

By the next morning, I'm half hatching a plot to knock Abby out with a lamp and repossess my watch. It's so frustrating to have lost it to Mrs. Grundy for weeks and now to have to wait for Abby to give it back.

"So how much longer is this going to take?" I ask at breakfast.

"I've almost got it. Have you finished reading the tablet?"

"I have a few more pages. I can't believe that Jill's father was your teacher. People would really frown on that in my time."

"It was pretty common when I was young," she says. "But even though our relationship was consensual, I can see why people might raise their eyebrows. He was the one with all the power." She clinks her dishes into the sink without even rinsing them and disappears upstairs, leaving me to take care of Sarah. I slip upstairs and put on my leotard under my frock so I'll be ready when it's time.

I feed Sarah lunch. I wait.

When I'm pacing the living room, about to go right over the edge with anticipation and frustration, Abby breezes in to take Sarah upstairs for her nap. Then she beckons to me. As I join her on the couch, I feel it right away, a kind of expectancy in the air, in the long call of a bird in the trees that makes me think of spring, of the fluttering in my stomach that feels like hundreds of butterflies rising at once. It's finally time.

Abby rushes around, locking the front door and slamming the windows closed. She engages the deadbolts on the back door and the kitchen door. As if preparing a formal farewell ceremony, she pours coffee. The delicate cups clink. Her hand is shaking so much that the liquid sloshes over the edge. She gives the spills a quick, perfunctory dab with a cloth.

And then she sits down and takes the two watches from her pocket. Mine with the black strap and her own nearly identical one with the white strap.

"I think I've fixed it." Her voice is hushed. "It was a slippage problem in the sequences of connections."

I'm going home, I think. *Home.* The word alone causes something to swell inside me.

But Abby calmly sips her coffee, staring absently at the window. I glance nervously at it, sure I just caught a movement outside, and she leaps up to tug the curtains closed. She sits again. Contemplates a cookie. Finally says slowly, "I think I got both watches fixed. I want you to take both of them with you. I want you to remove the temptation for me to go after Jill, or for Mrs. Grundy to get hold of this and do who knows what. I can't be responsible for screwing up people's lives any more than I already have."

"Of course." Relief feels like a long-held breath finally released.

"You do know that there will be a hole in our family when you're gone—you know that, right?" Abby says earnestly.

I nod. I've begun to see that I'll have holes too, no matter what I do.

She refills her coffee cup, then rises and strolls around the living room, pausing to pick up a sheet of newspaper, a child's ball. She appears deep in thought the entire time, rolling the ball around in her hand, scanning headlines without really seeing them. Then she paces to the back of the house and checks the window locks. She rattles the back door and comes back to twist the front door handle even though she already double-checked those locks earlier.

I skim the last few pages of her account, but I'm too excited to focus. Maybe I will never know the rest of this story. I'm relieved when she finally returns and balances on the edge of her chair, looking ready to sprint away at a moment's notice.

"I know that you want to go home," she says, taking a gulp and making a face as if the coffee was more bitter than she expected, "but if you ever meet Jill in your own time, I need you to tell her my story. Will you do that?"

I nod. "I only have a few pages." I show her where I left off.

"Okay," she says. She looks around nervously as if she's afraid of being overheard. Takes a breath, apparently making a decision. "I'm going to read you the rest, and then you can go."

I sigh and fidget impatiently, barely listening.

31

BRADFORD, PA, JANUARY 24, 1929
1 P.M.

I was surprised at how much I enjoyed my day job developing the fancy Chronowatch for Zippo. I loved the moment that the prototypes came alive and began to keep time. I imagined watchmakers of past centuries building every wheel and spring and winding mechanism, mounting the bridge on the balance wheel and witnessing the clock starting to pulse and beat and thrum. Digital watches weren't quite so dramatic, and yet still, there was that inspiring moment when it all came together, when life began.

As I gradually solved the glitches of the time-travel watch, I began to perform cautious experiments. You were coloring on the floor, scribbling pink strokes across a Smurf's head when I slipped into my bedroom and set the watch to five minutes in the future. I felt a whoosh like a rush of wind, glimpsed flashes of light as my body jolted and lifted and then fell backward with a thud onto the bedroom carpet.

At first, I didn't think I'd gone anywhere at all. I berated myself for deluding myself about this time-travel thing. Clearly, it hadn't worked. I stepped out into the living room again. You were still cross-legged at the coffee table. The coloring-book page had been attacked by five minutes' worth of red and blue scribbles, gleeful untidy blobs of color resembling clouds that showed no regard for the thick black outline of the Smurf. You were holding the page up for me to see.

I looked at my watch. I'd done it after all. I'd traveled five minutes into the future.

After a few more small successful trials, I prepared some larger experiments. I decided to travel to Olympic years to watch gymnastics competitions: 1920 in Antwerp, 1928 in Amsterdam, 1948 in London, 1960 in Rome. I even added a couple of future Olympics dates: I wanted to know if I could go forward in time also. I set three prototypes for these dates, one with a red strap, one with a white strap, one with a black strap. I left two in the kitchen drawer with the code I'd made up and a note: If I don't return, please come find me.

You were in the den watching cartoons the day I determined that I had gained enough mastery to zap myself to 1920 for a few hours. I intended to return to my bedroom to the same moment that I'd left, never leaving you unsupervised. Still, I'd been quizzing you for days about what to do in an emergency. Later, I discovered that the ultrasensitive device had trouble holding its destination firmly, malfunctioning in transit by resetting itself. I theorized that that was why, when I sent myself to 1920, I didn't end up in Antwerp.

Instead, I found myself on the site of my own house in Bradford, Pennsylvania.

"So that's how you ended up here," I say. Slowly her story has sucked me in again. But still I'm impatient to get going.

"I was more prepared than you," she says, heading to the kitchen to take bread out of the oven. "I'd dressed in what I thought was a more timeless suit, no bell bottoms or bright colors, so at least I didn't stick out quite so much, although I certainly didn't fit in either."

She sits back down, lifts the tablet, and takes up where she left off.

So there I was, on the sidewalk, and my first impulse was to shoot myself right back to 1976. But while I was hastily resetting the watch, a group of people all dressed in black and bearing covered dishes mounted the hill, staring openly at me. They knocked on the door of my future in-laws' house. A woman who turned out to be Luke's mother hovered in the doorway, eyes lingering on me after the others had entered.

"Are you coming in?" she asked, and so I went in too.

Luke's mother ushered us into the parlor, where a crowd of subdued, black-clad family members, friends, and neighbors ranged around, talking in low voices. The dining-room table was heaped with plates and dishes of food: hams and fried chicken, rolls and pudding, carrots and peas. "So good of you to come," everyone murmured as I circled the room.

They were too polite to ask me who I was, and it took me a little while to figure out whose post-funeral gathering I'd crashed. Someone asked me to hold the baby and passed six-month-old Catherine into my arms.

The sleeping baby's dead weight reminded me of you as a little baby, and in that moment, I felt a niggling fear. How had I ended up in Bradford in 1920 when I'd meant to go to Antwerp?

Suddenly, Catherine's eyes popped open and her whole body went stiff as she reared back to stare into my face. Her mouth opened, gearing up to wail and call attention to the fact that I was a stranger. I hurriedly embarked on a frenzied game of peekaboo. At first Catherine looked startled and suspicious, but finally she giggled, and from then on, she was my decoy, my co-conspirator, saving me from too much interaction with other adults.

"Which one are you?" asked a young woman. Luke's sister, it turned out.

"Which one what?" I asked as Catherine tried to grab one of the buttons on my suit.

"You are one of Delilah's cousins, right?"

Though I had no idea who Delilah was, I nodded and said, "Abigail."

Later, I would find out that Delilah was Luke's first wife, who had just died in the tail end of the flu epidemic, and that she was originally from New England. That she fortunately had a large and sprawling, not particularly close, family with many distant aunts, uncles, and cousins, and that there could very well have been one named Abigail. Expecting to be leaving soon, I went along with Luke's family's assumptions.

Later that night, when I met Luke for the first time, I was taken by his bright greenish eyes. After Catherine had eaten the peas I mashed for her, I noticed that her eyes were beginning to droop. I found a crib in an upstairs bedroom and gently laid her down. I felt sad for this baby who was now motherless, but it was time to get back to you. I slipped into the backyard, away from the lights and voices.

I'd thought that I had the return trip figured out, but now, fighting down panic, I saw that I'd made a rudimentary error. Dumb, dumb, dumb, I kept thinking. Since GPS satellites weren't going to be in place in the past, I had carefully set the coordinates to pre-identified traversable wormholes, but now I worried that there was some kind of pin-to-pin wire connection problem. This meant that times and dates and locations would slip randomly, and there was no telling where I'd end up.

Why hadn't I traveled with tools, spare parts, a high-precision microscope, notes, or my other prototypes in order to compare the location settings? I fiddled with the watch but couldn't even get it open, and of course I had no clue in 1920 how to confirm the watch's settings.

Luke's family was happy to put up Delilah's cousin, especially one who was so good with baby Catherine. I spent hours each day caring for her. The way she propped herself up on her arms as if about to take off crawling and how she ran her hands through water or along a blade of grass, enthralled. Everything reminded me of you.

Even when I used household items as tools to open the watch's casing, even when I thought I'd fixed the problem that caused it to vacillate between time and location settings, I still hesitated. Unable to confirm that any of the settings were correct, I feared that one more small malfunction would leave me lost in time forever.

I tried to reassure myself: I had, after all, left the prototypes in a kitchen drawer. Not the best place to leave them, but I hoped that someone, somehow, would find them, would get them to you—that you would figure out what to do with them, would come back and find me. I told myself they wouldn't malfunction like mine had, but obviously, I was in denial. Major denial, when it comes right down to it. Every day I watched for you, maybe a teenager, maybe an adult, maybe even an old woman, to appear and rescue me, and I thought maybe I could convince you to stay. Every time a peddler came to the door or a stranger greeted me in public, I felt that uptick of hope that maybe they were a messenger from the future.

For a long time, I thought about little but you and my work. I was uneasy with the comparatively idle days, fighting a barely restrained hysteria, feeling always on the verge of rending my garments and tearing at my hair with the profound grief of missing you, of failing you, of leaving you all alone, of you thinking that maybe I'd abandoned you on purpose.

But I was so sure that you'd arrive any day. Waiting, I found myself falling in love with Catherine. I gravitated toward Luke and his sorrow even while Luke's mother treated me with suspicion, plying me with questions about Delilah's family and my own plans to go back home. I offered vague replies.

It was treacherous, falling in love with people from the past when all I wanted was to return to the future. I knew that if you showed up with one of the other prototypes, if I could figure out how to return to that moment five minutes after I'd left, in 1976, I would grieve the loss of Luke and Catherine. But if I had to make this wrenching choice, I knew that it was you I'd choose. I felt so split between times, it seemed right that I'd become known in 1920 as Abby, not Gail, my name also split in two.

When I convinced Luke that life must go on, when I talked him into finishing construction on the house that he'd begun building next door for his young family and abandoned after his wife's death, maybe I was really giving advice to myself. Gradually, as you failed to appear, as my regrets compounded, the foolish adventurousness of my younger self faded. I was too familiar with the potential consequences. I was more hesitant. I found myself in a more conventional life than I'd ever expected. Secretly, I plotted and sketched inventions.

Then, horrified at the memory of my youthful, brash arrogance, I tore up those sketches, no longer in love with innovation for its own sake. I was often paralyzed by anxiety. The years went by. I could have suspended my life, could have waited, but what if I found myself waiting forever?

In an era in which contraception was just gaining ground, I had the other two children and couldn't imagine leaving them either, any more than I'd wanted to leave you. I wished I'd made a child-sized Chronowatch and brought you with me. But what if you'd landed somewhere else in time? Why didn't I see how dangerous this was? This is the greatest regret of my life. The loss of you.

I hope that you've made a wonderful life for yourself, even if I never see you again. I hope that somehow you get this letter, and that you at least know that nothing that happened was your fault. I never stopped missing you.

Love,
Your mother

32

Abby's voice is getting raspy. She stops reading and gently lays down the tablet. I've been listening so intently, only gradually does the room come back into focus, the abandoned coffee cups on the table, the cold pot, the napkins wadded alongside them, the smell of baking bread wafting from the kitchen. Sarah will be awake anytime now, I realize with a jolt, and the other kids are due back from school in less than an hour. We need to wind up this conversation so I can go.

"There is nothing worse than losing your child," Abby tells me, her anguish still audible after all these years. "Even if I could go back now, how could I? How could I leave Catherine, and Robert and Sarah and Luke? What kind of choice is this, between my first child or my other three?" Agitated, she leaps up to clear away our dishes.

I've been hanging on to the way she talks about Jill. I always imagined that even way back in the olden days, when the mortality rate was higher and many kids didn't live to adulthood, parents were just sort of used to it, just shrugged at the loss of a child and went on about their lives. I always imagined that people who gave up kids for adoption abandoned them casually, without much thought.

But clearly that's not the case. There's a faraway look in Abby's eyes, a deep sadness on her face. Maybe abandonment isn't a casual, pain-free act.

"Does anyone else know any of this?" I follow her to the kitchen, where she's checking the bread and resetting the timer for a few more minutes. "Did you ever tell Luke?"

She laughs, but with a bitter edge. "Of course Luke loves me. He likes that I'm so different from other women. But this, I just don't think he'd believe this. My mother-in-law isn't wrong that women who are different, women who have epilepsy or Down syndrome or too many ideas of their own, have been confined to mental asylums."

"So when I first came along, you thought I was Jillian." I lean against the counter, watching her rinse the teacups.

"Oh, as much as I've gotten used to suppressing my feelings, I could hardly conceal my joy," she says. "But I was terrified too, knowing that you being here might force me to make an impossible choice. What if I could go back to my own time after all? What if I could go back to the day I'd left and just resume my life? I should have looked harder for your watch, but I was a little afraid of what getting my hands on it might mean. But I should have found it. I should have kept it from getting into anyone else's hands."

I hand her the plates. "I can't imagine ever time traveling again. I just want to go home. But what if someday I can't stand not knowing where I came from? I was born here. In this house. But I don't think that Joan was my birth mother."

"I don't think so either." Abby looks thoughtful. "You got the watch from the kitchen drawer, right?" she asks. "Was there another one still there?"

I shake my head. But then I remember: there was another watch just like this, one with a red strap, in Jill's pink plastic purse.

I'm distracted, for a second, by a creak in the other room. Just one of those sounds that houses make, I decide. I often lay awake as a child, listening to the pops and groans of the house settling.

Abby pulls chicken and potatoes out of the icebox to prepare for dinner, and I hear that faint creak in the dining room again. This house is not that old. Do newer houses make these faint settling sounds? But I'm too absorbed in what Abby is saying to investigate, and anyway, I watched her lock and double-check the doors.

"Just in case you have any problems, I want to be sure that you know how to set the watch," Abby says as coffee begins to pump up into the glass dome at the top of the kettle and she removes it from the stove. I follow her back into the living room, glancing nervously at the time. We only have a half hour left. Abby, for all her paranoia, seems oblivious.

"So here's my prototype." She picks up the watch with the white strap. "It has all of the significant gymnastics moments programmed into it. But say you needed to reset it. Remember, you can only set it for locations where I've already identified traversable wormholes. When I first started my research, I found them all over Bradford, as you can see from the watch settings. So, say you want to go to some location there. Let's just pick a random date—how about February 5, 1978? Toggle this switch, and then be sure and fill in the location window correctly. Let's say Hanley Park, Bradford, PA."

I follow along, programming the same information into the watch with the black strap.

"There's a date here in 1988." She frowns. "That was way after my time. Must have been the malfunction. I remember that I programmed in the coordinates for a gymnastics center there—they held a zone qualifier in the early sixties. There was a really dramatic uneven bar collapse that I wanted to see."

So that's why it had been so easy to program the watch to find Jill in Dallas in 1988. Abby had already plugged in the coordinates, and I'd only had to add the date.

Abby enters the same date into the white-strapped watch. "I wish I had time to erase the history on both of these, but this is quicker. You can wear one watch and take the second as a backup. If they're both programmed exactly alike, then if there's a problem with one, you can just use the other. Or compare them to see how to reset the first one."

I wouldn't have the faintest idea how to do that, but I don't mention that. I'm impatient to get going. Everyone will be home in twenty minutes. "Where am I going to vault?" I ask, but she's not listening. Instead, she says, "Try another date." I randomly choose another place and lock that date into the black strapped watch: Callahan Park, Bradford, October 11, 1975.

Each time I enter a setting, Abby punches the same one into the white-strapped watch, checking to make sure I'm following the steps correctly. "So you get the idea," she says. "Okay, the date of your birth is already here. And look, the date that you left Bradford is automatically saved in your watch. That's the one we're going to set. Also, I've packed some things for you."

She hands me a cloth bag with a round canteen of water tied to the handles. The bag is stuffed full of bread and cheese and apples, and she's slid the tablet in there, too. "Someday, maybe you'll find Jill in your own time. I want you to give this to her," she says. In the bottom of the bag, there's a hairbrush and a toothbrush and some baking soda. "If you hold on to it tight it should travel with you. Just to be sure you don't get stuck anywhere without supplies."

My stomach drops. So she thinks there's a possibility of more malfunctions? And how am I supposed to vault while holding a heavy bag?

The timer goes off, and I follow her to the kitchen. I set the white-strapped watch on the counter in front of me while I check the date in November 2018 that I'm about to go home to. "Do you think there's any chance that this won't work?"

"I've tested it. Everything is in working order. But I want you to be prepared, just in case."

"So what about the vault? How can I vault if I'm carrying this bag? And how did you manage to time travel from your house? Didn't you have to vault?"

She snaps back to the present, giving me a skeptical look as she unloads the bread pans from the oven. "Why do you keep talking about vaulting?"

"That's how I got here. I vaulted through time. My friend Zach said I had to achieve . . . velocity."

"You don't have to vault," she says. "You just double-click the button."

Suddenly, Mrs. Grundy appears in the doorway.

Abby and I both jolt, hard, like you do when you're guilty. *How the hell?* I think. It's like that woman can literally walk through walls. My eyes dart in horror from her mild face to the hairpins securing her braids, to her checked dress and sensible oxford shoes.

"Mom." Abby falters. I look over at the basement door, the same door that I used to spy on Mom and Jill back in 1976. The same door that no one ever seems to remember to lock. It's flung open. How in the world could Abby have failed to engage that lock? It's like she secretly wanted Mrs. Grundy to overhear her.

But Abby goes pale. "How much did you hear?"

Mrs. Grundy doesn't answer. She's headed straight for me. I come to my senses and we both dive for the white-strapped watch. "I was hoping you'd get this fixed," she says, yanking it off the counter and knocking my hand away. "It worked before, but it was a little defective. I tried to go to Prague once and ended up in Dallas." Her eyes glint at me, and I can't tell if her expression is malicious or amused.

She turns to Abby. "I heard enough to know that you had a child out of wedlock. Enough to know what a mess you've made of things. But I had to run back to the house, so I missed the instructions."

I grab at the watch but she elbows me away, latching it onto her arm with surprising dexterity. I catch Abby's eye. Maybe if the two of us tackle her, we can retrieve the watch.

But Abby looks dazed, shaken. "What instructions?" she asks slowly.

"Is there some way to reset the watch? When I was trying it out before, I could only go to the times and places programmed into it, and like I said, sometimes it would switch settings on me when I was traveling. But it was certainly a fascinating way to see the world."

Abby and I exchange another look.

I edge toward Mrs. Grundy. I'll bet I could beat her at arm wrestling. I'm strong enough to take back the watch by force.

"Just give it back," Abby says. "There's no way to reset it. The only places you can go are gymnastics competitions, and I can't imagine you'd be interested in those."

I try to signal Abby with my eyes. Abby moves toward Mrs. Grundy, and I ease behind her. We'll sandwich her between us so she can't escape.

But all of a sudden, she ducks and sprints away. In a flash, she's out the front door.

Abby lets out a little shriek and after a beat we both whirl around, racing after Mrs. Grundy.

33

BRADFORD, PA, JANUARY 24, 1929
3:40 P.M.

Ahead of me, Abby jiggles the front door handle of Mrs. Grundy's house, then starts pounding on the door. It's locked.

Clutching the bag and my watch, I chase after her as she bolts from one door to the next. None of them yield. "She locked them all," Abby gasps, out of breath. "She never locks the doors."

At least someone *remembered to lock all of her doors*, I almost say, but instead I swallow my snarky retort and say, "I know how to get in." I race around to the side to push out the basement window. It's not loose like in my time, but it's also not locked, and I nudge it open wide enough to squeeze through. I drop to the ground in the dark basement and dash to open the back door. We pound up the stairs and through the house, our feet echoing on the hardwood floors, our shouts muffled by the heavy furniture. Abby pokes her head into the master bedroom. She loops in and out of the kitchen. She crashes up the stairs and I hear doors flying open.

I follow behind her more slowly, opening closets and checking under the massive bedframe and behind hutches, scanning each room to make sure Mrs. Grundy isn't hiding somewhere. I know this search is futile. Because she already knows how to use the watch, it would take seconds to transport herself out of here.

Especially since she doesn't have to vault.

One closet is crammed with men's suit jackets and pants, all neatly hung, a row of white-collar dress shirts and tweed pants and vests. Felt and straw hats and newsboy caps line the shelf above. Two-toned shoes face forward on the closet floor. The closet smells faintly of pipe tobacco, as if Luke's father, Mrs. Grundy's husband, just stepped out a few minutes ago.

Abby's footsteps batter the floor overhead. I gently close the door and glance into the bathroom, where some of Mrs. Grundy's checked house-dresses hang on a hook, identical to the one she is wearing today. The room smells of talcum powder and perfume; the counter is littered with small bottles and a hand mirror.

Doors slam overhead. Clutching my own watch, I think, at least I have this. At least she didn't take mine this time. I can still go home.

Abby appears breathless at the bottom of the stairs. "She's gone," she says. "She's gone." Her forehead is slick with sweat, her hair popping out like broken springs from her tight bun.

"That's what I figured," I say. "Maybe there were still places programmed into the watch she hadn't had a chance to visit."

Abby looks at me like I'm a total airhead. "If she's traveling through time, she could mess up everything. She could cause paradoxes. She could keep me from coming backward in time. What if she hates me enough that she wants to keep me from marrying her son? She could prevent my children from ever being born. But no—she loves those children. Why would she do that? Anna—Elizabeth—we have to find her!"

I finger my watch, trying to swallow my frustration and dismay. Everything seems to be conspiring to keep me from going home.

"This is all my fault," Abby moans. "Look, I'll just take your watch and go look for her. You wait here. Hopefully I'll be back in a few minutes. If I don't come back, tell Luke—"

"No," I say. She is not taking this watch from me. I will not risk her disappearing on me, leaving me stuck here forever. "I'll go find her."

"What if you can't? What if she does something terrible?" Abby, usually so unflappable, wrings her hands. It's like we've reversed positions: Abby, always the one in control, me the disheveled one half-crazy from homesickness.

But now there's a wild look in her eyes, and I'm so stunned, it feels like calm.

"You can't go. You have a family. You can't risk leaving them." I swallow hard. All I want to do is go home, but what might happen to the kids, or Abby, or Jill, or *me* if Mrs. Grundy changes the timeline?

"The watches are exact duplicates of each other, and you fixed the slippage problem, so this will be quick." I think aloud. "I'll just run through all of them. Check out all of the dates and locations until I find her, and then figure out how to get her back here. Easy peasy."

"This will be another burden on my conscience." Abby eyes my watch as she struggles with indecision. "If anything happens to you, how will I live with myself?"

"I'll be fine," I say as if I believe it.

And then I begin to realize the full implications of our predicament. I'm going to have to take a watch that has malfunctioned in the past and go after a woman I barely know, whose motives I can't fathom—a woman with the power to wipe out my existence, and Abby's, and the kids', a woman who has in her possession another watch that has malfunctioned in the past.

It all seems crazy and impossible. My hands are shaking, and then I have to suppress unearthly tremors that try to take hold of my body. I grit my teeth, shivering while Abby watches me anxiously.

And I was scared of vaulting?

Right now I'd rather be about to jump out of a plane with a broken parachute.

Or leap into the ocean with faulty scuba diving equipment.

I'd be more likely to survive those things.

Out the window, I see the kids trotting uphill, home from school. "Abby, I have to do it," I say firmly before I can change my mind.

Abby doubles over. "Oh, my God, I have the worst stomachache," she says. "Something's happening." Her eyes are wild, fevered. "Elizabeth, am I fading? Do I look translucent? Am I vanishing?"

"You look the same," I say. "But I have to go. I promise I'll find her."

"Be careful," she says. "And whatever time you end up in, if you don't see my mother-in-law, you have to move on. Don't risk changing anything. She doesn't know how to change the dates or times on the watch, so make sure when you go to each place that you arrive a few minutes before or after her so that you don't both land at the same time. And also, if you see her traveling around with the watch with a black strap, get out of there as fast as you can. That means you're seeing the version of her in the timeline that was trying out the watch she stole from you. And you can't allow the same object to be in the same place at the same time."

I remember Zach saying this: that an object can't intersect with itself. I look down at the black-strapped watch on my wrist and remember how it looked on Mrs. Grundy's wrist a couple of days ago.

"But if she's wearing the white strap, get her," Abby goes on. "And if you find Jillian, check to see if she has the other prototype with the red strap. And if she does, make sure she knows to be careful with it and—"

"Okay," I interrupt her. "I promise."

She fashions the cloth bag into a makeshift backpack, threading my arms through the handles. Then she grips my shoulders and peers into my face. "We'll probably never see each other again," she says. "I feel like I should say something wise." There are tears in her eyes as she kisses my forehead. I can only nod, my throat closing before any words can come out.

Maybe she'll never see me again, but if I'm lucky, I'll see a younger version of her as I travel through time.

This isn't good-bye forever, not really.

"I don't know how, but I'm pretty sure that Jill is your mother," she says.

"You mean Joan—" I start, but she shakes her head.

"Jill."

"But that would make you my grandmother," I reply.

There's a banging on the door. The kids, back from school, searching for us.

I take one last, wondering look at Abby, my thirty-five-year-old grand-mother, and double-click.

PART
3

TWISTING

34

BRADFORD, PA, JANUARY 29, 1929

4:00 P.M.

The first time I did a standing back handspring was at a middle-school play rehearsal. I was an orphan in a production of *Annie*. The director didn't like the way we were all just standing there in a row. He wanted the scene to be more dynamic, so when I finished my lines, I flipped over backward. At first he was worried about liability, but after everyone else begged, he finally let us keep it in the scene. I was pretty pleased with myself. It had taken me a long time to learn to do a back handspring without the momentum of a run or a roundoff.

Traveling in time without vaulting is like that. One minute I'm standing in Mrs. Grundy's front room, and the next it's like I've vaulted without the run to set it up, like I've recklessly thrown my body into space. Once again it's like I've been knocked unconscious, like I'm waking from a long sleep, lights flashing in my eyes as I feel myself landing.

35

MUNICH, AUGUST 31, 1972
8 P.M.

I'm in a stadium's outer hallway. My watch says I'm in Munich. A sign near the door gradually comes into focus. Olympiapark München, it says. My head is light and a little achy, and I feel like I need to sit down and rest for a few minutes.

Someone walks by me munching on a Weiner schnitzel and sipping a beer. Over a loudspeaker, an announcer pronounces syllables that sound harsh, all consonants and no vowels, and spectators' voices carry in a language that sounds like gurgling and hissing. German, I guess, wondering what my own language sounds like to non-English speakers.

I've got to get up, I think. I have to find Mrs. Grundy. If she's here, she would have arrived at the same time I did and slipped right by me while I was recovering.

But there are people everywhere. How will I ever spot her?

At least this time I've traveled where I meant to, and I didn't hear that shuffling sound, as if the watch was resetting itself in midair. I hustle from the doorless passageway into the arena, wondering if it's possible to remain inconspicuous in a flapper frock with a leo underneath, a bulky cloth bag, and high lace-up granny shoes.

But no one's paying any attention to me as I plop into a spot on the bleachers. I close my eyes, still a little dizzy. Gradually I get back my equilibrium.

The gazes of the spectators around me wander between events, the four-ring circus of a gymnastics meet, but I immediately fix my eyes on the bars, where a tiny girl with blond pigtails is about to make gymnastics history.

I'm only a few feet away from Olga Korbut. In Munich. In 1972. The adrenaline rush gives me goose bumps. I've seen Korbut in videos, pixie-like and fluid as if she has rubber bands in place of bones. She's wearing a white leo with red trim around the scooped neck. I remember that in the all-around competition, she made elementary mistakes on the bars, tapping the floor on her mount, missing a high-bar kip. By now, the event final, the audience's expectations are modest, their gazes detaching themselves from her and roving the gym.

I completely forget for a moment that I'm supposed to be looking for Mrs. Grundy. My eyes are on Olga Korbut. Maybe Abby, nursing Jillian at home while watching TV, will glimpse me in the crowd, though she won't know what she's seeing, because right now, in 1972, she has no idea who I am.

I watch Korbut execute a flawless mount to the low bar and rapidly fly between the unevens. I hold my breath, remembering how her routine culminates in a back flip from the high bar to the low, the first backward release move ever in women's competition. No one's allowed to compete this skill anymore because it's too dangerous, starting from a standing position on the high bar. I watch as, smooth as a dolphin, she arches backward and flips effortlessly, sleek and elegant and aerodynamic.

As she sails through the air, the audience of thousands erupts in screams. There's another high-pitched explosion of voices as she sticks the landing. The score pops up on the board: 9.8.

Which would be a great score if it weren't the Olympics, where everything comes down to a tenth of a point. A wind rises around me: the crowd is booing. They whistle and jeer and yell what are probably profanities in German. Feet begin to stamp. The risers vibrate. The whole stadium resounds with protest.

The judges look on impassively.

All of a sudden, I see her, a few rows ahead of me. A twist of braid on the back of a head. An arm encircled by a black band. A gray suit.

And then it registers. Her watch has a black band.

My watch has a black band.

We are wearing the same watch.

This is a version of Mrs. Grundy from a couple of weeks ago, the Mrs. Grundy who stole my watch and was experimenting with it.

And the same watch can't intersect with itself.

People around me are still muttering and grumbling as I rush out into the hall, away from the charged air, resetting the watch as I hurry away from Mrs. Grundy before the whole world can explode.

36

BRADFORD, PA, OCTOBER 11, 1975
5 P.M.

When my body jolts to the ground this time, it's on a neat green lawn behind a stand of trees on a warm afternoon. Once again, I feel dizzy, like I've been whirling in circles, and spots from the flashing lights jump in front of my eyes. This time it's several minutes before I can get to my feet. I set the time for a few minutes before Mrs. Grundy will arrive to give myself a chance to recover.

The ambient noise has downshifted from the pounding and yelling of angry voices to a mower droning nearby. And there's a wind I can't seem to feel but sounds as if it is blowing steadily: traffic on a nearby road, quieter but more insistently continuous than the occasional roaring engine and rattling carriages of 1929. No whistles and clatters of trains or clopping of horse hooves, but all of a sudden, the faraway drone of a swarm of bees—and then they are buzzing all around me. I fling my arms over my head and crouch, cringing and terrified, before I realize that what I'm hearing is a plane growling above me. It vibrates the ground I stand on, all of the leaves around me flinching. A snatch of music pounds from a distant car and this time the trembling of the leaves is barely perceptible. The air smells different too, less like the blend of livestock and crude oil of 1929, or the sweat and Weiner schnitzels of the 1972 Olympics. This year, 1975, smells more like exhaust fumes and fast food. These are close to the familiar smells of my own time.

As soon as my headache and dizziness subside, I circle the trees, following the sounds of kids shouting and a baby crying to a playground. For a minute I feel disoriented, as if surrounded by the ghosts of the kids who I've been with nonstop for the last week. I think I catch a glimpse of Catherine hanging upside down on the monkey bars, but she twists slightly and I see that it's another blond girl. I almost reach out to catch a dark-haired sprite in a terry-cloth playsuit who flies by, nearly knocking me over, but she turns her head and her features aren't Sarah's. A boy rumbling low as he propels a matchbox car through a sandbox raises his head, and he's not Robert. I think of muscle memory, that ability to perform tricks without conscious thought. Now my brain seems determined to reproduce not physical tricks but familiar features in the faces of strangers.

The clothes hurt my eyes: bright colors and funky patterns, checks and zigzags and prints dotted with sailboats and smiley faces, super-short shorts with halter tops or super-flared jeans. Even the adults are wearing rambunctious patterns. Parents doze or chat on benches while a dozen kids take turns sliding down a long silver slide, swing on cloth swings, and scramble up the rungs of a silver jungle gym.

A conversation between two mothers is suspended as they take in my flapper dress and catch each other's amused eyes. "Going to a roaring-twenties party?" asks a woman with long straight hair and a miniskirt, dragging on her cigarette right there on the playground and blowing smoke at the kids.

Then I see Jill. Her dark curls bounce as she pumps her swing up into the air, intent on rising higher and higher. She pendulums backward, throwing her head behind her and her feet forward. The chain pulls at the bar with a little thump. She tilts forward at the top of the arc. Then gravity pulls her back toward earth. I remember when I was little, wondering if I could sail high enough to make the swing fly over the bar, all the way around. If I could turn myself inside out.

Abby's not too difficult to locate, either, as the only other curly head among all of the super-straight hair that looks like it's been ironed. I recognize the distinctive splotch of freckles across her cheekbones. She's gripping the swing-set post with both hands, leaning out, staring at the sky. She looks pretty much the way she did when I left her only minutes ago, just younger and wearing a garish orange double-knit T-shirt.

This is Abby's alter ego, I remind myself. Gail.

Beyond her, in the parking lot, the cars are huge compared to my own time—lumbering gas-guzzling things. There are no SUVs.

"Push me," Jillian demands. Still gazing at the sky, Abby—Gail—ignores her.

Jillian appears used to this. She just scuffs her feet along the ground and hops out of the swing, darting for the jungle gym. Gail's eyes remain glazed. She takes a notebook and pen out of her pocket and jots something down.

Jillian is impossibly confident for such a tiny kid, skimming up a few rungs and then grabbing hold of the monkey bars. I edge closer, instinctively standing where I'd be if I were intentionally spotting her. She swings wildly forward, pedaling her small legs like she's on a bike as she reaches for one bar and then the next. Rapidly she sways along the overhead track of bars. I'm astonished that someone so little has that much upper-body strength.

Then everything happens fast. Gail glances up just as Jillian slips. For a split second, our eyes meet, and then I've leaped forward, catching Jillian.

Startled, she wraps her arms around my neck.

Then Gail is by my side, taking the child from me. "Thank you," she says. "Thank you so much. I was daydreaming and didn't see her. Thank you."

"She's strong," I say. Jillian is squirming in Gail's arms, wanting to be let down, completely unaware of how close she came to injury. Gail lowers her to the ground. "Be careful," she says, but Jillian is off and running, climbing again.

"She's kind of a daredevil," Gail says.

"Is she a gymnast?" I ask. I can't resist, but then I want to take it back: What if such an innocent comment ends up being the reason that Jillian becomes a gymnast? But what if my rushing forward to catch her when she fell has already altered the past?

"I've been thinking about putting her in lessons," Gail replies. "Harnessing some of that energy." Gail is staring at me funny. "You look sort of familiar. Are you from around here?"

"Yeah," I say, and for the first time when I say *yeah*, she doesn't wince.

At that moment, something catches my eye beyond Gail. A woman is approaching the playground, wearing a checked cotton housedress that looks out of place among the bright seventies colors and casual outdoor clothing. My eye travels to her arm, which holds a watch like mine except with a white strap. I lift my eyes to her face, to the gray braids coiled around her head.

My pulse rate rockets up. Mrs. Grundy. She's staring fixedly at Abby and Jill. She frowns at me.

What am I supposed to do now?

Abby and I didn't discuss that.

Should I approach her slowly and try to talk to her?

Grab her watch off her arm and hold it hostage so she can't escape?

Sneak up on her to set her watch back to 1929, then click it?

Yeah, like I could do that without her noticing.

I really haven't thought this through.

"Jillian, thank this nice girl for helping you," Gail says. Jillian ignores her as she wiggles her way up the jungle gym again. "And come on. We need to be getting home."

Gail turns to me. "Do you ever babysit?" She studies me again, like she is trying to figure out how she knows me.

Words fly out of my mouth. "Yes, I do." I'm keeping my eyes on Mrs. Grundy, willing her to stay put.

Gail reaches up and swipes Jill off of the jungle gym. Jillian erupts in indignant howls. "We've got to go," Gail says.

I stay beside them, like somehow I can protect them, as Jillian climbs into her red metal wagon and Gail pulls it out of the park and down the sidewalk.

Mrs. Grundy follows a few steps behind.

Gail pauses. Mrs. Grundy stops also, glancing at her watch and then scanning the street as if waiting for her ride.

"This is a holiday weekend, so the day care isn't open," Gail says. "And I have to go in to work for a few hours tomorrow and Monday. If you're interested in a babysitting job, I'd pay well."

"Sure," I say. I move closer to Gail, willing her to keep her voice down as she gives me directions to her house.

Mrs. Grundy stands there in her sensible oxfords, gazing up at the clouds and ahead at the hospital as if to disguise the fact that she's tailing us. I hope that she can't hear Jill. That she doesn't figure out that Gail lives in the same house she did fifty years ago.

"I'll be at your place by ten tomorrow," I say hastily, waving good-bye before I rush back to confront Mrs. Grundy.

"Why are you here?" Mrs. Grundy hisses at me, and we both watch the retreating backs of Gail and Jill.

Up close, I see for the first time that her eyes are the same greenish color as Luke's. The first time I ever saw her, I thought she looked really old, but now I realize that she has a fresh, clear complexion, with few wrinkles, like my own mother, if my mother had an evil twin. Maybe, I think with some shame, I just never looked at Mrs. Grundy that closely. I just saw her serviceable dress and her gray hair and the lines that framed her mouth and assumed she was elderly.

"Why are *you* here?" I volley her question back to her.

"You are just as ill-mannered as ever," she says, reminding me why I thought of her as old and stodgy.

"If you don't go back to 1929, you could mess up the timeline." I thought that pleading with her might work, but my words sound pretty lame even to me. "If you keep Abby from going back to the 1920s and meeting Luke, your grandchildren won't exist." *And you could prevent me from being born,* I don't add. "You don't want that, do you?"

"You have no idea what I want," she says. "Abby is the mother of my grandchildren. I'm doing this for them. All of them."

"Doing what?" I go cold all over.

What is Mrs. Grundy planning to do?

"Just go back," I beg her. "Leave well enough alone."

"You'd like that," she says absently, but she's not looking at me. Gail and Jillian are now far in the distance, disappearing around the corner of Interstate Parkway.

"Is this the first place the watch brought you?" I ask.

She laughs. "I left at least five days ago. I've been all over the world. Don't you remember our conversations at all of those Olympic competitions? I always wanted to travel."

I wonder what conversations she's talking about, but I'm distracted by the way she somehow reminds me of Mom, specifically of her tone when she's irritated with me. I imagine that if I cut the tension with the right joke, we'd both laugh uproariously.

No, I remind myself. *This is stern, sour Mrs. Grundy, who is nothing like Mom.*

"You forget," she says, flicking her eyes away from the receding figures, giving me a smug grin. "I can go to any of the settings on this watch. You won't know where to find me."

And then she double-clicks her watch and is gone.

So, I totally blew that one. Should I jump to another time right now, or bide my time here for a while, in case she comes back?

Suddenly I understand the impossibility of my task. Every setting on our watches is another possible place for her to hide. Where will I ever find her, and what will I do when we come face-to-face again?

My impulse is to race randomly through time, searching for her. But I remember the dizziness and headaches and fatigue that seem to get worse with every time jump.

"If you ever get separated from me, stay where you are," Mom used to say when I was little. "I'll come back and find you."

Does the same logic apply here? Should I stay put? Wait for Mrs. Grundy to show up again?

But I get the feeling that she could go on playing cat and mouse with me forever. Like, literally forever. Through all of time. Or at least all of the settings on the watch.

So maybe what I need to do is figure out which setting on the watch would allow her to cause the most damage. Does that mean I should focus on places where Gail is? Where Jill is?

Should I focus on the night I was born?

What if she comes back to this day? If she overheard Gail, she knows that she'll be working tomorrow. What if Jill is somehow at risk? Should I fulfill my agreement to babysit her and be there to protect her in case Mrs. Grundy comes back?

But if Mrs. Grundy comes back, it would be to the exact same moment in time. Wouldn't I have seen two versions of her arrive?

I don't think she's here anymore, and now it's getting dark. I need a safe place to hide.

37

BRADFORD, PA, OCTOBER 11, 1975
7 P.M.

U nder a tree, I polish off a pear and some cheese from my cumbersome
bag. I lighten it a bit more by gulping down some water. The air is
cool, and when it's late enough that there won't be kids playing in the streets
or grown-ups mowing or barbecuing in their yards, I set off toward my own
house, where Mom lives.

Do I have to stop calling her Mom? Should I call her Joan? But she's still
my mom, no matter what.

And here in 1975, she's been married to my dad for three years.

Instead of turning on Sanford, I veer up Kennedy Street. These big
houses on either side have burned down in my own time, leaving a row of
empty lots. I circle around on Leigh Street and come down Sanford from
the other direction so that I won't have to pass Gail's house and risk being
seen by her.

My pulse quickens when I catch sight of the two big cars in my own
driveway, a strange-shaped green car with a label on the back that says
Gremlin, and that big station wagon with wood panels on the side, meaning

that my dad must be home. I circle to our backyard, which has been cut into green stripes. Flowers bloom along the edges of the yard, which is much more neatly manicured than in my own time, with not a dandelion or bald patch in sight. The patio is a long, flat surface, not gap-toothed with missing bricks as it will be a few decades later.

I push the basement door hard, stumbling in as it gives way. In here, it looks the way I remember it from my visit to 1976: no freezer inside the doorway, and the carpenter's bench where Abby used to work, the bench that in my time holds some old electrical cords and a cat bed my cat Simone Biles won't use, is completely stocked with drills and saws and screwdrivers.

I tiptoe to the stairs. In 1976 the door was open, but now it's closed tight. Through the wall I can hear voices murmuring, the sound of the TV. I sit and listen, homesick for my own home though I'm sitting in it right now. For Mom, so much younger here, only twenty-two. For the dad I only met briefly in 1976, who has a low, gentle voice. For Simone Biles.

Once the house has gone silent and I'm pretty sure my parents are in bed, I test the door. Miraculously, no one turned the deadbolt. In the kitchen, someone has painted Abby's boomerang-patterned Formica countertops an ugly tan color. When I was young, Mom replaced these with granite.

I hastily scrounge some food from the refrigerator and cabinets, finding crunchy granola bars that look like the prototypes for granola bars in my time, bottles of Perrier, nuts, and cheese slices. I hate Perrier. I dump it out and fill two bottles with tap water. I'm going to ditch the canteen so I can travel more lightly.

Upstairs, a toilet flushes. My adrenaline surges. Grabbing a throw from the living-room couch, I slip back to the basement and spread the blanket on the grubby concrete basement floor.

I can't relax. I think of all of the mice Simone Biles will catch down here in my own time, leaving their tails on the basement floor, and I imagine their ancestors scampering around me now. I lie there in the spooky dark, my brain whirring. I miss my kitty. So sweet on the surface, but being down in the basement now, I am reminded of the time when I found the skeletons of a family of baby mice, and how I began to realize my cat was really a predator. When I pet her and she whips back her head to sink her teeth into my hand, I'm convinced that if I weren't a lot bigger than her, she'd probably eat me too. I remember when I was little how I couldn't understand how a cat—or people either—could be both affectionate and vicious.

One time I asked Mom if a woman we knew was a good person or a bad person. "There's no such thing as a good person or a bad person," Mom said. "Everyone has some of both. Even the nicest people have moments of cruelty. Even people who are abusive have dogs and children who love them."

I was irritated by that answer. I just wanted to know who was good and who was bad.

I think about Mrs. Grundy. Next time I see her, what will I do? What kind of person am I? If she won't respond to pleas or logic, can I just snatch the watch off her arm? Is there some way for me to get leverage, to force her to go back?

I shift into six different positions trying to get comfortable on the cold basement floor, but my thoughts refuse to settle down. Finally, I sneak back up the stairs, pausing in the kitchen to fish a flashlight out of a drawer. The refrigerator hums as I stand looking at a butcher block of knives. I vaguely remember Mom selling this in a garage sale years ago, and I'm pretty sure there were knives missing from it by then, so do I take one or not?

And am I predestined to do everything the same way, or can I make a different choice? How much free will does a time traveler have?

I can't imagine myself threatening anyone with a knife. I might have pushed Molly and gotten kicked out of the gym, but I'm not a violent person.

Am I?

A car passes the open window. I creep on up the stairs, listening, grateful for the thick walls, hearing only faint snoring behind my parents' closed door. I whip open the attic door and climb, and then, curling up on the floor with the old blue blanket, a little shaken at even considering violence, I finally drop off to sleep there above my sleeping parents.

$\ell\ell\ell\ell\sim\!\!\!\bigcirc\!\!\!\ell\ell\ell\ell\ell\sim\!\!\!\bigcirc$

After they've left for church, I return the throw to the couch, touching everything along the way. The stair railings, the car keys Mom has left on the coffee table, a jacket of my dad's draped on the back of a chair, all things they have recently touched. Resolving to ditch my flapper dress, I search through Mom's closet. She's so tall that there's no way her pants will fit me. I pull on a sweatshirt over my leotard, and then a skirt that's short on her but reaches my knees. It's a little ridiculous with my high lace-up boots, though this look will be way more in fashion in a few years. I wad a couple of extra T-shirts and some underwear into the bottom of my bag and leave my flapper dress behind some paint cans in the basement storage room.

Then I go back upstairs and slide a small knife out of the block on the counter. Just in case I need to defend myself. Although I'm not really sure I would even know how.

38

"Thanks so much for doing this." Gail opens the door of the yellow house within seconds after I knock. She seems harried, gathering books and papers and a bagful of what I now recognize as watch parts. Kissing the top of Jillian's head, already distracted and absent-minded, she darts out the door. I was just in this house a couple of days ago, but now, instead of stately dark furniture that casts shadows across the room, there's that low-slung couch with broken springs and the TV in a cabinet.

Jill's hopping and skipping across the room. She bounces up and down on her heels, twirls and leaps, then takes off running out into the yard. It turns out that my toddler mother never sits still.

She climbs the door frames and the back of the couch. She shimmies to the tops of cabinets.

She never stops moving and she never stops talking, asking me one question after the other, not waiting for the answers. "Why are your shoes so funny-looking? When will Mom be home? Do you want to meet my stuffed animals? Can we go outside?"

I scan the yard for Mrs. Grundy as Jill tears back and forth across the grass. Sitting on the porch steps, alert for any movement, I watch Jill pretending to be a dog, prancing around on all fours and barking. She turns into a meowing cat leaping after a robin, and then a train choo chooing along a track.

At lunchtime, we walk down to McDonald's. Still no sign of Mrs. Grundy. I don't quite get how time travel works. Is it even possible for her to return? Since she can't change the coordinates on the watch, wouldn't she have to zap herself back to yesterday again? Does she know that she can't let her watch intersect with itself? Anyway, if she'd tried that, wouldn't I have seen two of her in the park? Maybe there actually were multiple versions of her hiding in the trees and bushes, watching. I don't think so, because at some point I would have caught a glimpse of her. All of the possibilities boggle my mind.

At McDonald's I imagine that Jill will crawl through tubes and jump in the ball pit in the play place, wearing herself out. But there's no play place. I scan the menu, looking for a Happy Meal, but they don't seem to exist yet either.

By the time we head home, I'm pretty sure Mrs. Grundy isn't coming back here. And I feel a restless pressure to keep going, but I can't leave Jill alone.

After a brief nap, she's up and ready to go again.

"Do you know how to do a cartwheel?" I ask her, and she reaches for the ground and executes a perfect one. "How about a back walkover?" I try, and she flings herself backward, legs kicking up into the air. I show her how to do a roundoff into a back handspring. She doesn't quite get it, but I can tell she's intrigued. I wonder how I ended up so ordinary if I'm the granddaughter of two scientific geniuses and the daughter of a gymnastics prodigy.

After dinner Jill beats me several times at Hungry Hungry Hippos before she takes a bath and I help her into her Winnie the Pooh pajamas. Then we watch *Little House on the Prairie* until Gail gets home. I glance out the window at every passing car, every rustle of a breeze, but there is no sign of Mrs. Grundy.

lllee llee

In the dark I head up the sidewalk, still on the lookout for Mrs. Grundy, but she seems to have vanished into another time.

In my parents' driveway, a bright light attached to the porch railing glares down onto a car's innards. A screwdriver clatters to the ground and a man's voice says, "Damn it," before his head emerges from behind the hood. When I saw him in 1976, he was wearing a hat and sunglasses, and I didn't get a good look at his face. But now I recognize from the pictures his light, crew-cut hair, those striking blue eyes, a smattering of stubble on his chin.

My pulse races as I move up the driveway, imagining actually talking to him. I dive for the screwdriver just as he also bends forward, and our heads almost knock. I hand it to him.

"Thank you," he says. He has the kind of skin that crinkles up when he smiles, and startling thick white eyebrows that make his eyes look even more penetratingly blue, a contrast that's far more evident in real life than it was in photographs. "How's that little girl of yours?"

For a second I'm frozen there, all of the things Mom has told me about him flashing through my thoughts. How he was a person of few words, conveying his affection by doing things: putting gas in her car and changing the oil, bringing in flowers from the garden, fixing her oatmeal for breakfast. How broken up he was when their first daughter was stillborn, but how he still spared Mom the task of putting away the baby clothes and crib by doing it all himself before she came home from the hospital. How he called at the exact same time every day from the road when he was away.

I realize I've just been standing there, staring at him, and I struggle to recover my voice. "Oh, I'm not Gail," I say. "I'm Elizabeth." Then I realize that maybe I shouldn't use my real name. "I mean, Anna, the babysitter."

This is the man I've always thought of as my dad, and in the dark, he has mistaken me for Gail. Not so long ago I didn't know a single person I resembled. Not so long ago I had no idea what my dad looked like, and here he is, the downy hair on his arms glowing in the artificial light, his oily hands reaching to fiddle with knobs and switches.

"It's nice to meet you, Elizabeth Anna," he says, and I'm glad I slipped. It's nice to hear my name come out of his mouth. He smiles briefly and then returns to whatever he's doing. And I leave him there in the driveway. *That's my dad*, I think. I know he's not my biological father, but I will always think of him as my dad.

After he and Mom are asleep, I steal up to the attic again, where I spend hours toggling through the watch settings, trying to guess what would Mrs. Grundy do. WWMGD?

I think of her words to Abby: "You've made a mess of everything. Somebody has to fix it."

What did she mean? What is she going to do? That question nags at me constantly.

This is like a game of hide-and-seek—I have to go to all of the settings to find her. But why would she go to the Olympic dates?

It's like trying to figure out why someone would hide in the closet as opposed to the basement—like, maybe it's just random. But I remember her comment about our conversations at Olympic competitions. Those had clearly happened for her, but are in the future for me. Maybe I'm supposed to find her, befriend her, reason with her.

Since she told Abby that she was going to fix things, that makes me think I should concentrate my efforts on some setting that involves Abby and Jill. I don't think the Olympic dates and locations could possibly be integral to whatever she's planning, but I'm mystified by her comment about our conversations at them.

Trying to figure out what she's planning gives me chills. Is she going to Bradford to try to prevent Abby from coming back to the 1970s? But why? Then she wouldn't have her grandchildren, and she loves her grandchildren. She can't possibly want to cancel Abby's existence.

Even if she wants to, say, stop Jill from being born, she can't. She can only go to the settings that are already preprogrammed into the watch.

But Zach and I programmed my birth date into the watch. Does she want to stop me from being born?

Why would she do that?

A cold panic washes over me.

But my eye keeps landing on 1988. I mean, Jill did disappear and was never heard from again. Maybe Mrs. Grundy had something to do with that. Maybe, for some reason, that date is key.

I remember her saying, "I tried to go to Prague but I ended up in Dallas." But when I was in Dallas in 1988 before, I didn't see Mrs. Grundy, did I?

Then I remember that grandma with the crown of braids in the parent viewing area. Suddenly I'm sure that that was her. If I go back to that day, wouldn't I risk meeting myself also and causing the same watch to intersect?

I need to be systematic. Check all of the places set in the watch.

But I suspect that there's something I need to figure out about 1988. And how does that link to the other times and places in the watch? I finally put away the watch and nestle into my blanket. Closing my eyes, I think of my parents sleeping below me.

My dad. I spoke to my dad.

The only dad that I ever knew—up until two days ago—existed.

My dad.

39

It's 1978. I'm in Hanley Park, and it's snowing. My head throbs, spots of light still exploding in front of my eyes like someone just took my picture with a flash, and my stomach twists. I perch on the end of a stainless steel slide, waiting for the nausea to pass. Once again, I'm underdressed, bare legged in Mom's miniskirt now turned into my granny skirt. The cold almost feels good, settling my stomach.

Below me, a little girl, chubby in a down coat and snow pants, is dragging a plastic sled up the slope, a fluffy stuffed dog wobbling on top of the sled. It's Jill, I realize.

And then Mrs. Grundy appears from the other direction. She's coatless, wearing the same drab checked dress she had on that day she disappeared in 1929, the same dress she was wearing in that park in 1975, and the white watch.

She whisks past me, calling, "Have you seen a puppy?"

Obviously she's up to no good, trying to lure Jillian to go with her.

Jillian drops the plastic handle of her sled, lifting her stuffed dog to show Mrs. Grundy.

"No, that's not my puppy. She ran away. Can you help me find her?"

Jillian nods solemnly and takes Mrs. Grundy's hand.

I react without thinking. "No," I yell. "Stranger danger!" I race toward them waving my arms.

Mrs. Grundy glares at me. She fumbles around for a second, then taps her wrist.

She's gone.

Suddenly, Jillian starts screaming and a woman scrambles over the hill, slipping and sliding in the snow, yanking Jillian away from me. Her foster mom.

I totally blew that one.

But now I'm even more sure: Mrs. Grundy is after Jill. What does she want with her?

I duck behind some trees. No point in staying.

I tap my watch.

40

PRAGUE, JULY 5, 1962
9 P.M.

I meant to do a quick scan of the crowd in Prague, cross this place off my list, and then move on, but my stop here, where I timed myself to arrive ten minutes before Mrs. Grundy, has turned into two hours. I'm too queasy to do anything but sit completely still, leaning my throbbing head against a wall, waiting for the flashes of light to clear away, watching the doorway to an enormous outdoor stadium for Mrs. Grundy. I'm squeezed in with a crowd of spectators under the covered part that rattles with rain, which waterfalls down the uncovered exterior wall in great gushes. In the distance, I can see buildings with towers and spires like in a horror movie, alongside another building with a dome. They are surrounded by the low walls of simpler buildings. Everything looks really old.

I finally manage to rise to my feet and climb onto the bench of some bleachers, scanning the crowd for gray braids and a checked dress. Around me, people huddle in coats, eating a concoction with ground beef and vegetables from paper bowls or pastries shaped like chimneys, stuffed with strawberries, and covered with powdered sugar. The air is heavy with the smell of beer. The writing on the sides of food containers and cups has so many consonants and so few vowels I wonder how to pronounce the words.

I watch as, beneath a roof, in dim light, gymnasts continue their rotations. I don't think this is another Olympics. Maybe it's a World Championship? I can barely hear the voice of an announcer, talking in another language I don't know. It sounds a little like the German I heard in Munich, but less harsh, a little more like singing. It's almost impossible to hear the floor music over the clatter and whoosh of the downpour. A young woman walks to the edge of the floor and strikes a pose. She has a small ledge of boobs and a suggestion of hips, kind of like me, rather than the straight-up-and-down figure like those of the wispy gymnasts who will follow her. Her helmet of hair reminds me of pictures of Jackie Kennedy or Amy Winehouse.

I scan the crowd around me while a pianist on the edge of the floor brings his hands down on the keys, striking the first chords of a classical piece.

The music is interrupted by thunder that booms like a shotgun at a starting line. The gymnast ignores the crash. She begins to leap and turn in a slow ballet, languorous. I'm pretty sure I'm watching Larisa Latynina from the Soviet Union, moving as if in slow motion.

As I half watch her, passing my eyes over clusters of spectators, the stadium lights suddenly blink off and the floor goes dark. The pianist doesn't miss a note. A staccato flash of lightning spotlights Latynina twirling and tumbling. In the dark, I can see her shadowy form, the unhurried, slow, elegant movements: her split leap, her almost sluggish back handsprings into a back tuck, now considered comparatively easy tricks.

The crowd is a shadowy blur as lightning illuminates Latinyna's oddly languid tumbling with a kind of strobe-light effect. A crack of thunder, a flicker of light, another shudder, like flashbulbs going off, briefly highlighting the curve of an arm, the extension of a foot. Then all is dark, and there is just the sound of music and a shuffle of feet and the thud of a landing.

More quick lightning spotlights Latynina's calm grace, so seemingly impervious to the turbulent backdrop. It's like she's a mythological figure who planned the storm for dramatic effect, who choreographed her routine to these rolls and rumbles and crashes, these flashes and flickers and flares. A crack of thunder provides a dramatic finish. It drowns out her music and then fades, so that only the last notes are audible. A blaze of lightning illuminates her final pose.

Behind her, in the stands, a movement, and then everything is dark again. The crowd is on its feet, applause booming across the stadium.

As lights flicker on, I immediately see Mrs. Grundy making her way past me with a cup of beer. "Hey!" I shout.

She turns her head. I half expect her to run, but instead she lights up like we are long-lost friends and climbs the bleachers toward me. I take in her watch: it's the one with the white strap.

"That was amazing," she says, lowering herself to the bench beside me.

"Wasn't it?" I ask. I can't believe that Mrs. Grundy and I are actually sharing a moment of awe. I try to keep my voice casual so she doesn't know how nervous I am about what she might do. "How do you manage to seem so at home everywhere?" I ask her.

She laughs. "I spent quite a bit of time traveling around when you were living with Abby," she says. "I figured it out. But is there some way I can add new settings?"

"Nope. You can only go to the ones already programmed in."

She looks disappointed. So maybe she doesn't have any nefarious purpose. Maybe she really does just want to travel the world.

I can't buy that, though.

"Where are you going next?" I ask.

"I'm not sure." She sips her beer. "I'm not going to hurt anyone, you know. You don't have to be afraid of me."

I eye her suspiciously. "Then why were you trying to kidnap Jillian?"

She pauses as if searching her memory. "Oh, that," she finally says. "Look, I've got everyone's best interests at heart. Just stop following me. Everything will be fine." She bows her head, adjusting the buttons on the watch.

"But—" I start, but before I can formulate my questions, she's gone, and I feel more uneasy than ever.

41

BRADFORD, PA, SEPTEMBER 9, 2009
8 A.M.

I've always functioned best with a good night's sleep, but the thing about time travel is that there are no hotels or bed-and-breakfasts. It's also sort of hard to figure out when it's bedtime. After a few futile time jumps, I feel like I've been at a long gymnastics meet and could really use a nice hotel swimming pool and some room service. The next best thing, I guess, is a trip to a house I know will be deserted. And I know something that Mrs. Grundy doesn't: how to program new times into the watch, as long as I go to locations that are preset.

So that's why I end up at Gail's abandoned yellow house. I've started to feel feverish after a jolting series of leaps between watch settings. I curl up on the mattress in Gail's bedroom and slip out of consciousness, Mrs. Grundy flitting through my dreams.

At one point I think she's in the room. Shadow people spin and flip. I toss, moaning in the dark.

I wake, my skin burning.

When I open my eyes to early-morning sunlight and the sound of mice scrabbling in the walls, I feel better, refreshed, my head and stomach steady again. Guzzling some water in the kitchen, I hear a commotion outside and look out just in time to catch a little girl flying down the street, hoisting a backpack almost as big as she is. That's me. A boy's footsteps hammer the pavement as he calls for her to wait up.

Zach.

My heart squeezes when I see the way that little boy gazes at Younger Me, eager, tentative. Almost as if he has a crush on her. If he did, I never realized it.

I watch the two kids skid to a stop on the corner.

A school bus stops with a sigh like air escaping a balloon. I watch seven-year-old me board, followed by seven-year-old Zach. The bus lurches away.

I check the opposite window. Mom's car isn't in our driveway. I venture out.

Our side door is unlocked. Inside, I wander, feeling nostalgic. In my room there's a bookshelf where my desk will eventually be and a mattress in the cubby under the stairs where that younger version of me is still small enough to sleep.

There are only a couple of small gymnastics trophies, because I'd just started competing recently. I touch the toys, the Tickle Me Elmo, the tackle box full of beads, and the Barbie dolls my friends all gave me for my fifth birthday . . . I reread some of my favorite picture books. Digging through my toy box, I find a Winnie the Pooh backpack I carried back in kindergarten. I vaguely recall that it disappeared at some point and I never found it again.

I'm about to be the cause of that mysterious disappearance, because a backpack would be less awkward to carry than Abby's cloth bag. I transfer the tablet, toiletries, and remaining food to the backpack and scrounge up some more food downstairs in the kitchen, stuffing it as full as I can.

Sending psychic apologies to Mom, I dig through her change jar for coins with dates from the seventies and eighties to join my babysitting money from Abby. Opening the secretary in the living room, I find my birth certificate. Mom must have used it to enroll me in school, soccer, and gymnastics, but I don't think we'll need it again for a few years. I remember that it too disappeared. Is that because I took it for some reason? If I don't take it now, does that mean I won't have to search for it, won't have to break into the file cabinet in the attic? Would this prevent me from finding out about Mom's secrets? I shrug and tuck it into the tablet.

Back at the yellow house, I pick out some wide-legged pants from Abby's closet and ditch Mom's miniskirt.

I know I have to get back to my mission. But instead I take a break for a couple of days, spying on Mom's comings and goings. I see her passing before the kitchen window in the mornings, assembling sandwiches and fruit for my lunch pail and her own brown bag, hugging me good-bye every morning, then stepping out into the yard to hang wet clothes on the line or carry out trash bags. Her hair is often disheveled, her shirts askew, her lipstick faded by evening because she's so busy taking care of me. I never realized how busy.

And with her right there in front of me, I miss her more than ever.

42

ATLANTA, JULY 3, 1996
9:40 A.M.

At the Georgia Dome in Atlanta, Kerri Strug, in a V-neck leo patterned like an American flag, launches her first vault in the 1996 Olympic team finals.

When I landed out in the hall a half hour ago, five minutes before Mrs. Grundy was likely to arrive, I only had a mild headache and a slightly upset stomach. At first I thought that I'd discovered the trick to smoother time travel: taking rest breaks between jumps. I felt proud of myself for figuring that out. Then my head started to throb, I broke into a cold sweat, and my heart began to race. My mouth filled with saliva and I dashed for a bathroom instead of waiting for Mrs. Grundy.

I'm a healthy, athletic girl. Mrs. Grundy is older and less fit. How is she holding up? Where does she hide to recover? Once my stomach settled, I went to wash my hands, half expecting to find her throwing up in the next stall. But the restroom was empty. I was disappointed. I had hoped to talk to her some more, and I'm not sure why I never even tried before Prague. Not back in 1929 when, granted, she was always ignoring me and looking through me. In 1975 our exchange was weirdly hostile—almost like she was the one who thought I was up to no good. In 1978 I ran at her, screaming. I think of Mom advising me to respond to my teammate Molly by "killing her with kindness."

So what if I tried to get to know Mrs. Grundy?

I lay on the couch in the restroom vestibule, thinking about this. I love that bathrooms of the past often have these couches, as if women are so delicate that they never know when they might need to lie down.

Once I stopped shaking, I dragged myself through the stadium, checking bathrooms.

Finally I entered the arena, where I recognized Strug right away, even if I was too far away to make out the freckles on her chipmunk cheeks. Still, her cropped hair is distinctive, along with her look of determination as she flies down the runway, doing a roundoff into a back handspring onto the vault. Her block off the horse is a little flat and she completes her one-half twist but lands short, falling backward onto her seat.

"Kerri Strug is hurt," says an announcer.

She limps away for a consultation with her coach, and right away I recognize the guy with the mustache: it's the legendary gymnastics coach Bela Karolyi. I strain to see them from my place in the stands.

Strug limps back to the end of the runway. She stands there, twitching her leg. Coach Karolyi is chanting on the sidelines: "You can do it. You can do it."

I wondered why she would vault again if she was hurt. I remember something Mom said once about Kerri Strug. That she thought it was child abuse to convince her to vault again after being injured.

She salutes, sprints, throws herself into a hurdle, handsprings off the board, blocks off the table, and lands on both feet. One leg pops up. She hops on her other foot, salutes, and collapses to her knees. She lifts her arms triumphantly before pain crosses her face. She crawls off the mat as the crowd cheers.

I feel a little indignant on her behalf.

She didn't even have to do that vault. The American team would have won anyway.

No time to linger. I dread ramping up this headache and sick stomach again, but I have a new sense of purpose: I'm going to talk to Mrs. Grundy some more. Maybe, instead of clicking on all of the time stamps methodically, one after the other, I need to go back to the beginning.

This thought fills me with terror about what I might discover, but before I talk myself out of it, I'm headed to the night of my birth.

43

BRADFORD, PA, JANUARY 3, 2002
6 P.M.

I feel like I've shrunk and arrived in a snow globe, a quiet little world where in front of my house snow falls thickly, blowing into my face. Sleet ticks onto roofs and I'm shivering there without a coat, listening to the clatter of frozen trees, squinting at the silent, shiny street, sheeted over with ice that turns it into a slippery chute.

I don't throw up this time, but my nausea is still cresting and receding when a girl steps out of the shadows of a fir tree next door. I move deeper into the shadows of a twin tree, sinking to the ground. I hate this weak, im-mobilized feeling on first arriving, like it's all I can do to keep from passing out.

I can't see the girl's face, only that her belly is too large for her small frame. She's wearing a coat with sections like a caterpillar and bell bottom pants that tent over her feet. How can this be Jill? Jill would have been in her thirties in 2002, but this is not a grown woman.

This is a teenager, a girl close to my age.

I'm startled by a movement at the back edge of the yard.

Mrs. Grundy, arriving five minutes after me.

What if she really does want to keep me from being born?

But it's not like I can sit down with her and have a conversation here.

If Mrs. Grundy sees me, so will the girl.

If Mrs. Grundy sees me, chances are she'll disappear.

If the girl sees me, I run the risk of altering the past.

I reach for the watch. But before I can push the button, Mrs. Grundy is gone.

44

BERLIN, AUGUST 11, 1936
2:15 P.M.

I come to on the grass outside an outdoor stadium. A woman is leaning over me, talking fast. I recognize the language from Munich, though back then, I thought that German sounded harsh. The woman has a kind face. Whatever she's saying, she doesn't sound mean at all. I raise myself to a sitting position, but when I try to stand, darkness closes in. I abruptly sit again.

The woman offers me some water. Her head pivots around as if searching for medical assistance.

"I'm okay." I stumble to my feet, weaving drunkenly away before she can call more attention to me.

Flags with swastikas unfurl from the round roof of the stadium. I feel uneasy, remembering history lessons about the Nazis. I pass between two tall columns with the Olympic rings suspended on a sign between them, and another sign that says Olympiastadion Berlin. I slip into the bleachers under a roof with the center cut out so that the sky becomes the ceiling.

Minutes ago, I was standing only a few moments from my own birth. Mrs. Grundy was there, and yet I still exist here, so maybe her plan doesn't involve me at all. Before me, women in one-piece suits that remind me of old-timey gym uniforms wave their arms in dance moves. They pause in the midst of bar work to sit still on the low bar. They take running leaps over a narrow horse. The equipment and outfits are less sleek than in my own time. They look cumbersome and clumsy, but the women move effortlessly through their routines.

"Anna," a voice calls, and I'm startled to see Abby rushing across the field toward me. She's wearing the white Chronowatch on her arm. She throws her arms around me, and I'm so surprised and overjoyed to see her, I reciprocate, even though we never had a very touchy-feely relationship.

"The watches work!" she says. "I got them fixed! Last time I saw you, you were reading in your bedroom. I'd better get back to 1929 and make some coffee and tell you what's going on!"

"Right." I can barely get the word out. I'm overcome with joy to catch a glimpse of this version of the Abby that I know, this version who knows me back.

She zips away before I can warn her about Mrs. Grundy. But if she were to go back to 1929 and stop Mrs. Grundy from stealing the watch, what would happen to this version of me in 1936?

Maybe, instead, I should have asked her what I should do when I find Mrs. Grundy.

But even that question could throw things into chaos. I take a rest, gearing up to move on to the next location.

45

MONTREAL, JULY 18, 1976
9:20 A.M.

The girl on the bars is Nadia Comaneci. I instantly recognize her big brown eyes and dark bangs, hair tied with yarn into crooked pigtails. I would have been able to identify her by her waif-like figure alone, or V-neck suit with piping the colors of the Romanian flag. Mrs. Grundy is sitting next to me in her checked dress. It's looking a little raggedy, with a small hole near the hem. I stare at her hand.

She's still wearing her wedding ring.

I'm actually chowing down on hot dogs with Mrs. Grundy as we watch the competition together. Go figure.

I timed it so that we'd arrive at the same time this time, even though I was afraid I'd be too sick to detain her. Landing, I had to lean against a wall. I was so dizzy, my head throbbing. As long as I held totally still, I felt fine.

"You look like you were hit by a bomb," Mrs. Grundy said. She was hovering over me.

"The time jumps make me a little queasy. Aren't they bothering you at all?"

"I usually wait a few days between them," she said. "Do some sightseeing, get some rest. Do you know that you can get a hotel room and then just leave in the middle of the night without having to pay the bill?"

I felt a grudging admiration that the straitlaced Mrs. Grundy has become an outlaw. Not that I'd ever approve of sticking a hotel with the bill under normal circumstances, but under these weird ones, I was a little envious. It would be much harder for a sixteen-year-old to get her own hotel room. For a second, I entertained the idea that we could join forces and see the world together.

But then I remembered that she's not just doing random pleasure time traveling. She's got something up her sleeve. Something that is probably not in my best interests.

"Do you want to go check out the competition?" I asked, gesturing toward the building shaped like a flying saucer before us. And that's how we ended up sitting side by side here in the stadium, watching Nadia Comaneci. I sneak a few glances at Mrs. Grundy, the big white-strapped watch on her small wrist, the prominent veins in her hands, the tight braids that she has bobby-pinned to her head. I wonder if the pins hurt her scalp.

OMG. I can't afford to start feeling sympathetic toward her.

Mrs. Grundy fends me off with a glare, and I turn my attention to Comaneci. I try to focus on her straight lines, her perfectly vertical handstands, her complete control. I try not to look at Mrs. Grundy, though I am braced in case she makes any sudden moves.

Comaneci swings into her dismount, landing several feet in front of the bars, sliding a little forward on the landing. She throws up her arms in a salute, arching deeply. The crowd cheers, but she doesn't even seem to notice as she dashes back to her team.

The digital scoreboard flashes a 1.0. Heads turn, a coach rises, necks crane toward the judges' table.

"A 1.0?" Mrs. Grundy looks confused. "Isn't that pretty low?"

"I've heard about this. The scoreboards can't display anything above a 9.99," I explain. I look down at the way I'm pressing my watch to my arm with my opposite hand, as if I'm afraid that Mrs. Grundy is about to rip it off. Mrs. Grundy follows my eyes and smiles at my nervousness. She's definitely up to no good.

The loudspeaker announcer says, "Ladies and gentlemen, for the first time in Olympic history, Nadia Comaneci has received the score of a perfect 10."

Comaneci runs out to wave at the crowd. Then she escapes back to her team. The cheering continues. She returns and waves again. Rejoins her team and marches on to her next event.

"That was so cool," I say, pretending to be totally comfortable sitting there being all friendly with a woman I don't trust.

"I think it's rather warm in here," Mrs. Grundy replies. "Oh, wait, did you mean like the cat's pajamas?"

"Yeah." I know that I've got to take advantage of this opportunity to pretend to have a friendly conversation. "So hey, remember when you said you were going to fix the mess that Abby made?" I ask. "What exactly are you planning to do?"

"It's nothing for you to worry about," she says, her voice so stern that she is obviously telling me to mind my own business.

Except isn't this sort of my own business?

She seems so mild mannered. She bought me a hot dog. What if I'm overreacting? Maybe time travel is just allowing a lonely widow to have a little fun. Maybe she's not going to do anything terrible.

Yeah, right. This is exactly what she wants. Me to let down my guard so she can pull some surprise attack. I watch her warily.

"I'm going to run to the powder room." She stands, gazing down at me with a long, calculating look that gives me a little chill.

"But—" I say, as she hurries down the stands, threading herself between other spectators. I'm pretty sure she's not coming back, and she doesn't.

46

P ast a row of palm trees, bundles of leaves balanced on tall stick-like trunks, I enter Pauley Pavilion. For once all the signs are in English, but I still feel overwhelmed by the maze-like halls crowded with spectators lined up at concession stands. I wait a few minutes for Mrs. Grundy, but when she doesn't show, I make my way into the arena just in time to see Mary Lou Retton vaulting her front handspring pike front half. I would recognize that powerful, aerodynamic body anywhere, her broad muscular shoulders tapering down to a tiny torso supported by legs that bulge with muscles like a body builder's.

I turn and scan the crowd in the rows behind me, my eyes landing on a woman in an elegantly tailored gray silk crepe suit with a drop waist, a side open collar, and a faux gemstone necklace. From a distance, she looks like a fashion plate from a twenties magazine, and I idly wonder if people in the US in 1984 were reviving twenties styles.

Then I leap to my feet. It's Mrs. Grundy, the version of her who stole my watch out of the planter and held it hostage for a couple of weeks. It is so exhausting to always have to be so vigilant, to keep the black watches from intersecting with themselves.

I whip around and hurry toward the nearest door, relieved that at least I'm in the lower part of the stands.

"Wait!" Mrs. Grundy calls, and I glance over to find her waving wildly. "Isn't this the elephant's eyebrows? The gnat's whistle!"

I spent enough time in 1929 to be able to interpret her slang: she's finding time travel to be the bee's knees.

If I didn't know better, I'd think she was a fun, harmless person. I go on scrambling toward the door, even though she's in the middle of a row, blocked on both sides by full seats of spectators, purses and jackets and water bottles no doubt obstructing her path out. I glance back one more time. She doesn't seem to be making any attempt to come after me. My eyes sweep over the gym where Mary Lou Retton completes her full twisting layout Tsuk. She goes bouncing off the mats, arms raised in a triumphant wave.

I could swear she looks right at me the moment before I double-click and fling myself through space and time.

47

After six time jumps in a row, I feel like mush. Like I got hit by a car. I ache all over, my skin feels as if it's covered in bruises, and my head throbs as if some projectile slammed into it. And unlike Mrs. Grundy, when I need to sleep, I can't just check into hotels. Which is why I landed here, in the yellow house, the day before I first left. It seemed ingenious, like maybe I wouldn't feel quite so homesick if I could be near my house and Mom and Zach, even if they don't know I'm here.

My adrenaline is pumping so hard I startle awake after a short time. I'm becoming convinced that Mrs. Grundy is really not that dangerous. That there wouldn't really be any harm in going back to the day I left. She'll have her time-traveling fun, she'll miss her grandkids, she'll go back to 1929.

Or am I just trying to convince myself of this because it's what I want to believe?

I try to suppress the ominous feeling that there's something that I'm missing.

Trying to make a decision and feeling restless, I retrieve a flashlight from the kitchen junk drawer. I shine my way across the living room, to the window. Mom's Toyota Corolla is parked on the street. The plants in the porch box sag, twines of brown stalks, the way they get in the fall after we've forgotten to water them for weeks. In the window, my shadowy self opens a drawer, looking for a butter knife.

That's me, a few days before I traveled to 1976, 1988, and then 1929.

I remember seeing a flash of light next door. I thought I was hallucinating, not knowing that I was only a few feet from myself, wandering through time.

I feel such a wave of longing for my real life, it almost knocks me over.

And without pausing to think about it, I set my watch and double-click.

48

My feet pound the floor. I automatically arch into a salute as I hop forward on the landing. A laugh bubbles up. I rush forward to meet Zach. Except he's not there, and neither is any of the gymnastics equipment, as far as I can tell in this dim gym.

Suddenly everything is swirling around me. I drop to my knees, check my watch, check the clock on the wall.

Did the watch malfunction again? It says I'm at the gymnastics gym, but this isn't it.

Outside, a storm is revving up. Rain splatters then crashes onto the roof. A rumble of thunder shakes the building. A flicker of lightning illuminates basketball hoops mounted on opposite walls. Confused, I follow the lines on the floor to the double door that leads into the hall.

An old mop, its ropes stiff and brownish, leans against the door of a glass-front office across the hall from a classroom piled with broken desks. I check my watch again. Maybe I accidentally sent myself to 1970 instead of 2018.

But according to the watch display, there were no accidents, the display stubbornly insisting that this is 2018.

This is the building that was refurbished into our gymnastics center. But for some reason, it hasn't happened. I'm in a long-abandoned old school building.

I grit my teeth and plunge out into the rain with a déjà vu feeling. Rain pummels me until Abby's wide-legged pants drag me down, clinging like a wet bathing suit to the leotard beneath it. They feel so tight that peeling them off will be like removing a layer of my skin. I imagine emerging like a butterfly, a whole new person from the one I was the last time I set off from home in a rainstorm.

Reflections of light stretch down into the pavement. An occasional set of headlights approaches me before cars whoosh by. Tires throw up small fountains of water.

I'm cold and miserable and sore, with a fever flaring up, but I propel myself forward.

It feels like I've been walking for hours by the time I finally reach my own street. When I see the green street sign, joy surges through me. I remember from eighth-grade English class how Odysseus finally returns home after wandering for twenty years, disguised as a beggar, and nobody but his dog and nursemaid recognize him.

Anxiety prickles as I wipe stray spits of rain from my face and thrust my way up the hill. Just a few more steps and I can collapse.

And then I catch sight of the empty lot next door to my house. The yellow house is gone.

A car splashes along the street and swings into Zach's driveway.

A figure emerges: it's him. I take off running.

"Zach," I call, flooded with joy.

He inches over to the edge of the driveway, squinting at me as I approach. He's wearing a McDonald's uniform. "Do I know you?"

"It's me!" I'm giddy, about to throw my arms around him, greasy polyester shirt and all.

He backs away. "I think you have me mixed up with someone else. Or maybe I'm having a weird dream."

He goes into his house, slamming the door in my face.

That slam reverberates all the way through me. Shock and disbelief pummel me like fists that I can't fend off.

How could Zach not have recognized me? It feels like his blank stare erased me from the earth. Completely obliterated me.

I try our front door. It's locked, so I go around back to the basement door. A thick padlock is looped through the handle.

A faint light glows in Mom's bedroom window. I return to the front to pound on the door. More lights flash on.

Through the front window, a shadowy figure appears at the bottom of the stairs and shuffles toward the door, unhurried. She unlocks it and peers out, squinting.

It's not Mom. It's an old woman. A pencil spears her white hair, resting behind an ear. There's a book of crossword puzzles in her hand.

"Who are you, and why are you banging on my door in the middle of the night?" she demands.

"Do you live here?" I must sound like a complete moron. "Where's Joan?"

She snaps on the porch light. "Joan who?"

"Joan Arlington?"

"Joan Arlington?" She sounds skeptical. "My step-cousin Joan? She's in Ohio. Where she's always been. Are you one of the foster kids?"

"The foster kids?" I'm stumped. Mom has foster kids? And a step-cousin?

Her gaze lights on my wrist. "That watch," she says. "They said those were destroyed." She raises startled eyes to my face. "Do you want to come in?"

I step inside the door and gaze around the living room, furnished with the kind of sectional couch and pressed wood shelves my mom hates. Before I can ask how she knows about the watches, she bustles up the stairs. She returns momentarily with a dry shirt and pair of elastic-waisted jeans. These clothes smell like powder and perfume, like old ladies, and they're totally not my style, but she and I are about the same height and size. My leo is still damp, but I leave it on to avoid having to explain. I think I'm getting a rash underneath it.

"Should I call Joan?" she asks me. "Will she be looking for you?"

I shake my head. "Who are you? What do you know about this watch?"

"I should be asking you the questions. Hang on, let me get my cell phone. Do you know how to work this? I wish I hadn't given up my landline. I can't hear on this thing." She vanishes into the kitchen, and idly I reach out and pick up a piece of mail on the table next to the door.

It's addressed to Elizabeth Grant.

Horror dawns.

For some reason I have a different last name, but the old woman rattling around in the kitchen is me.

I run. Bolt out the door and down the hill, legs churning, desperate to escape this 2018, where there is no gym and I'm a woman in my eighties.

What did Mrs. Grundy do? It's like the timeline has split and created a parallel universe. That woman, that version of me, would have been born around 1930.

Is that what she's planning?

I skid to a halt near the park and inspect myself. My arms, legs, and feet are all still here. So Mrs. Grundy didn't destroy my existence exactly.

She just left me homeless and timeless, with no choice but to wander in time forever.

Maybe I'm so tired that I'm hallucinating. I need to think.

At least the rain has let up, so I'm only slightly damp when I find a garage to take refuge in. Like most Bradford garages it's a stand-alone structure, this one with a regular side door in addition to those big heavy wooden ones that rumble as they lift up. There's no car in this one, just a bunch of broken furniture and a rolled up rug and a ladder on its side. The roof is leaking, a thin stream of water pouring down steadily.

I pull out Abby's tablet, flipping through the pages.

My birth certificate isn't there. It has disappeared. In this alternate universe, it has never existed. I turn the pages one at a time, shake the tablet, check the bottom of the backpack, frantic.

There is no me who was born in 2002 in this reality.

The seat cushions off a broken rocker make a half-decent pillow, but I'm too wired to sleep. I lie and watch water flow down from the ceiling, plunking to the floor, ricocheting off of it to splatter against an old armoire hulking in the middle of the floor.

I empty my backpack, taking out items one by one. The tablet, the knife, my food and water, my toothbrush. I confirm again that my birth certificate isn't there.

When I was five, I had strep. I remember trying to get up, then slumping back to my mattress. "This is terrible, terrible," I kept telling Mom. I remember hours of burning with heat and shivering with chills and feeling like my head and stomach were both trying to spin away like flying saucers.

This is even worse. This is terrible, terrible, and Mom's not here this time to bring me aspirin and tuck blankets around me.

Mom, the Mom I know, isn't anywhere.

Joan, a woman I don't know, lives in Ohio. And for some reason, she is my step-cousin.

A bad feeling has wedged itself between my ribs. I feel like I can't breathe. As the sky turns light, I haven't slept a bit.

Why did I think I could trust Mrs. Grundy?

I let her lull me into complacency. I didn't complete my mission. And this is the result.

I think about the gymnastics center. Why is even that gone? My existence or lack thereof shouldn't have affected the Y's acquisition and remodeling of that building, should it? It's not like I was in any way instrumental in bringing that about.

As soon as the public library opens, I claim a corner computer and google madly. Turns out that the gymnastics team fizzled out about five years ago. I remember how, when I was eight, the Y was getting ready to discontinue our team before I became the first level-3 competitor in western Pennsylvania. I remember how all of my older teammates told me that I was only allowed to compete because the Y wanted my money. How Mom reassured me that I was improving my skills and helping to save the team. "It's a win-win," she said.

I never really believed her. But now, having seen an alternate reality in which I never competed at the Y, maybe I really was the first domino in a chain reaction, falling with an impact big enough to knock down the next domino, and the next, and the next: one factor that caused the team to revive and then, finally, thrive. Even if minuscule, a factor.

When I google Elizabeth Grant, someone by that name pops up in the 1940 census. She was born in 1929 here in Bradford. Her mother was named Jillian Grant. I can't find any birth records for her, but then, beyond googling, I'm not really sure how to look.

But in this 2018, there are still news stories about a gymnast named Jillian Clayton who competed at the Olympic trials, was disqualified, and then dropped out of sight.

I still find references to Abigail Key, who was born in 1950 and worked at Zippo. Mentions of her stop completely after 1976. I can't find any death records.

I can't find any Harry Crakes, but there are four Harry Cranes in the Boston area.

I think of the name on the jersey of the boy Jillian was talking to outside the gym. There are hundreds of people with the last name Martin in Dallas.

My adrenaline abruptly wears off. I lay my head down on the table beside the computer and close my eyes, shutting out alternate 2018. I'm so tired that within seconds I doze off, obliterated entirely by sleep.

"Miss?" A librarian is standing above me, cautiously touching my shoulder. I snap awake and blink at her. The bright overhead lights burn my eyes. I wipe my mouth, afraid that I had been drooling. I don't recognize this librarian. In real 2018, my 2018, she would have been one of Mom's coworkers.

"Sorry," I mutter, staggering to my feet. Lean my whole body to push open the door and plunge out into the cool autumn air of this 2018, where a scattering of leaves still clings tenaciously to trees. The creek beside the library is full, rainwater rushing, spilling over its banks, so loud it's as if it's still raining.

A memory flashes: I'm walking with Mom in the park, holding her hand, the popsicle I'm eating breaking off and melting into a pool on the pavement. Bees float above the sweet puddle and the honeysuckle bushes. My sandals scoop up dirt, getting my feet dustier with every step.

I miss Mom so powerfully I feel like I'm moving through water, barely able to lift my heavy feet or push against the current.

Right down the street is the Dairy Queen where Zach and I ate ice cream and stared out at this same creek. That was only yesterday but a whole lifetime, a whole world, ago.

Everything looks the same, but Zach is a stranger and Mom is far away. And even if I found her, she wouldn't know who I am.

Maybe I could enlist the help of Alternate Zach. I invent an entire conversation with him in my head. I know exactly what he'd say, at least if he's anything like the real Zach. He'd tell me that if I have any hope of returning to a world where I'm my mother's daughter, I'm going to have to complete my mission.

I have to go back to the night of my birth. Maybe then I'll figure out how I ended up being born in 1929.

49

I'm standing in snow under the pines in the middle of a field. My house is next door, looming out of the shadows, all the windows dark.

I'm on the lot where the yellow house should be. The wind bites my cheeks and snow spreads out around me, a long flat surface with a few hilly drifts, untouched snow with no footprints. There's no place to hide, but no reason to either. I don't see my earlier self crouching behind a tree. There's no girl with a rounded belly stepping out of the shadows. No rustle of movement, of Mrs. Grundy appearing and then disappearing.

I'd be chilled to the bone even if I weren't standing up to my calves in snow.

I'm in an alternate timeline. There's no Jill. No me. No Mrs. Grundy.

What do I do now?

1988, I think. Mrs. Grundy is going to have to turn up in 1988.

I double-click.

50

I arrive in 1988 moments after I left what feels like years ago. I land on a pile of pre-vault mats.

It's early morning, the gym still dark and quiet. I hold myself complete-ly still even though my thoughts are whirring. What if this is a different 1988 from the one I visited before?

I ease my backpack toward me, unzip it, and feel around inside. Pull out the tablet and flip through its brittle pages.

A white page falls out. My birth certificate.

I break out in a cold sweat of relief. I still exist. In this 1988, the timeline hasn't split yet. There is still hope.

When I finally pull myself to a sitting position, I'm still shaking. It feels like shock has formed a shell around me, trying to protect me from knowing that my whole life as I know it could be wiped out in an instant.

Even when the dizziness and nausea pass, numb paralysis holds me there on the edge of the mat, weighing down every bone in my body. Moonlight slices across the room. Faraway traffic swishes. A door slams somewhere in the building, the last janitor leaving, probably. I ease out into the hall, cautiously sliding along the wall, prepared to duck into a doorway. I slip toward the stairs and then stagger up them as fast as I can go, which isn't very fast on shaky legs. My heart jackhammers. Blood thumps loudly in my ears.

And then I'm there, at the top, only feet from the closet.

Please let it still be open, I think, remembering how I popped the lock before I left.

It is. I tumble into the dark space, crashing into my corner cave under the mats.

In my dreams, the world is spinning, tilting toward the sun, then away again, spinning, spinning, always in motion, and then my cat Simone Biles is battering the door, trying to get into the closet.

At home, if I close my bedroom door at night, she throws herself against it, thudding repeatedly, until I wake up enough to let her in. Then she races past me, scolding me with a little trill in her throat, circling back to butt her head at me until I pet her.

I open my eyes, overcome by anxiety. But there's no cat pounding against the door, no cat lying beside me, snoring faintly. Just the sound of a janitor rattling the doors up and down the hall, making sure that they're locked.

I drop off to sleep again. I wake to find the sun directly overhead. Gulping down water, I pass out again, as if there are weights on my eyelids. Not even the hunger pangs that gnaw at me, not even the new urgency of my mission, motivate me to get up.

What if I do the wrong thing, make the wrong choice? What if no matter what I do, I never see Mom or Zach again?

I try to remember what day it is. I left 1988 on a Friday night, so it must be Saturday now. Jill is due to compete in Atlanta this weekend. My coaching job starts on Monday morning.

I slip into the bathroom, then return and pull my knees up in a fetal position, wrapping my arms around them, shrinking myself as small as possible. The smaller I am, the less I will feel that gut-twisting, immobilizing sorrow that grabs hold of me unexpectedly, sending chills through me. My teeth chatter uncontrollably. Even when I make myself a blanket of sorts from some locker-room towels and a roll of spring floor foam, I still can't stop shivering.

I've never lost a grandparent, like some of my classmates have. I've never even lost a pet. I had no idea that grief could be like this—this sharp ache, this constant churning. This feverish sensitivity across the surface of my skin. This feeling that I can't cry or run or do anything to release the tension that just keeps building and building.

I wake early Sunday morning from a kaleidoscope of disturbing dreams I can't remember. I turn my swirling thoughts to practical matters. I haven't refilled the Winnie the Pooh backpack in a while, and my supplies are getting low. The gym is closed on Sundays and the janitorial staff has vacated.

Still, I'm cautious. I dart from one doorway to the next, backing into shadows and listening. The fact that I'm working so hard not to get caught is a good sign, right? A sign that I haven't given up altogether. A sign that I still have hope. I listen to the silence a good hour before I dare feed coins into the vending machine. They clatter through the slot. The whir of the motor that pushes items off the trays is unbearably loud. Sandwiches, apples, chips, and granola bars drop to the bottom. I open the flap to retrieve them, stuffing them into my backpack. My heart feels like it's about to cartwheel right out of my chest as I refill the water bottle.

No one is here, so I take a long shower and scrub my hair, feeling as if I'm coming alive again as I rinse off days of grime. I wish I had a bar of soap, shampoo, and deodorant, but I make do with liquid soap from the dispenser and am grateful for the thin white towels the gym provides. After I'm clean, I rinse out the elastic-waisted jeans and long-sleeved pullover from my elderly self in alternate 2018, switching into the lost-and-found warm-ups I'd left hidden behind some old trophies in the supply closet.

My improved mood doesn't last. Lying in my cave, I'm desperately lonely. I spend another long night chasing away terrified thoughts and hot tears, unable to fend off the hollow sadness that seeps through me.

I think about how, when I was little, I worried that Mom would die and leave me alone in the world. It never occurred to me to worry that our whole relationship could be erased.

That everything could be gone, that the person I was and the person I most relied on no longer existed, just like that.

I relive the moment in Alternate 2018 that I called out to Zach in his driveway. Over and over, his face plays in my mind, looking at me without recognition.

I've always taken for granted that Zach would be there when I needed him.

That I could even ignore him for years and still pick up where we left off.

During my travels through time, I've anticipated the moment when I will land and find him there, waiting for me. I've rehearsed the stories I'll tell him. I've envisioned how proud he'll be of me. How eager to hear about my adventures.

I've imagined getting up the guts to kiss him.

But now what if I never see him again either?

Trying to lull myself back into sleep, I channel Mom, who used to walk me through deep breathing exercises when I was nervous before a meet.

"Your feet are so heavy," she would say. "Your legs are so heavy, they're like bricks, your feet and your legs feel so heavy it's like they're going to sink right through the mattress down to the floor."

And I'd feel every muscle relax, one by one as she named them. Feel my feet, my calves, my thighs, my pelvis, my torso, my neck, all of me go limp, and finally I'd drop over the side of a precipice into unconsciousness.

I want that now: that feeling that I'm floating there in space, caught by a cloud of sleep that holds my weight.

I lie on the mats, and in my head I try to recreate Mom's soothing voice.

51

DALLAS, MAY 23, 1988

7 A.M.

On Monday, when I finally emerge, I feel a little better. It's like when I arrived I was just an outline of myself, but gradually the color is filling in, and I'm becoming me again, with new hope. My limbs loosen up as I demonstrate cartwheels to preschoolers and my voice starts to come back to me as I praise pointed toes and straight legs. I keep glancing out the window of the gym, imagining Mrs. Grundy passing by.

I find some baked goods in the break room and half a granola bar someone tossed into the trash. My mood lifts. I'm starting to feel a little more like myself again.

Whoever that is.

The next afternoon, working with a five-year-old on beam, I'm distracted by every person who passes the window. I keep turning my head, looking for Mrs. Grundy. My student has neat cornrows woven with beads that click together as she takes careful steps, arms extended, touches her toes, and then rolls down to stand on her heel as she focuses on the end of the beam. She high-fives me good-bye outside the door when her mother comes to collect her. I turn, smiling, and come face-to-face with Jillian, standing there with her arms crossed.

I knew she was back. I've been expecting to run into her. Still, I almost drop my clipboard in the face of her up-close, real-life presence, with the gloss on her lips and the calluses on her hands and the bruises on her hips, the reality of her unaltered by the soft glow of magazine photo lighting.

And then she's actually talking to me, despite my misstep last time I saw her. "Hey," she says. "So you're the freak show who everyone says is my twin." She raises her hands to steady my clipboard. Hardened chalk has dried in her cuticles.

"We do look kind of alike," I choke out.

This is my birth mother, is all I can think.

"I know we're probably not related or anything, but someone said you're from Pennsylvania. I lived there when I was a little kid."

I know, I almost answer, but I'm busy searching her face for resemblances to Abby and to the little girl I met in 1976.

"A town called Bradford. Have you heard of it?"

Before I can formulate an answer, she says, "So how'd you end up here?" She sounds overly casual. She obviously suspects that something is up.

"My dad got a new job."

"I know this is a long shot, but in Pennsylvania, did you know someone named Gail?"

Now that we're face-to-face, I can see the two tiny freckles on her cheekbone. I wish I could tell her everything I know and ply her with questions, but if I announce that I'm her daughter, I'm pretty sure she'll think I'm totally crazy. I mean, who wouldn't? And I have to be cautious, anyway, remembering what Zach said about not changing the timeline. Except how do you know which actions are so big that they'll change everything, and which ones will just create insignificant adjustments?

So I just shrug. "Pennsylvania is a pretty big state."

She looks at her watch. "I gotta go." But then she looks back at me and calls, "I have a dinner break at five. Want to meet me?"

Suddenly, I feel optimistic.

Instead of telling myself over and over that things will be all right, for the first time in a long time, I think maybe they will.

In the athlete lounge, Jillian pops open her Tupperware container of leftover chicken and raw veggies, scrutinizing me the whole time.

"Did you know that I'm adopted?" she asks. "I feel like we must be related somehow."

"We might be." I watch her eat. I'm so hungry. I'm never not hungry.

"So tell me about yourself." She pops some broccoli into her mouth.

"What do you want to know?"

"I don't know, like when were you born? What are your parents' names?" Then she giggles, as if she realizes that those aren't exactly normal questions to ask someone you've just met.

But she doesn't apologize or change direction. She just fixes her stare on me, holding her ground until I answer.

I quickly select a date that would make me a couple months younger than her. I tell her that my parents are named April and Andy. She still doesn't look convinced.

"So are you originally from Pennsylvania, or Cleveland?" She shoves some broccoli spears toward me, a row of miniature felled trees.

Cleveland? She's obviously trying to figure out how I'm connected to Gail.

I just shrug, chewing the broccoli's rubbery stalks all the way up to the heads that crumble in my mouth. It's been a while since I've had fresh vegetables. I think how appalled Mom would be, so I eat every bite.

The thought of Mom casts a shadow over me.

I stop eating.

But Jill plows on. "Do you have a boyfriend?" Now she sounds more like a normal teenager.

"Not really. My best friend is a guy. Zach. He's kind of cute. What about you? Who was that guy I saw you talking to the other day?"

She hops up to heat her chicken in the microwave. Other gymnasts are filtering in for their dinner breaks, and she greets them and jokes with them before returning to the table with a steaming container.

"Can you keep a secret?" she asks me in a low voice, and I nod. "My schedule's really too busy for dating. But that guy was my boyfriend. He goes to my school. We were really serious." She looks at me speculatively, like she's trying to figure out how much of their conversation I overheard. "The breakup was mutual, though. I just didn't have that much time for him, and he didn't like that."

I nod. It's like we've both decided to pretend that I don't know that this is mostly a lie. That I didn't witness the moment they broke up. Or confront her afterward and embarrass her.

"I imagine it's pretty tough to fit in guys," I say carefully.

She shovels a last bite of chicken into her mouth. "Gotta get back to workout. We'll talk more later."

52

Early the next morning I slip into the viewing room to watch part of Jill's first workout. Her gaze rarely extends beyond her own small force field where she is intensely focused on the job at hand, the mechanical repetitions and adjustments of each skill. With a Walkman plugged into her ears, she warms up with stretches and a dance routine, lifts weights, jumps rope, runs the track. On floor, she works with her dance coach, then gives each apparatus forty-five minutes. Twenty to thirty vaults, five or six bar routines, eight beams, two runs all the way through her floor.

She's on autopilot, seemingly casual as she throws an effortless round-off back-handspring double-back dismount off the beam, then fudges the rest of her tumbling, not bothering to complete all of her runs or ham up her performance on floor. Her practices are boring, regimented, as if she's ticking off one task after another, like she's not really that into it.

Her coach murmurs to her quietly enough that I only catch some of his words. He wants her to work on containing her power so that she doesn't knock herself out of bounds. He doesn't seem too concerned about the way

she slides forward on her landings, I guess because, in competition, she salutes while she does it so that it looks like a stylistic choice rather than a
mistake. The judges still credit her with a stuck landing, the way they did
back when Nadia Comaneci did the same thing.

A couple of days go by without any opportunities to talk to her. Early
every morning, I'm tempted to just sleep, to shut out the world for a little
longer, but often I drag myself up and go to watch her again. I walk up and
down the halls periodically throughout the day, peering into every gym for
a sign that there's someone else here, hiding like me. I check every nook and
cranny of the locker room.

I jiggle the handle of the janitor's closet door. It's unlocked. It's much
smaller than the supply closet, with no place to hide.

In my practice leo and a second old baggy one that I retrieved from the
lost and found, I easily blend into the gym, but it seems like Mrs. Grundy's
age and old-fashioned clothes would make her more conspicuous.

Between teaching my classes, observing others, and studying for certification, I surreptitiously scavenge lounges, the viewing area, the space under
the bleachers for books, newspapers, change, and half-empty potato-chip
bags as well as expired yogurt and forgotten sandwiches from the fridge. I
am always on the move, looking for food, looking for Mrs. Grundy.

As soon as I get my first paycheck, I skip Jill's workouts and go out to
buy breakfast sandwiches at McDonald's and a pair of cheap sneakers at Tar-
get. I toss Abby's cracked leather lace-up shoes into a trash can. It's such
a relief, after ten days, to walk out in sunlight again, although I feel rattled
by traffic and horns and screeching brakes and changing lights after being
cooped up inside for so long.

That afternoon Jill approaches me in the hall. "How come you didn't
come to early practice?" She's pouty, like a little kid who's happiest when
someone's watching.

"Mom needed me to do chores the last few mornings." I hold my breath,
afraid she'll ask me where I live. But she doesn't. The word "Mom" feels like
ashes on my tongue.

"Well, come by tomorrow. You can meet me for dinner and tell me what you think of the changes we made to my beam."

And just like that, a routine develops. More often than not, I meet her for dinner after my afternoon classes. Jill's school has just let out for the summer, so she's in the gym for eight hours most days, and seems desperate to take a break by the time five o'clock rolls around. It's like she takes it for granted that spending time at the gym is just what you do when you love gymnastics. She doesn't ask why I'm there even on afternoons when I'm not coaching.

But while she doesn't question my constant presence, she does pay way too much attention to my vending-machine sandwiches. At first she just wrinkles her nose, but after a few days, she starts bringing double helpings of her own dinner, offering me half. I wonder if she thinks that my family is too poor to feed me.

Some days I walk to a nearby mall and branch library, just to look in windows or page through books in a comfortable chair. Everywhere I go, I'm on the lookout for Mrs. Grundy's glare and crown of braids. I've never been a patient person, and now it's torture that all I can do is watch and wait.

I feel certain that Mrs. Grundy is here somewhere, but as time stretches on with no sign of her, I doubt myself. My stomach clenches up like a fist that won't uncurl.

53

DALLAS, JUNE 3, 1988

5 P.M.

"So, I always thought that gyms like this made you weigh in." I watch Jill fish from her duffel a small bag of chips and a brownie, which she cuts in half. "I thought they were really strict about snacks. I thought that they banned junk food and searched your bags to make sure you don't have any." I've read these horror stories.

They made me glad I wasn't an elite gymnast.

"I've heard that about some places." Jill wolfs down her dinner. "Also, coaches who yell at their gymnasts and tell them that they're fat."

I've heard about this too. Coach Amy would never say anything like that, or Mom would have pulled me out of gymnastics a long time ago.

Jill snaps the lid on her Tupperware and tosses it in her gym bag. I notice that she has tied the frayed black shoelace to the zipper of her bag, turning it into a pull. "We do have to weigh in once a week, but I don't think anyone makes a big deal about it. Of course, I always weigh pretty much the same." Then, without any pause, she says, "I actually lost some weight right after my boyfriend and I broke up. I think it brought up all of my abandonment issues. Adopted people have a hard time dealing with abandonment or rejection. It makes us think about the first time we were rejected, when our parents didn't want us."

It feels weirdly ironic to be having this conversation with my own future birth mother. And to know how much Abby did want her. "How do you know your parents didn't want you?"

"Well, my mother disappeared and never came back." She stretches her leg out in front of her and dispassionately examines her feet.

"Maybe she couldn't come back. Maybe she got stuck somewhere."

"I did a school research project on adopted kids," she says. "We often feel like we can't get enough attention. Maybe that's why I'm a gymnast. Because I like it when so many people pay attention to me."

"Yeah, maybe." I hate it when people pay too much attention to me. At the same time, I was essentially adopted as a newborn and never knew it. It's only recently that I've felt abandoned, but I don't know who to blame. I no longer exist in my own timeline. My home, my whole life, has disappeared. Can you blame time?

I've been abandoned by time.

"Are you sure you never met my mother?" Jill leans forward, like she's never asked me this question before. "She disappeared when I was four."

"That would have been what, 1976? How would I know her?"

She narrows her eyes speculatively. "There's something about you. I can't quite figure you out." She examines me as if she's devoting the same single-minded focus to deciphering me that she applies to mastering her gymnastics routines. "You know how I told you that the breakup was mutual? It wasn't really. I think he was freaked out because he thought I was getting too serious."

"Really?" I carefully modulate my tone, making sure I sound detached.

"I thought Kyle was the one." She practically whispers the words.

Kyle, I think. That's his first name.

"The one what?" I ask.

"You know. The one and only."

"Oh." I don't want to say anything stupid and scare her away, but we're both way too young to think that way. I push away thoughts of Zach, the Zach I knew who may no longer exist. "You're barely seventeen."

"Some people meet the loves of their lives when they're even younger." She sounds defensive.

"He was the love of your life?"

I'm glad she doesn't think of him as a random hookup, this guy who I suspect is my birth father. But still, I don't buy it. Kyle, the love of her life? What if my crush on Zach isn't so silly after all? What if he's the love of my life?

I blush at the thought, it's so ridiculous.

Jill plops her feet back down on the floor and leaps up. I follow her out to the hall.

"I know you don't believe me," she says.

"I guess it's a really romantic idea."

"I thought he loved me. He said he did." She's walking so fast, I can barely keep pace with her. "You know, when you do this, when you live a life like this that's so totally focused on one thing, sometimes you wake up and realize that eventually this is all going to end and you'll have to start all over again and figure out what you want. Sometimes I think about that and I just freak. Like I just don't know what I'm going to do. Sometimes I imagine just changing my name and starting all over again, with no one else's expectations on me."

I think of the anguished boy I spoke to briefly in the entryway to the building. "Maybe he did love you," I say. It's obvious to me that she loves him. It's obvious to me, from that brief interaction, that he loves her. But if I tell her that, will my interference change everything?

I think of Alternate 2018 and swallow my impulse to help. I wonder if, in my own 2018, Zach was devastated when I never came back.

"You'll figure it out," I say to Jill, wishing I didn't sound so lame. All I know is that she will disappear from the news in only a few weeks, and I don't know where she'll go.

She shrugs and ducks into the gym, the lingering hurt abruptly erased from her face, and the next thing I know, she's back in the zone, swinging up onto the bars.

54

E very morning I prowl around the building, going into every bathroom, squatting to look at the feet at the bottoms of the stalls, peeking in every closet, examining every parent and grandparent waiting in the hall or the viewing room. I open all the lockers missing padlocks. Someone has left a tube of toothpaste in one of them. Could it be Mrs. Grundy's?

She has completely vanished. She couldn't be staying in a hotel without paying indefinitely, could she? If she's in 1988, where is she sleeping?

Jill catches me on my restless rounds, yanking me away to have lunch or dinner with her, talking nonstop as if she urgently needs me to know her story. How at ten she was adopted by the foster family she's lived with since she was four. How she took gymnastics classes from the time she was little, how her family relocated to Texas for her training, and how by nine she was an Olympic hopeful.

I know all of this, of course. It was in the Wikipedia article I practically memorized in 2018. I pretend that I'm just hearing it all for the first time. She tells me how she won junior championships, attended international camps, calculated how she could break into the top ten to qualify for World Championships and get a spot on the Olympic team for 1988. And now she's almost done it. She came in second at Worlds and she's getting ready for the Olympic trials, one event away from the one to which she and her family have devoted their entire lives.

Sometimes my mind wanders, spinning out plans. Like maybe I'll interview moms in the waiting area. Make up some story about why I desperately need to find Mrs. Grundy. She's my grandmother who has dementia and has wandered off. She's a stranger who dropped something valuable.

But either of those schemes might call attention to my search. I need to find Mrs. Grundy without her finding me.

As the days pass, I have to fight to hold on to my hope. I feel like I'm in limbo, stranded here with no control over what happens. I eye my watch but resist the urge to make myself sick again searching futilely for her.

After practice one night, Jill drags me outside. I haven't been outside at night in ages. As we sit on a bench outside the gymnastics center, something in me begins to revive. I'm mesmerized by the stars above and the breeze on my cheeks and arms. It feels so normal, as if my whole world hasn't been shattered.

When I stare up at the sky, I think how here in 1988, Mom is somewhere on this planet. This continent. Maybe she's looking at these same stars. I wonder what would happen if I went looking for her in this time.

But then what? She wouldn't know who I am.

She'd look at me the way Zach did, polite but uninterested.

"Sometimes I feel like a total fake," Jill confesses. She's stalling going to her car, returning home to bed, though she knows she has to get up early. This lack of discipline isn't at all like her. "I mean, I'm not that strong or fast. I just work really hard."

I notice how torn her hands are from the friction on bars. My teammates and I used to compare our rips, proud of them, but they were nothing like hers.

She has serious callouses. Her hands are tough as horses' hooves.

"But you're so good." We lean our heads on the back of the bench. The scoop of sky is like the valley of another universe, the world turned upside down. Some nights the homesickness feels unbearable.

"I'm really not that good," Jill says earnestly.

As we stretch out our legs and stare up, it feels like there's something about sitting side by side, not looking at each other, that encourages intimate conversation. "You seem so normal," Jill goes on. "I want to be like you. I've never been anything like other kids. My only friends are here in the gym, really, but they're not real friendships. I mean, we compete against each other."

After all of my time in the fluorescent lighting of the temperature-controlled gym, there's a gently mesmerizing melancholy about the summer night, the sound of crickets, the headlights of cars that slide to a stop over on the street, their doors opening to engulf freshly showered girls toting gym bags. I'm so tired, but in a different way from the way all of my time jumps make me tired. It's more a mental fatigue caused by stress and homesickness and sleeping lightly and trying to stay alert so I don't get caught hiding out in the closet. By tossing and turning and struggling to figure out my purpose, what I'm supposed to be doing, whether there's really a person named Mrs. Grundy or I've just dreamed her.

The life I knew from 2018 is feeling like a distant memory too. Like someone else's dream.

When I stop to count, I realize I've been time traveling for two months now.

"I've always felt sort of different too," I tell Jill, but she waves me away, disbelieving. I feel a little resentful that she's so caught up in her own drama that she doesn't fully see me, that I am something of a blank slate to her, her sounding board, someone she projects her own feelings onto.

But then I remind myself that I have cultivated this role in her life. That I can't risk her knowing me too well.

"I wish I *were* you, Anna," she bursts out. Most of what I've told her about me has been generic and super wholesome, presenting myself as someone nothing much ever happened to, a girl from a two-parent family who participates in gymnastics as a hobby. "I feel so pressured all the time. I'm going to the Olympics, you know."

She waits for my reaction. "Yes, I know," is all I say.

Of course I would know this even if she hadn't already told me. But she's repeated it to me several times with a mixture of pride and bewilderment and anxiety, as if she doesn't quite believe it herself.

You don't want to be me, I wish I could tell her.

"Gymnasts never feel good enough," she goes on. "You're so conscious of all of your flaws. Of every single fraction of a point you'll lose if you make the tiniest mistake. You know you can always be better. You can always improve your skills, you can always be higher in the rankings. You can never stop and rest and just be proud of what you did. You have to keep going or someone else will beat you." She yawns. "I know I need to get home, but this feels so normal, you know? Like if I weren't a gymnast, we could talk on the phone every night about boys and go to the mall on weekends. Do you know, I don't even have your phone number?"

"Oh, yeah, I need to give that to you," I respond vaguely.

The glass doors open and close, occasional blasts of air-conditioning reaching us. More girls flock out into the warm summer evening, some in groups, some with their mothers or fathers. Wearing street clothes and clattering bracelets, their hair wet, they cross the sidewalk to the parking lots or wade across a field of bluebonnets toward the cars parked on the street. All of them with homes to go to.

Jillian absently bites at her cuticles. "I keep having these nightmares. Like I'll dream that I do a perfect tumbling pass and then land out of bounds. Or that I can't do anything at all. I'm totally frozen."

"What if you did? What would be the worst that could happen?"

We stare into the wide expanse of sky, dark blue and velvety, like a blurry reflection of the bluebonnets.

There's such a long silence, I don't think Jill is going to answer. But finally she says, "I guess I've always worried that if I don't get the highest placements or best grades, my family will be disappointed. I'm so worried that I won't make the Olympics, and they'll feel like all of their sacrifices were for nothing. I'm so afraid of letting them down."

"I've felt kind of that way too," I admit, which sounds crazy since I know that the pressure on Jill to be perfect has always been so much more intense.

"Really?" As if she can't quite grasp this, Jillian repeats, "Really? You? But you have such a good relationship with your parents, right? Not that I don't. I mean, they do a lot for me," she adds hastily. "It's just that I was four when they took me in, so I remember my life before them. And if they could choose me, couldn't they unchoose me?"

I never for a second doubted that Mom wanted me. I never for a second doubted that I was the center of her life.

I can hardly bear to think about Mom, the ache of loss is so fierce.

No, I think. *I'm going to fix things. Somehow.*

I study Jillian, wishing I could tell her the truth. That Abby never got over the loss of her, that she missed her every day. That maybe someday, Jill will find a way to meet her too.

But I clam up, always unsure of what I can and can't say, what would inadvertently change all of our lives.

"When Mom disappeared, this social worker sent me over to the house next door where this woman lived, and we just sat and colored pictures. It was so peaceful and soothing," Jill says.

Jill has obviously gotten some of the details wrong, but I remember listening to her and Mom when they were coloring in the kitchen. I remember the pages I found in Mom's attic file cabinet: unicorns and stars and dolphins, the gray elephant and yellow daisies, the green elephant and purple daisies, the rainbow-striped puppy.

Jill looks dreamy, her gaze far away. "I just wanted to stay there. But then I was sent to foster care at Jim and Anne's. Eventually they adopted me, and I guess I had a pretty happy childhood. But I've never stopped missing my mom. And I've always remembered that woman next door. This is going to sound sort of cheesy, but I have this memory of her telling me there was more than one way to do things. Like trees don't have to be green and you don't have to color inside the lines. I think of it whenever I get a deduction for stepping out-of-bounds. Whenever I feel all boxed in."

Sometimes, out of nowhere, regret slams into me all over again, followed by terror.

Why didn't I appreciate Mom more? What if I never see her again?

Jillian tips her head back like she's gulping in the whole night, swallowing it up. It's so absurd to think that this teenager is my biological mom, this teenager who I mother more than she mothers me.

"Maybe someday I'll go to medical school," Jill says. "Like my dad. After I retire from gymnastics. And I want to do all of the normal stuff. Date, go to parties. Get married. Have children."

A little while later, back inside in my closet, I climb up on the mat pile, stand so that my eyes are level with the window, straining to see stars. Streetlights drown out their light.

The lonely, despairing feeling that comes on me every night begins to crowd in. But I remind myself that the stars are there, beyond the glare.

All the things I want are still out there, somewhere.

Once again hope pokes through my fear and grief like the points of faraway winking stars. Hope and determination.

I will figure this out. I will restore my life and never leave it again.

55

I've been here more than two weeks, and still not a single glimpse of Mrs. Grundy. I wonder if she's found some source of money, enough to rent a room or buy a car to sleep in. She got money from somewhere to buy me that hot dog back in Montreal.

As an adult, she can blend more easily into the outside world. I feel envious, on edge after a couple of close calls when a janitor appeared in the hall right after I'd escaped the storage closet in the morning, people popping into my makeshift home at all hours to grab stuff, and someone coming in and rooting for a long time while I held my breath in my corner behind the mat pile. My patience is wearing thin, but I go on searching every corner of the gym. "Taking a power walk?" ask janitors and coaches who I pass on my rounds each day.

I smile and walk faster, pumping my arms, taking deliberate breaths, watching for Mrs. Grundy.

When Jill invites me to her house for dinner and a sleepover, her mom picks us up at the gym. They both raise their eyebrows at my Winnie the Pooh backpack, but they're too polite to say anything.

The Claytons live in a huge, airy house with no separate rooms downstairs, just big open areas flowing into each other. Jill's doctor dad is balding, with a fringe of hair around his pink scalp. He's wearing a really ugly plaid tie. He makes jokes about the expensive care and feeding of gymnasts, and Jill just laughs. She is more moody toward her stay-at-home mom, who has fluffy honey-colored hair and a tanning-bed tan and seems anxious to make me feel at home. She seems like someone I could confide in, if I could confide in anyone without doing further damage to the timeline.

"Do you have a cold?" Jill's mom asks her when she sniffles. "Do you want any more salad? You need to put your warm-up suits in the laundry. You're starting to run low."

Jill bristles. "Stop babying me, Mom," she says.

I want to yell at her to be nice to her mom. To stop taking her parents for granted.

Both of them are very attentive to me. "That's so odd that you're both originally from Bradford," her mom tells me.

I glance sharply at Jill. "I looked up your job application," she says.

"That's weird," I choke out. "We're actually from the same small town?" I pretend to be shocked.

"We were just there a few months, but that's when we became Jill's foster parents," her mom says, and then, as an aside to Jill: "You were really too young to remember living there."

"I remember some things. Mom watching gymnastics on TV. And this babysitter who taught me to do a back handspring." She fixes her gaze on me thoughtfully.

After dinner she asks me if I want to see her room. As we climb the stairs, she runs ahead. "Wait a sec." She reaches inside the door and snaps off the lights. We enter a room that feels like a haunted house, everything glowing in the dark, emitting a faint greenish light.

There's a whole shelf full of dinosaurs and glow necklaces and alien figures with big bulging eyes, ghosts, a light saber, a model of a brain, a yo-yo, bouncy balls, a mobile. As their green glow fades and the room settles into darkness, Jill impatiently flicks the light back on and flops onto her bed, flipping a grimy, indeterminate stuffed animal as if it's a gymnast tumbling over the spring floor of her stomach. I sort through an overflowing bin of new, intact stuffed animals. "What *is* that?" I ask her as she tosses the animal into the air and watches it plop back to her bed.

"It used to be a dog," she says. All that's left of it is plush skin, most of its stuffing gone. I remember the fluffy stuffed animal she was carrying when she was sent to foster care. "I've had this since I was little."

"It's kind of more of a pancake than a dog now." I stretch out on the other twin bed.

"Yeah, I know, like one of those animals in a cartoon that's been flattened by a piano. One time when I was little, I was in a park and this woman came up to me saying something about dogs. Mom dragged me away. She said that the woman was probably homeless and harmless but I shouldn't talk to strangers."

She sits back up, still clutching the remains of her stuffed dog. "Here's the weird thing: I swear I've seen her since, or someone who looks like her, but then I think I'm just imagining it."

My heart quickens. "You mean recently?" Relief spills over me. So maybe Mrs. Grundy isn't a figment of my imagination?

"Yeah, this woman approached me at the gym the other day and started chatting about the Olympic trials. At first I thought she was a reporter and I kept dodging her questions because Mom is supposed to set up all of my interviews. But there was something familiar about her."

"Was she wearing a checked dress? Kind of old-fashioned looking? And coronet braids?"

"No, she had on jeans and a polo shirt. And she was really creepy. She kept talking about the trials and then suddenly she said, 'I know you're in trouble. I can help you.'"

I feel triumphant, surer than ever that 1988 is where Mrs. Grundy plans to wreak havoc. "Back up. Can you describe her? How old was she? What color was her hair?"

"I don't know, like a grandma? Kind of a gray color?"

That was my mistake, looking out for Mrs. Grundy's checked dress when of course she'd be savvy enough to blend in wearing updated clothes.

"You should be careful," I say. "She might be dangerous."

"Wait. What was that about a woman in a checked dress?" Jill doesn't wait for me to answer. With a funny look on her face, she continues, "The woman who Mom thought was homeless and harmless when I was little? I always remembered that she was wearing a dress that reminded me of our kitchen floor. We had a black-and-white-checked floor. And I remember there was something funny about her hair. Something different and really, I don't know, old-fashioned? Like in a book. I thought it was pretty. I guess maybe they were coronet braids. I didn't know that word."

My mind is racing. "So this week, where exactly did you see her?"

She flings her shell of a stuffed dog into the air again without answering. Maybe I pushed too hard, because she gives me a suspicious look and retreats, changes the subject. "Do you want to watch a video?"

She busies herself with a really chunky TV, a huge videocassette recorder, and a fat videotape while I stay silent, afraid of revealing too much. Afraid of going home next time and not finding any version of myself at all.

Jill lies on her stomach in front of the TV, laughing at some movie about a bunch of elderly people about to be evicted from their homes and tiny extraterrestrial creatures who arrive in flying saucers to save the day.

Where could Mrs. Grundy be? Could I have seen her and not recognized her, since I assumed she'd look the same in 1988 as in 1929?

Or, more likely, she's purposely dodging me.

By the time Jill falls asleep with her chin resting on the remains of her stuffed dog, I'm even more wide awake, mulling over how I'm going to track down Mrs. Grundy.

56

E arly one morning after tossing with nightmares and hunger and home-sickness and frustration, I slip out of the supply closet, sleep in my eyes. I ease the door closed and turn, crashing right into Jill. I startle so violently, it's obvious that I'm guilty.

"What were you doing in there?" Jill regards me sternly, arms folded.

An answer pops right out. "Just looking for another practice beam for my class."

"Wow, at seven a.m.? That's really dedicated." Her eyes narrow. "Have you been sleeping there?"

She storms away before I can answer. I wonder if she'll report me. I wonder if she'll ever talk to me again.

Worry gnaws at me all day as I pace through the building, treading the same path I walk every day. Maybe I should get out of here before Jill turns me in. But where am I going to go?

I think of Alternate Bradford in 2018. In 2002. Will everywhere programmed into the watch now be an alternate version of itself?

I slip into the lounge at dinnertime on the pretext of retrieving an expired yogurt from the refrigerator. Jill is there, waiting for me. As if nothing has changed, she doles out food for both of us and says, "This is so weird. I haven't been eating any more than I usually do, but I've gained a couple of pounds. And I'm so tired all the time."

She doesn't look to me like she's gained an ounce.

After she heats both of our portions, she flops down in an office chair. "My parents are convinced that we're somehow related."

She swivels from side to side, the chair squeaking rhythmically. She's always twirling and bouncing and jiggling her foot, but today is even worse than usual. I'm not sure if it's excess energy or nerves that keep her always in motion, always agitated.

"I told Mom and Dad that your parents travel a lot in the summer but you want to stay here for your job at the gym, and could you stay with us? Mom said that's fine. She wants your mom to call her."

I rein in my drifting thoughts. "Oh. That's nice, but—"

"But you'd rather sneak around and live at the gym? Or is it that you don't have a mom who can call her?"

I eye her warily.

She leans forward confidentially. "Okay, so here's what we're going to do. You're going to impersonate your mom and make arrangements with mine."

Suddenly, she blinks. Her eyes widen. She sits up straight. She swallows hard.

"Are you all right?" I look around for a coach or athletic trainer as Jill retches, then springs to her feet. She races to the small bathroom connected to the lounge. I hear her gag and heave some more.

When she returns, paler than before, she chooses a new, stationary chair to plop down in.

I suddenly feel queasy too. What if it's me that's making her sick? The beginning of me forming inside of her?

"I must have gotten some stomach bug." She takes deep breaths, holding her head steady. "I feel nauseated all the time."

"Maybe you shouldn't twirl around in chairs," I point out, then clam up. I'm not going to inadvertently do anything else that might change the timeline, even something as innocuous as being the one to plant the idea that maybe she's pregnant.

After Jillian tells her coach that she's feeling sick, we slip out of the building and walk down the street to the atrium of a closed bank where there's a phone booth. I poke the dime into the heavy rotary phone and let Jill dial. Her mother picks up right away.

"Is this Jill's mother?" I pitch my voice a little lower than usual. I close my eyes, imagining Mom inhabiting me, feeling her spirit, her words, take over. "This is Anna's mom. She says that your daughter invited Anna to stay with you while we're traveling for my husband's work? That's so kind."

I try to hurry the conversation along, but Jill's mom keeps asking questions. "So when are you leaving? Where are you traveling to? What does your husband do? How long will you be gone? Is it okay if Anna comes with us when Jill goes to Olympic trials, in July?"

Outside the scratched glass of the corner booth, Jill paces. I send her a frantic look, but she can't see me.

She sinks down onto the carpet and lies down, right there, flat on the carpet of the bank atrium.

I answer her mom's questions as best I can. "We're going to—um—Istanbul for a couple of months. My husband's in the international trucking business." I want to kick myself. Who drives their eighteen wheeler to Istanbul? I picture my blue-eyed dad taking a ferry across the ocean, sitting in the cab of his big truck.

"We're leaving first thing tomorrow," I stumble on. "Well, it sounds like there's someone at the door! Gotta go. Toodle-ooo!"

I slam down the phone, leaving a sweaty palmprint on the receiver. I'm pretty sure Mom has never said *toodle-ooo*, especially not in a fake British accent. Where did that come from?

But I'm excited, thinking about Jill's extra twin bed, with a mattress softer than a mat. I can't wait to burrow under all of the blankets, to sink my head into the plump pillow, to stay warm all night away from the over-air-conditioned gymnastics center, and to sleep soundly, unworried that someone is going to burst into the room and hear me snoring.

And, of course, now I can be closer to Jill. Be her bodyguard when Mrs. Grundy surfaces.

I think again of that knife in my backpack with a nervous flutter and wonder what lengths I will go to in order to preserve my own existence.

57

Whenever I encounter gray-haired women, mostly grandmothers who drop off and pick up their gymnasts, I feel downright rude, staring boldly into their faces. I'm embarrassed to admit that I might not recognize Mrs. Grundy even if I do see her, since I've never really looked at her that closely. I've always just thought of her as a collection of characteristics: a crown of braids, a shapeless figure in a checked dress. Even if I do see her, I might not recognize her face.

The gym closes for the Fourth of July. At a nearby park, Jill and her mom spread a blanket on the ground and we wait for dark, Jill dozing. "Do you think she's working too hard?" Jill's mom whispers to me.

On a sidewalk, kids light smoke bombs that trail exhaust and Roman candles that fizzle. Their sparklers carve through the dark, their light forming a ghost-like dance. It still makes me giddy to breathe fresh night air, even with the burnt smell that hovers, even with the pops and bangs around us that unnerve me as if I've just entered a war zone.

Jill's mom nudges her.

"Geez, Mom," Jill mutters, and struggles up to a sitting position, grass imprints wrinkling her cheeks. Just then, the fireworks finally begin to explode across the sky: the ghost of a Ferris wheel, a green gushing waterfall, a red blossom sprouting in one forceful heartbeat, petals of light drifting, autumn leaves cradled on the wind.

I wrap my arms around my knees, feeling that ache of homesickness as white lights shatter like popped bulbs raining sharp splinters of glass. The lights flicker, tremble, a sky full of jazz hands, a sky full of stars falling, falling, falling.

When I first came to stay at Jill's, I was braced to dodge dozens of questions, but she's generally too tired to ask them. She comes into her room after her shower each night, towel wrapped around her head, wearing a pair of pajamas with stripes that glow in the dark. She snaps off the light and hops into her bed, glowing like a ghost, and we gaze at the constellations pasted to the ceiling while she chatters about her day and then drops off to sleep seconds later. There's no transition: she goes straight from boundless high energy to immobile sleep.

Despite her exhaustion and bouts of nausea, as we near Olympic trials, she soldiers on, faithfully driving off to the gym for daily workouts. If I'm not teaching till afternoon, I take a bus to the center and walk up and down the halls, peering into the faces of older women.

One night, catching movement through the window of a small gym, I duck in to find Jill napping on a mat.

I don't disturb her. I wander on, scanning the faces in the parent viewing area, in the lounge, in the lobby and the pro shop, along the upstairs track.

Back downstairs, Jill stands blinking, her cheek creased, murmuring with her coach in the hall. "You need to take care of yourself and keep up your focus," her coach says. "You seem distracted, and you've gained a few more pounds."

Jill looks down at the floor, nodding.

"Everyone's going to think I'm bulimic," she tells me that night. "I think it's just stomach flu or something, but I can't seem to shake it. And why have I gained three pounds?"

I will her to figure it out. I want her to get prenatal care. But she's already moved on to complaining about her coach and the pressure she feels to make the Olympic team. Then she skips to Kyle. "Can you believe he dumped me? I thought what we had was real."

I wish I could tell her about seeing him the day after they broke up. From what she's said, it doesn't sound like she's spoken to him since. I feel bad for him. I wish I could urge her to talk to him. If she's pregnant, shouldn't he know about it?

And then she's off again. "I think it's just that being dumped by him made me feel insecure because it reminded me of being dumped by my mother."

"I'm sure your mom didn't mean to leave you. I'm sure something happened to keep her from getting back to you," I say for about the millionth time.

I feel resentful that I'm reassuring her about her mother while she's being totally callous, oblivious to the fact that she's about to become mine.

I'm drifting off when Jill says, "Anna? Are you awake? I can't sleep. My period is really late. Do you think I could be pregnant?"

I jolt all the way awake. Once again I'm glad that it's dark so she can't see me roll my eyes. I try to keep my voice steady. "How late are you?"

"A couple weeks."

"Didn't you start wondering two weeks ago?"

"Oh, gymnasts are always missing their periods. We don't have that much body fat."

"Didn't you and Kyle use protection?"

"Sometimes." Her voice is small. "We weren't always that careful. He was bad about it—he kinda expected me to take care of it. And I kept thinking, whatever happens happens, and maybe I'm not meant to do gymnastics forever, you know?" After a silence, she says, "Can you help me get a home pregnancy test?"

"Shouldn't you go to a doctor?"

"But I don't want anyone to know."

"If you're pregnant, they'll probably eventually figure it out."

"What am I going to do?" She sits up in bed. " I can't have a baby. That would destroy everything I've worked for." She dissolves into tears. "And can you imagine how much it would hurt to have a baby?"

I lob a box of Kleenex toward her. I want to be nice and compassionate, but this is me she's talking about.

"Do you know that if I had a baby, it would be the only person in the world I know who is my blood relation?" She narrows her eyes at me. I hold my breath. Then she lets out a sob and glances, alarmed, toward the door, lowering her volume. "I'm pretty sure it's against the rules to compete in the Olympic trials if you're pregnant," she says.

I remember a stray fact from my research. "You know that Larissa Latynina competed while she was pregnant at the 1958 World Championships?" When I was working on my paper, I read something about how she liked Borsht and Ukrainian dumplings but still looked like a ballerina.

"So maybe I could still compete?" Jill says hopefully.

"Well, probably not." I think better of my Larissa Latynina fact.

Jill thumps her leg rhythmically on the bed, another nervous habit. "What if I go to trials and make the Olympic team? If I'm pregnant now, I'd be what, three months along by the Olympics? What am I going to do? God, maybe I'll just drop out of gymnastics and disappear. Say I have an injury." She sounds briefly hopeful before her tone becomes dejected again.

Then, all of a sudden, she's sound asleep, her breathing soft and even.

Unbelievable. I'm wide awake and stressing out, and she's sleeping like a baby.

58

T he next day during Jill's practice, I slip out to a drugstore to buy a pregnancy test, stuffing it way down into the dark depths of my backpack. That night, by the time I finish helping her mom with the dishes, it's time for *The Wonder Years*, a show that Jill likes.

But she's not in the family room. I find her instead in her room, on the bed, staring at the plus sign on the stick. She looks up at me with swollen, bloodshot eyes.

"You got the test out of my backpack." I wonder what else she found, rooting through my stuff in order to retrieve the drugstore bag. The knife, the tablet, the watch, my birth certificate?

"It's positive," she says dully, stating the obvious. Though I knew she wasn't going to welcome the news of her pregnancy joyfully, my stomach still feels all shriveled up, tight and tense, knowing that my birth mother's first reaction is a negative one.

Jill drives us to Planned Parenthood early the next morning where she finds out that she's six weeks along. I already guessed this, but still can't wrap my head around it and the idea that I should have been born in 1988, not 2002. Not 1929.

That's me in there. An embryo, the size of a pea, according to the pamphlet the clinic gives Jill. I have little buds where my arms and legs will be and dark spots where my eyes and nostrils are developing.

"This is going to be all over the news," Jill tells me, her keys dangling from the ignition because she has forgotten to start the car. "As soon as people find out, my gymnastics career is over." She gives me an assessing look. "So," she says, suddenly calm. "What do I do?"

"Well, I think you should—"

She leans forward and interrupts with a hiss. "No, I don't want to know what you think I should do. I want to know what I DO do. You know, right?"

"I don't know what you're talking about," I say evenly.

She slumps back and closes her eyes.

All day, I desperately try to formulate answers if she asks this question again. I think of Zach's rules. *Don't try to save loved ones. You can't undo the past.*

But would it break the rules to encourage the past to unfold the way it's supposed to?

That evening, Jill lies in bed, agonizing. "My parents relocated for me," she says. "They moved to Texas so I could train. How can I let them down like this after everything they've given up?"

I can't summon up any words. I'm not sure I would have any wisdom to impart even if I weren't so afraid of interfering.

"I've never had a normal life," she says. "And now I'm going to be a teen mother? What would you do if it were you?"

Sometimes I just want to crack. Split apart.

Stop having to be so detached, such a good friend.

Sometimes I'm so tired I can hardly stand it.

She's so quiet that I think she's fallen asleep. She sniffles.

"I can't do it," she says. "I can't. I can't do this."

I'm trying to be patient, but I'm angry. She's not thinking of her baby at all.

If I were her, maybe I wouldn't be having profound maternal thoughts either, but it still makes me irrationally mad that she's not.

"I always felt so lucky," she sobs. "My timing was so perfect. I was set to peak at exactly the right time—seventeen during an Olympic year. I used to wonder how I could possibly be any luckier." She flops over, burying her face in her pillow.

After a while, I hear her get up to pee. She comes back to bed and seconds later is up again, back to the bathroom.

She's up and down for a couple of hours while I doze off and then wake again and again.

She snaps on the bedside lamp. The light shines right in my eyes, startling me.

"Wake up, Anna," she says. "There's something I need to show you."

I sit up, blinking and groggy, while she rummages through a desk drawer, finally extracting a small pink plastic child's toy purse. It's dingy and its clasp is broken.

She pulls out a ring, silver with a murky black stone affixed to it, an old mood ring that no longer seems to change colors. "These were my mom's. I have no idea why I took them. I mean, I was four. I guess anything that had been hers was comforting."

I sort of get that. I wish I had something that belonged to Mom. Even a shoestring.

Next Jill removes a Chronowatch—the third prototype, the one with the red strap.

"This was my mom's too," she says. "Her job was designing watches for this company. I guess this was one of her designs. But actually"—she fixes her gaze on me with disconcerting intensity—"I think it had something to do with why she disappeared."

"Why do you think that?"

"I just have this vague memory of her tinkering all the time with a watch like this. I used to think of it as her magic watch, like it could make her invisible or something, because she'd put it on and then I wouldn't be able to find her and then suddenly, there she'd be again. Don't you think that's weird?"

I don't reply.

"You know what's even weirder?"

I just shake my head.

"You have one just like it. In your backpack. I wasn't meaning to snoop. I was looking for the pregnancy test. But why do you have a watch just like this one?"

I think back to the day I confronted my mother with questions about my origins. How pale and nervous she was, how quickly she changed the subject.

Maybe that was because this is all too weird, too impossible, too unbelievable.

I remember how careful Abby was about telling me the truth. Now I understand both of them better. How can any of this make sense? And how much can I safely reveal?

Every time I'm tempted to spill everything, I think of eighty-something me, and my stomach clenches, and I clam up.

I can't do anything else that might change the timeline.

"You know that woman I saw at the gym?" Jill asks. The question is vague, but of course I know right away that she's talking about Mrs. Grundy. "She was wearing a watch like this, too."

"If you see her again, you have to tell me right away," I blurt out, and then, before she can ask any more questions, I leap out of bed. "I'm going to the bathroom."

Jill yawns and lays her head down on the pillow. I know that she'll drift off in seconds. I know that she isn't capable of staying awake long enough to demand answers from me.

I pace, agitated, marking a path between the sink and the bathtub. Where is Mrs. Grundy? Patience has never been my strong suit, and right now, with so much energy pent up inside me with no release, I feel about to fly right out of my own body.

I picture myself on the uneven bars, flowing from the low bar to the high bar, swinging around them in circles, leaping across the floor, channeling some of this excess energy that threatens to burst me wide open.

59

I miss the bars, but mostly, when I think about gymnastics, I miss the dancing part.

When I moved up to optionals a few months ago, I talked Mom into contacting a custom music company for an arrangement of the song I'd chosen, "A Thousand Years." It was too slow, really, for a floor routine, the custom music company told her. Beautiful, elegant, not suited for showing off tumbling power and skill.

But I didn't want to tumble, I wanted to dance. I asked Mom if we could hire a local dance teacher to help me with choreography.

In the evenings Mom drove to Red House Beach at the state park after it was deserted for the day. I'd put on my music and dance in the sandy dirt while Mom read under a tree.

I liked practicing when it was just me, stretching and turning, flipping into my aerial cartwheel, doing a roundoff and two back handsprings, avoiding the back tuck I was supposed to include. I swam out to the dock and danced from one end to the other, thinking about Zach even when I tried not to. I liked dancing out there, just me on those wood planks floating on the water, my own island.

Now, desperate to ward off my constant agitation, at dinner I tell Jill that I want to get back into the gym. She's way more enthusiastic than I expect.

"We should get you ready for a zone meet," she says.

"An elite qualifier? Oh, no, I'm not close to good enough for that," I protest. I remember being so excited about competing at a USAG meet alongside gymnasts on elite tracks.

Was I really excited about the competition itself—or about impressing Zach?

"You don't know until you try," she singsongs.

"Oh, I know," I say, but she won't believe me.

In fact, she won't stop talking about it, like she's seized on this as a distraction from her pregnancy, and I totally regret ever bringing it up.

"We have the same body type," she says. "I'll bet you're way better than you think you are."

"I'm not," I keep replying, but she won't listen.

"Let's see what you can do before I go back to practice." She smiles expectantly. I haven't seen her smile in ages.

Reluctantly, I follow her to one of the small gyms.

"I'm out of shape. I can't really do much." I lean into what feels like the freefall of my front hip circle on the low bar, then execute a wobbly squat on before I miss my kip to the high bar.

"You're just out of practice," she says, sounding doubtful as she watches me. "Let's see what else you can do."

I show her part of my beam routine. I'm steadier than I expect, but mostly I walk through it, narrating my tumbling passes.

By now she's having trouble keeping the shock off her face.

"I told you," I said. "I'm not like you. I'm not anywhere near as good as you."

We move on to floor, where I once again run through the choreography but leave out my tumbling runs.

"Oh, sometimes I skip the tumbling too during practice," she says, letting me off the hook. "I like to save my energy for competition."

She's being nice, I think, sounding a little like a mother though she has no idea that she's actually mine. She makes suggestions about my hand and head and foot positions, compliments the intricacy of my footwork, and sometimes asks me to repeat moves so that she can try them out herself, like my pops and locks and my running man.

"So cool," she says. "Where did you learn this?"

"They're hip-hop moves," I answer without thinking, and her brow furrows.

"Hip-hop?"

"It's popular where I'm from," I say.

"Like rap?" she says. "I always thought Bradford, Pennsylvania, was pretty white."

"Well, yeah," I say, and execute a barrel roll, thereby shifting the subject to ballet. We practice some jetés and pliés. Dance steps are actually something I'm better at than Jill. I remember wistfully the ballet lessons I took when I was young.

"Okay, I think we should start with some conditioning." She shifts into take-charge mode, planning a program of conditioning, running, push-ups, and jump-rope exercises that sound perfect for tiring me out so that at night I can't lie awake fretting.

Sometimes it seems like Jill is two different people. An anguished, terrified teenager at night, worrying aloud and crying while the glow-in-the-dark items, after absorbing light all day, glow greenly in the room, fading slowly. A confident gymnast by day, all business, completely focused on her preparations for the Olympic trials.

After my classes and some conditioning, I meet Jill for dinner, where she talks nonstop about the trials. "Forty percent of our scores will be from the US Championships, which means that sixty percent will depend on how I do at the trials," she says. "There's no coach's discretion this time—our scores will determine who's going to get the seven slots for Seoul."

A couple of other gymnasts are giggling in a corner, and another is hovering near the microwave, so I speak as quietly as possible. "You're going to be what, more than two months along by then?"

"Two months what?" she asks, as if she's forgotten that she's pregnant. "There are twenty-three women and seven slots. So even if I weren't going in as a favorite, I'd have an almost one in three chance of making it. Phoebe Mills already has a pretty strong lead. The real fight is going to be for the fifth and sixth spots, and the alternate position."

I sigh, knowing that Jill will drop out of the trials.

That for some reason she'll be disqualified, though I don't know why.

That night Jill comes out of her denial to agonize, asking me again and again questions she doesn't really expect answers to. "How am I going to tell my parents? How am I going to tell my coaches? I wish I could just disappear and have this baby and then go back to my life. Everyone's going to be so disappointed in me."

What if she could? I wonder as we lie there in the dark.

What if she could just travel to 2002, have me, then return to 1988 and resume her life as it is? Come back to the brink of the Olympic trials, no longer pregnant, and continue her training?

But that's not what happened, is it? If I were to help her do that, we'd be creating another alternate timeline.

It bothers me that she's so focused on the end of her gymnastics career, the disappointment of her parents, and the pain of childbirth that she can't conceive of her baby as real. It gives me a bad feeling, knowing how little attachment she has to me. But then, she's young. What if it were me? How mature would I be? I try to forgive her at least a little, since her mother abandoned her when she was little, and she doesn't have the comfort of knowing that her mother's disappearance was an accident.

All she knows is that she didn't start out with a mother that she could rely on, and maybe, as a result, she doesn't know how to be reliable herself. Except she's had her adoptive parents all these years, and I can't imagine any other parents you could count on more.

I wonder if she is ever going to tell them. I wonder when she's going to start making decisions. But honestly, if she had owned the fact that she was pregnant, if she'd let herself fall in love with me, would she have left me with Joan? Maybe her disbelief and denial are a good thing, even if it hurts.

On Tuesday afternoon, following an older woman through the halls, I open my mouth to shout out Mrs. Grundy's name. Then I realize I don't even know Mrs. Grundy's real name.

60

Dallas, July 13, 1988

9:45 a.m.

J ill's mom is always fussing over her, insisting that she sit down and eat a healthy breakfast before workouts, packing vegetables and lean chicken for her lunch, reminding her to get to bed early. "Okay, Mom," Jill says impatiently, brushing her off. I look away, swallowing my envy.

After Jill leaves for the gym one morning, I'm reading in the breakfast nook when her mom bustles in to neaten the room. She gathers the butter dish and salt and pepper shakers, whisking away my empty cereal bowl just as I leap up to carry it to the sink.

"Oh, no, finish your chapter," she says, but I'm distracted watching her wipe the table and clear away newspapers, and I can tell that she wants to say something to me but is reluctant to interrupt.

I set down my book.

"Do you think—" She busies herself running a dust rag over the hutch and china cabinet before she turns back toward me.

For a second the expression on her face is familiar: wistful, uncertain, her narrow nose and ruddy cheeks reminding me, briefly, of Luke, though right now her features are pinched with worry, with none of his carefree charm. Of course, I'm primed to see resemblances in everyone around me.

Jill's mom moves her mouth soundlessly for a moment until I rescue her. "You're worried about Jill," I say.

"Is something going on with her? Is she all right? Am I allowed to ask these questions without making you feel like you're betraying your friend?"

"She's going through something, I think. But she'll be fine." I hope that's true, since I don't really know whether she'll be fine.

"The Olympics were always her dream," her mom says. Anne. She keeps telling me to call her Anne, but I'm self-conscious about it, and in my head, I still think of her as "Jill's mom." "We've put so much into this. Left our life in Illinois behind, moved here, sacrificed so much. But if this isn't what she wants, if it's too much for her, her well-being is the most important thing to us. We want to do what's best for her. But she's come so far. It would be a shame to just throw it all away."

She rushes on: "I'm glad she has a friend like you. Thank you for looking after her."

At first I think that the conversation is over and that she's going to return to cleaning the kitchen, but she paces back from the door and sits down at the table. "I swear that you and Jill have to be related somehow," she says. "But I never got much information about Jill's birth mom or her family."

She rises and sinks a couple of slices of bread into the toaster she keeps on a tray right next to the table, goes back to the kitchen to retrieve the butter dish she put away.

"But you lived in Bradford at one time?" I ask.

"My father was from there," she says.

It feels like small firecrackers are going off in my brain. Like there's something I'm not quite getting.

"What was your dad's name?" I ask her. "Maybe I know him."

"Oh, no, he would have died long before you were born," she says.

The toast pops up and she plucks it out, buttering it but then leaving it uneaten on a plate.

"This is going to sound really crazy, but my grandmother told me on her deathbed that I was going to adopt a little girl. She was oddly specific about it. I was only seventeen, and I'd made the trip back to Bradford with my dad to say good-bye. He was expecting to be appointed the executor of her will, and thought he was going to inherit one of the houses that she owned since he was the oldest boy. He was already making plans to move back there. So, anyway, I was sitting by her bed and she told me that there was going to be a child who needed a home here in Bradford someday, and I needed to be ready to foster her. I was pretty sure it was all just the ravings of a woman on morphine, but that conversation planted a seed. I wasn't even sure if I'd heard her right."

"So your dad inherited the house? And that's why you moved back to Bradford?"

"Oh, no, that was the thing. For some reason, his mother left all of the property to her stepdaughter's daughter. Both houses. You'd think she would have at least divided them up between her kids. He was pretty bitter about it. He'd already sold the house in Illinois at that point. My parents were divorced and I was living with Mom, but I visited him in Bradford occasionally. And then when he was diagnosed with early-onset Alzheimer's, Jim and I moved back to be near him for the last year of his life. That's where we became Jill's foster parents. The best thing that ever happened to us during one of the worst things that happened to us."

"Well, everyone pretty much knows everyone in Bradford." I try to sound offhand, but my heart is thudding. "Do you know the name of the step-granddaughter? And who did you say your dad was?"

"I'm embarrassed that I don't remember my grandmother's first name—I just knew her as Grammy. My step-aunt, the one whose daughter ended up with the house—I just knew her as Aunt Wren. I don't remember her married name. Or honestly, her daughter's name. We visited sometimes when I was little, but the family kind of splintered after Grammy's will."

I feel my brow furrow as I take all this in. I repeat my question again. "What was your dad's name?"

"Bob," she says. "Bob Grant."

"Robert," I breathe.

"Yeah, yeah, Robert Grant," she says.

"And your name is Anne," I say. "Like Anna."

She gives me an odd look.

"Sorry, it just occurred to me that we have almost the same name. Is Anne a common name in your family?"

"No, my father always said I was named after a distant cousin. Someone he knew when he was small. He always had such fond memories of her. It made me wish I'd known more of his family, but they were all pretty scattered."

I'm trying to put it all together. Anne is Robert's daughter—and my namesake? At least the namesake to my fake name? And Wren?

I puzzle for a second, and then I know.

Catherine. Who was Catherine's daughter?

Why would Abby have left everything to Catherine's daughter, causing such bitter feelings, causing a split among her kids?

Unless she knew that the house next door needed to be vacant in 1972 so that her alter ego, Gail, could move in.

Unless she wanted to be sure that when Jill was left all alone, there would be someone next door to take care of her.

But it still doesn't make sense.

Why not leave everything to Robert, or Anne and Jim, the ones who ended up raising her?

Unless Catherine's daughter was my mother, Joan.

61

I'm supposed to go to the gym to work out and then teach, but instead I find myself making notes, examining all of this information from every possible angle. My mind racing around and around in crazy circles, I sketch out a family tree.

The result is always the same: Mrs. Grundy is my great-grandmother and Jill's step-grandma. Luke is my grandfather and Jill's stepfather. Anne is my cousin and my grandmother. My mother's step-grandmother is my great-grandmother and my step-grandmother. And so on and so forth, and my brain hurts.

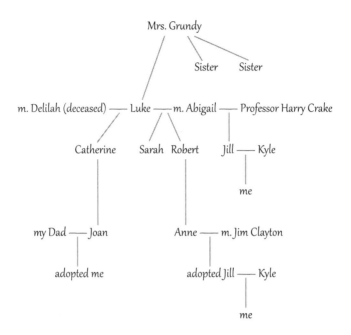

62

SALT LAKE CITY, AUGUST 3, 1988
6 P.M.

W e arrive in Salt Lake City on a hot July afternoon.
"You two can share a room if you want," Anne says as she checks us in at the hotel desk. "But no talking at night. Jill, you need to get as much rest as possible."

Jill hasn't been talking much lately anyway, busy at the gym for up to nine hours a day, constantly willing her body to cooperate, pushing through her fatigue and bouts of nausea. The tension in my body has been so acute I can't even work it off on the bars or the track.

She continues to give interviews. She's still a favorite for the Olympic team. She is still, by all appearances, working hard. But she's cautious and distracted, and she does the minimum amount of tumbling she can get away with. Jill's coach seems exasperated and puzzled about her slipping commitment.

At bedtime she goes straight to sleep every night without saying much. She and Anne both seem out of sorts because Jill's coach isn't allowed to go with her to trials. A coach has been appointed for her by the Gymnastics

Federation. She flops on a bed in our hotel room while I unpack. I can't believe we're here. I can't believe that Jill thinks she's going to go through with this.

For about the millionth time, I wish Mom were here. I spent my life ignoring her advice, but now I want it. I want someone wiser than me to tell me what to do.

Jill snaps on the TV and we listen to coverage of the trials on ESPN.

"More than fifty gymnasts are here for ten days of intense competition," a reporter breathlessly explains. "And right now, anything can happen. Will Kristie Phillips be able to come back from her disastrous World Championships? Will Michelle Berube, returning from retirement, make her second Olympic team? How will Tim Daggett do after shattering his left leg nine months ago at the World Championships?"

There's a clip of Tim Daggett. "The sound of my bone snapping was like a gunshot," he says, grimacing.

The camera flashes back to the reporter. "Will the back injury that kept Sabrina Mars out of US Nationals also make it impossible for her to make the team? What about Scott Johnson, who's competing with a pin and two screws in his right hand?"

Jill and I exchange a glance. The media hasn't gotten wind of the biggest story: Will Jillian Clayton actually try to compete while pregnant?

At nine we turn the lights out. I can hear Jill sighing and flipping from one side to the other.

"Mom used to talk me through relaxation exercises when I couldn't sleep," I tell her. "Try this. Imagine that your feet are getting heavy, like weights, like fifty-pound barbells, they're so heavy they're sinking down into the mattress, making it sag. Your calves are heavy, so heavy . . ."

Even when Jill breathes softly and steadily, my brain won't settle down. I roll over from one side to the other and back again. I put a pillow over my head to block the tiny red light of a smoke alarm flashing near the ceiling. When I finally wake up mid-morning, Jill has left for practice. I grab a bagel from the breakfast room and go in search of the arena. Outside, it's sunny and at least ninety degrees, but inside, it's dim and cool and airy.

I flash my pass and perch on a padded metal seat halfway up the risers, quickly caught up in the dramas unfolding before me. I groan with the rest of the crowd when 1988 world champion Dan Hayden falls twice on his final event and loses his slot on the team.

I cheer with eight thousand people when Tim Daggett sets off on his choppy run down the vault runway, the first time he's competed a vault since his injury.

I watch closely, holding my breath, worried that he's going to break his leg again.

"He hit the board firmly and squarely," says the announcer. At first his voice is hushed, but then it rises in excitement. "Did you see the strength of that heel drive into his handspring before he snapped the tuck and then kicked out? That landing is right on! One hop, a step—the triumph of a courageous will over an incalculable fear!"

The crowd leaps to its feet. I'm swept up with them, rising without planning to, clapping like mad, moved and inspired by this feat.

I could stay rooted to this seat for hours, caught up in the stories of all of these guys as, one after the other, they face down obstacles, failing with dignity, succeeding with aplomb.

I temporarily forget about myself and my own obstacles, though I never shake off my constant low-grade dread.

There's a lull. My dread blossoms into a full-blown ominous feeling. Watching all of these cute, muscular gymnasts lift and throw themselves up high and slam themselves to the ground, all I can think of is what this will do to Jill's body, and mine.

When I go looking for Jill, a coach blocks me from entering the women's locker room. "You can't come in here, athletes only."

"It's okay, she's my sister," Jill calls. She's swaying forward, doubling over, on a corner bench. Lockers slam while other gymnasts come and go, glancing at her with concern.

When our section empties out, she murmurs, "I've been keeping my tumbling pretty light, but just now, when I did a back handspring, it felt like I stretched my abdominal muscle a little bit. I'm so afraid I'm going to pull or strain something."

Another gymnast passes us, and Jill raises her voice to a normal volume. "At least I'm not scheduled to go first," she says. "The girl who goes first always gets the lowest score."

"This is such a bad idea," I whisper. "You should be avoiding anything high impact."

Even though I'm whispering, she looks stricken and waves at me to keep my voice down. "My stomach hurt when I did a back tuck too. I don't think I can go through with this. But if I don't, the media's going to find out and then everyone will know."

"Ma'am, you can't be in here," calls out the coach who has appointed herself the guardian of the locker-room door. We watch her escort out a brown-haired woman in a black pantsuit.

Jill leaps up, seizing my arm. "That was her," she hisses. After a split second I take off running, arriving at the door just in time to see a fit, tan older woman rush off down the hall, threading between clusters of people.

I skid to a stop when a toddler wanders into my path. A woman blocks my view as she retrieves him.

By the time I maneuver around them, Mrs. Grundy is gone.

She dyed her hair? I keep thinking. Why didn't that possibility occur to me?

I've always thought I was good at identifying people by their physical features, but all I was looking at were her hair and clothes. How could I have been so blind?

lllll lllll

"What are you going to do?" I prod Jill that night in the hotel room.

"I don't know," she says miserably. "I'm supposed to start on vault tomorrow. Vault is quick. Maybe I can do that at least."

"That's a terrible idea." I'm getting angry. We've come all this way because Jill refuses to face her predicament and make a decision. If she were a friend who were behaving this irrationally, I would probably spill to her mother.

But sometimes it seems like I don't really have any control. Like events are going to unfold the way they want to unfold regardless of my intervention. Like all of the events of my life are predestined.

But then I think uneasily of my attempt to return to 2018. Somewhere, somehow, something took a wrong turn, and it changed everything.

Doesn't that mean that we still have choices?

All I know to do is caution Jill to be careful of Mrs. Grundy, but repeating my warnings a million times doesn't cause a magical shield to form around her. It just irritates her.

Despite every sign that competing is a bad idea, she shrugs off my concern and shuts herself into the bathroom to take a hot bath. She emerges in a billow of steam that races out to cloud the mirrors in our room. In her glow-in-the-dark pajamas, she is sound asleep, curled up on her bed before the steam has even had a chance to dissipate and while the pajamas are still glowing.

63

SALT LAKE CITY, AUGUST 5, 1988
6:25 A.M.

Jill leaves the room before sunrise, tiptoeing so as not to wake me, but I spring awake anyway. I'm too wired to go back to sleep. Instead of taking the time to wash my hair, I braid it tightly and throw on a baseball cap. I toss on a T-shirt and shorts and grab a bagel at the breakfast bar. I'm too on edge to eat.

I hit the pavement as a tip of sun appears above the clouds, scattering light across them, turning them pink and yellow and orange. The calls of birds are louder than the traffic at this time of morning.

What if I finally come face to face with Mrs. Grundy? Shouldn't I take the knife? The thought makes me queasy, but I turn back. In the hotel room, I reach for the knife.

It's not there. I empty the backpack. The watch is there, and the tablet. But not the knife. And not my birth certificate either.

I strap on the watch, my uneasiness sharpening as I walk to the arena. There, I check the locker room, the practice gym. I scan the faces of gymnasts as they run through practice vaults and tumbling passes. I can't find Jill.

If I weren't so tense, I'd be moved by the cold emptiness of the competition gym before the crowds arrive. A work crew makes last-minute adjustments, running final safety checks on the bars and vault. Anne is one of the sparse spectators who has already claimed a seat in the stands. She hurries over to me. "Did Jill come with you? Do you know where she is? No one has seen her."

That bad feeling rises in my chest again. Maybe Mrs. Grundy has gotten to her. Maybe they've both disappeared without a trace.

"She missed her equipment touch a while ago. This isn't like her," Anne says.

I offer to look around the arena while Anne checks the hotel again. I poke my head into all the banks of lockers, the showers, the restroom stalls. I pass a girl staring at the wall as if deep in meditation, headphones in her ears. Another girl practices jumps in the corner. A third one is sitting in front of the mirror while a stylist puts the finishing touches on her braid. None of them is Jill.

In the wide downstairs halls where merchants are selling T-shirts and doughnuts and hot dogs, I peer intently into faces. I scan for a black pantsuit and brown hair, though it's obvious Mrs. Grundy is smart enough to change up her outfits and wigs.

An official bars me from the warm-up gym. "I have an urgent message for Jill Clayton," I say.

He disappears inside and comes back, shaking his head.

I keep looking. Locker room, restroom stalls, shower stalls. A door sign that says Staff Only.

Maybe because I lived in a storage closet till recently, that sign catches my attention, or maybe I hear a faint noise, the sound of a voice saying, "No!" I twist the knob and am surprised when the door swings open. I stare into a dark space overtaken by brooms and mops and buckets. I detect movement as my eyes adjust to the dark.

Mrs. Grundy towers over Jill, who crouches in a corner. "Stay away from me," Jill says.

Jill's holding the knife. It trembles in her hand. Its blade glints a reflection of the hall light. She looks as ridiculous brandishing a knife as I imagine I would. It occurs to me that a weapon might be more dangerous in the hands of someone who has no idea what they're doing.

Except that Jill doesn't look very threatening, because with her other hand, she's clutching her stomach. She moans, bending over, loosening her grip.

Mrs. Grundy and I both lunge for the knife, but she's closer.

"Close the door," Mrs. Grundy hisses at me. She dangles the knife from one hand, clutching the wooden handle, blade down, as she crouches next to Jill. She doesn't exactly look comfortable holding a weapon either.

The door clicks shut. My fingers fumble to find the switch for the overhead light.

As it flares on, Jill shields her eyes. I eye the knife in Mrs. Grundy's hand. She's eyeing me back, dropping her gaze to study my watch. She's wearing her identical one with the white strap. It seems out of place next to her expensive-looking suit jacket and scarf with jeans.

She looks totally different from the person I've been searching for. I was expecting gray old-fashioned hair, not this new chestnut brown color. It falls neatly into place, finely layered so that the sides look like feathers. Despite my realization many jumps ago that Mrs. Grundy didn't look older than Mom, despite the moments I sat beside her in the stadium in Montreal and stared at the wedding ring on her finger, I've still had it in my head that I was looking for someone with age spots and skin like wrinkled paper, with gnarled hands and stiff movements. Someone really old, like ninety. Not the woman before me with smooth skin, almost invisible fine lines radiating out from her eyes and forming parentheses around her mouth, with a tan as if she just returned from a cruise.

It's like she's a shapeshifter, not a stodgy 1920s grandmother, a sour old woman who was easy to paint in my head as a villain. She's startling in her ordinariness. And she looks almost concerned, crouching there next to Jillian, who is moaning softly.

I think about my cat Simone Biles. She can be a gentle purring creature until she spots her prey. You can turn in an instant to a monster when there's something you want.

"I know you have no reason to trust me," Mrs. Grundy says to Jill in a soothing tone. "But I'm here on behalf of your birth mother. She's looking for you."

"Abby did not send you," I reprove her. I move slowly toward Mrs. Grundy and the knife.

"My birth mother? Who is Abby?" Jill raises terrified eyes to me.

"Gail. Abigail," I say.

Her eyes widen. "You knew something about her and didn't tell me?"

Fending off guilt—what choice did I have?—I quickly redirect the conversation. "You can't trust Mrs. Grundy," I tell her. "Are you okay? Do you need to go to the medic's room?"

"Mrs. Grundy?" Mrs. Grundy asks just as Jill says, "No, no, I'll be okay."

"Look, Jill, I know you must be so scared and desperate and not sure what to do and worried about what people will think," Mrs. Grundy says. "Your birth mom would want to help you. I can take you to her."

"Where?"

Warily, Jill glances back and forth between me and Mrs. Grundy, like we're in cahoots.

I lower myself to sit beside her. "Okay, you know the watch?"

"The magic one I have that matches yours? And yours?" Her gaze sweeps over the watches on our arms. "They have something to do with time travel, don't they? I remember Mom talking about that."

"There's no time right now to tell you the whole story. But when your mom disappeared, she accidentally went back to the 1920s and got stuck there."

Jill's eyes widen again in shock and then narrow suspiciously.

"She has a family," Mrs. Grundy takes up the explanation. "You have three siblings in 1929. And your mother misses you desperately. It would mean everything to her if you went back. You could have your baby in the bosom of a loving family. You'll be safe. The world never has to find out about your shame."

"Shame?" I roll my eyes.

Mrs. Grundy continues to address Jill as if I'm not there. "Your mom loves her family, but she'll always be incomplete without you. Come back, have your baby, and then decide what you want to do. You can go wherever you want to if you decide not to stay in 1929."

She makes it sound so simple. Jill can just travel back to join Abby in the past. Then I'll become that alternate version of me, born in 1929. I'll grow to be that old woman with a pencil speared behind my ear and a crossword puzzle book in my hand.

So this is how it happens.

There would be worse things than growing up in Abby's family. But that would mean I might never know Mom, or Zach. I'll never do gymnastics. I might not ever go to college or have a career.

Instead, this version of me will just go on wandering through time forever. Will my memory of my life in 2018 eventually be erased?

"I'll have my baby and then come back here?" Jill says. "Back to this day, and Olympic trials, and I can compete."

"If that's what you want, of course." Mrs. Grundy's tone is so soothing. "You can stay there with your baby and get to know your birth mother for as long as you want. Or you can also always leave her there, surrounded by a good family, and go wherever you want. Whenever you want."

"Her?" Jill says in wonder. "My baby is a girl?" Her eyes flicker over to my face. She stares at me intently, as if arrested by a realization.

"Don't listen to her," I manage to choke out, though my voice sounds strangled. "If you do what she says, you'll mess up timelines. Create alternate universes. You could alter events so much that you could never come back here. Think about that. You might never have the chance to go to medical school. And what if you could never see Anne and Jim again?"

"And you?" she asks. "What would happen to you?"

"She'll be fine," says Mrs. Grundy.

"My whole life as I know it would cease to exist," I correct her.

"Like murder?" Jill breathes. She looks stricken enough to make me hopeful. Mrs. Grundy doesn't have a chance now. There's no way Jill will be tempted by her plan.

But Mrs. Grundy isn't giving up easily. "Don't be so dramatic. You'll still exist," she tells me. Jill's head swivels back and forth between us, uncertain again. "Your mom would be so overjoyed to see you again," she cajoles Jill. She's doing a pretty convincing impersonation of a concerned mother and grandmother, one who's just as stubbornly afraid as I am of what she has to lose, afraid that Abby will leave or that her grandchildren will be erased.

I search Mrs. Grundy's face for some sign of duplicity or evil, but all I see is a woman who is terrified of losing her family, who is desperate to keep them safe and together.

But I can't afford to sympathize.

A voice comes on over a crackling loudspeaker, barely audible from the hall. "All competitors, please register with the judges."

"I've got to finish getting ready." Jill rises to her feet. Her tone is mechanical. Her face is pale and there's a sheen of sweat on her forehead. "I have to think but I can't right now. I have to go vault."

Mrs. Grundy raises the knife awkwardly. I hold my breath as we all follow it with our eyes.

"You can't," Mrs. Grundy says. Her voice is shaky and the knife trembles in her hand. "Vaulting would endanger your child. You could induce a miscarriage."

We all watch as the knife vibrates violently. She's just as scared as we are.

Why didn't I use some of my spare time to take lessons on how to disarm a knife-toting madwoman? Why did I take this stupid knife at all? Unless she's learned some new skills on the streets, Mrs. Grundy is as wimpy as the rest of us.

But that doesn't mean that, if driven far enough, she won't do damage.

Her eyes still fixed on the knife, Jill sinks back down to the floor.

If she goes with Mrs. Grundy, if they both disappear, if the person I am now no longer exists, at least my mother won't have to grieve, because she'll never have known me. Zach will grow up and marry someone else.

This thought takes me by surprise. Marry? What do I care who Zach marries? That's years in the future.

The loudspeaker voice blasts through the hall. Our heads all whip around as we strain to hear: "Jillian Clayton, please report to the competition area."

And then, without any forethought, I lunge for the knife handle. Mrs. Grundy lets go of it a little too easily, like she's relieved that she doesn't have to slit anyone's throat after all. I'm surprised at how effortlessly I seize the knife. What am I going to do with it?

Use your words, Elizabeth, I hear Mom say. *Even the nicest people have moments of cruelty.*

And in that moment, I know that I have a choice. I know that there has got to be a better way.

So often, events during my time travel journey have felt predestined, like they're going to happen the way they happen no matter what I do. But not always.

I loosen my grip on the knife.

Jill has quick reflexes. She reaches out and snatches it away, then looks surprised. She holds it in front of her. Her hands appear to be steadier than Mrs. Grundy's or mine.

"I'm going to go vault." Jill backs toward the door. "Don't anyone try to stop me."

She reaches behind her to turn the doorknob, swings around and slides the knife into the waistband of her warm-up shorts, and takes off running to the locker room.

Mrs. Grundy and I exchange an alarmed look. "Stop her," she says. "She can't vault."

"I know." I leap into action, tripping over a bucket in my haste to get to the door.

"Try to convince her to come with me," Mrs. Grundy says. She sounds feeble. Defeated.

"I know you really love your grandchildren." I stop in the doorway. "But I'm your great-great-granddaughter. What about me?"

"If she vaults, she could miscarry," Mrs. Grundy says. "Then you'd stop existing anyway. Wouldn't it be better to send her to Abby? You'd just grow up in a different era. And you love Abby. She'd be so happy."

Either way, I'm screwed. "I didn't even think you liked Abby," I say. "But you love her. You really love her and your grandchildren."

"Oh, posh," she says gruffly. "Whatever that means."

She would sacrifice everything to keep her family intact. Even me.

I make up my mind, sprinting out the doorway, tearing down the hall.

"Stop her," Mrs. Grundy calls after me, and it's almost as if we're on the same page, except for the part where she wants to obliterate my life as I know it.

64

SALT LAKE CITY, AUGUST 5, 1988
3:57 P.M.

Racing along the slippery floors of these back halls still clean and unscuffed by the shoes of thousands of spectators, I keep thinking about Mom, random memories rushing through my head. How she used to play Candyland with me when I was little, carefully stacking the deck of cards beforehand so I'd draw one purple card after the other. She found the game hopelessly boring and figured out that if she did that—reverse cheated—I would win in just a few moves.

I think of how terrible she always was at festivity, at decorating and preparing for holidays, at making sure the tooth fairy and Santa Claus came. Once she accidentally left some of my presents in her bathroom closet and tried to convince me that Santa Claus had gotten lost and left them in the wrong room. The Easter Bunny never came to our house. She told me when I was older that she just couldn't face another gift-giving occasion. When I was really little, she'd buy herself presents for her birthday and Christmas and let me wrap them to give to her. "For single moms, there's no other adult to take our kids shopping for presents, so I just did it myself," she told me.

I wonder if she's doing that now, still buying herself presents since I'm not there to do it.

I remember the look on her face the day I confronted her about the circumstances of my birth, the way she steeled herself against my anger, trying to contain the hurt and fear struggling across her face, like she was afraid that she was about to lose me.

I'd give anything to go back to that moment and assure her that whatever had happened, I knew she'd done the best she could.

Mrs. Grundy keeps intruding on my memories. When I met her, she was a new widow, just like Mom had been, carrying on after her husband's death when it must have killed her. She didn't go to bed and not get up. She just went on about her life, took care of her grandchildren, fiercely trouncing them at games. When I met her, I had no idea that she was probably grieving. She's like Mom that way, with a surface calm that hides the multitude of thoughts going on underneath. I think of how proud she was when one of her grandchildren managed to beat her at a game. How pleased she seemed to be to know that one of them might be smarter than she was.

I feel a grudging respect for her. Under other circumstances, maybe I'd even feel affection for her. I wish, fleetingly, that I'd taken the time to get to know her. That I'd made her love me as she does her grandchildren, that she would fear messing up my life as much as she fears that Abby will make yet another decision that will alter hers and her grandchildren's lives forever.

In the locker room Jill is hastily pulling her competition leo off a hanger while she kicks off her shorts. The knife clatters to the floor. Neither of us makes a move to retrieve it.

"When I put this on, everyone's going to know." Jill smooths out the leo, covered with Swarovski crystals that catch the light and bounce it back into my eyes. "They're going to notice my pouchy belly and the rumors are going to start. I can't go out there, can I?"

I shake my head.

"What should I do? I need you to tell me what I should do. I mean, what am I supposed to do? What DO I do? I saw your birth certificate. It says you were born in 2002."

"Do you have it? When I looked earlier today, it was gone."

She shakes her head, and cold realization washes over me: my birth certificate has disappeared again.

"You're going to travel to the future to have your baby," I say, my voice shaky, because I'm not sure that that's true anymore. "To 2002. Do you remember the woman who told you it was okay to color outside the lines? I'm going to tell you where to find her. She's really a good person, I promise." Maybe I'm telling her too much. But isn't it the job of time travelers everywhere to ensure our own births?

"Won't Mrs. Grundy just follow me to the future and try to stop me again?"

"Not if I can keep her from it," I say slowly. "Do you have your mother's Chronowatch prototype?"

"I carry her stuff with me everywhere," she says. "But it's back at the hotel."

"You need to go back to the hotel," I say, talking fast. "Wear my clothes and pretend to be me, and go gather some things. Go to the hotel ATM and the breakfast bar. Use the emergency credit card your mom gave you and get as much money as you can. Also, pack as much food as you can fit in your gym bags. Don't bother with any clothes. When you get to where you're going, you can wear your mom's."

"But if I don't show up to vault, everyone's going to be looking for me. How will I have time to do all of that?"

She's right. Somehow, we have to stall everyone. We have to give Jill time to get out of here.

Jill watches with wide eyes as I pull off my T-shirt and shorts and pass them to her. I fit my baseball cap onto her head.

I hold out my arm to show her how she's going to set the prototype with the red strap. And then I freeze.

"The red prototype hasn't been fixed," I say. "It's still going to have the slippage problem."

What if Jill ends up having me in medieval times or in a cave?

Resolutely, I rip my watch off my arm. "You're going to have to take this one."

I check to be sure it's programmed for seven months before my birth.

"Won't you be stranded here in 1988?" She looks alarmed.

"Don't worry about me." I push away the uneasy memory of Zach's voice: *You can't do anything that might change the past. You can't kill Hitler or compete in the early Olympics or run over your grandpa with a tractor.*

But what if I'm just ensuring that a past that already happened happens again the same way?

I give Jill a quick tutorial on how the watch works. "When you get to 2002, lay low in the house until you're full term," I instruct her. "You can make a trip or two to the grocery store during the day when everyone on the block is at work, but mostly you've got to stay hidden. Be sure you get prenatal vitamins and eat healthy, because you're not going to be able to go to a doctor. You have to be careful that no one sees you. When it's time, you'll go next door to Joan's and have the baby."

"And then what?" She's watching me incredulously, like she doesn't believe any of this but she doesn't know what else to do.

I want to tell her to stay. Stay with Joan and help raise her child. But that's not what happens.

"Come back. Go back to Texas with Anne. Use your middle name. Find your biological father. His name is Harry Crake. He's at MIT. Go to college and med school. But whatever you do, don't turn your back on Anne and Jim either. They love you. They'll support you. Just go and do all the stuff you've dreamed of."

"Except the Olympics," she says. "Can't I just come back and resume the trials?"

"You'd have to hide out and lose the baby weight and train somewhere. Is that really what you want to do?"

She bites her lips. "No," she finally breathes. "No. I want to be done with this."

"So go." I push her toward the door. Watch her saunter out into the hall, passing a pacing Mrs. Grundy. "Jill's headed into the arena," she calls. "She's going to scratch it."

Mrs. Grundy's forehead furrows with worry. She knots her hands together. Taps a tooth with a fingernail. Glances at the arena doorway, then retreats, staying staked there in the hall as if to try to nab Jill again as soon as possible.

Impersonating me, movements lighter and freer in my clothes, cap pulled down over her eyes, my watch strapped to her arm, Jill disappears into the crowd. I may never see her again.

Am I insane?

I almost run after her before she reaches the outside doors. And then she pushes against them and disappears, taking with her my only way to get home.

"Wait here for me, I'm coming with you," I murmur to Mrs. Grundy as I pass her, and she halts, standing there in the middle of the hall, her sagging shoulders straightening, her head lifting.

PART
4

LANDING

65

SALT LAKE CITY, AUGUST 5, 1988
4:45 P.M.

"Jillian Clayton, please report to the judges' stand," comes another loud-speaker announcement, and as fast as I can, I wiggle into Jill's expensive bejeweled competition leo, glad that my hair is already braided.

Several gymnasts are stationed near a TV in the locker room, where they'll watch the competition, while the warm-up gym has come alive, animated with girls stretching and swinging and executing practice jumps. I beeline through the athletes' entrance into the arena, straight to the judges' stand to check in.

Thousands of people loiter near the entranceways and fill the metal seats, buzzing and eating pastries and waving signs.

Anne is standing in the front row, sweeping her gaze worriedly over the gym, craning her neck toward the door. When she sees me, she raises her eyebrows, clearly perturbed. Then she ducks down into her seat, talking to another mom, refusing to look at me.

Jill's Federation-appointed coach meets me. She doesn't know Jill that well, and all she says is, "Where have you been? Your mom and I were about to send an army to search the building and the streets and the hospitals and the hotel."

I pretend to be puzzled. "I was right there. In the warm-up gym."

"But we all looked there," she says. She catches sight of a news photographer and whispers, "We will talk about this later."

As crazy as all of this is, I feel oddly calm as flashes pop around me. The crystals on my leo sparkle, dazzling my eyes. I try not to look self-conscious about being photographed, but I can't wait for the competition to start and the flashes to be banned.

There are twenty-three women in the competition, representing ten private clubs and one university, all vying for the seven slots on the Olympic team. Jill's Olympic dream is dead, but I know what I'm going to do.

I'm going to compete at Olympic trials.

Even though I'm about to make a fool of myself, I feel totally pumped, even if this is probably not a story my grandchildren will ever believe.

I will never be a great gymnast, but I'm the granddaughter of a brilliant inventor and the daughter of a spectacular athlete and the daughter of a courageous single mom who sacrificed everything for me. Now's the time to draw on whatever I have inherited from each of them.

I feel a surge of strength. During the last few months, I've performed feats I would never have imagined when I was living an ordinary life in 2018. I know that my vault is going to look ridiculous next to the high-flying fancy feats of the real competitors. It won't look a thing like Jill's Tsukahara full. I've never even practiced on a narrow horse like this one.

But for just a second, I feel calm and confident and proud, no longer drowned by Jill's light.

Kristie Phillips opens the competition with her first vault while Missy Marlowe from Rocky Mountain Gymnastics in Utah is up on the unevens. She's on her home turf and the crowd is wild, clapping and stamping and whistling and cheering and waving frenzied signs even before she begins to chalk her hands. She swings through her routine, executing an impressive handstand on the straddle back before she sticks her landing and smiles and waves at the crowd. A 9.850 flashes on the scoreboard. None of the gymnasts look at anyone else's scores. Some barely even look at their own.

Kelly Garrison Steves executes her vault for a 9.775 while national champion Phoebe Mills makes a 9.882 on bars. "She swings with the strength, the stretch, and the confidence of a national champion," the announcer says.

Now Sabrina Mars is on bars. "This is an all-or-nothing situation," says the announcer. "Because of a back injury caused by a congenital spinal condition, Mars is competing in the trials without scores from the Houston Nationals, so one hundred percent of her scores here in Salt Lake will count. Every mistake will be magnified, every bobble potentially crushing, but she's fighting gamely, with dignity."

I watch, breathless, as she misses her handstands and receives a 9.338. I cringe each time a score appears that ends a competitor's dreams.

Doe Yamashiro, still recovering from a leg injury, lands low on her vault and scores a 9.075. The crowd is subdued.

If they think these scores are bad, wait till they see mine.

Brandy Johnson finishes her bar set. She slips into her jacket and pants. Then she plugs in her Walkman headphones. She barely glances at her score, a 9.926.

Though she strolls away without cracking a smile, nodding her head in time to her music, the crowd roars. They're pumped again.

Then Joyce Wilborn sails high and long and gets a perfect 10 on her vault. At the same time, Stacey Gunthorpe falters on bars.

"Oh," the announcer groans. "She went over the top on the beat swing after the cast pirouette. What an error." She scores a 9.0.

For a while I watch all of this, detached, but my nerves are getting to me. One second my legs feel stiff and inflexible and fragile as uncooked spaghetti, like I can't walk without stumbling, and the next second it's like my spaghetti is cooked, my legs so weak I'm afraid they'll collapse under me. My heartbeat is drumming in my ears. It feels like a million bees are buzzing in my head.

I am going to vault. Not through time, but into another reality.

I close my eyes. Imagine Mom telling my pulse to calm, my fluttering stomach to stabilize.

"You're up next," my coach says. "Just give it all you've got, okay? Do what you did at Worlds."

A hysterical giggle tries to bubble its way to the surface: I, a YMCA gymnast from small-town Pennsylvania who was unable to complete a vault in a dinky local meet, am going to fling myself over a horse at Olympic trials.

I manage not to collapse in hysterical laughter. Instead, I nod. I stroll to the end of the runway, fixing my eyes on the judge in the crested blue blazer.

I don't have time to think about my pounding heart or my weak legs or that breathless feeling like I've been running too fast and hard for a long time.

The judge raises her hand. I salute and squint at the runway.

I could just scratch the vault. I don't really have to go over. I don't really have to obtain a score. I just need to distract everyone until I'm sure Jill has had time to gather her things and go. I imagine Jill landing in early 2002, a random year she must have originally chosen in a hurry, without a whole lot of forethought.

That is, if there was an original reality when she didn't know me, when Mrs. Grundy wasn't chasing her, when she was simply a terrified teenager running away. Or maybe our fates have always been intertwined in an endless loop.

I don't really need to do this, but I take off anyway, my legs churning as I launch myself toward the vault, feeling as if I have something to prove.

66

My feet pound the mat as the horse looms ahead. All of my might, all of my determination to find my way home again are concentrated in this moment as I run, blocking out the crowd, the judges, my memories of all the times I've screwed up, scored low, given up.

My foot twinges.

I bounce on the springboard.

Reach all the way through my shoulders to land squarely on the horse.

I feel my back arch a little as I pitch over and then land, with a thud, right on my butt.

I mean, I'm totally out of shape. I haven't vaulted in ages. I never really imagined that I'd stick the landing.

But I didn't tank it. I went over. It felt like the most amazing feat of my life.

I hobble to my feet in the dead-silent arena. There are eight thousand people in the stands, and I'm pretty sure I hear an isolated cough. A pen dropping to the floor. A toilet flushing down the hall.

That's how quiet it is. I have stunned the crowd. Though, I'm pretty sure, not in a good way.

A judge rears back and casts a sharp glance at another judge, who is motionless, her mouth dropping open. The two lean their heads together, whispering. My coach catches up with me and we jog side by side back to the head of the runway.

"What was that?" she asks. Her tone is incredulous, like she has no idea where to begin to critique my performance, since just about everything was wrong with it, like she's not sure whether she's in a parallel universe or something. Which, in a way, she is.

"I don't know what happened," I say. I glance toward the stands, but Anne is so far away, I can't see the expression on her face.

The judges wave at my coach. "You need to approach the judge's table," she hisses at me.

I return the way I came, seized by another spasm of hysterical laughter. I put all of my energy into maintaining control.

"We're not even sure how to score that," one of the judges says. "Miss Clayton, with that little performance, you're on the edge of being disqualified."

"I'm sorry," I say, trying to sound contrite. "I'm really nervous."

After some whispering and gesturing, the judges turn back to me. They're letting me make my second run. "Don't let us see another stunt like that," one of them says.

I zoom back to the beginning of the runway, sending a silent apology to Jill. I stand for a long second, taking a deep breath, closing my eyes.

Imagine drawing energy from Mom, and Abby, and Jill.

Imagine telling Zach that I vaulted at the 1988 Olympic trials.

That I actually went over. Not once, but twice.

My eyes pop open when Jill's Federation coach murmurs next to my ear. "I'm sure you'd be more comfortable if you'd been able to bring your own coach, but you have to focus," the coach says. "Let's see the vault you did at Worlds."

I nod. Wait for the judge's signal. Salute. Launch my run again.

I don't have time for fear. I don't have time to imagine consequences. I just run. Ignore that little throb in my foot.

Pound, jump, spring upward, crash my hands against the horse, keep my body straight, soar through the air. My legs are a little bent and I'm aware of flailing my arms sloppily.

Then, whomp. I'm on my feet.

Against all odds, I've stuck the landing.

I'm exuberant as I salute. That might have been my best vault ever. In a western Pennsylvania competition, I'll bet it would be at least a 9.5.

By now it's like someone has pushed the pause button. A shock reverberates through the gym before the silence finally gives way to a cresting roar of voices. The coach is consulting with the judges. They're shaking their heads. The other gymnasts have all stopped chalking their hands, warming up, adjusting the bars. Everyone is staring at me.

I feel a flush rise to my cheeks as I prepare to walk the gauntlet of horrified witnesses toward the locker-room door.

A score flashes up on the board.

1.0

The bewildered crowd doesn't cheer or boo or stomp their feet. If I could see the expressions in the blurred faraway faces, I'm pretty sure I'd see raised eyebrows and looks of shock.

But I might be just as happy as Nadia was when she saw a 1.0 on her scoreboard. I know that my 1.0 isn't a substitute for a perfect 10 that the scoreboard isn't equipped to display. My 1.0 is just a 1.0. But it's a score. I made a score at Olympic trials.

"Ms. Clayton has been disqualified from competition," the announcer stammers out, stating the obvious. He leaves it at that rather than going on to say, as he has after other athletes made mistakes that ended their Olympic dreams, *What a disappointment.*

"I'm just not feeling well," I tell my coach. I fight a smile as I cast one final glance back at the board.

I made a score at the Olympic trials. So what if it was dismal? I still did it. This has got to be at once the most embarrassing and proudest moment of my life.

But that vault? It was nothing next to the challenge that I have ahead of me.

In the bleachers, Anne stands, looking dazed, then wades through the aisles toward the steps. She's coming.

I feel bad. But when she gets back to the hotel, she'll find Jill returned from 2002, waiting for her.

Be there, be there, I silently beg Mrs. Grundy. I'm afraid I'll find the hall empty except for a few bathroom goers and spectators stepping out to smoke.

But she's there, waiting.

67

SALT LAKE CITY, AUGUST 5, 1988
6:45 P.M.

"Let's go." I grab Mrs. Grundy's hand and tug her toward the locker room.

"I can't believe you did that," she says. "Do you need to see the medic?"

"No time. Wait here." I race to grab my bag from a locker. Dash to the door and yank Mrs. Grundy down the hall, catching sight of Anne's face bobbing in the crowd exiting through the arena doorway.

Together, Mrs. Grundy and I fly up the stairs and around the corner, into the back hall.

We face each other. "Are you sure you're okay?" she says.

Her expression slips back and forth between worry and a triumph she tries to quell but that keeps reappearing, like the sun constantly shimmering behind a cloud.

"I'm fine. Let me see your watch." I tap in Thursday, October 24, at 2:00 p.m. "This way my baby will be born in the spring."

Her mouth drops open. "I didn't think you could put in new settings," she says.

"Well, you can." I keep a tight hold on the watch lest this information lead to some new disaster.

"And what about your watch? Is it back at the hotel?"

"No time for that. We can both use this watch. Anna says you can travel with whatever you're carrying."

"You want me to carry you?" She takes a step back, eyebrows knitting together.

"I'm a gymnast. I'm light."

"All right," she says with a sigh, and I leap up into her arms. They close around me. I'm surprised how soft her skin is, how it feels less like I'm being imprisoned and more like I'm a small child she's carrying to bed.

"On the count of three," she says. We count together, "One, two, three."

And we're in front of the house, and she's dropping me to my feet, and it's been so long since I traveled through time that I only have a little headache that starts to clear quickly. It's autumn, on the eve of the Great Depression, the air crisp, the trees half clothed.

The sidewalk is slick with a plaster of yellow leaves, the yard piled with orange and yellow and brown scraps that crunch underfoot. Mrs. Grundy leads the way up the porch steps.

A face appears in the window and then the door is hurled open so hard it hits the wall behind it. Abby heaves herself out, crying out, drawing both of us into a hug.

"Mom," she says. "We've missed you. And Anna—"

"This isn't Anna," Mrs. Grundy says in her gravelly voice. "This is your daughter, Jill."

"My goodness," Abby says. It's felt as if I was starting to forget her face, and now here she is, real again, freckles, curly hair, wiry frame. I'm so happy to see her.

She peers closely, questioningly, at me. She knows that I'm not Jill, but she plays along. "It's uncanny how much you look like our previous visitor," she says. She swallows hard, searching my face for confirmation that we found her daughter. "Jill," she says softly.

"Jill isn't really showing much yet," Mrs. Grundy says, "but she's, er, in a family way. I told her that you'd take her in."

"Oh!" Abby's voice is shaking as she ushers us both into the house.

I catch her eye and then give Mrs. Grundy's watch a hard stare, hoping that Abby will pick up on my telepathic messages. Somehow, Abby gets it. She takes Mrs. Grundy's arm and unstraps the watch. "I think that'll be enough traveling through time, Mom," she says.

"Oh, thank God," Mrs. Grundy says, sinking to the sofa. "This has started to get harrowing. You wouldn't believe how many times I've barely escaped getting arrested for shoplifting and skipping out on hotel bills. All I wanted to do was reunite you with your daughter." She looks smug. "I thought then maybe you'll keep your focus where it belongs. On your husband and your home."

"You're right," Abby says. "Thank you, Mom."

"But you know," she says, "I think I was wrong about that. I didn't understand how you could have a family and still be restless. But I had so much fun. When the children are older, you ought to get a job. I think I'm going to get a job. I had the best time."

Abby looks a little alarmed, like she thinks that Mrs. Grundy is going to time travel away again at any moment.

She quickly slips me the watch. I put it in my pocket. I want to ask Mrs. Grundy more questions, but Abby says to me, "I think you'd better go. If the children get home from school and see you, they'll never let you out of their sight again."

Mrs. Grundy looks up sharply. "But I brought her to you," she protests. Catching the look that Abby and I exchange, realization dawns on her. She lunges forward toward my pocket. "You're not Jill," she accuses me. "You're Anna."

"I'm sorry," I say, and this time, I genuinely am sorry for the way her pride in her achievement is abruptly replaced by despair.

"You're right, Mom, this is Anna," Abby says. "But please don't worry. I'm not going anywhere. I'm not going to take the children away from you as long as you promise not to try to have me committed to an asylum. You're stuck with me. But Anna has got to go."

Mrs. Grundy sputters, doing several double takes. Maybe she hasn't looked at me any more closely than I ever looked at her.

"You two," I interject. "I swear, it's like you two love each other but are too stubborn to be the first to admit it. It's like you're afraid to talk to each other but you secretly want to. I mean, why else did you let it slip that you had my watch?" I address Mrs. Grundy. "And why else did you accidentally leave the basement door open?" I ask Abby.

But I'm like that too. Too stubborn to be the first to admit how I feel about people.

"If I try to have you committed to an asylum, they'll commit me too, after all of this," Mrs. Grundy says in her gruff voice, the one she uses, I realize, whenever she's overcome by emotion. "Who's going to believe this story?"

Fleetingly, I wish I could hang around for a while. See the kids. Compare notes with Mrs. Grundy about our travels through time. "I have questions," I tell her. "What was with all of those stories about women and sanitoriums?"

"I was trying to protect her," Mrs. Grundy says. "I was terrified someone would realize that there was something not quite right about her. Wait—you think I would have tried to get the mother of my grandchildren committed to an institution? What kind of person do you think I am?" She looks at me incredulously.

I don't bother to respond. I have so little time to get my questions answered. "Where did you get all of the nice clothes? Where did you stay when you were in Dallas for so long?"

"I got a job," she says. "I was the social director for a cruise line out of Galveston. I specialized in roaring twenties parties. Mine were the most authentic. It was a blast." She turns to Abby. "Do you think there are any jobs like that here?"

"You're my great-grandmother," I say to her. "But I don't even know your name."

"Elizabeth," she says.

There's a long silence as I take this in. "That's my name," I finally choke out. "My real name, I mean. Not Anna." I am, inadvertently, her namesake. "I was sort of named after my badass great-grandmother," I say in wonder.

"Are you calling me a donkey?" She sounds baffled, maybe even a little hurt.

"No, no, in 2018, a badass is a good thing. It's like a—a—"

"A sockdolager," Abby supplies. "Someone who's a real humdinger."

A smile breaks out on my great-grandmother's face.

It's hard enough to say a final good-bye to Abby. I know that I can't wait for Luke, my grandfather, to get home from work, or the kids, my aunts and uncles, to arrive from school. To have to say good-bye again to Sarah, and to Catherine, who will someday have a daughter named Joan. To Robert, who will someday name his daughter Anne.

So I keep it simple. I set the watch and strap it to my arm. Then I hug the first Elizabeth, my great-grandmother, and am surprised that she doesn't just endure my hug, but that she squeezes back. I kiss Abby, my grand-mother and step-great-grandmother, on the cheek.

"Have a good life," Abby says to me. Her tone is joking, but she frames my face with her hands and gives me a long look.

I double-click.

68

I'm standing knee-deep in snow, in the shadow of a pine tree. My stomach feels unsettled; a new headache is gearing up, blasting my forehead, and I lower myself into the snow under branches that slump toward the white ground, which glows with a kind of odd phosphorescence. Jill has stolen out of the house where she has camped now for several months, no longer the tiny girl I saw only yesterday and a lifetime ago, now misshapen in an old down coat, heavy with pregnancy. She crunches across a new layer of snow. Flakes flurry around her head, swirl so hard that I can barely see her. They settle on the ground, turning the world clean and new.

I catch a sudden movement across the yard. It's me, months ago, looking for Mrs. Grundy, who appears at the edge of the yard. My great-grandmother's gaze lands on Earlier Me just as Earlier Me spots her. And all at once, they both vanish.

Jill doesn't notice any of it. She trudges on across the yard, pant cuffs sweeping the snow, bell bottoms that I now know belong to Abby, toward Joan, the woman who will become Mom.

69

I stand close to the living-room window of the yellow house, straining to hear a faint, high-pitched rhythmic baby's cry.

A day later I'm at the window again when Jill, sitting in the kitchen, swivels her head and looks straight at me. I duck out of sight, crouch behind a bush, wondering if she saw me.

The side door opens and Jill steps out onto the porch. She's cradling a tightly swaddled bundle. I hold my breath. She should not be out here without a coat. She should not be bringing a newborn baby out into the cold. She looks out over the yard, scanning.

For me, I think. She saw me.

The snow glows in the moonlight. It's bright, unearthly. It's like a whole field of light, pierced by the pine needles scattered across the ground and shadowed by the scrawls of branches and twigs that, sleeved by ice, contrast sharply against the white winter sky.

Jill cradles the baby. She looks sad. Older, somehow, since the last time I saw her, and not just by seven months. I search her face, but she's a few feet away, and I don't know if the love and regret that passes over it are real or my imagination.

"Little Bug," she says to her baby, but really, I'm sure, for the benefit of my teenage self. "I'll come back someday."

My heart stalls in my rib cage like the snow caught in the branches. *But you never did*, I want to say. *You never came back.*

The door opens. "Are you okay out here?" asks Mom.

"I'm just saying good-bye," Jill says.

"No, wait—" Mom takes the baby as Jill brushes past her. "Don't go yet. We have to talk about this—You don't even have a coat on—"

"Tell her it's okay to color outside the lines," Jill says, and then she's gone, and Mom is standing there, confused, peering off into the distance, and then down into the face of the baby she holds. Me. The baby wails again. "Did she call you Elizabeth?" she says. *Little Bug. Elizabeth,* I think.

Around me, all the trees hold snow in their branches like steady arms that manage not to bow under the weight. Joan presses the baby against her shoulder. She goes back into the house.

70

It's the month before I suspected that I might be adopted. My house is still here. Mom's car is in the driveway. I see myself in the kitchen window, washing dishes.

I'm poking my toe slowly into the water of time, weak with the relief of finding life as I know it playing out before me. I lie there in the yard, listening to all of the familiar sounds, recovering from my time jump, before I creep into the basement where the freezer hums and the furnace pops. I pull the light chain and the basement springs to life: the cold concrete floor and the litter box. Simone Biles leaps from the ceiling insulation and noses up to me. Hands trembling, I unzip my backpack and pull out Abby's tablet.

My birth certificate is right there, the top edge poking out of the tablet.

When everyone is asleep, I pull a throw off the couch and steal up to the attic, wading around the dead bees on the floor. I wrap myself in the blanket and conk out for twelve hours, waking just enough to listen to the buzzes and hums of our house. Me, Mom, the plumbing, the TV, the phone. The comforting sounds of ordinary life.

71

In a dark auditorium in a junior high school in 1965, a hushed audience focuses on a stage. In the foreground, in the spotlight, the hero and heroine toss back and forth lines of dialogue, but that's not what I'm here to see. I'm watching the two girls in overalls, playing stagehands in a show about putting on a show, at the back of the stage moving chairs around. I had to throw up in the bathroom when I arrived. Now I ease along the side aisle of the shadowy auditorium for a better view, knowing this will be my last time jump.

Mom always used to tell me that she grew up before Title IX really kicked in, before girls were encouraged to do sports. "Do you think we'd be friends if we'd met in middle school?" I used to ask her, and she'd laugh. "Oh, you'd think I was weird. You'd make fun of my pleated pants. You'd tell me they were grandma pants." The tallest girl in overalls is gawky and awkward, with long frizzy blond hair.

Mom was wrong. That girl looks like someone I would have liked to be friends with.

Now the boy and girl in the foreground are launching into a song while the two girls at the back of a stage pick up a chair at the same moment. They yank the chair back and forth, the blond girl rocking forward, pulling back, rocking forward, letting go, then tumbling into a back shoulder roll, ending up so close to the edge of the stage that the audience, meant to be paying attention to the singing central characters, gasps loudly.

I remember Mom telling me this story about the choreographed fight over a chair, the gasp of the audience. Even years later, she was still amused and a little self-satisfied at the memory. I used to laugh, finding it hilarious that her great gymnastics skill was a back shoulder roll.

But now that I've witnessed it, I'm kind of proud of her, at the way she stole the scene.

And now I'm more impatient than ever to see Mom, the grown-up version of her I have always known.

72

BRADFORD, PA, NOVEMBER 10, 2018
10:02 P.M.

When I land in the gym, Zach's back is turned to me, facing the vault table, the direction where he last saw me. He whips around.

I'm on my feet, and the world has righted itself.

Zach turns. A rush of something—Love? Affection? Relief?—swells in my chest. I drink in his face, his hair, the cowlick more prominent than usual so that it sticks up as if he's been running his hand nervously through it. I take in his ears, the same ones that stuck out when he was a kid until he grew into them. His big, clumsy hands. His big, stinky feet. He's beautiful. I fling myself into his arms.

"It worked," he says, hugging me hard. "You were gone for five minutes."

He holds me at arm's length. He looks spooked. "I mean, you totally disappeared. That was the longest five minutes of my life."

"Five minutes?" I roll my eyes. "Zach, you asshole," I reply, and I catch the surprised look on his face before I grab him again.

He holds me tight. So tight, my heart is pounding. The room starts spinning around me. I think I'm going to pass out. "Just give me a minute."

I lie down on the mats. His concerned face looms over me, but I put up my hand. When I can speak again, I say, "You know I didn't really have to vault. All I had to do was double-click."

"Yeah, I just told you that to help you overcome your fear," he replies.

"You asshole," I say again. I'm too weak and sick to put much force into it, and it comes out sounding more like an endearment than an accusation.

I know what to expect: waves of nausea, a hammering in my head, dizziness, the edges of everything closing in before I pass out if I get up too soon. I know that if I wait it out, the pain will clear, leaving only a profound fatigue.

This is the last time I will ever experience it. I'm never leaving my own time again. I recover enough to talk fast on the drive back to my house. There's so much to tell, I don't know quite where to begin, and my words tumble over each other.

"Are you making all of this up to mock me?" Zach accelerates as he sends skeptical glances my way. I just want to stare and stare at him. I want to touch his arm and his cheeks and his hair and make sure that he's real, but I restrain myself. I remember my resolution not to tell him how I feel, not to risk our friendship. I remember my resolution to play it cool.

"Hey, this was all your idea, so now you have to believe me," I protest, and whether he believes me or not, I can't stop my words from spilling over, I have so much to say. "When I went to Alternate 2018, you were there, but you didn't know me. And get this: you were working at McDonald's. I can't believe that without me in your life, you got a job at McDonald's, of all places."

"Uh, Liz," he says. And just looks at me.

"Wait, you work at McDonald's?"

"Yeah, only for the last year."

I gape at him.

"I'm saving for college," he says.

"Oh. That's really—um—mature," I admit.

I scoop up my Dairy Queen wrappers from the car floor. It was at least a year ago and only yesterday that I wadded them and threw them there.

Idly, I pick up the pocket watch that belonged to his grandfather from the console between the seats. It's gold, carved with branches hovering over a snow-covered field.

With a déjà vu feeling, I pull it closer. Examine the strange lettering on the back, in a code that I recognize immediately. I pass my eyes over it, deciphering one letter at a time.

Abby Grant, it says.

So Abby did become an artisanal clockmaker.

Zach smiles, looking a little too pleased with himself. "Well, maybe you didn't have to vault, but you overcame your fear, right?"

"I competed in the frickin' Olympic trials," I reply. We don't need to discuss my score.

And when it comes right down to it, I'm still afraid of vaulting.

But now I know that fear doesn't have to stop me.

I get more and more impatient as we get closer to home. To Mom. My room. Simone Biles.

We turn the corner onto Sanford. And my house is there. Still standing. Still the same. There are lights on in all the windows.

I turn to Zach. Screw my resolutions. "We'll talk later," I say, and lean over to give him a quick kiss on the lips.

He looks startled. Then he reaches over, pulls me close. Leans down and gives me a real kiss that leaves my lips soft.

Under normal circumstances, I could stay there forever. Under any other circumstances, I'm not sure I would ever be able to tear myself away.

Then I glimpse a face in my living-room window. He follows my gaze. "Go," he says with a gentle push.

And then I'm running, up the porch steps, to my front door.

73

"The meet went late," Mom says, laying down her knitting and rising as I spring into the room, lobbing myself into her arms. "I missed you!" I cry out. I still don't feel good, but at the same time, I feel great. Better than ever in my life.

Mom is obviously startled but adapts quickly and hugs me back.

And sitting by the fire, I tell her my story. Her eyes are wide, disbelieving, even a little alarmed, as she casts worried glances toward the phone as if she's trying to decide whether I've gone off the deep end and she needs to call 9-1-1. But then I mention Catherine, and she smiles.

"Mom," she says. "When she was in high school, she renamed herself Wren. She said that she always wished she could fly."

I remember how I taught her to do a cartwheel and told her that gymnastics was like flying.

She settles back against the cushions and tells me about her Uncle Bob, who used to talk about his cousin Anna, and her Aunt Sarah, who spent a few years in her early twenties doing acrobatics with a circus. And her

step-grandma, Abby, and her grandfather, Luke, who helped raise Mom after her parents died when she was young. "Somehow, she knew to buy IBM
and Disney and McDonald's stocks, and was one-hundred-percent accurate
at predicting who would become president. Grandpa used to joke that Abby's psychic powers missed the boat when it came to sports, except for gymnastics. She had no idea who was going to win the Kentucky Derby or the
World Series, but she always knew who would win gold in gymnastics at the
next Olympics."

Mom vaguely recalls her great-grandma who lived next door, Elizabeth.
She lived well into her nineties. She had a late-in-life career as an activities
director on luxury ocean liners.

"Abby told me that someday I would adopt a daughter. I thought it was
just the ravings of a senile old woman. I always felt guilty that I couldn't take
in the little girl next door when her mom disappeared. So that was actually
Abby?" Mom keeps shaking her head, trying to wrap her brain around all
of this.

"She knew that Jill would be okay," I said. "I think it was me she wanted
you to be here for."

"She left everything to me," Mom says. "With a provision that I had to
live here and rent out the house next door to a woman named Gail Lynn Key
in 1972. It was so oddly specific."

"And you're still paying to keep all of the utilities on and have the place
cleaned. Why?"

Mom looks pale and ghostly in the firelight, dark erasing the lines
around her eyes and the softening of her jawline. "I wanted her to be able
to come back. For your sake. But I've also been terrified every day of your
life that she'll come back and try to claim you. I even thought about moving, going somewhere she'd never find us, but I knew you'd have questions
someday. That I'd be protecting myself, not you, if I ran away."

I can't fathom the courage that must have taken. If I'd been her, I would
have run away. I wouldn't have risked anyone taking my baby. But Mom was
thinking about me, not herself.

When we're so sleepy and we can barely stay awake, we google names to try to find if Sarah and Anne and Jim are still alive, along with Dr. Harry Crake and his daughter, Dr. Lynn Crake from Buffalo. I can't find Kyle Martin. There are too many men with that name.

I'm disappointed. I'm going to have to do more detective work to track him down. Maybe someday I'll go find everyone. In real time, getting motion sick in cars and buses, not time sick flinging myself to the past or the future. But right now, I'm just happy to be home.

After Mom goes to sleep, I empty my backpack. Slide the knife into a kitchen drawer. Head down to the basement, where I find, behind some paint cans, a flapper dress, stiff and dusty. Then I go to the living-room secretary and return my birth certificate to where it belongs.

74

Bradford, PA, November 12, 2018
3 p.m.

Zach yanks the gearshift to park in front of the gym. He acts all casual, but there's a new expression on his face, like he can't quite believe the turn our relationship is taking, like he's hopeful.

"I can't do it," I say. "I'm like the piranha of the team."

"The what?" He looks confused. "Do you mean the pariah?"

"Whatever," I say. Why is it that I only mix up words when I'm talking to Zach? Maybe because he's so cutely earnest and I like it when I make him smile.

"So you, like, time traveled to all of those time periods and competed in Olympic trials and you're nervous about this?"

"Yeah, I know, totally illogical." I gather up my courage and hop out of the car.

When I go into the locker room to gather my things, I almost run smack into Molly, who comes storming out, glaring thunderclouds at me. Inside I find Callie, sitting by herself on a bench.

There's a look on her face like someone just struck her.

"Hey, Elizabeth," she says, the first time she's acknowledged my existence and greeted me by name in months.

"Hi Callie," I return. "Is everything all right?" She seems so young. I don't really have any desire to be friends with her anymore, but I feel bad for her. The way she twists her hands together makes me think that maybe Molly has turned on her too.

"I'm fine," she says in a small, squeaky voice. "See you at Tuesday practice?"

"I'm not sure if I'll be there," I say absently, but I'm pretty sure that I won't. "Hey," I say after I scoop my grips and scrunchies and nail polish remover into a bag. Callie looks at me with tear-filled eyes. "Don't let her get to you," I call back.

Coach Amy is in her office, talking to someone on speakerphone while she sorts ribbons for an upcoming meet. "I've never had to ask someone to leave," I hear her say. "But she was bullying other kids and—" She breaks off abruptly when she catches sight of me. "Let me call you back," she says.

My hands are clammy. So she's going to kick me off the team.

Maybe I deserve it. But I think of the knife, and know that I don't have it in me to hurt anyone else on purpose.

"Hey!" Coach Amy beckons me into her office. "You never brought me your birth certificate."

"But—I thought that Molly—"

"Molly isn't on the team anymore," she says crisply. It takes a second to sink in. Molly's the one who's been bullying other kids. "And you're usually one of our top scorers. We've got to work on your tumbling. But your overall technique is so strong—"

"I'm really honored," I have to talk fast, or I might never get the words out at all. "But I think I have to take a break from gymnastics."

Her eyes rake across my face. She sighs. "Well, we know what that means. Hardly anyone ever comes back. Gymnastics is something you have no choice but to outgrow, eventually."

"Maybe I'll miss it so much that I'll be back in a couple of weeks," I say.

She gives me a lopsided smile, clearly unconvinced. "Well, let me know. And there's always a coaching job for you here," she says.

Back in the car, I tell Zach to take me to the dance studio. I'm going to sign up for hip-hop and jazz.

75

BRADFORD, PA, NOVEMBER 29, 2018
NOON

The woman who appears in the restaurant doorway is slim and small, with oversized glasses that make her look smart and somehow even more glamorous. "You look just like my childhood friend Anna," she says, lowering herself to sit down beside me.

"And your babysitter Anna," I add.

"And like me when I was your age," she says.

I can't stop examining her face, imagining that I will someday look like this, her curly hair bundled up into a bun with wisps escaping and hints of gray at the roots.

I present her with the tablet containing her mother's story, and the translation I've typed up for her.

Her eyes pass over it wonderingly.

"Didn't you ever want to come back for me?" I ask.

"Of course," she says. "I used the time-travel device one last time. You were six. I hid out in the house next door to you for two weeks."

The five-year-old yogurt Zach and I found: that was Jill's.

"You seemed happy," she goes on. "You seemed to have a tight bond with your mom. I couldn't take that away from you. But then, a few months ago, I saw you compete."

The woman in the stands the day I failed to vault.

"I did so badly that day," I say.

A smile plays about her lips. "I knew it wasn't going to be your last vault," she says.

"Isn't it funny that we do the same gesture before we do backward blind elements?" I ask, flicking my fingers. "Why is that?"

She shrugs. "Why do we both have a sweet tooth and like cats? Maybe it's genetic. Or maybe you saw a video of me and unconsciously imitated it. Who knows?"

"Parking was a mess," says a man as he approaches our table. He has shiny dark hair and skin that matches mine. I can see the tall, gangly boy in his confident frame. I stand awkwardly as he closes his hand around mine, shakes it solemnly, holds on tight for just a second too long without releasing it. His dark eyes look misty.

"Elizabeth," Jill says. She's standing, too. "Meet my husband. And your father."

"Kyle," we say together.

Someday soon, I'll visit Dr. Jillian Lynn Key Clayton Crake Martin and Kyle Martin at their house in Buffalo. Kyle promised to show me how to make Chinese dumplings the way his mother used to, and I imagine that I'll babysit their little girl, my sister. I can picture her room, decorated with glow-in-the-dark stars and dinosaurs that let off an eerie green light when we first turn off the lights. I'll show her how to do back handsprings and we'll color together: me a dinosaur with paisley markings, hers with bull's-eyes. There'll be a fire in Jill and Kyle's fireplace. Outside, trees will cast long shadows on the snow.

Somehow, in this fantasy, Mom is there too, counting stitches as she knits, murmuring with Kyle, who hauls in an armful of firewood, and with Jill, who tends the fire.

Acknowledgments

This book started as a project to keep me entertained during very long gymnastics meets when my daughter was competing, some years ago, on the same YMCA team as Elizabeth.

I owe many thanks to my daughter's coaches and her teammates who took the time to sit beside me during meets and answer my millions of questions about skills and scoring.

I consulted a number of books and articles in order to write about gymnastics and the 1920s as authentically as possible. I found especially helpful John Arend's detailed account of the 1988 US Olympic Trials, "High Drama: The 1988 U.S. Olympic Trials Soared to New Heights of Heart Stopping Dramatics," from the September/October 1988 issue of *USA Gymnastics*. The announcer's commentary is derived from Arend's engaging storytelling. General gymnastics-related books that I read include American Girl's *Girls Love Gymnastics*, Andrew Donkin's *Going for Gold*, John Goodbody's *The Illustrated History of Gymnastics*, Dan Gutman's *Gymnastics: The Trials, the Triumph, the Truth*, Linda McDonald's guides for gymnastics spectators and parents *Struggling in the Stands* and *Stressing in the Stands*, and Dvora Myers's *The End of the Perfect 10*.

Autobiographies by gymnasts proved informative as well: *Winning Balance* by Shawn Johnson; *Mary Lou* by Mary Lou Retton, Bela Karolyi, and John Powers; *Heart of Gold* by Kerri Strug; and *Chalked Up* by Jennifer Sey.

I looked at several useful books about the 1920s—picture books like *Ticket to the Twenties: A Time Traveler's Guide*, written by Mary Blocksma and illustrated by Susan Dennen; and *If You Lived 100 Years Ago* written by Ann McGovern and illustrated by Anna Divitos. I also consulted more-detailed histories by David Kyrig (*Daily Life in the United States: 1920–1940*) and Frederick Lewis Allen (*Only Yesterday: An Informal History of the 1920s*).

Many fellow writers offered me feedback on multiple drafts of this manuscript, including Karen Bell, Darlene Goetzman, Andrew Harnish, and Dani Weber. Sara King offered encouragement on an early draft. I owe a huge debt to Edie Hemingway, who brought her expert eye to an early draft and gave me suggestions that helped me to reshape the manuscript. In a class she offered with Harold Underdown, Eileen Robinson was attentive to helping me with my novel's emotional trajectory. I continued to meet with fellow writers Ellen Jellison and Stephanie Theban after the class was over, both of them reading this novel through twice and offering helpful feedback. Writer, former gymnast, and current gymnastics mom Jill Kelly Koren checked the manuscript for accuracy, though any mistakes that remain are my own. Taylor Tarahteeff inspired me with his enthusiasm about local history and answered some related questions. Anna Smith's knowledge and advice related to publishing resources proved constantly inspiring and invaluable.

The University of Pittsburgh at Bradford's Office of Academic Affairs provided me a sabbatical and support to attend the Rutgers Council on Children's Literature Conference. My colleagues at Pitt Bradford as well as those from the Naslund-Mann Graduate School of Writing at Spalding University have taught me and provided inspiration and support.

I feel very fortunate that this novel landed at CamCat. Many thanks to Sue Arroyo and Helga Schier for believing in this project, to Elana Gibson for her work on the manuscript and cover, and to Kayla Webb and her incisive eye for both fine details and larger issues. I am so grateful for all of the work she did to help me hone this manuscript. Thanks to Maryann Appel for the layered attention to detail in the covers you create and other members of the CamCat team, including Bill Lehto, Laura Wooffitt, Meredith Lyons, Gabe Schier, Abigail Miles, Jessica Homami, Nicole DeLise, and Camryn Flowers. Thank you also to Ellen Leach who copyedited the manuscript into tip-top shape.

Finally, thank you to Steve, who totally bought the time travel despite his skepticism about what I thought were much more believable details. He listened to me read this whole manuscript aloud on a drive to Massachusetts, and that's the tip of the iceberg when it comes to his support. And thanks to Sophie, who inspired the best parts of Elizabeth.

About the Author

An adoptive parent and former longtime gymnastics mom, Nancy McCabe is the author of six books for adults, most recently *Can This Marriage Be Saved? A Memoir* (Missouri 2020), *From Little Houses To Little Women: Revisiting A Literary Childhood* (Missouri 2014), and the novel *Following Disasters* (Outpost 19 2016). She has also written two books on China adoption. Her work has appeared in *Newsweek, Salon, Writer's Digest, The Brevity Blog*, and the *Los Angeles Review of Books* in addition to numerous other magazines. She's a Pushcart winner with eight recognitions on notable lists of BEST AMERICAN anthologies. Her two most recent nonfiction books are also available as Audible Audiobooks.

She is a recipient of a Pennsylvania Individual Artist's Fellowship and two awards from Prairie Schooner, and has worked as a regular blogger for Ploughshares. With MFA and PhD concentrations in fiction writing, McCabe directs the writing program at the University of Pittsburgh at Bradford and teaches in the graduate program at Spalding University's Naslund Mann School of Writing.

Her extensive teaching experience includes workshops in elementary and secondary schools as a Writer in the Schools in three states and community workshops for libraries, bookstores, and writers' centers. She is the author of the handbook *Making Poems: Writing Exercises for the Classroom*. She currently regularly teaches online for the Creative Nonfiction Foundation as well.

This is her first novel for young adults.

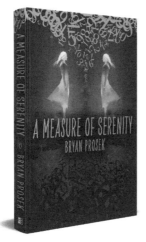

CamCat
Books

VISIT US ONLINE FOR MORE BOOKS TO LIVE IN:
CAMCATBOOKS.COM

SIGN UP FOR CAMCAT'S FICTION NEWSLETTER FOR
COVER REVEALS, EBOOK DEALS, AND MORE EXCLUSIVE CONTENT.

CamCatBooks   @CamCatBooks   @CamCat_Books   @CamCatBooks